THE REMNANT TRILOGY | BOOK 1

NOAH
MAN OF DESTINY

TIM CHAFFEY &
K. MARIE ADAMS

THE REMNANT TRILOGY | BOOK 1

NOAH

MAN OF DESTINY

TIM CHAFFEY &
K. MARIE ADAMS

First printing: August 2016

ISBN: 978-0-89051-972-1
Library of Congress Number: 2016913246

Cover design by K. Marie Adams; cover illustrations by Ben Iocco

Unless otherwise noted, Scripture quotations are from the New King James Version (NKJV) of the Bible, copyright © 1982 by Thomas Nelson, Inc. Used by permission. All rights reserved.

Please consider requesting that a copy of this volume be purchased by your local library system.

Printed in the United States of America

Please visit our website for other great titles:
www.masterbooks.com

For information regarding author interviews,
please contact the publicity department at (870) 438-5288.

Master Books®
A Division of New Leaf Publishing Group
www.masterbooks.com

CONTENTS

Dear Reader,

Most people recognize Noah as the man who built the Ark, but have you ever wondered what he was really like? How did he have the necessary skills to accomplish such an overwhelming task? Who were Noah's parents? When and how did he meet his wife? Was she a godly woman?

The Bible tells us he was a righteous man, but was he a faithful believer from a young age? Were there plenty of righteous people in his life as he grew up or was the world already filled with violence and depravity?

And while we're on the subject, how did Noah age? During this time, many people lived more than 900 years. Such a concept is difficult for us to imagine, but what might it have been like to live so long? Did people back then age at a slower rate so that at 600 years old, Noah could pass for someone who's only 60 today?

More than a fourth of all of human history passed by the time the Flood devastated the earth, yet this period is compressed into just six chapters of Genesis. So we are left to wonder about how many things might have been. In some cases, the Bible gives little clues on which we can build our speculations, but we must be careful to always distinguish between Scripture and our own ideas. For example, many Christians believe the Bible teaches that Noah was mocked while he built the Ark, but even though this idea is often repeated, you will never find this anywhere in the Bible. While it is certainly believable that a righteous man would be scoffed at by a wicked society, the Bible just does not tell us this about Noah. So even though it makes sense, we must realize that idea is merely speculation instead of Scripture.

As strange as it may seem, one of our main goals in writing this novel was to help readers distinguish between fiction and biblical fact. Yes, you read that correctly. We want to use fiction to teach how to discern between fiction and biblical, historical account. To help in this goal, we will include a non-fiction section at the end of the book that includes answers to multiple questions that may arise as you read, as well as some surprises for readers who have visited or plan to visit the Ark Encounter theme park in Kentucky. But we are getting ahead of ourselves. First, you need to meet young Noah. So join us as we respectfully imagine what life for the man who built the Ark might have been like.

— Tim Chaffey and K. Marie Adams

CHAPTER 1

Iri Sana — Noah's 38th year

Wood shavings dropped to the floor like the curls of a child's first haircut as Noah repositioned the chair seat he was carving. He examined each edge, then pushed his blade along the perimeter, carving away a wafer-thin slice. Tilting his head, he examined the result, then, satisfied, exchanged the carving blade for a polishing stone and began the long process of smoothing the wood.

Having done this numerous times before, Noah allowed his mind to wander as his right fingers felt the scratchy grain of the wood and his left hand guided the polishing stone in confident, careful strokes.

He had been only 30 when his father, Lamech, declared his intention to build a new, larger shelter for their family's expanding herds. With a grimace, Noah remembered the effort he had exerted to persuade his father to include the woodshop. Only after many revisions to the building drawings — wherein father and son went back and forth — and after much reassurance that Noah's woodcarving projects would not get in the way of his helping on the farm, had this room become a reality.

Noah looked around the small space. It was well worth the many heated discussions. Here, in the place with barely enough room for him to stretch out on the floor, there was sufficient area for him to work and ample space to dream. His few tools hung neatly along one wall, their shadows dancing in the flickering light from his lamp. They weren't much, but they were enough. Each tool, each completed project, gave him a small measure of hope that he would not always have to work in the fields with his father. Still, Noah's restlessness increased as his Rovay approached, the ceremony in which the community officially recognized him as a man.

This warm season was his least favorite. The longer days meant the stolen time before sunup afforded Noah his only opportunity to work on something he really enjoyed. Not that he hated his farm duties. In fact, he liked working the ground. It was hard work, but there was gratification in planting seeds, tending the shoots, and watching them grow to produce a harvest. But none of these labors brought the same degree of satisfaction as selecting the proper piece of wood and revealing, chip by chip, portions of the form until the final product took shape.

Noah set the stone down and ran his palm across the seat. He grinned, thinking of what could ensue if a guest happened to sit on this chair without all the splinters removed. Pleased with his work, he turned and stared out the open window. A gentle breeze cooled his sticky skin and carried the scent of springal blossoms, a welcome relief from the barn's customary pungency. An almost-whole moon bathed the earth with its soft light, and a faint glow on the horizon indicated that the sun would be up soon.

Another long day in the fields. It was up to him and Jerah to prepare the orb plant field today. A stab of rebellious energy pierced him at the thought of the tedious work stretching before him. He resolved anew to speak with his father, only to deflate moments later at the thought of his father's look of disappointment. Noah shook his head, muttering to himself as he returned the stone to its place on the shelf. "He just won't understand."

Noah gazed at the quickly fading stars. Following the example he had witnessed countless times from his grandfather and father, he offered a quick prayer. *God, thank You for providing in abundance everything I need. Help me to remain faithful to You in all things today. May my work —*

A shout from inside the house shattered the silence. Noah's head jerked up. Why would his brother be creating so much noise this early in the morning? He strode to the doorway of the barn just in time to see the silhouette of a man crash out of the door of their house and into the dusky terrain. Moments later, Jerah ran out the door and yelled again.

"Stop!"

The shadowy figure ran across the yard in Noah's direction as Jerah gave chase. Alert, heart pounding, Noah tightened the knee-length cloth wound around his waist before he sprinted away from the barn. The stranger spotted him and turned left toward the row of springal trees Noah's mother had planted on the north side of the house. Knowing that only 20 of the short, bush-like trees were in that row, Noah altered his course and dashed down the other side of the trees, hoping that Jerah would pick up on his strategy and flank the fleeing man.

The row of trees between them made judging the man's speed in the faint light difficult, but hearing sounds of brush cracking under feet nearby, Noah guessed they were nearly even in their pace. He sped toward the last tree, hoping to tackle the man as they came into the open. As Noah attempted to plant his left foot to cut in front of the stranger's path, he slipped in the dew-covered grass and slid to the ground. The intruder jumped over him, but Noah shot his arm out in a desperate attempt to thwart his escape. He barely missed as the man twisted to avoid Noah's grasp.

While the man's maneuver prevented his capture, he landed awkwardly and stumbled. He splayed in the long grass and skimmed across the moist ground ahead and to Noah's right. Both men scrambled to gain their footing as Jerah approached.

"Stop!"

The invader ignored Jerah's command and ran into the malid orchard, which was about one hundred paces from the house.

"Come on, Noah," Jerah said as he sprinted past. "Try to keep up."

Needing no further taunts, Noah bolted into the trees. *There's no way my little brother is going to outrun me.* Ducking under branches as he ran, Noah struggled to keep the stranger in his sights, thankful it wasn't later in the year, when he would need to dodge the large fruit that would dangle from the limbs. He strained to hear the man's footsteps, but his own breathing and his brother's yelling blocked out any other sounds.

Knowing the wide river at the edge of the orchard would likely force the man to head right in a few moments, Noah cut across the second-to-last row of trees, aiming to put himself directly in the path of the trespasser. If Jerah continued his pursuit directly from the rear, the fleeing man would be trapped between the stream and the two brothers.

Slowing his pace slightly, Noah broke free of the orchard just in time to see the darkly clad man veer right to avoid the river, exactly as he had guessed. The stranger took several steps in Noah's direction before spotting him. He was only 20 cubits away when he stopped. He glanced first at Noah and then at Jerah, who emerged from the orchard and closed in.

Now that his eyes were well-adjusted to the dusky morning light, Noah saw a loaf of bread in the man's hand. "Who are you?"

The burglar looked at the brothers, dropped the bread, and then raced toward the river.

Noah shook his head before continuing his pursuit. Jerah, who had not slowed, tackled the man, sending them both toppling down the waist-high riverbank into the mushy silt of the river's edge below. Undeterred, the thief punched Jerah's cheek and then kicked himself free.

As the morning sky turned from pink into a lighter, brighter hue, Noah caught his first good look at the man. Dark, unkempt hair draped over his forehead. He possessed a muscular, but wiry, build. Noah clenched his fist. *Who is this man who thinks he can steal from us?*

Upon clearing the last several patches of tall orchard grass, Noah jumped down the embankment and used the drop as well as his anger to fuel his force as he slammed into the man. They fell into the cool, shallow water with a splash.

Keeping a grip on the stranger was more difficult than Noah had imagined. Quickly sizing up his opponent, Noah concluded the man was a little shorter and lighter, but he was solid and quick. Noah would have to use his height to his advantage if he wanted to maintain control. He gripped the man's shoulder and pressed his weight down to keep the challenger off balance in the soft, muddy river bottom, which squished and shifted constantly beneath their feet. Before Noah could react, the thief grabbed him around the neck with his left arm, and with his right, he delivered a sharp elbow into Noah's ribs, knocking the wind out of him.

As Noah staggered back, he saw Jerah attempt another jump on the man. However, this time, the man dodged the attack, causing the momentum of Jerah's body to slip right over him and drop in the deeper portion of the river. Anxious not to lose the intruder, Noah fought for air, but nothing seemed to enter his lungs. With great effort, he lunged toward the man and clipped his foot just as he exited the water. Any air left in Noah's lungs whooshed out as he landed flat on his stomach.

Gasping, Noah expected to hear sounds of the man scrambling away, but he only heard a splat as the thief landed in the nearby muck. Noah wanted to get to his feet, but the breathless sensation in his midsection caused him to contort in pain instead.

Jerah trudged through the water's edge and bent over to give his brother a hand up. "Ouch. That can't feel good."

"Go." Noah whispered, each word taking great effort. "Get him."

"There's no need. Look."

Fully sitting up now, Noah took in a deep breath and turned. He spotted the motionless man lying face up on the shore only a few steps away. "What happened?"

"You tripped him, and he got knocked out by that big rock. I don't think he's going anywhere for a while."

"Make sure he's still breathing."

Jerah walked over to the still figure and knelt down. "He's breathing." He checked the man for further injuries. "He's a little torn up, and already he's got a pretty good knot on his head. But nothing looks broken."

"Are you both alright?"

Noah looked up to see his father standing on top of the bank, wheezing from the sprint. "We're fine. That's more than I can say for him."

Lamech studied his two sons and then the man who had broken into his house. "Looks like you did a good job. Tie him up, and let's get him back to the house. We'll have to keep an eye on him."

Noah untied his belt and handed it to Jerah. "Here, use this." He wound his knee-length tunic around his body a little tighter and tucked the end of the cloth into the fold at his waist.

Lamech stepped down next to his sons as Jerah took the pliable leather strap and bound the man's hands together with a series of tight knots. "Tell me what happened," Lamech said. He reached out his hand to help steady Noah, who slowly climbed to his feet.

"I woke up early and heard some noise coming from the main room," Jerah said. "I assumed it was just Noah heading out to the woodshop, but decided to check because it seemed too late for Noah to be starting out. When I came around the corner, I saw him" — he gestured with his thumb to the prone man — "in our house. He was grabbing some food." He glanced at Noah before adding, "It's a good thing Noah was already out in the barn. I wouldn't have caught him alone."

Lamech frowned, though whether because of the invasion of his home or because of Noah's activities in the barn, Noah couldn't tell. Not caring to discover the source of his father's displeasure at the moment, he turned away and began climbing up the embankment. He paused at the top to pick up a soggy loaf of bread lying in the tall grasses. As he held it up to show his father and brother, it began to separate and slop into pieces down his raised arm. Quickly dropping the rest of it, Noah shrugged, "I doubt he'll want this anymore."

Jerah's quick grin lit up his face. "He won't miss it."

Lamech put a hand on Jerah's shoulder. "Come on, let's get him back to the house."

CHAPTER 2

Noah emerged from his room wearing a clean work robe. He strode from the side hallway into the main living area, where he watched as his mother, Nina, pulled two rounds of bread from the back of the brick oven.

They had lived in this home for only 20 years now. Noah remembered watching as his parents planned for the expansion soon after his sister, Misha, had been born. On more than one occasion, he had peeked through a break in the curtains that sectioned off Jerah's and his bed pallets to see his parents sitting at the low table, heads bent, as his mother sketched in the dim light from nearby oil lamps. His father would point at a few places on the sketch and comment. Their soft voices carried no discernable words, just excitement.

Noah and Jerah, as young as they were, had helped build the expanded timber-frame house. The back half of the large, single room was separated into two equal-sized bedrooms. Two other sleeping quarters were added, along with a hallway connecting all four rooms. The hallway turned at a right angle, opening into the large room at the front of the house, which contained the kitchen and dining area, and was the hub of family activity. Growing up, Noah liked that his room was the closest to the kitchen. That meant fewer steps to get to the food.

"Noah."

Noah jolted at his mother's voice.

"Can you get some honey on the table?" she asked. "Firstfeast is almost ready."

"Of course." Noah passed by the low table where the family ate their meals, noting that it was already filled with food. The clay oven on his right held a prominent position, dividing the table area from where the main room extended back in an "L" shape — the place they now kept their food stores. Noah moved to the right of the oven where he had installed the wooden cabinetry he built for his mother a few years ago. He inhaled the fresh aroma. *Mmm. There's nothing like the smell of fresh-baked bread.*

Noah opened the cabinet closest to him and reached on the topmost shelf, fumbling around the containers of dried figs and preserves until he found the honey. Stomach grumbling, he retrieved a crock filled with golden goodness. Had he been a bit younger, he might have given in to the urge to sample the contents.

The door opened. Lamech entered and hugged his slender wife. "Looks delicious, Nina."

Brushing back a strand of wavy hair that never would stay out of her face, she leaned in, gave him a quick kiss, and pointed to the table. "The fruits, nuts, and herbs are out, and the rest will be ready soon."

"Here's the milk. I'll go wash up."

Noah took the warm, fresh milk from his father and placed it and the crock of honey on the table. He walked over to the far side of the main room, where they kept all their dried goods stored in large earthenware pots and woven baskets. Jerah and Misha looked up at him from where they kept watch over the unconscious intruder, who lay on a low cot usually reserved for visitors. Noah had constructed the wooden frame of the bed, and Misha's talented fingers had tightly looped many cords around it in a diamond pattern, weaving and knotting them to provide a firm base.

Jerah stood at the head of the cot, one leg casually crossed over the other, and leaned his arm on the wall. Misha sat on a stool close to the injured man and checked a bandage on his arm.

Sunlight beamed through the large, open window next to Jerah, giving Noah an opportunity to get a good look at the prostrate man. He looked younger than Noah had guessed — perhaps just a few years older than Noah. Dark, curly hair spilled over a bandage covering the wound on his head, and a short scraggly beard gave the impression that he hadn't groomed himself much in recent days. Noah saw scratches and other marks on his limbs from the tussle early that morning. Peering closer, he noticed other scabs and scars, indicating deeper wounds that had mostly healed.

Noah glanced at Jerah. "How is he?"

"He's groaned a few times, but other than that, he seems to be resting well."

"And you?"

Jerah smiled and touched the bruise that swelled on his cheek. He winced but kept his grin. "This? This is nothing. I'll be fine."

Misha nudged Jerah with her bony elbow and looked up at him. "The girls at the market are going to think you look tough now."

Jerah laughed, stuck out his chest, and placed his hands on his waist, elbows out.

"Well, except those skinny arms will betray him," Noah said pinching his brother's biceps.

Jerah turned red as Noah and Misha laughed. "Hey, you would've never caught him by yourself."

Noah nodded. "That's true. You were pretty brave this morning. You should've seen him, Misha."

"Yeah, I jumped on him twice."

"And got thrown off twice." Noah smiled, turning up just one side of his mouth. "I'm the one who took him down."

"You just got lucky that he hit his head when you tripped him. Otherwise, as slow as you are, he would have been long gone."

Before Noah could fire his next comeback, Misha pointed. "Look."

Noah looked down at the bound man and called out to his father, "He's waking up."

The stranger briefly opened his eyes and then squinted hard. He tried again, looking toward Misha and blinking several times.

Lamech strode into the room and stood next to Noah. "How is he?"

Noah shrugged.

The young man attempted to see where the voice had come from, but flinched and quickly rested his head back down. He tried to move his hands, but the binding held fast. "Where am I? Why am I tied up?" His speech slurred a little. "Who are you?"

"Why don't you tell us first who you are?" Lamech placed a hand on Misha's head. "Let your mother know that we'll be there soon."

Shoulders slumped, Misha walked out of the room.

"Who are you?" Lamech resumed his questioning as he sat down on Misha's stool.

Rolling his head slowly, the stranger looked up at Noah and then at Lamech. "My name is Aterre." He opened his mouth to speak, but then stopped and closed his eyes. "Are you the ones I fought with?"

Noah nodded. "I'm Noah." He motioned to his brother, who was still standing by the window. "And that's Jerah."

Aterre shifted slowly and placed his bound hands unsteadily on the edge of the cot. Using them as a prop, he carefully scooted himself into a more upright position and leaned his back against the wall. With clenched jaw, he squinted into the sunlight, trying to see Jerah better, then he turned guarded eyes back to Lamech as the older man continued.

"I'm their father, Lamech. What were you doing in my house?"

"I was trying to find something to eat."

Noah noticed Aterre had a different accent. He pronounced some vowel sounds much more quickly than Noah had ever heard. *If I'd been able to travel, maybe I'd know where he was from.*

"And you thought to steal it from us?"

"I was hungry. It's how I've been able to survive these last several whole moons." He shifted again in obvious discomfort. Noah couldn't tell if it was because Aterre was uncomfortable over getting caught or if his injuries caused the distress.

"What about before that?" Noah asked.

Aterre shook his head. "I was never a thief, but lately I've had to." He paused and closed his eyes, his whole demeanor hardening. "All because they came."

Noah and his father exchanged glances.

"Who came?" Lamech leaned closer.

Aterre sat there stiffly.

"Young man." Lamech's voice firmed in a way Noah knew all too well. "I'm asking because I'm trying to decide whether I should turn you over to the town protectors. So unless you want to be punished by them, you need to start talking. Who came?"

"Men. They attacked my village one night. It happened so fast. I heard screams and saw bodies strewn everywhere." Aterre's eyes fixed on nothing, and they were filled with hatred. "My mother and sisters are gone. They would've killed me if I hadn't grabbed the knife I keep under my pallet and swung it at the face of the man who grabbed me. Judging by the amount of blood I felt, I think I cut him pretty bad. He screamed and let go of me." He slumped, his voice falling to a whisper. "I fled and kept on running until I was sure no one was following me."

Lamech gently placed his hand on Aterre's shoulder. "Do you know who the men were?"

Aterre shook his head, wincing at the sudden movement, and then shrugged off Lamech's hand. "No. There were just too many. They came so suddenly."

"Were they from around here?" Noah asked.

"I doubt it." Aterre sighed and looked at the wooden poles that comprised the main frame of the peaked thatched ceiling. "I've been on the run for nearly six whole moons, so I'm not sure if I know precisely where 'here' is. We lived in the land of Havilah, on the southwestern side of the Blue Sea. With no family left and no clue who attacked us, I just wanted to get far away from that place. I thought I'd take my chances and go to the land of Eden. I knew no one would even try to find me there."

Noah knew rumors about the land of Eden, which was located far away to the northwest, following the Hiddekel River up through the land of Asshur. Still he was curious to know what Aterre had heard. "Why there?"

Aterre raised his eyebrows. "You don't know?"

"Tell me." Noah knelt down to be at his eye level.

"There are tales that the land was cursed in ancient times and is haunted by the spirits of everyone who has died attempting to enter it. They say that anyone who goes there will either die or lose their mind."

Noah raised his eyebrows. "And you aren't afraid to go there?"

"My mother always taught us not to believe the legends. She said spirits of people couldn't harm anyone — that when we die, we just go to the ground and stay there. I guess I trust her more than the stories."

"We have our stories about Eden here too." Jerah leaned in.

"What stories?" Aterre tried to scoot closer but his jaw clenched and he quickly abandoned the attempt.

Jerah sat at the foot of the bed. "My great grandfather was named Enoch. He spent a lot of time in the land of Nod warning people that the Creator would judge the wicked."

"Of course, they mocked him," Noah said. "Father says the people there are pretty evil."

"One time he decided to go to the land of Eden with my father's uncle, Berit." Jerah lowered his voice. "But Enoch never came back."

"What happened to him?"

Lamech held his hand out to stop his second son from continuing. "My uncle says that he was walking behind my grandfather. He looked to the side for a second, and when he turned back he only saw a flash of light and my grandfather was gone."

"Really?"

Lamech nodded. "My uncle thinks he crossed the border to Eden and was turned into a spirit."

"Is that where the rumors come from?" Aterre looked more awake now.

"Maybe, but I don't think that's what happened. My grandfather walked closely with the Creator."

"What do you mean? They took walks together?"

Lamech shook his head and smiled. "No, that's our way of saying he faithfully followed the Creator's ways. So, my family and I believe that the Creator took him because he was so faithful."

"Why would He do that?" Aterre asked.

"Maybe to spare him from all the wickedness in this world."

Aterre raised an eyebrow. "By killing him?"

"He didn't die. He was taken so that he didn't need to face death. Now, he lives with the Creator."

Aterre let out a deep breath.

Lamech studied the young man for a long moment. "Do you have any idea what happened to your mother and sisters?"

Sadness swept over Aterre's face. "If they're still alive, my guess is that they're slaves."

"Slaves?" Lamech asked. "That's happening in Havilah too? My grandfather said that some places in Nod took people as slaves, but I didn't know anyone else would do something like that."

"I'd heard rumors about it," Aterre said, "but I never imagined it would happen to my family."

"I'm sorry about what you've been through." Lamech paused, looking critically at Aterre. "How would you feel about staying with us?"

20

Aterre looked up with widened eyes. He appeared as stunned as Noah felt. "With you? But I just robbed you and fought your sons. Why would you be so kind to me?"

"The Creator expects us to be kind to others, particularly to those in need." Lamech shifted in his seat. "If what you told us is true, then it seems to me that you need to be part of a family again." Lamech motioned to Aterre's hands. "Noah, Jerah, untie him."

"Yes, sir." Noah worked to untie the leather belt that had secured Aterre's hands together while Jerah undid the one at his feet. Misha entered the room again and stood next to their father.

Aterre stretched out his hands and gingerly flexed his arms. "Thank you."

"You're welcome. You know, there are other ways of getting food around here." Lamech motioned to Noah and Jerah. "I'm sure the boys wouldn't mind having some more help in the fields."

"The fields?" Aterre's eyes lit up ever so slightly. "You're a farmer? I'd love to help." Aterre attempted to sit up straight but quickly changed his mind. "I guess my head is still spinning."

Lamech lightly patted Aterre's shoulder. "Just take your time. I'll have Misha bring you a plate."

Misha jumped to her feet and smiled at Aterre. "You talk funny."

Aterre grinned. "I might say the same about you."

She laughed and hurried into the kitchen.

Lamech stood up. "Here's my proposal. Take some time to heal up, and then as long as you're willing to work on the farm, you're welcome to stay with us. Noah can teach you what you need to know."

Aterre looked at him steadily. "I don't know what to say."

"Don't thank me just yet," Lamech said. He smiled and put an arm around Noah and pulled him close. "You haven't had to work with my son yet."

CHAPTER 3

Noah set the stone blade of the hoe on the ground and leaned against the staff as he scanned his surroundings. A light breeze carried small, fluffy white clouds across the great blue expanse. The sun neared its high point of the day, but the air remained mild and comfortable. The beautiful weather would soon give way to the hottest days of the year, so he wanted to enjoy this while it lasted.

Thanks to Aterre's hard work over the past several weeks, they had not only planted grain in the two fields still fallow when he arrived, but they had cleared, plowed, and planted a brushy area Lamech had long been desiring to convert to useable land.

Noah looked at the small, healthy orb plant shoots at his sandaled feet and then up in the direction of the house. Although it was blocked from view by the barn, thinking of the house brought to mind the midmeal preparations going on inside. Noah's stomach grumbled. The table was always so full of good things this season that sometimes Noah pictured the carved wooden joints he had labored over giving way to the weight of the food. Midmeal provided the family a chance to gather together while they rested and let the hottest part of the day transition into the sun's descent. It gave Noah the energy he needed to finish working late into the evening.

Nestled between the Hiddekel River at its back and the barn in front, the house was the heart of the growing farm. The malid orchard and smaller river that emptied into the Hiddekel, where Noah had chased and tackled Aterre, lay to the right. Rising high above the north side of their house was Sacrifice Hill, as his father called it. At its crest, their family made regular offerings to the Most High: fruit, grain, and occasionally the best of the flock. While the hill hosted the most solemn occasions, it also was the location of some of the finest playtimes for Noah and his siblings.

Taking in the view, Noah visualized himself and his brother as boys, chasing each other down the slope. Sometimes they would race, seeing who could roll down the large mound fastest. The two boys competed at everything, and being the older brother, Noah usually came out ahead, but Jerah was never far behind.

Noah also thought back to the countless times he'd climbed that hill just to be with himself and his dreams. He remembered the boyhood ritual he'd observed whenever he got his chores finished early. He would climb Sacrifice Hill and watch for the small cargo boats on the river, carving replicas and longing to be on one. They rarely passed by, but Noah's mind raced with the potential for adventure that each one carried. Where did they come from and how far up or down the river would they travel? Perhaps they would encounter bandits and would have to prove their strength. What would it be like to visit other lands and see other peoples?

Alas, for now he was confined to the vicinity of Iri Sana, a town just up the Hiddekel. His father called it a small town, but it was the largest Noah had ever seen. Home to a few hundred people, it boasted a large farmers' market and a handful of specialty shops along its main road. What he wouldn't give to see the world, but that would have to wait for at least another year — until he turned 40. He sighed. *If Father lets me.*

Immediately ahead, the pale green stalks of gold and brown pebble fruit were already knee high, and in a whole moon would tower above him. To the south, fields of long grass would grow tall before being harvested about three times a year. Beyond that, several cattle and other livestock grazed on the rolling hills that stretched to the forest.

Something smacked Noah in the back of the head.

He spun and barely blocked a second clod of dirt before it reached its intended target. Brushing off his hands, Aterre laughed. He had recovered from his wounds in a few days and had joined Noah and Jerah in the farm work for the past several weeks. Though he tired easily at first, Aterre was a quick study and easy to get along with, despite their less-than-ideal meeting.

"Are you going to work or just daydream?"

"I've been working all morning, just like you. But I think it's almost time to head in for midmeal."

"I was thinking the same thing." Aterre put down his hoe. As he adjusted the upper portion of his robe, Noah noticed, not for the first time, a dark image on his back before it disappeared once more beneath the fabric covering.

"What is that?"

Aterre looked confused. "What's what?"

Noah closed the distance between them. "That mark on your back. I've never seen anything like it. It looked like a tree."

Aterre exposed his back again so Noah could see the inked image more clearly. The tree symbol began at the base of Aterre's shoulder blade. The trunk curved as it followed the shallow lines made by that bone. Leaf representations spread out gently to the right, and made a bolder statement as they crossed the rounded boundary made by his spine. "It is the mark of Sepha. Back in Havilah, the young men who join Sepha receive this symbol on their backs."

Noah furrowed his brow. "I've heard of Sepha before, but only in a negative way. My father says they distort the teachings of the Creator."

Aterre tucked the cloth into the fold at his waist. "With all due respect to your father, I don't see how that's possible. Sepha just teaches us how to calm our minds and focus our thoughts. My order also taught us some defensive and attacking moves. That doesn't go against the Creator's ways, does it?"

"Not that I know of," Noah said. "But that explains how you were able to take on Jerah and me at the same time."

"That might've had something to do with it." Aterre flashed a sly grin. "Although you farm boys are pretty tough."

As the two headed off toward the house, Noah wondered why his father would have spoken negatively about the group if they were not truly bad. "So Sepha doesn't have any kind of moral or spiritual teachings at all?"

"Well, we're taught to protect our families and our fellow members. We're told that if we focus properly and clear our minds of any distractions, then we can discover true wisdom."

Noah arched an eyebrow. "True wisdom? From inside yourself?"

Aterre shrugged. "I don't know. It never really made sense to me. I ignored a lot of those things and just concentrated on the personal combat skills. I thought they might come in handy someday." He paused. "Turns out when I needed those skills most, I was too late to save anyone but myself."

Noah was silent for a while. "From what you've shared, it sounds like you did well to get out of there alive."

"I guess. Anyway, that's what I know of Sepha."

"Well, the idea of wisdom from within is probably why my father disagrees with it. I think he'd say that true wisdom can only come from the Most High."

"But what if the two beliefs aren't really incompatible? What if when we block out distractions and calm our minds, it's the Creator who shows us true wisdom?"

Noah scratched the back of his head. "That's a good question. I don't think that's how it works though. We should talk to my father about it sometime."

A pair of young bovars skipped about their sturdy wooden pen as the young men approached. When grown, these animals brought a supply of milk to the family or helped with the plowing, but this pair had a different purpose. They were being kept safe and fed in this pen so that Lamech could one day sacrifice them to the Most High.

As Noah rounded the barn corner and headed toward the house, a small, gray, long-eared bounder stared at them as it nibbled on tall green sprouts growing close to the barn. Both young men walked to the well to wash up. Noah rotated the windlass he'd crafted, quickly drawing up a pail of the refreshing, underground spring-fed water.

"These blisters are finally getting better." Aterre held out his palms to receive the clean splash Noah offered.

"That's good," Noah said, rubbing his own hands together to get them clean. "Maybe now you'll finally stop whining about them."

Aterre playfully shoved Noah and the two laughed.

"You and your family talk about the Creator a lot," Aterre said when they had sobered. "How do you know what He's like, or that He's even real?"

Noah hesitated before speaking. It was true that his family often spoke of the Creator. His existence had never been something Noah questioned. But Aterre's words were not cynical or confrontational. He

25

seemed to have a genuine interest in finding an answer. Noah decided to respond with a question of his own. "You don't think He exists?"

Aterre shook his head. "No, I didn't mean that. I don't have any problem with the idea that an all-powerful Creator made us. That makes a lot of sense. But you and your family talk about Him as though He's right here, as if He cares deeply about you and this world. How do you know that He's really like that?"

"What else would He be like?" Noah asked.

"Well, the way He's talked about in Havilah, it's as if. . . ." Aterre ran his fingers through his hair. "It's as if He were distant, unconcerned. It's almost like we made up this concept of God so that we'd have someone to blame when things went wrong or someone to call out to when we need help." Aterre looked straight at Noah. "So when I see your family having such complete trust, not only in God's existence, but in His goodness, it makes me wonder how you can be so confident about it."

Noah shrugged. "I've always believed in Him." Noah motioned to the expanse of the farm. "Growing up where I have, with these people around me, I've always taken those things for granted. Everywhere I look I see the Creator's handiwork — the animals, the plants, the stars, and mankind. I've never bothered to ask how anyone knows the Creator exists because I just *know* that He does."

"So are you saying that it's just a feeling you have? You feel like God's real?"

"No, it's more than that." Noah looked up as he searched for the right words. "It's a deep conviction of my soul. Somehow, deep down, I just know. That probably sounds a little weird, although not as weird as finding true wisdom within yourself." Noah laughed.

"Fair enough." Aterre took a small cloth out and dipped it into the water before wiping sweat from his forehead. "I'm not trying to be obnoxious, but with all I've been through, I don't see how I can believe the same way you do. Do you know any way to show me that your view is true?"

"If my great grandfather were still around, I'm sure he could tell you. The Creator spoke with him." Noah stared off into the distance. "I wish I could hear directly from the Most High."

Aterre gave a nervous laugh. "No, thanks. That would scare me too much."

"Why?"

"Think about it. If the old stories are true — that the Creator banished the first two people because they ate a certain fruit, then I don't even want to think about what He'd do to me."

Finished with his washing, Noah smiled as he returned the bucket to its place. "You sure have a way of seeing things from a different perspective than I do. The way my father tells it is that they did the one thing God told them not to do. It was their fault. They rebelled against Him and brought death and the Curse into this world. Then He banished them so they wouldn't eat from the tree of life and live forever."

"Doesn't that seem harsh to you?"

"I guess it depends on how you look at it. It seems merciful to me."

Aterre's eyes widened as he cocked his head. "Merciful?"

"Yeah, can you imagine how miserable it would be to live forever in the world they broke? We work hard for our food. People commit all sorts of atrocities. If you could never die, then there wouldn't be any hope of being free from pain. It would eventually become an awful existence. And imagine how much worse the wicked would become with no fear of death."

"Hmm, I never thought of it like that."

As they neared the door of the house, Misha peeped her head out. "Noah, Mother wants you to bring some water in." With both hands, she thrust out a large clay container.

"Alright. Thanks, Meesh." Noah grinned at Aterre as they retraced their steps. He stepped back over to the waist-high, circular rock wall and once again lowered a bucket down the middle of the pit.

Aterre leaned against the well. "So how do you know your great grandfather told the truth about hearing from the Creator?"

Noah filled the jar as he spoke. "I trust him. I wasn't there to hear the Creator speak to him, but according to everyone who knew him, he was a very honest and upright man. So I don't believe he would lie about the most important issues."

"I guess when you have people you trust, it helps. Your family is becoming that to me." He grinned at Noah and slapped him on the back. "Well, except for you." Aterre grabbed onto one of the attached braided leather handles. "This place and your mother's baking — maybe I really did reach Eden after all."

CHAPTER 4

Iri Sana — Noah's 39th year

Noah reached over the side of the wooden cart to stabilize the baskets and clay pots that jostled against each other. The large wagon was filled with a variety of produce grown on the farm to be sold or exchanged at the weekly market in Iri Sana.

His father placed a steadying hand on the front corner of the cart. "Whoa. Easy, Meru," Lamech said as he used his other hand to tug lightly on the reins to slow the lunker through the rough terrain. The large, gawky beast stood a head taller than Noah at its shoulders and stretched about six cubits from the tip of the proboscis above its mouth to the end of its unimpressive tail. The short brown and white fur around its torso rippled above muscles as the creature towed the fully loaded wagon with ease.

Noah glanced up to the top of the hill and spotted more deep ruts cut into the path. "That rainstorm really tore up the trail."

Lamech nodded. "It sure did."

The early morning air carried the fresh, sweet aroma that lingered after it rained. His father said the smell came from oils produced by the plants, which, when mixed with rainwater, gave the earth a pleasant scent. He was probably right. This particular stretch of the trail smelled the best and it boasted the most vegetation. Massive trees lined both sides of the route. Early in the year, before they budded, these trees would be tapped to extract their sap, which Noah's mother would convert into syrup or sugar.

Long strands of gray fibers and green ivy draped themselves across random branches. Low-lying ferns and a colorful assortment of weeds, grasses, and flowers threatened to overtake the trail heading north from Lamech's farm to Iri Sana's main thoroughfare.

"Aterre and I will fill in the ruts before next week."

"Good." Lamech glanced back at Noah. "You two work well together. He's already like one of the family."

"Yeah." In a little over a year, Aterre had helped Lamech's farm thrive. The barn had been expanded again. They prepared and planted three new fields, which meant they painstakingly removed dozens of stumps. Noah thought about how sore his shoulders had been from the time spent hacking at roots so the stumps could be pulled away. Of course, a hard day's work in the heat was often capped off by a refreshing swim with Aterre and Jerah in the Hiddekel. Noah smiled. Those swims usually turned into some sort of crazy contest between the three of them.

"I'm proud of you boys," Lamech said. "You've really done some great work."

"Thanks." Aterre had made life on the farm more enjoyable, but his stories and descriptions of other parts of the world made Noah's heart grow even more restless. He had to see it for himself. He swallowed hard. *Creator, please give me the right words, and help my father understand.*

They crested the hill. In harvest season, after the leaves fell from the trees, parts of Iri Sana could be seen, but the lushness of the forest prevented any such view at this time. The path leading down appeared to be in better shape. Lamech eased the rein and Meru resumed her lumbering gait. It would not be long before they joined the main road.

"Father, with my 40th birthday coming up next whole moon, there's something I need to talk to you about."

Lamech took a deep breath and let it out slowly. His face showed a hint of sadness. "What is it?"

Noah looked down and kicked at the packed dirt inside one of the ruts, leveling the rough ground. The silence stretched. Finally, he looked up and held his father's gaze. "I know you prefer it when we get straight to the point, so here goes. I'd like to become a carpenter's apprentice."

Lamech pursed his lips and nodded. "I feared this day would come. You have a knack for woodworking, and it's easy to see how much you like it. But, Son, what's so wrong with farming?"

"Nothing." Noah shrugged. "I don't mind working the fields, but carpentry is different. There's a certain. . . ." He paused, eyes on the canopy above, searching for the right word. "A certain *satisfaction* I gain whenever I get a chance to build something. I just love doing it."

"I know you do, and you do great work. Why don't you continue working the farm? I could cut back some of your responsibilities to give you more time to build things."

"Maybe Jerah would have to pull his weight then." Noah chuckled, and his father rolled his eyes. "In all seriousness, I'm not looking for a lighter workload."

"But haven't things been better since Aterre arrived?"

"Oh, no doubt about it. The three of us have a great time." Noah stared at the trail. *How can I help him understand?* "I believe that the Creator has given me this passion for a reason. Maybe I'm supposed to pursue something different than you did. And I've learned all I can on my own. I want to study with a master."

"Have you sought the Creator about this matter?" Lamech asked.

"Yes. Almost every night I pray for guidance."

"And has He responded?"

Noah held up his hands. "I'm not sure. He hasn't spoken aloud to me, but it seems that the more I pray about it the more certain I become that this is what I want to pursue."

Looking down the road, Lamech scratched Meru's shoulder. They walked in silence until they reached the bottom of the hill. A hint of shame nagged at Noah for disappointing his father. However, Noah realized, there was a blend of some relief at finally broaching the topic. He straightened his shoulders.

Lamech halted the beast and turned to face his son. "Do you know what my prayer was when you were born? And why I named you Noah?"

Noah nodded and watched as his father's eyes welled up.

"Of course you do, I've told you before that I prayed you'd be the one to bring us rest from the Curse on the ground that our greatfather brought about when he sinned." Lamech reached down and picked up a fist-sized rock from the path and then whipped it into the undergrowth to their left. "How can you do that if you aren't a farmer?"

Noah let the question hang for a few moments. "What if that's your plan but not the Creator's? And how can I possibly bring rest to ground that the Almighty has cursed?"

Lamech hung his head and shook it. "I don't know. Maybe it's just the wishful thinking of a proud father." He looked Noah straight in the eyes. "I'm still proud to be your father, always." He coaxed the lunker forward again.

"And I'm grateful to be your son." Knowing his father's dissatisfaction, Noah remained silent for many steps. Yet he'd finally brought up the subject, and he wanted an answer. "Father, I know this is hard for you. Will you give me your blessing to become a carpenter's apprentice?"

"Where will you go? Who do you know that would be willing to train you?"

Noah held his palms up. "I don't know. I'd really like to see the world, but if there is someone nearby, then I'd settle for that."

"What about Darge? I'm sure he'd train you."

"I thought about that, and I'd love working with him. But Darge only does fine carving. He doesn't build large items like I want to."

The lush vegetation on the trail thinned and the road to Iri Sana came into view. A short, white-haired man, plodding next to a small cart towed by a spotted brown pack animal, crossed the intersection.

"Looks like Nuca and his load of roasted beans is going to beat us into market today." Lamech cracked a smile. "He must've had two helpings of his famous brew this morning."

Noah laughed and sensed that his father was happy for the subject to change. "Yeah, he moves pretty well for someone in his 800s. We'd better not forget to buy a pot of beans from him, or you'll be sleeping in the barn 'til next week."

Lamech snorted. "Your mother certainly takes her morning brew seriously. Don't let me forget."

The storm had carved another large groove just before the intersection. Lamech carefully guided Meru around the short, but now difficult turn. With her considerable strength and size, Meru had little trouble negotiating it. The problem Lamech faced was slowing the beast down enough to keep the goods safe in the wagon behind. Once again, Noah steadied the cart to the best of his ability until they reached the smooth, well-traveled road. Nuca and his cherished beans were now even farther ahead. Far behind them, Noah spotted two more farmers toting their produce to the market.

The damp coolness from all the shade and vegetation on the path had given way to a warmer, drier air. The sun stood about a fourth of the way to its peak and bathed the earth in a soft morning light. Multiple fields with crops at varying stages of growth stretched to their left, while to their right, the grass and weed-covered uneven ground gradually descended to the river.

Iri Sana stood directly in front of them. Initially established on the banks of the lazy Hiddekel a century earlier as an outpost for adventurers, the town gradually grew into the economic hub of the entire farming region. Quiet and slow every other day of the week, the town bustled with activity on the sixth day as nearly every farmer within walking distance gathered to buy, sell, or trade.

More than a dozen shops lined either side of the main street, each offering unique goods or services. At the end of the row, the road veered right and led down to the dock. The first building ahead to their left was Noah's favorite store — Darge's Crafts. The quaint wooden building outdated the town itself and was originally just Darge's home before he transformed the front room into a shop, selling various wood-carved toys, puzzles, and trinkets. He had farmed many of the nearby fields until, a decade before Noah was born, a falling tree crushed his right leg, which had to be amputated below the knee. Armed with an odd sense of humor and a kind spirit, Darge carved a variety of peg legs designed to look like animals from the region — he even used wood from the tree that injured him to make several of the artificial legs. At first, he made them to ward off the bitterness of losing a limb, but he soon found children flocking to his front door every market day to see what animal his leg sported that week and to hear the corresponding tale he would tell. He began carving other items, everything from toys and puzzles for the children to bowls and utensils for their parents.

Years ago, Noah had been one of those children. One day, the peg was in the shape of a fish, complete with detailed scales and fins, and Noah couldn't keep his eyes off it. His hands itched to try to imitate Darge's craft. He begged his father to buy him a set of woodcarving knives — a decision Lamech probably questioned several times and

32

especially regretted after this morning's conversation. After some brief instructions from Darge, Noah honed his craft and before long could whittle anything he set his mind to.

As Meru lumbered near Darge's door, Noah reached into the wagon and withdrew a wooden limb he had carved to look like a fish, similar to the one he remembered from so long ago. He'd made it as a gift for the man whose imaginative carvings had made such an impact on him. Noah held the fish up for his father to see. "You think he'll like this?"

"I'm sure he'll love it." Lamech winked. "As long as he isn't envious of your work."

Noah chuckled and slid the fish into his bag. "I don't think there's much chance of that. He's far better than I am."

"If you say so. It's hard for me to tell the difference. I just don't have an eye for that sort of thing."

"Maybe, but you can grow a crop of beans in a weed-infested field." Noah climbed the short steps to Darge's front door. "I'll meet you at the market after I'm done here."

"Very well, Son."

Noah opened the door and stepped in. A wave of memories blasted him as the familiar wooden scents struck his nostrils. How many times had he explored this small shop looking for a new contraption to occupy his free time? How many times had he listened to Darge weave tales of adventure to the children who came to see his leg? A smile tugged at his lips as the fond memories flooded his mind.

"Ah, young Noah. Morning peace." Darge stood up behind his counter and smiled. On a shelf farther back rested two dozen pegs that the children enjoyed the most. "Did you come to see my newest leg?"

Noah's smile widened, and he stepped across the room, skirting wooden toys set in piles around the floor. "Morning peace, Darge." The two men exchanged a firm hand-to-forearm grip before Noah reached into the sack slung around his shoulder. "It's great to see you. I'd be happy to see your latest work, but first I wanted to give you something."

"What's this?" The middle-aged man cracked a broad smile as he took the gift. "You made me a fish peg?"

It pleased Noah to see the man's delight. "Not just any fish peg. I tried to make it like yours from so many years ago — the one you wore the day my father bought my first set of carving knives from you."

"Your craftsmanship is remarkable." Darge held the gift up close to his face and turned it slowly, inspecting the quality. "Well, let's see if it fits." He bent over and replaced his current prosthesis with the wooden fish, locking it into place. He gently placed his weight on it and then took a couple of steps. "It's perfect. Thank you for this."

Noah nodded. His eyes moved from Darge's face to the previous peg now resting on the counter. "And is this your latest?"

"It is." Darge handed it to Noah. "What do you think?"

Now it was Noah's turn to marvel. It was clearly a bird with its wings spread out — the two wingtips corresponding to the two ends of the peg. The feathers had been exquisitely cut into the wood. A sharp hooked beak and a pair of perfectly formed clawed feet jutted out from the middle. "It's magnificent."

"Do you recognize it?"

"Yes, it looks like a soaring taroc. Spectacular." With no small effort, Noah pulled his gaze away from the bird and caught Darge's eyes. "What tale will you spin today to go with this?" Noah gently returned the masterpiece to its designer's hands.

Darge grinned. "I've been dreaming up a good one. The children will love it. You should stick around for old times' sake."

"I'd love to, but I need to help my father in the —" Noah's eyes focused on an intricately designed box on the counter. "What's this?"

"I wondered how long it would take before you noticed my latest invention." Darge picked up the miniature chest and handed it to Noah. "It's a puzzle safe."

Noah flashed a quizzical look. "A puzzle safe?"

"See all of these small cubes on the top? Each of these can twist and move around. When they are arranged in just the right sequence, the box will open."

About 30 little blocks were nested in the cover. Noah moved some of them and twisted others. "Fascinating. What's it for?"

"You can put valuables in there or anything that you'd want to keep from the prying eyes of your brother or sister." Darge flashed a half grin. "Just put them in the puzzle safe, spin a few blocks, and they'll never get into it without breaking the entire thing. But it's pretty sturdy. What do you think?"

"It's amazing, but I can't open it."

"That's because you don't know the arrangement." Darge reached out and placed the box on the table. "I used slightly different colors for the blocks so that they would create a picture when it's finished." He quickly spun parts and slid them into place. The pieces soon formed a recognizable shape, which filled out more and more as Darge worked.

"It looks like a long-eared bounder," Noah said.

Darge slid the final piece into place. "Because that's what it is. Watch this." He flipped a latch on the front of the box to the side and lifted the lid. About a span in length and width, the well-oiled interior drew out the deep colors in the grain.

Noah let out a quiet whistle. "Is it for sale?"

Darge nodded. "One silver pikka, but for you Noah, I'd sell it for three copper pikkas."

Noah's pulse quickened in excitement. "Only three pikkas? I'll take it." He unfastened the leather strip around his neck and counted the small flat piks and round pikkas of copper and silver that were strung on it. After some quick calculating, Noah slipped off a silver ball and handed it to Darge. "I don't mind paying full price for something like this. Besides, the Creator has truly blessed our farm this year. I can afford it."

The shopkeeper dropped the silver pikka into a drawer beneath his counter. "Thank you, Noah, and may He continue to bless you and your family."

"Thank you, and may He do the same for your family." Noah turned to leave. "Farewell, Darge."

"Farewell, Noah. Don't be a stranger."

Noah slipped the unique box into his bag and left the store. After his eyes adjusted to the morning's brightness, he hurried down the street, passing several shops and a handful of farmers with their carts or wagons in tow. He turned right at the end of the street and made his way down the hill. The famers' market was just getting started. Wagons, booths, and tables of every type of fruit, vegetable, herb, and nut Noah had ever known were on display. He spotted Meru among the animal stalls to his left so he knew his father had arrived. The Hiddekel flowed softly behind the market. One small dock extended about 30 paces into the water. Beyond the river lay rolling hills covered with forest as far as the eye could see.

Noah wove his way around multiple tables and greeted each vendor he passed. He recognized all of them, but some were mere acquaintances.

He found his father busily organizing their wagon for a day of trading and sales. "Sorry I'm late."

Lamech looked up from his work. "Actually, you're right on time. Help me with these."

One by one, Noah and his father unlatched each side wall of the wagon and allowed them to hang beneath the flatbed. They slid their wares to the edge, and using a low table Noah had built, they elevated the fruits and vegetables in the middle of the bed so that every item could be easily viewed.

"So what did Darge think of his gift?" Lamech asked.

"He really liked it."

"Noah." A deep voice resonated behind him.

Noah knew that voice. He spun quickly to greet one of his father's friends. "Master Toman, it's great to see you."

The broad-shouldered, barrel-chested man stood a handbreadth higher than Noah. His wavy jet-black hair and deep brown eyes complemented his dark complexion. If any man was as strong as Meru, this was he. Toman nodded. "And it's good to see you, young Noah, son of Lamech. Your father tells me that you want to be a carpenter's apprentice."

Noah glanced back at Lamech, who turned away and acted as if he weren't paying attention, but not before Noah saw the gleam in his father's eyes. Noah fought back a smile and faced Toman again. "Yes, sir."

"Well, as I told your father, my brother is a carpenter and lives a one-day journey from here. I don't know if he's looking for an apprentice or would even want one, but I'd be happy to send word to him to find out. That is, if you're interested."

Noah instantly pictured himself as an apprentice who quickly made a name for himself because of his work. It took a moment for his mind to come back and configure a response. "Yes, please find out for me."

The man nodded again. "Your father tells me that your Rovay celebration is next whole moon. Hard to believe you're that old already."

"Yes." Noah stood tall. "I'll officially be a man."

"I'll try to get word from my brother before that." Toman held out his arm.

Noah cringed internally and braced himself for the vice that would soon crush his forearm as he extended his hand. He squeezed Toman's arm tight, but his fingers didn't seem to make a dent in the man's muscle-bound forearm. At the same time, Noah imagined his own hand going numb from the man's mighty grip. Finally, Toman released the vice and Noah felt the blood flowing back to his hand.

"I will see you soon," Toman said.

"I'm looking forward to it. Thank you!"

Noah turned and walked over to his father, who was arranging some of their first crop of leafy vegetables. When he was sure Toman was no longer looking, Noah stretched out his fingers and arm, hoping to loosen the muscles up again. "Father." He waited for the man to look up. When he did, Noah gave him a tight hug. "Thank you." After releasing him, Noah looked him in the eye, and cracked a smile. "I'll finish setting up. Why don't you visit Nuca, so we get some of those beans before we both forget."

CHAPTER 5

Noah darted across the yard, slowing just enough for Misha to stay right on his tail without catching him. Playfully, he taunted her as he zigged and zagged just out of her reach. "C'mon Meesh. You almost caught me."

More than two dozen young people cheered her on, waiting for her to tag him so another game could start. "Go, Misha!" "Get him!" "He's an old man now!"

Noah dashed behind a syringut tree. Misha stopped, waiting to see which side he would come out. She giggled as he faked one way and then the next. Noah surveyed his options as the others slowly closed in, making his escape more difficult. He sprinted to the right and easily avoided his sister. He looked back to see how near she was. As he spun back, he caught Jerah out of the corner of his eye.

"Watch out." Jerah pushed Noah to the side and laughed.

Noah lost his balance and tumbled to the ground. He got on his hands and knees, but before he could scramble to his feet, Misha jumped on his back and screamed in triumph.

Noah stood up as easily as if his sister weighed nothing at all. She let go and he turned to hug her. "You got me." He grinned at Jerah. "I'm not sure if it was fair, but you got me."

Misha jumped away. "Let's play again."

"Just one more," Noah said as he brushed some grass and dirt off his robe. "Who wants to start?" Since Noah had been the last one caught, he won the right to pick who would start the next game. He looked at his brother and tapped a finger on his chin, faking a tough decision, but then turned and pointed at his cousin, Dunal, who was about the same age as Jerah. "You start."

The youths scattered to avoid Dunal, who had started counting.

Aterre came around the corner of the house. "Noah!"

"Is it time?" Noah asked.

"That's what your father sent me to tell you."

"Okay, I'll be right there." Noah caught Dunal's attention. "You're in charge now."

"Alright," Dunal said. "I'm looking forward to your big night."

Noah nodded and followed Aterre. His friends and close relatives had gathered to celebrate his Rovay today. By this evening, he would be considered a man. Every part of the day was designed to celebrate this rite of passage. In the morning, he played games with all those under 40. Now he would meet with his father and some other godly men. They would pray with him and for him as he prepared his mind and heart for the evening events. Then he would bathe and put on his father's cere-monial clothes to offer, for the very first time, sacrifices on behalf of his family. When it was complete, neighbors and friends would join them for a great feast in his honor, and they would celebrate late into the night. Noah glanced back at his younger relatives, feeling the symbolism of leaving them behind. *I'm no longer a child.*

"You look nervous." Aterre nudged him with his shoulder.

"Because I am." Noah cracked his knuckles. "This is important for my family and for me. My grandfather says that we've practiced this for many generations."

"So you'll offer the sacrifices tonight, and then what?"

"Then once I get married, it'll be my responsibility to offer them for my family each year."

Aterre stopped and motioned to the crowd of young people running around the yard. "You have your eye on any particular young lady?"

Noah laughed. "Honestly, I haven't given it much thought yet." It was fairly common for a man to marry a close relative, and Jerah occa-sionally teased him about their cousin, Pivi. Although she had grown quite lovely, Noah had never had more than friendly feelings for her. He knew that the teasing was really due to Jerah's own interest. He scanned the grounds — sure enough, Jerah seemed more interested in flirting with Pivi than the game. He looked back at Aterre. "I'm more nervous about what Toman might say tonight."

"And if his brother wants an apprentice, you're just going to leave me here?"

Noah shrugged his shoulders and laughed. "Maybe. At least you like farming. Besides, this way you and Jerah could fight over who gets to marry Pivi."

Aterre pushed him and then sprinted for the house with Noah close behind.

* * * * *

The fire crackled and an overpowering aroma of burning flesh assaulted Noah's nostrils as he raised his arms. "Almighty Creator, please look with favor on this sacrifice and continue to bless Your servants."

A thick gray cloud enveloped him as he opened his eyes, causing them to burn and tear up. The smoke blocked any view of the house or barn at the bottom of the hill and obscured the early evening sun. Pulling part of his robe over his nose, Noah bent low and picked up the blood-soaked knife he had just used to kill the fatling. He had watched his father perform the sacrifice annually. The grain was offered first, and Noah had little trouble putting the firstfruits of their harvest on the fire. But the blood sacrifice was always painful. Even when his father did the actual killing, Noah's heart ached as he watched their best young bovar squirm and kick during its final breaths.

He had just learned how much harder it was to slit the animal's throat and hold onto it while its life flowed out. Blinking back tears, he glanced at the burning sacrifice, haunted by the stare of betrayal the young bovar had fixed on him in its final moments, horrified anew at the cost of sin.

As the fire burned lower, Noah stood and wiped the knife and his bloody hands on his apron. Head low, he stepped away from the flames and joined his family, who knelt around the earthen altar. Lamech placed a hand on Noah's shoulder and said a prayer of thanksgiving for the Creator's provision in spite of the Curse on the ground.

The annual sacrifice came to a close after several other men prayed. Noah rose and looked again at the offering. The fatling was nearly burned up and the fire smoldered. As they descended the hill to prepare for the feast, several family members congratulated Noah on a job well done.

His ceremonial duties complete for the day, Noah focused on the crowd gathering near the house. One man in particular stood out, or rather, above the others. Noah fought the urge to run toward Toman, but he could not resist picking up his pace. The large man spotted Noah and made his way through the crowd to him.

"Master Toman, thank you for coming."

"Congratulations, Noah. You have grown into an honorable young man." Toman held out his hand for his customary painful greeting.

Noah held up his blood-stained arm. "My apologies, sir. I haven't yet had an opportunity to wash up."

Toman pulled back his hand, unaware of Noah's relief. "I well remember my first sacrifice."

Noah nodded and a solemn feeling came over him as he reflected on his first sacrifice. "Indeed." An awkward silence hung for a moment as Noah tried to figure out how to shift the conversation. He decided a direct approach would be best. "Master Toman, have you received word from your brother about an apprenticeship?"

The smile vanished from Toman's lips. "I'm sorry to be the bearer of bad news on your big day. I wish it could be better. My brother said that he just took on a young charge earlier this year, and as long as it works out, he won't need another one for nearly four years."

Noah unsuccessfully fought against showing disappointment. "I understand. I appreciate you asking him."

"I'll be sure to let you know if the situation changes." Toman put an encouraging hand on Noah's shoulder. "I know you have your heart set on this. Trust the Creator. If He wants you to learn carpentry, then He will guide you to that when the time is right."

The corner of Noah's lip curled up in a half-smile. "Thank you, Master Toman." Noah believed his tall friend was correct. The Creator would make His will known when the time was right. But that did not make it easy for his restless heart to wait. Still, a feast in his honor was about to begin, and he wasn't ready for it. "I'd better wash up." Toman nodded and turned to greet others.

Noah entered the house, determined to hold his head high this night, even though his hopes had been dashed. On his way to his room, he dodged several women, who were scuttling about in final preparations for the feast.

He entered his room and went to the bucket of water. Scrubbing the bloodstains off his hands and arms took longer than he anticipated, and despite his best efforts, thin semicircles of dried blood lined his fingernails. Eager to get back to the celebration, he put on the brand new robe his mother had woven specially for this evening. Deep blue strips stitched onto the light brown fabric gave this outfit a more distinguished look than his ordinary work clothes. Noah closed his eyes, took in a deep breath, and then let it out. *Creator, thank You for bringing so many loved ones here today. Help me to see past my disappointment so that I may see Your goodness. Help me to trust You in all things.*

Noah avoided several women again as he moved through the kitchen. A hundred scents filled the air as trays and dishes were filled and delivered to their destination outside. Amid the cacophony, Noah heard his mother's voice. He turned just in time for her to smother him with a hug.

"I'm so proud of you," Nina said, tears suddenly appearing in her deep brown eyes. "You did wonderfully today."

Noah looked into her dark eyes. They always gave the impression that she knew exactly what he was thinking. "It was a great honor."

She let go of him. "And it's an honor for your father and me to watch you become the man you are." She smoothed a loose part of his garment and fussed with the way it draped over his shoulder. "Do you like your new robe?"

"I love it."

She kissed his cheek. "Now, get out there and enjoy your celebration."

Noah stopped Pivi's mother as she attempted to step past them with a woven tray of cakes. "I'll take those for you." He grabbed the tray and headed for the door.

"You'd better not eat all of them," she said.

He flashed a mischievous smile. "I'll be sure to save one."

Noah walked outside, and after thanking half a dozen well-wishers, he found an open spot for the desserts he carried on one of the four large rectangular tables that stood waist high. Setting the cakes down, he licked a finger that had "accidentally" scraped against one of the treats. Most of the guests found seats around the dozen rounded, low-lying tables in the yard. The more elevated platforms, including the one on which the recently delivered cakes sat, were laden with the largest array of food Noah had ever seen at his home. It was as if the farmers' market from Iri Sana moved to his house for the night. The women had outdone themselves. The smells of spices enticed him to inspect closer. He saw many of his favorite sauces, ready to be placed on grains or scooped up with pieces of bread. There were savory stews, generops, and stuffed peppers. Gourals were cut in half and steamed, then lavishly sprinkled with a variety of herbs; their yellow interiors looked like cheery suns. All this made his stomach growl.

He had been to Rovay celebrations before, but never paid close attention to the details. He had always been too busy playing with his friends. But now it was his turn to be at the center of what many considered to be the most important celebration in a person's life. He took his seat at the head table and scanned the crowd, which had doubled in size since the sacrifice.

Jerah had a small cluster around him, and he clearly enjoyed being the center of attention, especially since Pivi was part of the group. She and Misha laughed at something his brother said. Toman reclined on a cushion nearby, looking like a small mountain next to his diminutive wife. Aunts, uncles, cousins, and longtime family friends chatted, laughed, and reminisced. Noah paused to treasure the moment, but then furrowed his brow. *Where is Aterre? And Father?*

The flurry of activity near the door of the house slowed as the last of the trays and bowls were carried out. His mother motioned for Jerah and Misha to join her at the place of honor. The other women soon took their seats as well. *There they are.*

Noah's father, grandfather, and Aterre came around the side of the house and made their way to the head table. "Where have you been?" Noah asked as Aterre sat in the chair to his left.

Aterre raised his eyebrows and shrugged.

Noah tried to read his friend's expression. *What is he hiding? Is it good news or is he in on some sort of mischief?* Noah decided it was most likely the latter and determined to stay alert during the rest of the evening to make sure he wouldn't be caught unaware.

Lamech stood behind Noah and spread his arms out wide, waiting for the crowd to quiet down. "Dear friends and family. Thank you for honoring our home with your presence here tonight." He put his hands on Noah's shoulders. "As you know, my oldest son became a man today, and you honor him tonight as well."

"A fine son you've raised," someone said from the back.

"A fine son, indeed," Toman said. "The Creator has blessed you."

Others nodded or shouted in agreement.

Lamech held his arms out again. "Yes, the Creator has blessed Nina and me richly with such fine friends and family."

Noah nudged Jerah with his sandaled foot to get his attention and leaned in close. "Well, maybe not you."

Jerah shook his head and smiled. For once, he seemed to struggle with finding a comeback.

Lamech continued to speak. "Forty years ago, the Creator entrusted us with our first son." He looked at Noah. "At that time, I never could've imagined how much my love for you would grow over the years, and how proud I would be as a father, watching you grow into the man you've become." He wiped a tear from his eye. "Seeing you offer the sacrifice today, knowing that you love and trust the Creator and want to follow His ways, is the greatest joy of my life." He paused as Noah stood to embrace him.

"Thank you."

Lamech's tears flowed freely. He nodded to Methuselah, who took that as his cue to stand.

"One hundred and eighty-two years ago, I stood up at a party like this one to bless one of my sons," Methuselah said gesturing in Lamech's direction. "I know you're all looking forward to eating, so I'll keep this short. Lamech, you've followed the Creator's ways and, along with Nina, have faithfully begun to raise your beautiful children. I pray that God will bless you with many more." He approached where Noah stood with his father. "Lamech, you'll remember this. At that celebration, my father Enoch asked you to publicly commit yourself to follow the Creator."

Lamech nodded. "I remember."

Methuselah smiled. "And you've kept that promise. Now, if you don't mind, I'd like to ask my grandson to do the same."

Noah put an arm around his father and grandfather.

"Noah, son of my son, before all those gathered here tonight, do you vow to serve the Creator with all of the days He gives you?"

Noah took a deep breath and nodded. "I do."

Methuselah placed a hand on his shoulder. "And if God grants you a wife and children, do you promise to lead them in following the Creator's ways?"

"I do."

"As you know, my father, your great grandfather, spoke boldly against the growing wickedness in this world. Enoch was the godliest man I've ever known, and I see the same sort of spirit in you, Noah. Do you pledge to stand against evil and to stand for the truth no matter what it might cost you?"

Noah took another deep breath and affected the most serious tone he could muster. "I promise to stand against evil and to stand for the truth, even if it costs me my life."

"May the Creator give you the strength and courage to honor these vows." Methuselah hugged him tightly.

The crowd stood and applauded. Noah noted that the first star had made its appearance amid the backdrop of the still blue sky, and he bowed his head in silent prayer.

Lamech once again held his arms out. "Before we eat, I just have one more announcement. Please, everyone, have a seat."

Aterre tapped Noah's shoulder and grinned, a knowing look in his eyes. Confusion spread across Noah's face. *What are they planning?*

"Hearing my son commit to following me in serving the Creator makes me the proudest man on earth." Lamech fought to keep his composure. "He does not wish to follow in my footsteps as a farmer. Instead, he feels called to become a carpenter's apprentice."

Expressions of surprise and confusion registered on faces in the crowd. Toman nodded. This wasn't news to him.

"I trust the Most High is guiding him in this decision," Lamech said. "And as much as I'd like to keep him nearby, I've learned that my father's cousin is a carpenter and I'm giving my blessing for my son to become one as well."

Everyone present clapped, but Noah only sat up straight, his eyes wide.

"Let the celebration continue for my son, a carpenter."

As the crowd's focus dispersed, Noah leaned in to the circle formed by his father, grandfather, brother, and friend. "A carpenter?"

Methuselah unbound a leather strap wound around his forearm. "Of a sort. My cousin Ara is a shipbuilder in Iri Geshem. He builds the boats you see on the river once in a while. If you're interested" — he waved the leather strap — "I'll give you my armband as a pledge for Ara that you come with my blessing. I'm sure he'll have a place for you."

Noah could hardly contain his excitement. "Of course I'm interested." He paused. "Iri Geshem? Isn't that all the way at the end of the river on the Great Sea?"

"Yes, it will take you about two whole moons to travel there," Methuselah said. The thin lines around his eyes deepened in a shrewd look. "Are you still interested?"

Noah thought of all the time he'd spent watching for the boats that occasionally passed by. He'd often wondered where they came from, where they went. His heart pulsed with excitement of the discoveries such a journey would bring. So soon after being crushed, his dreams were becoming a reality.

Aterre's kick brought Noah back. "Yes. Yes, I'm interested. It sounds amazing. And you're really letting me go, Father?"

"On two conditions. First, you keep the vows that you just made. And second . . ." Lamech hesitated. "Take Aterre with you."

"But what about the farm?"

"Jerah's still here, and if this is truly of the Creator, then we'll have enough hands to do the work that's here. I'd rather know that you have a companion for this distant adventure of yours. And it would be good for Aterre."

Noah looked at Aterre. He was beaming and nodding his head. *So that's what they were planning.* Noah hugged his father as hard as he could. "Thank you, Father. I'm happy to accept."

"Good," Lamech said. "Now let's eat."

CHAPTER 6

Land of Havilah — Noah's 40th year

Naamah sat in the corner, rocking back and forth. She idly twisted a thin lock of her silky, rich black hair between her fingers. She blinked dully, not wanting to think, not wanting to care.

"What's wrong?" Tubal-Cain knelt in front of her.

To block him from view, Naamah lowered her head, letting her hair become a barrier.

"You know, sitting here moping isn't going to help things. Let's go for a walk. We've got time."

"No."

"Talk to me," he said, his voice gentle.

Peeking through the curtain of hair, she could see that he hadn't moved. Knowing his concern made her feel just a little better. "No."

His knees straightened and she heard him stride over to the window of her spacious bedroom. The dreary, gray sky matched her mood perfectly. "Come on, Amah. Being sullen won't help anything. What's ever been so bad that we haven't been able to get through it together?"

Silence. Too mad, she would not give in by speaking to him.

"This isn't my fault and you know that."

Not one word, she commanded herself, tightening her full lips.

"You know you'll feel better just talking it out. So talk."

With head still bowed, Naamah caught a smile just in time before it crept up the corners of her mouth. She liked this. He was worried about her. That felt good. And there was something else too, but she couldn't quite place it. Influence. That is what it must be. She had some effect in another person's life. Lifting her head slowly, she looked at her tall, handsome brother and sighed. "I just feel helpless. And so worthless, you know?"

"How do you feel worthless?" he asked and sat down on one of the many large cushions scattered around her room.

"It's been different ever since *she* came here." Naamah spat out her words. "We were a family and a happy one. Sure, Da wasn't always involved, but it was good. When we'd go to the little retreat home, we had such fun times." Naamah got up and began to pace. "But then Da had to bring her home. What? Wasn't Mam enough for him? He had to have another wife? And what did Mam do about it? Nothing. She just let things happen and accepted it all. Da practically ignores Mam because he's so enamored with *her*. And Mam just lets him. She sits around and does nothing about it."

Naamah stopped and stood directly in front of her brother. "I can't do it. I don't want to." Knowing she wasn't finished, she lowered herself onto her soft, opulent bed. The words kept pouring out. "Do you know what it's like when I'm around town now? People look at me strangely. They know our family is different, and they look at me as if I'm different, as if I'm tainted somehow. And now with Da becoming more involved in the city council, that just makes it worse."

"I agree that Adah feels like an intrusion on our family, but it wasn't her choice either. Da brought her here after one of his trips." Tubal-Cain's care for her was evident in his eyes. "Plus, it's not like this happened yesterday."

Naamah ignored the reason in his comment and pointed to the middle of her chest. "The hurt's been here ever since she arrived. I guess today makes it feel like someone's taken the pain, sharpened the edges, and jabbed it into a fresh part of my heart." Naamah's quivering voice grew louder as she spoke. Angrily she wiped away tears that appeared in spite of her wishing them not to. "Don't you realize what this means? She's having a baby. It's not just Mam that's being replaced. Now we're being replaced too."

"Come on, it's just a baby. You like babies. You can cuddle and help care for the little one, and we can both teach him what it means to be part of our family."

"You'll see. It's not 'just a baby.' Things will only get worse around here."

"No, Amah. Things don't have to be that way. It'll depend on what you make of it. No matter the circumstances, you can always choose to have the right attitude; and that makes all the difference."

Naamah plopped one of the many pillows that fluffed about her bed into her lap and gently fingered the rich purple fabric. "So you're saying that if I change my perspective all this will go away? You know that's impossible, right? Even if that woman and her newborn were banished from Havil, things would still be different."

Tubal-Cain sighed. "I'm not saying the situation would change. I'm saying how you view it would change." He walked over to her and gently placed a hand on her cheek. "Why don't you try it? What's the worst that could happen?"

She glanced up at him, sadness in her eyes. "It doesn't work."

"So you'd be right where you are now."

"Yeah, I guess."

"With one difference." He grinned at her.

"What's that?"

"You wouldn't have this pillow because I'm taking it." He snatched the pillow from her lap and hit her soundly with it on the side of her head.

"Ow! Hey!" She threw her arms up in protection. "You're too old to do that."

"Oh, am I?" He laughed as he continued to swing it at her.

"Yes," she mumbled through a mouthful of one of his pillow attacks. She sat up straight. "And at 30, I'm too old too."

"You won't be 30 for another eight whole moons and you know it. Trying to make yourself sound like you're not still a child. Ha. I know better."

"Well big brother, do you know enough to avoid this?" She snatched up a sturdy pillow in each hand and returned blows, one to his head and another to his waist. She giggled. "Direct hit."

"Children, stop. Your father has summoned us to the birthing room."

Naamah looked up. Her mother, Zillah, had entered the room. The dour look on her face showed she wasn't any more pleased about the situation than Naamah. She crossed her arms and huffed. Clearly, her agenda

49

did not include patience at this time. Tubal-Cain and Naamah dropped their makeshift weapons and quietly followed her out of the room.

As Naamah walked behind her mother and brother down the narrow hallways and up several couplets of stairs, the painful feelings rushed back. She dragged her feet as her chest tightened and her breathing grew heavy. She didn't care that she lagged behind. All too soon, they reached the birthing room and Zillah opened the thick, ornately carved wooden door. The three stepped inside and stayed in the back of the room. Naamah placed her hands behind her back so that they touched the wall; she liked the comfort it brought to know that she was as far away as possible.

Naamah hated how each aspect of the room showed her father's preference for his new wife, Adah. While her own room was by no means small, this room dwarfed it, making hers look like a closet in comparison. She saw the vaulted ceiling, as well as two columns that formed three openings to a balcony overlooking the city. Sunlight flooded into the room. Hanging metal orbs caught the light from the balcony and reflected it around the room. A raised platform supported the bed and colorful curtains dropped from the ceiling surrounding it. Naamah was grateful for the obscured view. Not ready to pay attention to the occupant or the reason why they were all there, Naamah focused on the dais, which was large enough to support a bed three times the size of her own. Yet it still seemed like a small portion of the room.

Everything about this room showed care, prestige, comfort, even pride. *So this is what Father's been building in all these renovations.* She knew that the size of their original home had almost tripled, but she had always stayed away from Adah's extensive quarters.

The sounds of painful effort from the woman in labor rang out. Suddenly a new cry broke through. It was the squeal of a healthy baby. Naamah looked over at her own mother, who blankly stared at her slippered feet. Though her eyes did not hold their old spark, she was still stunning. Her body still sported the curves that had originally held captive the attention of a young warrior — the same warrior who now had shoved her aside for his new conquest.

At that moment, her father yanked apart the curtains and lifted the baby. "A son!" Naamah heard the exultation in his voice and saw his pride as he held the tiny bundle high above his head. He proceeded to the balcony and announced the arrival of yet one more of his progeny to whomever happened to be passing by.

Naamah looked at Tubal-Cain, her eyebrows raised. He shrugged but did not look as at ease as earlier. Several more people hurried into the room. Adah struggled and writhed in pain. Concern spread across the faces of those attending her. Naamah nibbled her little finger. *Maybe she'll die and we can go back to the way things were.* She shook her head. *Come on, Naamah. How could you think that? That's not fair.*

Fighting to rein in her thoughts, Naamah focused on the turmoil at the bedside. Adah groaned weakly several times, and one of the attendants rushed to summon the father and his new son back to the bedside. He leaned close, whispering something to his wife. She sat up and gripped the sheets tightly.

"There's another one!" a midwife shouted to no one in particular. After a few agonizing moments, another cry broke the air.

A nursemaid examined the newest addition. "A second son!"

Naamah's father exchanged the first twin for the second and held him up. He looked at Adah. "Two boys! You are indeed worthy to be my wife." He turned to face his older children. To Naamah it seemed as if he were on the stage and they were merely shadows whose only value came from his attention. "Zillah, Tubal-Cain, Naamah, come see my two sons."

Slowly, Naamah separated from the wall and followed her mother and brother. The painful grip that had been squeezing her heart ever since Adah's arrival intensified and dug in its fingernails. Her breath caught in her throat as she tried to keep her composure. Feeling a hand on her shoulder, she looked into the caring face of her brother and exhaled, the pain just a little less because it was shared.

Chapter 7

Iri Sana — Noah's 40th year

I'll miss you too." Noah bent low and wrapped his arms tightly around his sister.

"I don't want you to go," Misha said.

"I know, but this is something I have to do." He kissed her cheek, let go of her, and turned to his brother.

"It's about time you leave." Jerah smiled and hugged him.

"I love you too." Noah laughed. "Take care of our sister."

"You know I will."

Noah pulled back, put his hands on Jerah's shoulders, and looked him in the eyes. "I'll miss you broth —" He choked up and then swallowed the lump in his throat. "Honor the Creator."

While Aterre said his farewell to his stand-in parents, Noah took in the familiar surroundings one more time. The early morning sun was mostly hidden behind light gray clouds that released a soft drizzle. The gentle current of the Hiddekel lapped the side of the boat, which was partially beached on the shore at the edge of their property. Taht, their trusty pack animal, stood unsteadily on the deck, apparently unsure what to make of the lightly swaying surface. She was secured in a small pen next to their bags. Red and pale green malids sparsely populated the trees in the orchard. Sacrifice Hill rose to their right, its top obscured by fog.

When Aterre turned his attention to Jerah, Noah stepped to his mother and held her fast.

"I can't believe how quickly the time has gone." She kissed his cheek. "Be safe, Son."

"I will. I love you, Mother." He kissed the top of her head and freed his grip. "I'll miss you."

"I love you too."

Lamech embraced Noah. "Never forsake the Creator's ways. He will guide your steps as you walk with Him."

"I won't forget." Noah wiped his face to remove some of the light rain as well as his tears. "I love you, Father. Thank you for everything."

"I love you, Son." Lamech released Noah and his eyes welled up. "Remember, if things don't work out. . . ."

"We'll be on the first boat back home." Noah backed away and looked at his family against the backdrop of the only home he had ever known. He inhaled deeply and then exhaled. "I can't believe this is really happening. I'll miss you all so much. May the Creator keep you safe and well."

Each family member said their farewell. Noah wanted this moment to extend longer — at least part of him did — but he also wasn't sure how much more of it he could take.

"You ready then?" Aterre asked, as if reading Noah's thoughts.

Noah wiped his eyes again and nodded. "Let's go."

He couldn't believe how the days had passed by so swiftly. At the onset of the agreement with his father to wait until after the harvest, the delay felt long. But now that time seemed to have vanished like a night fog on a sunny morning. Noah was satisfied with what they had accomplished. The majority of the produce from the garden had been gathered for Misha and Nina to preserve for the land's rest season. The grains and grasses had also been harvested and properly stored. During the last few weeks, Noah and Aterre trained two young hired hands on the inner workings of the farm. They caught on quickly during the harvest, leaving Noah confident that his father would be able to maintain productivity in the next year.

As Noah and Aterre walked up the small incline onto the boat, Noah looked the vessel over. It stretched no more than 20 cubits from bow to stern, yet was the biggest boat he had ever boarded because it was the only boat he had ever been on. His father had made arrangements and paid for this trip during a previous visit to Iri Sana, and Noah had eagerly met the crew when they loaded their cargo moments earlier.

Deks, the leader of the ship's three-man crew, gripped Noah's forearm. "Allow me to officially welcome you aboard my boat."

"I'm glad to be here. Let us know if you need any help along the way."

"I'm sure we'll find plenty for you to do." Deks pointed to the ramp. "You can start by giving me a hand with this."

"I got it." Aterre bent down and grabbed one side of the wooden incline while Deks picked up the other side. They stowed it along the inside edge of the boat.

Noah slipped the bag off his shoulder and set it next to the rest of their gear, which was packed under a hide to keep it from getting soaked. Looking to occupy himself with something other than the sorrowful thoughts of missing his family, he scratched the back of Taht's neck, just beneath her short black mane, comforted by the familiarity she brought. "How you doing, girl?"

One of the crew shoved the boat away from the shore and jumped in, splashing the deck and soaking the hem of his garment in the process as the small craft drifted backward. The other crew member spun the boat until it faced downstream by stabbing a long, sturdy pole into the water.

Noah's family stood near the shore. His mother waved while wiping a tear with her other hand. His father appeared stoic, but Noah knew the man agonized over his departure. Jerah waved both hands above his head while sporting a crooked smile.

Misha ran next to the river, her long dress flapping against her heels. "It's not too late to stay, Noah!"

Noah forced a smile and couldn't stop a couple of tears from appearing. "I love you, Meesh!"

Aterre moved close to Noah. "So do I, little sister!"

She continued along the Hiddekel's edge, struggling to stay even with the boat yet not giving up. She passed the orchard and slowed when she neared the bank of the stream that emptied into the river, where a little over a year ago, her brothers had fought with Aterre. Misha stopped at the stream as if finally acknowledging that she had to let go.

A flood of emotions rushed through Noah. He ached for Misha and wondered if he was making the right decision. He had known it would be difficult to leave, but he hadn't realized it would hurt so much. And he hadn't considered how much it would affect his little sister. She was only half his age, and there was so much of her childhood that he would miss. For a brief moment, he considered jumping out of the boat and swimming to her, but the thrill of adventure and conviction that he was following the Creator's will overrode his emotions.

Noah's family became smaller and smaller as the boat drifted farther away. Jerah had reached Misha and put an arm around her. She clutched him tightly. His father remained where the boat had launched, holding his wife close.

The river carried the vessel around a bend, blocking Noah's view of his loved ones. He closed his eyes and turned around. *O Most High, please watch over them and keep them safe. Please help Jerah and Misha to follow Your ways.* Noah took a deep breath and let it out before opening his eyes. The sun peeked out from behind the clouds before quickly retreating, and a light breeze blew across his face.

"That was harder than I expected," Aterre said, breaking the silence.

Noah forced a half smile, appreciating Aterre's frankness. "Much harder." He scanned both sides of the river and felt a surge of energy course through his body. "But look. We're really doing it."

"Yep, you finally get to see the world."

"And what do you want?" Noah looked at his friend, suddenly realizing that Aterre might have goals and dreams of his own.

"I'm not totally sure. I know I eventually want to find a place to call my own."

"You could have done that by staying with my family."

"True. But being a part of your family has made me long to know what really happened to mine. I assumed they were killed like the others in my village, but I don't know that for sure. If they are still alive, I need to find out somehow. I don't know how to begin, but I do know that Iri Sana is too small and too far away to get word of them. Who knows? Maybe someone we encounter on this journey will be able to help. Plus, we're going to a seaport. I'll have a better chance of running into someone who knows something of those raiders and their prisoners there."

"I'll do what I can to help." Noah clapped Aterre on the back. "Well, future, here we come." He bent down and ran a finger along the ship's deck. "I can't believe that I'll actually get to build these." He grinned up at Aterre and increased his volume in confidence and excitement. "I'm going to be a shipbuilder."

"You say you're going to build boats?"

Noah turned to see the ship's captain lumbering toward them, his uneven gait slow and purposeful. "Yes, sir."

Deks pushed back a lock of black hair that had stuck to the side of his wind-hardened face. "Then you must be heading all the way to Iri Geshem to work for Ara."

"You know Ara?"

"Met him one time, when I bought this rig." He scratched the dark stubble on his chin. "That would've been about 20 years ago. Nice fellow, that Ara. You know him?"

"Not yet. He's my grandfather's cousin. I'm planning to become an apprentice."

"Well, I hope you have the talent." Deks stamped his foot on the deck. "Ara's craftsmanship is without equal." He turned to his assistant on Noah's right. "Valur, if all goes well, our next boat might be built by our passenger here."

Valur looked at Noah. The muscles on his sun-darkened forearms rippled as he gripped the long pole he used to keep the boat from gliding too close to the shore. His dark hair was loosely tied up behind his head. "Is that a fact? Well, youngster, make it a good one, and if you can figure out how to make these things larger, we'd make a lot more profit on each of these trips."

"I'll drink to that," the other assistant said.

"You'd drink to anything, Recharu," Valur said.

The portly man's belly jiggled as he chuckled. "That I would. But I'd drink double to a larger boat because I could afford it."

"Only if you did double the work," Deks said. "In your case, that wouldn't be too hard since double of nothing is still nothing. I'm surprised you haven't asked for a break already."

Recharu waved him off. "I was just getting ready to ask our guests if one of them would like to fill in for me so I can take care of the sail."

"I would." Noah hustled over to the heavyset man. "Show me what to do."

"The river opens up in a bit, and we'll steer with the rudder then. But for now, take this." Recharu handed Noah the long rod. "Just keep pushing down into the water to make sure it's deep enough for the boat. This thing has a draft of about three cubits."

"That means that it sinks three cubits into the water?" Noah asked.

"That's right. If you see us drifting toward the shore, push us back toward the middle."

Noah steadied himself and plunged the pole into the water. He drove it at least eight cubits deep, without finding the bottom. He brought it back up and waited until Valur put his pole into the water to repeat the action.

Recharu and Deks untied the small sail attached to the mast. They quickly hoisted it and fastened it in place, angling it to catch the wind. The boat lurched forward.

"I'll steer, Boss," Recharu said. He walked to the front of the ship and grabbed the navigating mechanism, which was essentially a waist-high rod connected to a post that ran below deck.

"How does that control the steering?" Aterre asked.

"Have a seat," Deks said. "Noah, you can put that down and join us."

Noah found a spot near Aterre as Valur went into the small cabin near the rear of the boat.

Deks pointed to where Recharu manned his post. "That shaft is connected to another rod down below through a series of gears, and that one runs to the back and connects to the rudder."

"Rudder?" Noah asked.

"It's a fairly small piece of wood at the rear that steers the entire ship. So when Recharu moves the shaft, it turns the rudder, allowing us to steer wherever we want to go."

"I would never have thought of that," Aterre said.

"Like I said, Ara is the best," Deks said.

"This may seem like a silly question." Noah scratched the back of his neck. "Obviously, the current and sail propel us downriver, but how do you make it back against the current? I've watched your boat go up and down the river over the years, but I was never sure how that worked."

"That's not a silly question. We use the sail, which usually means moving in a zigzag across the river to continue catching the wind properly. It takes longer; what takes three days going downriver becomes nearly twice as long to return, and that's only if we have some wind. If it's a calm day, we don't go very far."

Soon the morning fog lifted and the light rain stopped, revealing the tops of the trees on either side of the river. With no sign of civilization, the land's ruggedness heightened Noah's sense of adventure. He leaned forward, wrapping his arms around his knees. "You said earlier that you've only met Ara one time."

"That's right," Deks said.

"Why don't you sail all the way to Iri Geshem? I'm sure the people there would want some of the products from around here."

"I'm sure they would." Deks leaned against Noah's small pile of belongings. "It just wouldn't be worth the trouble to take the boat that far. Not far beyond Birtzun, the river gets pretty rough, and I don't want to risk wrecking my source of income."

"So you just travel between Birtzun and Iri Sana?" Aterre asked.

Deks nodded. "Mostly. There are a few small stops along the way that we occasionally make."

"It's a three-day journey to Birtzun, right?"

"That's right."

Aterre rubbed his eyes and yawned. "So what's Birtzun like?"

"In the daytime, it's a lot like Iri Sana, but a little bigger." Deks flashed a mischievous smile. "But when it gets dark, well, let's just say that good boys like you wouldn't want to be part of the night life. It can be a pretty rough place, especially around the taverns."

Recharu looked back at them. "I love the taverns. You just have to keep your head down and guard your money."

Noah raised an eyebrow. "What time will we arrive?"

Deks laughed. "No need to worry, young Noah. We should get there in the middle of the day. You'll have plenty of time to pick up provisions at their market, and then take the southern road that leads toward Iri Geshem."

CHAPTER 8

Birtzun — Noah's 40th year

Thank you for taking us this far. We appreciate your help, and I really enjoyed learning about the boat." Noah deposited three silver pikkas into Deks's hand and waved to Recharu and Valur, who busied themselves unloading cargo to sell at Birtzun's market.

Valur grunted as he struggled to stabilize his awkward load. "Farewell." Recharu set down the tall crate he was carrying and waved. "Remember, Noah. Bigger boats."

Noah laughed. "I'll see what I can do."

Deks held out his empty hand and met Noah's eyes squarely as the two men gripped forearms. "Buy what you need and then head out of town on the south road. You'd do well to be a good ways out of town when it gets dark. And guard your belongings."

Noah nodded, unconcerned. As Deks had promised, they had arrived with plenty of time left before the sun went down. "I hope to see you again someday."

"Likewise. Farewell."

Noah and Aterre walked beside Taht toward one of the fruit stands. The beast pulled a small two-wheeled cart, laden with their belongings, up the gentle slope. The market was about the same size as the one at Iri Sana, but the tightly spaced structures that made up the surrounding town were larger and more established. The buildings occupied either side of the wide street like eager animals lined up in the barn, ready to

59

greet whomever passed by. Colors abounded. Dozens of small flags hung in rows, connecting one rooftop to another. At least six shops proudly displayed their wares of brightly dyed garments. A few buildings boasted vibrant awnings, under which were round crates displaying produce of varied type and quality.

A dizzying array of sounds filled this marketplace. People clustered in groups, laughing and talking. Loud bartering punctuated the pervasive hum of voices as merchants argued the value of their wares with savvy customers. A calic barked as it chased behind a small child. Noah looked in the direction of a sudden bleat and saw rows of animals tethered at one end of the long street, each waiting for its master to return.

"Deks said the next river town is about a two-week journey and that we'd be able to take a boat from there to Iri Geshem," Aterre said, leaning closer to be heard. "So let's be sure to buy items that won't spoil in that time."

"Less fruit and more grain. I like that." Noah stepped along quickly, his energy fueled by the bustle around them.

A shadow from one of the taller buildings fell across them, and Noah glanced up. Upper windows were curtained closed, while a few customers in the dim interior of the ground level sipped their beverages with sullen focus. Just the feel of the place seemed dirty. He guessed this was one of the taverns Deks had warned them of and looked at it with curiosity. *What would make men choose to spend their time in such a place?*

Deks's other warnings came back to him, and he placed a hand on the edge of the cart and peered inside. "Let's also keep an eye on the wagon at all times."

Aterre looked back at the place they had just passed. "I agree."

They stopped at two fruit stands to purchase a few fresh items before searching out a grain merchant on the next street over. Before long, Noah and Aterre had purchased their provisions and made their way toward the southern edge of town.

The buildings here were smaller and farther apart, though there were still quite a few people hurrying about their business in the street. Noah led Taht around a woman leading three young children — the eldest looked no more than 20 — then had to yank the animal to a halt to avoid an old man who stepped right in front of him, one shaky hand extended. "Excuse me, boys. Might you have time to help out an old man?"

Touched by the wavery voice, Noah looked the man over. He was probably in his seventh century. His back was slightly hunched, and he shifted on his feet as if trying to regain as much of his former height as possible. His face was speckled with tiny darker brown spots, like spice sprinkled over flatbread.

"I'm sorry to trouble you lads, but my cart broke down on my way from the market, and I was wondering if you might be able to help me." Although narrowed by the steady sloping of aging eyelids and wrinkles, his deep eyes held concern as he shifted his gaze between Noah and Aterre.

They silently sought each other's council, and Aterre gave a slight bob. "Of course we will help. How far away is it?"

The man pointed a shaky finger back over his shoulder. Next to one of the more established buildings on the road Noah and Aterre had just traversed, Noah could see a cart tipped forward and listing to one side. Several crates had fallen and lay beside it in the grass. A grey-coated nuzzler stood beside the upset load, looking dejected. As the three headed to the cart, the old man pushed his hat farther back on his head. "It's kind of you boys to go out of your way to help a stranger."

Aterre scanned the man's face. "We don't mind at all. You asked the right people. Noah here is great with carpentry. He should have you on your way in no time."

"And Aterre is good at volunteering other's services."

The man grinned. "Well, I'm Ebal. Here, let me tie up your animal next to mine while you get started."

Noah dropped on all fours and examined the bottom of the small wooden wagon. "Looks like this support is badly splintered. It's going to need something to hold it together." Noah stood and scanned his surroundings. "Aterre, stay with our things." Noah fumbled around in their cart before finding a small axe. "I'll be back soon."

Noah jogged toward a large grove of trees several hundred cubits beyond the edge of town. Noting that the sun's power had already begun its waning, he quickly searched the ground for a fallen branch that could make a suitable repair. Before long, he spotted a large piece that, with some minor fashioning, would probably work.

Rushing back to the wagons, he held it against the broken wood, eyeballing the new piece and figuring out how to shape it. Noah glanced at the old man. "This shouldn't take too long." Noah quickly cut the wood to the appropriate length and chipped away a few rough edges to approximate the form of the original piece before it broke. "Aterre, can you come help me attach this?"

"Of course."

When Aterre joined him, Noah slipped under the cart while Aterre supported its weight from the outside. After some time of steady work, punctuated by Aterre's grunts and Noah's occasional instructions, the cart stood evenly once again.

Standing back, Noah admired their work. "That should get you home at least."

"Home? That would get me across the earth and back if I so chose. I'm indebted to you both."

Noah dismissed that comment with a wave of his hand. "It felt good to be able to construct something again. I have to admit I enjoyed it."

"Evenfeast." Ebal inserted the word suddenly.

"What?" asked Aterre.

"Let me buy it for you. See that place across the street with the lamps inside? They have the best meals in town. I'm a regular when my stomach can handle it. Go in there and tell them to fix you up a plate and to place it on my account. Show 'em this." He handed over his carved armband as a token. "I'll be inside in a moment and will join you both."

Aterre slowly accepted the offered talisman and led the way across the street. He ducked through the doorway and Noah quickly followed.

"Hello, travelers. What can I get for you?" A tall woman sidled over to them and ran a finger down Aterre's arm, her eyes flirtatiously following the line her finger traced before returning to his face.

Aterre's look never changed, and Noah couldn't decide if he was amused or unaffected by her forward manner. He cut in. "We're here as Ebal's guest" — he pointed to the armband that dangled from Aterre's grasp — "and we'd like something to eat. Please."

"Right this way." She led them toward the center of the room to one of a dozen or so tables in the establishment. As they followed her, Noah noticed that about half of them were full with what looked like contented townspeople. "Have a seat. I'll bring out your meals in a moment."

Waiting until she was a little farther away, Noah leaned across the table and spoke in low tones. "It's impossible to see our cart from here." He glanced at the window. "I know that it's still fairly light, but Deks's warning makes me nervous."

"I thought of that. Anyone could just walk by and take something."

Noah stood quickly. "I'll check on Ebal and make sure our things are safe."

"Good idea."

Noah hurried to the door. Taht stood at the hitching post, but the contents of their wagon were not as they had left them. "Aterre!" Noah motioned to him, and he quickly scrambled over. "Look."

They bolted out the door and ran to the cart. Everything had been ransacked. Clothing and other items were strewn all over not just the back, but the ground as well. A barrel of malids had been shoved roughly aside. Several of the round fruit had rolled around the floor of the cart, coming to rest against whatever pile of clothing or food stopped their progress.

"That happened so fast!" Noah slammed a fist against the side board, causing Taht to flinch. "Sorry, girl." He turned to Aterre, who had started to put things back in their places.

"Some of our food is gone. And your axe. It looks like they made off with my extra tunic." Aterre narrowed his eyes. "Deks wasn't kidding. We were only in there for a few moments. I don't see how someone had the time."

"Unless that someone had been able to look at our things while I was fixing his cart," Noah said slowly.

"Ebal? But he's — no, you're right. Why else would he be gone? At least he only got a few things."

Noah jerked his head as a thought hit him, and he frantically searched around for the puzzle safe Darge had made. It lay askew under an overturned basket. Noah snatched it up and with fast-moving thumbs, he flipped the pieces to their right places in order to open the lid. His stomach clenched. "Gone. All of our money is gone. I just have the small amount I always carry." He shook his head. "I don't understand. Only you and I know how to open this."

Aterre grinned and slapped him on the back. "I have our money. I pulled it from the box when you went to get the wood to fix his cart. I didn't suspect Ebal, but just thought it would be best to be safe."

Noah exhaled, too relieved to be annoyed by his friend's highhand-edness. "That was good thinking."

Unhitching Taht, Aterre took the lead rope. "What do you say we get out of here?"

Noah walked beside him. "I'm thinking evenfeast on the go is sounding pretty good."

Chapter 9

They followed the dusty trail as it passed over low rolling hills. A handful of trees on the side of the road provided intermittent shade from the late afternoon sun. At first, pastures and fields filled the countryside marked by an occasional dwelling. Noah recognized all of the crops but two.

Eventually, the road forked, just as Deks had told them it would, and they stayed on the trail closest to the river, which soon narrowed to a single lane as it descended into a forest. The evergreen trees grew tall and straight, and their sharp, resinous scent filled the air. A variety of birds flitted through the treetops. Noah only caught a glimpse of them as they darted from perch to perch.

"We'd better let Taht get a drink here," Noah said as they approached a small stream that meandered through a shallow channel.

"I need one too," Aterre said. "This dry air is making me thirsty."

Noah let the animal drink as long as she wanted. He bent down, scooped some water with both hands, and after an initial taste, he gulped it down. "Oh, that's so good."

Aterre leaned his face to the stream and sucked up a mouthful.

"Did Taht teach you to drink like that?"

Aterre grinned. "You should try it."

As he bent in for more, Noah pushed Aterre's head into the creek and chuckled as his friend came up sputtering and gasping.

Aterre coughed several times, trying to clear his throat. When he finally caught his breath, he threw a handful of water at Noah, who lunged to one side, scooping up another round and hurling it at Aterre. Having now received two barrages in the face, Aterre launched a full out attack. By the time Noah called for truce, they were both half-drenched and laughing.

Noah leaned back to catch his breath. "How much farther do you want to walk tonight?"

"Let's try to find a place to camp before dark." Aterre wiped his face with his robe. He looked around. "I wonder how much longer we'll be in this forest. It'll grow dark sooner in here."

"Well, let's press on and see if we can find the end before nightfall." After filling their leather containers, Noah stood and guided Taht slowly across the stream while Aterre braced the cart. "Easy, girl. Nice and steady."

On the other side of the brook, the damp ground rose sharply. Noah looped Taht's lead rope in the harness and joined Aterre in pushing the wagon from the back, guiding it away from the mushiest portions of bank. Upon reaching the top, Noah stood up straight and studied the trail ahead. "No end in sight yet."

"That's what I was thinking." Aterre sighed. "Well, we may as well keep going."

They continued through the still forest, each taking brief rests in the wagon from time to time. As the light became fainter, the noises picked up. The squawks, chirps, and sporadic cries led the men into a game of guessing what sort of animal made each sound.

The woodland eventually thinned. Noah spotted two large birds soaring above the canopy. He watched as they flew straight ahead and then dropped. "Look." He pointed up. "It's either a clearing, or we've made it to the end of the forest."

"I think we've finally made it," Aterre said. "Just in time. Let's go."

"C'mon Taht," Noah said as he stroked the creature's neck. "Just a little farther tonight."

With renewed energy, they made their way to the edge of the forest. A flock circled in the sky ahead, and Noah heard screeches coming from the far side of a small hill.

"I've never seen so many tarocs in one place. What's going on?" Aterre asked, concern etched across his face.

"I'm not sure. Something huge must've died. Let's check it out." He ordered his obedient animal to stop and tied her to a mature tree before following Aterre to investigate.

The squawking increased as Noah and Aterre crept up the hill on their hands and knees. When they reached the top, Noah pushed some long grass out of his way.

"I've never —" Aterre broke off, shaking his head.

It took a few moments for Noah to realize what he was looking at. More than two dozen tarocs clambered over a huge carcass splayed out in the field. Countless flies buzzed about, adding to the cacophony. The creature's long neck was ripped open about halfway between its body and its seemingly undersized head. The tail, which Noah estimated to be at least 20 cubits long, stretched to the bottom of the hill, where the clearing gave way to more forest.

Aterre stood on his knees to get a better look. "I've never been so close to such a large creature before."

Noah let out a low whistle. "My father called them earth shakers because the ground seemed to move whenever the larger ones walked. I used to see them occasionally come to the river's edge for a drink when I was younger, but I don't know if any were that big. What do you suppose happened to this one?"

"Tarocs don't kill large animals; they only eat them after they're dead. I think it was attacked by something pretty large." He pointed to the exposed rib cage. "Look at how those bones are broken. There's no way birds did that."

"Right." Noah looked up and saw a few more tarocs join the circle above them. "We shouldn't linger."

"While you get Taht, I want to get a closer look."

"You want to get closer to that smelly thing?"

Aterre shrugged. "Guess my curiosity is stronger than the stench . . . at least for now."

Noah turned and hurried down the hill, the cries of the boisterous birds filling his ears, and the carnage lying on the other side of the ridge fresh in his mind. He had seen seared muscles and the inner workings of animals lying loose on the outside of the livestock they had sacrificed. But somehow on this grand scale, in this setting, it unnerved him. He shook his head, trying to clear the uneasiness of what he felt. *Violent.* The word suddenly came to him. *That's the difference between the deaths I've seen and this.* Even though he had not witnessed the final moments of this towering creature, everything about the scene said violence: from the splintered branches and saplings surrounding the clearing, to the prodigious amount of dried blood under the neck, to the large missing hunks of flesh where the thighs joined the hips, to the contorted way the body lay now.

Noah reached Taht, untied her, and then slowly led her up the hill, giving wide berth to the feeding frenzy to his left. Even with the distance, Taht's feet danced nervously as they passed, and she tugged at the rope, eyes rolling. He could not have taken her closer to the mountain of a carcass even if he wanted to. Ahead and to his right, he noticed more broken branches and a pathway of small broken trees leading into where the clearing became woods again.

Aterre rushed over, brandishing something sharp over his head. "Look at this. I found it lying close to the carcass."

Noah took the dagger-shaped object and turned it over in his hands. It was nearly a span in length. He pointed at some blood and a small chunk of flesh at its thicker end. "Is this a tooth?"

Aterre nodded excitedly. "I think so. But I don't want to find out what it's from. Let's get out of here."

"I agree." Noah urged Taht to pick up the pace but suddenly stopped after a few steps. "Look at that. Those branches are split at least ten cubits up. Whatever broke them was pretty tall."

"You aren't kidding." Aterre pointed to his feet.

Noah did a double-take. Aterre was standing inside a shallow depression in the ground that was unmistakably a giant footprint, about a cubit and a span in length. Three long toes pointed toward the trail of the broken branches. Fear gripped Noah. "That's a footprint."

"Exactly. It went that way, and I don't want to be here if it comes back."

"Me neither. Thankfully our trail is straight ahead and not that way." Noah motioned to the broken branches. "C'mon Taht."

Noah handed Aterre the tooth and then drove his beast forward at a quickened pace. Entering the forest again, they found themselves in much darker surroundings. The light of the setting sun was evident in the distance, but did little to help them see much as the shadows of the forest merged with the deepness of the evening. As they pressed on, the noise of the tarocs grew quieter while the typical forest sounds increased. He felt more secure with the familiar sounds.

Aterre held up the tooth again. "Can you believe the size of this thing?"

"I can't imagine. You could make a knife out of that."

"That's a great. . . ."

A blood-curdling roar cut him off, and in an instant the forest grew silent, with the exception of a slight echo, which alone had the courage to mimic the terrifying sound. Noah stared wide-eyed at Aterre as they both instinctively grabbed tighter onto Taht to keep her from scampering. Unexpectedly, dozens of flying creatures bolted from their perches in the trees. The clatter of shaking branches above bombarded his ears. Noah hitched a thumb over his right shoulder. "It came from that direction, but it sounded far away."

"I don't care how far away it is, it's not far enough. Move."

Another roar filled the air, and then a new sound registered in Noah's mind. *Footsteps.* Massive footsteps. And their rumbles were getting louder. Noah kept his voice low. "It's coming back."

Taht let out a several nervous snorts, and hitched her back legs like she was getting ready to flee. Noah spoke to her soothingly as he tightened his grip on her rope.

Aterre rubbed her neck behind the tall bony protrusions at the top of her head as they hurried away from the approaching danger. "C'mon girl, steady now." He paused briefly and looked back down the trail. "I think it's heading for the dead earth shaker."

Noah glanced back, but couldn't see the clearing anymore. Tarocs flew overhead, and to Noah it sounded like they were screeching in anger at having their meal interrupted. "Let's just make sure it can't hear or smell us."

They continued walking in silence. After a short climb that put a small ridge between them and the dead earth shaker, a sense of relief rushed over Noah. Behind them, branches snapped and thudded on the forest floor and footsteps pounded before all went silent. Noah stopped Taht and held up a hand to stop Aterre. "Did you see it?"

Aterre shook his head and spoke softly. "No, but that's a good thing. It would probably haunt my sleep forever."

Noah forced a half-smile. "I know what you mean."

They walked in silence and when it became too dark to see, Aterre lit a small lantern and moved in front of Taht to guide the way. They arrived at another small stream, and Taht continued drinking long after they filled their water containers.

Aterre returned to the cart and grabbed the lantern again. "We should go just a little farther, get off the trail, and set up camp for the night."

"What's wrong with staying here?" Noah asked.

"Well, it's on the path, so it'd be easy for anyone passing by in the night to rob us."

Noah shook his head. "That's right. We aren't in Iri Sana anymore."

"Exactly. And we don't want to be too close to the water in case any predators come for a drink."

"Good idea. Let's find a place soon though. I'm exhausted."

"Enough adventure for one day?"

"Definitely." Noah stored his drink and led their animal away from the brook. "Can you imagine what this world would've been like if our Greatfather Adam hadn't sinned?"

"What do you mean?" Aterre asked.

"Originally, all of the animals ate only vegetation like we do. Those tarocs wouldn't have been scavenging on the earth shaker, and it never would've been killed in the first place."

Aterre held the lantern up and looked side to side. "And we wouldn't have had to flee from the owner of this." He pulled out the massive tooth and stared at it next to the light. "What should we call it?"

"What? The one with those kind of teeth?"

"Yeah. How about razor mouth?

Noah laughed. "Well, we haven't technically seen it yet. So let's go with what we heard. How about thunder step?"

"Or rumble throat? Tree smasher? Dagger tooth?"

"I like dagger tooth," Noah said.

"So do you really believe that?" Aterre slowly rotated the tooth next to the lantern, and the light revealed the jagged sides.

Noah's face registered confusion.

"That originally the animals only ate plants."

"Oh, yeah I believe that. It's what my grandfather said." Noah scratched his head. "Plus, it's hard to believe that the Creator would make a world where one creature needs to kill another."

"Then why'd He make them with teeth like this? This monster seems to be designed to kill and eat flesh."

Noah shrugged. "I'm not sure. Maybe those teeth are useful for eating fruit with thick shells, like melons, or maybe He changed the beasts when He cursed the ground."

"I have a different theory," Aterre paused thoughtfully. "I think that these beasts are gradually becoming more vicious. My mother told me many years ago that tarocs used to eat fruit. She said her grandmother remembers a time when they had one as a pet, and it only ate plants. Then one day they saw a carcass in the field, and several of the birds were eating the dead animal. That's the first time she'd ever seen anything like that."

"Interesting."

Aterre held the lantern to their left and took a few steps in that direction. "This might work. Let's head over here to see if we can find a good place to make our camp."

CHAPTER 10

Thankful for the change of scenery and climate, Noah breathed in the moist air and gazed at the vast array of vegetation around him as he and Aterre entered a dense tropical forest. They had spent the last week fighting through tall grasses and muddy trails of a wildly beautiful prairie after leaving the forest where they had encountered the dead earth shaker. On their third day traveling in the open plains, a heavy rainstorm drenched them and inhibited their travel.

While this new habitat offered a measure of relief from the elements, it was not more conducive to a faster pace. As the cart slowed to a stop, Noah jumped off to assist Aterre in removing yet another overgrowth in the path. While he hacked at the obstruction, he noticed the animals were different here too. Instead of an abundance of small, furry creatures skittering across the branches, green and brown-scaled reptiles sidled over the ground and in the trees. He ran his fingers along a leaf that was as long as his arm. "Have you ever seen anything like this?"

Aterre nodded. "We have trees like this where I'm from. And I also saw some while I was on the run."

"Did you take this trail during your journey?"

"So far none of it looks familiar. I tried to stay off the roads as much as possible and away from the river. I think I was probably farther west than we are."

Noah took a drink. "I can't believe you traveled all this way on your own. I would've been bored out of my mind. Except for that family on their way to Birtzun, we haven't seen anyone."

Aterre slowly turned the large tooth in his hand. Noah had wrapped its root in leather, and Aterre spent each evening honing one edge to create a dagger. "I hope they heeded our warnings about that creature." He paused before continuing. "Sometimes I can't believe I fled so far either. I guess I was so terrified at first and then so heartsore that I didn't realize how far I'd gone and how many weeks had passed."

Noah cuffed him on the shoulder as they started moving again. "I'm glad you're here. I may be sore and tired, but this trip's been amazing so far. I've always wondered what the world looked like beyond Iri Sana."

"Just wait until you look upon the Great Sea."

"What's it like?"

"I don't know really know how to explain it. Crystal blue water as far as the eye can see, and when the sun rises above it in the early morning. . . ." Aterre shook his head. "It's beautiful."

"I can't wait."

"And the sea creatures." His eyes lit up with excitement. "You won't believe this. Some of the great fish are even bigger than the earth shakers. Much bigger. And then there are the supergliders."

Noah cocked his head sideways. "Supergliders?"

"Yeah, they are sort of like giant birds without any feathers. I'll bet their wingspans can be over 15 cubits."

"You're teasing me, aren't you?"

"No, I'm serious. I told you that you wouldn't believe me."

Noah stared at a bizarrely scaled creature, with eyes protruding from the side of its head. It clutched a branch a few cubits away. Suddenly, its colors changed to match the background and Noah nearly lost sight of it. "No way," he said to himself.

"Really, I'm being serious," Aterre said.

Noah laughed. "No, it isn't that. Would you believe me if I told you that I've seen an animal that changes colors?"

"What? Now you're making up stories to try to outdo mine?"

Noah pulled Taht to a stop. "Think so? Look at this." He pointed to the odd creature still resting on the limb.

The cubit-long reptile slowly stretched one of its front legs forward and regripped the branch. One eye remained still while the other moved around, looking forward, up, and then down.

"That is the strangest thing I've ever seen," Aterre said.

"The Creator's artistry never ceases to amaze me. Keep watching."

Several moments later, the green near its belly turned orange and then purple.

Aterre laughed. "Crazy."

"Isn't it? I guess maybe I'll believe you about those supergliders and great fish."

The reptile focused its eyes ahead, opened its mouth, and sluggishly stuck out a strange-looking tongue. Without warning, the tongue shot forward and snatched a bug off a leaf more than a span away. Instantly, the bug was in the creature's mouth.

Noah and Aterre looked at each other in disbelief. Aterre put his hand on the top of his head. "That's incredible."

"It really is, but I guess it's not just the large animals that are changing their diets." Noah pulled lightly on Taht's rein. "Let's go girl."

* * * * *

Throughout the rest of the day, they continued on the trail, clearing some occasional vegetation, and marveling at many colorful birds and exotic creatures they had never seen before. As the sky grew darker, they arrived at a large clearing. About a dozen modest wood-and-reed homes formed a circle in the middle. Next to each of these buildings was a small garden. A taller and much larger wooden barn stood on the far side of the village. Several children laughed while they chased each other in a dirt field spotted with grass.

"Hello, travelers."

Startled by the voice, Noah turned and saw a middle-aged man strolling toward them. "Peace to you, sir." He looked different than anyone Noah had encountered before. His skin was light, and his thinning hair reminded Noah of the sand along the Hiddekel. *And what color are his eyes? Gray? Blue?* A knee-length garment hung about his waist, but his torso was bare — at least of clothing. His skin sported a variety of intricate designs and images.

"Ah, if you are men of peace, then I welcome you to Zakar." The man placed his fingers on his forehead and bowed slightly in greeting. As he straightened, his uniquely colored eyes met Noah's in a way that seemed to measure his character. "My name is Varelk." He motioned toward the huts. "I'm one of the elders in our village."

Aterre returned the bow. "Greetings, Varelk. It's good to meet you. My name's Aterre. Indeed, we mean you no harm."

Noah also greeted the man. "And I'm Noah, son of Lamech of Iri Sana."

Varelk's gaze drifted up as if he were thinking deeply. He shook his head. "Iri Sana? That's not familiar to me, but from your bearing, I would guess it's north of here."

"Yes, sir," Noah said. "We've been on foot for the past week, and before that was a three-day journey by boat."

"No wonder I've never heard of it. You've come a long way." He put his hand on Noah's shoulder. "Would you care to lodge here for the night? We'll have a small celebration to welcome you."

"We appreciate that, but don't go out of your way," Aterre said. "We don't require anything special."

Varelk laughed. "Nonsense, my boy. Around here, we look for excuses to celebrate. Come."

Noah and Aterre met at least two dozen citizens as they gathered around a pile of wood that was set up for a bonfire on the outskirts of the village. The people all shared Varelk's light-colored features, and the men bore similar markings on their arms and shoulders.

A young boy, who Noah estimated to be a little younger than Misha, stared at Aterre's knife, his blue eyes wide. He slowly reached out to touch the long tooth that hung from Aterre's belt.

Aterre spun and put a hand up. "Whoa. Careful, child."

The boy yanked his arm back and turned to run away.

"Wait. What's your name?"

As he tilted his head down, the child's curly, light-brown hair dropped over his eyes. "Elam."

"Hmm, I've never met an Elam before." Aterre pulled the knife from his belt and held it out to the boy. "You wanted to see this?"

Elam nodded and wrapped his fingers around the handle. He held it up and inspected both sides of the large tooth. "Grandfather, look!"

Varelk stepped to Elam's side. He carefully took the knife, examined it, and looked at Aterre. "Where did you get this?"

"Near a dead earth shaker." Aterre motioned to Noah. "We never saw the creature that it came from. We heard it roar, but fled before it came back."

"Yeah, we saw some three-toed footprints that were about one-and-a-half cubits long," Noah said. "Do you know what it was?"

Varelk grinned and tousled Elam's hair with his free hand. "My young friends, if I'm not mistaken, this is the tooth of a grendec."

"A grendec." Aterre took the knife as Varelk handed it back to him. "We just called it a dagger tooth."

The older man snorted. "That's a fitting name, indeed. Grendecs are terrifying. They stand more than ten cubits high and are about as long as our barn." Varelk motioned toward the large building with his head. "They have a mouth full of those daggers, but I've never heard of one of them attacking a person before. So you probably would've been safe if it saw you."

"That's a relief," Aterre said. "Can you imagine having to face one?"

Noah shivered and shook his head. "It makes me wonder why the Creator would make something so fearsome."

Varelk gave a knowing smile. "I used to wonder the same thing. I concluded that He made creatures like that to humble us when we realize how powerful He is."

Just then, an elderly man moved near the center of the gathering and raised his hands. "Your attention, please!" His long white beard bounced up and down as he spoke. When the crowd quieted, he said, "We are delighted to celebrate tonight in honor of our two guests, Noah and Aterre. I am Mehul, and I welcome you on behalf of the Zakari." As Varelk had done, Mehul placed fingers on his forehead and gave a slight bow. Then he turned to face the other side of the circle. "Let us thank the Creator for His blessings."

With the exception of Mehul, the Zakari dropped to their knees. Noah and Aterre glanced at each other and knelt.

"O mighty Creator," Mehul said. "We thank You for giving us life and a home. And we thank You for our two guests tonight. Please grant them safe passage to Iri Geshem. We ask for Your blessing on this evening. Teach us Your ways."

Immediately the Zakari repeated in unison, "Teach us Your ways." Then they stretched forward, putting their forearms and the right side of their faces on the ground.

Aterre looked at Noah, his eyes full of confusion. Noah shrugged and made a quick gesture by tilting his head, urging Aterre to follow their example. While unsure why the Zakari struck such a pose, he didn't want to offend. Noah held the side of his face to the ground for several awkward moments before closing his eyes and offering a silent prayer. *Creator, thank You for protecting us and providing for us on our journey. And thank You for the hospitality of the Zakari. Please bless them for their generosity.*

"Thank You, Creator," Mehul said. The Zakari repeated his words.

Noah opened his eyes and realized the prayer had ended when he saw people getting to their feet. He tapped Aterre's shoulder and stood.

Varelk stepped in front of them and motioned to a large board, laden with food, being carried by two young men into the circle. They set it on two sizable tree stumps that reached a little higher than their waists. "Please. Our guests eat first."

Noah and Aterre each filled a dish with fare from the makeshift table. Noah recognized most of the food options, and decided to select samples of those he had not seen before. Once everyone had filled their bowls, the board was moved away. Meanwhile, a plump man eagerly grabbed a torch and lit the pile of wood.

Seated on one of the many logs placed around the fire, Noah enjoyed his meal while he and Aterre talked with Varelk and other people of the village. As the evening wore on, mothers took their children back to their homes. Out of the corner of his eye, Noah saw Elam slowly get off his perch on top of a high stump as if not wanting to leave so soon. His mother waited patiently for him before leading the way to their hut. She, along with many other women, soon rejoined the festivities.

A steady beat caught Noah's attention. He spied a tall, thin man tapping a small drum. A woman, whom Noah guessed was the man's wife, set down her dish and picked up an instrument formed from a plant stem. She placed her fingers across some holes on the top of the reed, and blew into one end, producing a high-pitched, yet melodic sound. Soon another woman picked up a ringed object with several thin metal pieces inserted into it. She rattled it and clapped it against her hand in rhythm with the drum beat. The three musicians marched around the fire, prompting others to join with them.

Varelk rose and smiled. "Do you boys like to dance?" He hurried into the moving line that had formed behind the musicians.

"Count me in." Aterre jumped up and followed Varelk. "Come on, Noah."

Noah held up his hands. "Let me watch first."

Mehul approached. "Mind if I join you?"

Noah gestured to Aterre's recently vacated spot. "Please do."

The village elder gingerly took a seat. He looked at the celebrants dancing and yelling around the fire and laughed. "I'm a little too old for that."

Noah smiled. "Thank you for your hospitality. I'm delighted to know that your people worship the Creator."

"Indeed we do. That's one of the reasons we live so far into the jungle."

"What do you mean?"

"My older brother, Varelk's father, founded this village when I was a child. He said that the people of our city were no longer concerned about following the Creator, so he led a small group to this place so that their children could be raised to know the ways of the Most High."

Noah shook his head. "People turning away from the Creator — that's becoming more common." He stared at the fire and allowed the leaping flames to carry his thoughts from one idea to the next before settling on his next question. "Where did your people come from?"

Mehul pointed across the clearing. "A city called Bothar. It's a three-day journey west through the forest. I've heard things have only gotten worse since we left. Some of our young families have moved back there. I fear they've rejected the Creator and are following Sepha."

Noah spotted Aterre dancing around the fire and breathed a sigh of relief that his garment was still wound around his torso, covering the tattoo. Noah faced Mehul. "Why 'fear'? My father spoke ill of it, but . . . a friend told me that the group just teaches discipline and self-defense."

The older man arched an eyebrow. "They do much more than that. They're now in charge of Bothar. The leaders completely control their followers, who pledge to obey any command without question. They steal from travelers and murder men who oppose them. And I even hear rumors that they practice the dark arts."

"The dark arts?"

Mehul leaned back and sighed. "The dark arts refer to people trying to gain supernatural power and understanding by communicating with the dead or with spiritual entities."

"My father said the group was evil, but I don't think he had any idea they believed such things."

"Indeed they are wicked, but enough about Sepha. We're here to celebrate what the Creator has given us." He swept his arm out to the people happily weaving amongst each other, keeping time to the music. "What do you think of Zakar?"

"Your people have truly blessed us, and we're happy to have met you."

Mehul gave a slight nod. "Likewise."

Noah scratched the back of his neck and stared at his dusty feet. "Do you mind if I ask you a question about your people?"

"Not at all. Please, ask."

Noah lifted his eyes and held the man's gaze. "When your people prayed, why did they. . . ." An orange light far behind Mehul caught Noah's attention. His mind raced as his mouth fought to form the word. "Fire!" He pointed past the man to the village barn.

Mehul turned back and jumped to his feet. "Fire!"

The music suddenly stopped and everyone stared momentarily at the conflagration before springing into action. Noah and Mehul rushed to the barn. The thatched roof blazed orange, but the main part of the structure had not yet been engulfed in flames. Men and women scurried into the barn and then back out with arms full of food and supplies, many of them coughing from the smoke.

Noah wrapped the end of his garment around his face and darted in. Shelves of foodstuffs were stacked against the far wall, and large baskets of berries and vegetables sat on the floor. Noah spotted a wide board leaning against the left wall. He grabbed the arm of the nearest man. "Help me with this."

Noah moved quickly to the wooden panel. "Grab the other end." They picked it up and carried it to an open spot on the floor. Noah quickly lowered his end. "Here, fill this up!"

Within moments piles of food were loaded. Noah snagged the attention of two other men for their assistance. The four men hefted the platform and carried it a safe distance away from the burning structure.

"Dump it and let's make one more trip," one of the men said.

They hustled back to the room, which was now hotter, brighter, and smokier. Noah felt as if his hair would soon be singed. Thanks to the hasty work of the townsfolk, the barn only had a fraction of what it held before the fire. The men swiftly loaded up their table again. As they headed for the door, a large flaming beam fell from the ceiling and crashed to the ground right behind Noah. They rushed out of the inferno and into safety.

Noah fought for fresh air and collapsed, causing the food to crash to the ground beside him. Between his coughs, he heard many others doing the same. His lungs burned. When he finally caught his breath, he saw many of the Zakari watching helplessly as the barn succumbed to the fire. The center of the roof fell first, followed by the two end walls that collapsed inward.

"Is everyone unharmed?"

Noah turned and saw Mehul moving hurriedly among his people, checking on their condition. Some of the men fanned out around the building, stamping out any embers that managed to escape.

Aterre walked over to Noah. "Are you hurt?"

"No, I'm alright. What about you?"

The flickering light reflected in Aterre's eyes. "I'm fine."

Noah looked around the crowd. "It doesn't look like anyone's seriously injured."

A scream pierced the air. The door of a nearby house flew open, and a woman bolted through it. "Where's Elam?" She ran toward Varelk and another man, whom Noah thought might be Varelk's son, Elam's father. "I can't find Elam." Trying and failing to catch her breath before speaking again, she gasped out the rest of her words. "He was in bed . . . now he's not there!"

"Our son is missing?" the other man asked.

Varelk placed his hand on her shoulder, while Elam's father hurried toward their hut. "We'll find him. He probably woke up with all the noise and is out here somewhere."

Elam's mother cupped her hands to her mouth and yelled her son's name, echoed by her husband. Varelk moved off in another direction, also calling for the boy.

Suddenly, a cry rang out from the other side of the village. A petite woman ran toward the field where the children had been playing earlier in the evening. "Kani! Where are you? Kani!" A man hurried to her and joined in shouting her daughter's name.

Mehul clapped his hands and directed the villagers to make sure their children were accounted for.

Noah and Aterre ran around the edge of the clearing, calling out for Elam and Kani, while the distressed parents hastened to their homes.

Before long, the people gathered near the bonfire where their dancing had heralded peace just a short time ago. As Noah moved toward the crowd, several parents frantically waved their arms and shouted, while others knelt, weeping.

Mehul tried to calm them, but to no avail. "We won't stop until we find the four missing children."

Elam's father pointed at a couple of men. "You two, take some torches and check the east road. Look for any signs that they might have gone that way." He turned to the man who had been shouting Kani's name. "Liun, come with me. We'll check the northern trail. They couldn't have gone far."

As the four men raced off, fear and confusion gripped Noah. *Where can they be?*

"Do you think they're just hiding as a joke?" a short man with a bushy beard asked.

With tears streaming down her cheeks, a woman stepped forward, "Were they in the barn?"

"No," Mehul said. "It was nearly empty when it collapsed, and everyone made it out."

"Maybe they accidentally started the fire," the crying woman said, "then ran because they were afraid."

Another woman shook her head. "But they were all in bed, right? I put Kani there myself. She's never snuck out before."

"What if they were kidnapped?" the short man asked.

Aterre clenched his fists. "Then we go rescue them."

The conversation became impossible to follow as the frightened men and women shouted over one another. Noah turned and looked toward the north road. A man and woman near the edge of the clearing shouted out the names.

"Please. Please, try to calm down," Mehul said, his arms held up, slowly quieting the group. "I don't like to assume the worst, but I think we must consider kidnapping. Maybe the barn fire was a diversion."

"No!" Kani's mother threw her hands over her ears and shook her head, as if the words could somehow be unheard. She sobbed and dropped to her knees.

"Listen," Mehul said. "We aren't doing them any good standing around here. Go back and check your homes again, search every place you can think of." He motioned to Varelk and another man. "Grab some torches and let's search the edge of the forest."

"What should we do?" Noah asked.

"Do you have any tracking skills?" Varelk asked.

Noah dropped his gaze and shook his head.

"Then plead with the Creator that the children might be found."

Aterre hit Noah's shoulder. "I'm going with them."

The crowd quickly dispersed. Kani's mother slowly stood and returned to her home, calling her child's name as she went.

Noah stared into the night sky. "O Most High, please keep the children safe. If they are lost or hiding, help the Zakari to find them soon. If they're kidnapped. . . ." He felt his face redden with anger, and he gritted his teeth. "If they were taken, then please help us rescue them, and may the kidnappers receive justice."

CHAPTER 11

Something squeezed Noah's shoulder. He paused as his mind clumsily drifted from dreamland to reality. Someone was shaking him.

"Noah, wake up."

He blinked a few times, trying to get his eyes to adjust, but darkness filled the room. Aterre's voice eventually registered.

"They're getting ready to leave."

"Who's leaving?" A short, fitful night of sleep fogged his thinking. Noah felt like he was clawing at many vague concepts, trying to land on what was solid. Thus far, a losing battle.

"The Zakari. The men are heading out to track down the missing children. You said you wanted to go with them."

Noah sat up, the memories from the late evening finally rushing back. He stood quickly and shook his legs in an effort to wake his tired body for what lay ahead. "Of course." With the grogginess slowly fading, he girded his waist and wrapped the remainder of the robe over his shoulder. Then he slipped on his footwear and followed Aterre out of the guest hut. The day was dawning, but the stars held their nighttime posts like trustworthy sentinels posted across the sky, except in the east, which was painted with faint swaths of pink and red.

Stopping Aterre, Noah leaned close so as not to be overheard. "I forgot to tell you last night. Don't let them see your tattoo. They have a very negative view of Sepha."

"How do you know that?"

"Mehul talked to me about it. Be careful."

"I will. Thanks."

They jogged toward a small group at the west side of the clearing. The cool morning air filled Noah's lungs and invigorated him. As they neared those who had gathered in the stillness of the morning, Noah counted eight men and four women. The men were armed with thick, cubit-long blades with short handles. Two of them carried bows and each sported a quiver of arrows.

One of the men held a torch aloft, and with his other hand he pointed toward the edge of the trees. "This is where they passed into the forest."

"Are you sure?" Varelk asked.

"Yes, Father, the footprints lead up to here, and look at the broken blades of grass and that snapped twig."

Noah recognized him in the faint light as Elam's father. *Korel? Vorel? What was his name?*

Varelk turned. "Ah, Noah and Aterre. Thank you for joining us. Please know that you're not obligated to help us."

"We want to. No child deserves —" Aterre broke off. Tilting his head back, he took a deep breath and clenched his fists. "No child should ever be taken from their parents."

"We're glad to help." Noah stepped beside Aterre.

"And we're grateful for your assistance," Varelk nodded and looked to his son. "Parel, we'll follow you."

Parel. That's it.

"Father, I don't think it's a good idea for these men to join us." Parel angled his blade in Noah's direction.

Varelk crossed his arms. "We can use all the help we can get."

Parel glared at Noah and then Aterre. "How do we know that they weren't part of a plan to kidnap our little ones? What if they came as a diversion, knowing that we'd take them in and celebrate their visit? Then somebody else set the barn ablaze to keep us busy?"

Unable to believe what he was hearing, Noah opened his mouth to defend himself, but closed it when he realized that from Parel's perspective, the scenario made sense.

"Then why would they risk their lives running into a burning barn?" Varelk asked.

Parel held his torch higher and looked Aterre in the eyes as he spoke. "Maybe to make the deception even more believable."

Varelk stepped between the two men. "But why stay?" His voice was gentle. "Couldn't they have run off during the fire or while we slept?"

"I don't know." Parel's scowl turned to Noah. "Maybe so they could lead us off the trail today."

Noah refused to look away, thinking that a failure to hold his stare would seem like an admission of guilt. "May I speak?"

The man nodded.

"I understand why you don't trust us. If I were in your position, I'd probably think the same thing." Noah paused, searching for the right words. "We're willing to do everything we can to rescue the children, even if" — he glanced at Aterre — "even if that means staying behind. But if you want our help, be assured that we'll follow your lead."

"I'll take responsibility for them," Varelk said.

After a long moment, Parel sighed and nodded. "Very well." He met his father's eyes. "But I still don't trust them. They stay to the middle of the group and no one goes off alone with them."

"Agreed. Now, let's get going before we lose more time." The older man turned to the four women. "Pray for us."

Parel waved his torch in a circle over his head. "Let's go."

Noah fell into line behind Aterre as the company marched into the forest. After about 20 cubits, Aterre dropped back and walked beside his friend. "I can't stop wondering about what happened to my mother and sisters. What if they weren't actually killed like I initially assumed?" Aterre looked up and spoke softly, as if to himself. "If they were only kidnapped. . . ."

"Then we'll see what we can do to find them," Noah said. "Just like we're doing here."

Aterre snapped out of his contemplation. "Right."

Progress came slowly at first as Parel and another man regularly paused to look for signs of recent activity, a task made more difficult by the semi-darkness. Using their long blades, the men hacked their way through a few places where the forest was densest. As the sun rose higher in the sky, their tracking duties became easier.

The farther from the village they traveled, the more convinced Noah became that the children had not wandered off. When Varelk pointed out a man's footprint in the soft terrain next to two smaller prints, it only confirmed Noah's fears. Shortly before midday, they stopped when Parel discovered a shredded piece of cloth and a carved wooden hair rod not quite as long as his hand. He held them up. "Anyone recognize these?"

The muscles in Liun's cheeks bulged as he clenched his jaw. "Those are Kani's. The carved butterfly on the end is her favorite." He took the item as tears welled in his eyes. "She had two of these."

"You've got a smart girl," Varelk said. "She's leaving us a trail to follow."

Parel faced Liun. "We'll find them."

"Indeed we will, but first let's take a short break." Varelk sat on a fallen tree. His cheeks sagged in a face grown haggard overnight. "We'll need to eat to keep our energy up."

Erno, the thin drummer from the night before, slipped his pack from his shoulder and handed a small bag of food to each person. Erno's son had also been snatched in the raid. The man had said very little during the morning, but his countenance spoke volumes in its look of pure determination.

Noah found a spot on the log near Varelk. Very little was said while they hurriedly ate their meal. The combination of hunger and fear set the pace and subdued their tongues. No one smiled, and no one laughed.

During the temporary reprieve, Noah took a chance to look at his surroundings. Here were the same kind of large-leafed trees from the day before. Insects skittered across the giant foliage at various speeds. A green and yellow buzzbird zipped in and out among the white blossoms of a broad bush. Noah marveled at the tiny creature as it darted to a blossom, hovered, and then darted to another flower. Songbirds sang to each other in the canopy above. A faint cry from an animal echoed in the distance, but he couldn't discern the source.

Aterre stood and shoved the last of his rations in his mouth. He motioned for Noah to follow. "Come with me."

Noah swallowed his last bite as he trailed Aterre to an open area several paces away from the group.

"Where are you two going?" Parel asked.

"Just to the other side of these trees," Aterre said.

Varelk motioned for his son to sit back down. "I can see them from where I am. They're fine."

"What?" Noah asked when his friend stopped in the small clearing.

"I've been thinking that we may have to fight the kidnappers to free those children."

"And?"

Aterre cocked his head. "And you're a farmer. You've never been trained to defend yourself."

"I knocked you out." Noah gave him a half smile.

Aterre rolled his eyes. "You got lucky. But this could be a life or death situation." He spread his feet a little more than shoulder-width apart, left leg in front, and bent his knees slightly. "Take a defensive stance, like this. And put your hands up." Aterre raised his fists to the level of his chin, the left slightly ahead of the right.

Noah mimicked his friend's stance.

"Good." He pulled his knife from the side of his belt. "Now, if I was going to stab at you, how would you get out of the way?"

"Run." Noah chuckled. Aterre was not amused, so Noah got serious. "I guess it depends on how you attacked."

"Here."

Noah took the tooth dagger that Aterre handed him.

"Now stab straight at my chest."

"Are you sure?" Noah asked.

"Yeah, just go about three-quarter speed, and I'll show you what to do."

"Okay, here goes." Noah lunged forward.

In an instant, Aterre twisted sideways and grabbed Noah's arm. Planting his left hand under Noah's elbow, Aterre put downward pressure on Noah's forearm with his free hand.

"Ouch!" Noah dropped the knife.

Aterre released his grip.

"You could've broken my arm."

Aterre grinned and nodded. "I know." He picked up the blade. "Now you try."

Noah assumed the stance. "Go ahead."

As Aterre lunged at about half speed, Noah shifted to the side and grabbed his friend's arm. He locked Aterre's elbow and pushed down on his wrist.

"Not bad for a start. You're a quick study."

Noah let go of him. "Thanks."

"Let me show you what to do if he slashes at you from the side."

Parel ducked under a branch and stepped into view. "Are you boys ready?"

"Sure." After picking up the knife, Noah handed it back to Aterre. "Let's go."

Continuing due west into the early afternoon, the group came across a narrow road running north and south. The forest had thinned, and the air warmed with more sunlight breaking through the canopy. Parel and Liun studied the scene for a few moments.

"There are footprints heading north," Liun said.

Parel walked a few steps in that direction, bent down, and picked up the matching hair stick. He handed it to Liun. "Looks like your daughter left us another clue."

"Follow Liun." Parel motioned for the group to pass him and then fell into step next to his father, just behind Noah and Aterre.

"What is it, Son?" Varelk asked.

"Is this the way to Bothar?"

Varelk hesitated a beat before answering. "It is if we turn west after a while."

When Parel spoke again, something in his voice sent a chill through Noah. "If the rumors are true, that would mean. . . ."

The older man cut him off. "Don't even think about that. We'll get to them first. Let's pick up the pace."

Parel said nothing more but jogged back to the front of the pack.

Varelk caught up to Noah and Aterre. "Can I ask you a question, Aterre?"

"What is it?"

"Those fighting stances you were teaching Noah — where did you learn them?"

Aterre glanced at Noah and then stared at the ground. "I, um, I learned them a long time ago."

Varelk gave a small chuckle. It sounded forced to Noah's ears. "You aren't old enough for a long time ago." After an awkward silence, he spoke again. "Tell me, where did you learn them?"

Slowing down, the three men allowed the rest of the group to move out of listening range, and Aterre spoke softly. "I grew up in Havilah, where I was part of a group called Sepha. They taught us how to defend ourselves. But I left the group after . . . many seasons ago."

"But you bear their mark?"

"You know about them?" Aterre asked.

"More than I'd like to. They've become a very sinister group in Bothar."

"Do you think they had something to do with the children?" Noah asked.

"I hope not, but I strongly suspect them." Varelk rubbed his chin. "Do all followers of Sepha know how to fight like you?"

"That was part of the training — at least where I'm from."

"I was afraid of that. Our men aren't trained to fight. We're a peaceful people. Much of the reason we left Bothar was to get away from the evil and violence there."

"What rumors was Parel talking about?" Noah asked.

Some deep emotion crossed Varelk's face, and Noah felt again the chill of dread. "Some of the people of Bothar — those who follow Sepha — practice the dark arts." He swallowed. "We've heard rumors that they've recently started sacrificing children in the name of Sepha."

Noah's stomach clenched. "How could. . . ." He lowered his voice. "How could anyone do something so evil?"

"This world's growing darker all the time. When I was a boy, such an abomination would've been unthinkable, but in Bothar. . . ." He shook his head.

Noah looked at his friend. He'd worked beside Aterre for more than a year, journeyed with him, played and laughed and eaten with him. Yet it was hard to keep the accusation from his voice when he asked, "Aterre, do you know anything about this?"

Aterre scowled. "No. Never something so twisted and sickening. Like I told you before, I only knew about certain disciplines within Sepha." He pulled his shoulder wrap to the side, exposing part of the tattoo for Varelk. "If it's connected to such evil as you've said, then I can no longer be proud of this."

The older man stared at the mark. "Why did you leave?"

Aterre looked away and kicked at a twig lying on the trail.

"Sir." Noah's heart filled with compassion for his friend. "His family was attacked in the night, much like the children of your village. He was the only one to escape."

Varelk pursed his lips as concern spread over his face. He turned back to Aterre. "I'm sorry about your family. I hope you understand the reason I had to ask."

Aterre met the older man's gaze with a long, intense stare. Finally, he nodded. "Thank you. I'm sorry about your family too. We're going to get them back."

"A word of advice: don't let my son see that mark. If he doesn't trust you now, imagine how he'd behave if he knew."

Aterre nodded again. "I won't."

Hiking north, the party reached a fork in the road. The sun was low in the sky, causing a small signpost at a fork in the path to cast a long shadow. The marker indicated that the trail ahead and to the right led to a place unknown to Noah, and the route to the left went to Bothar. Parel and Liun examined the paths closely for a few moments, and then, unsurprisingly, headed left.

Chapter 12

As daylight faltered, Noah and Aterre followed the Zakari on the wide path's ascent through the woods. Parel and Liun exchanged a series of whispered conversations, and Noah sensed they were gaining ground.

Parel held up a hand and gathered everyone close. Keeping his voice down, he asked, "See that light up ahead? It looks like a campfire, and I'd be surprised if it isn't the kidnappers."

Noah squinted and barely identified a small orange flicker through the trees in the distance. *How'd they spot that?*

"We need to get off this trail, but don't make a sound," Liun said, and they all followed his lead. He gestured to Parel. "We'll sneak up there and check it out. The rest of you wait here for us." In an instant, they were gone.

Varelk herded the remaining search party members a little farther off the road. "Try to rest a little, but stay low and be on alert."

Noah's feet and legs ached from the long march. He plopped down and leaned back on his elbows, closing his eyes. *Creator, please protect the children and help us rescue them without a fight.*

"Noah, tell me about your relatives and where you grew up," Varelk said. "It'll help me keep my mind off all this."

Noah sat up. Talking about his family made him long for home. Nearly two weeks had passed since he said farewell. He shared about growing up on the farm, and that he often wondered how Jerah and Misha were doing.

Varelk stood and stretched. "I can see you're a godly young man, Noah. I'm certain my son has misjudged you."

Noah shook his head. "I don't blame him, but I will do whatever I can to earn his trust." He rubbed one forearm vigorously and then the next to warm up. "Besides what we saw yesterday, what is life like in Zakar?"

As Varelk talked about his town, Parel and Liun returned. The eight other men crowded around them, leaning in to catch every bit of their report.

"It's definitely the kidnappers," Liun said.

"Did you see our children?" Erno asked.

Parel nodded. "Yes, they appear to be unharmed but are tied up near one of the tents."

"How many kidnappers?" Varelk asked.

"We counted four, but it's possible that there were more in the tents or standing watch."

"Only four?" Erno clenched his fists. "We can overpower them."

Varelk held up a hand. "Not so fast, Erno. You know the followers of Sepha are fighters. We have no such training. We need to be careful."

"So what's the plan?" Liun asked.

After a short pause, one of the other men spoke. "Wait until they fall asleep, then sneak in and untie the children."

Liun shook his head. "Maybe, but if they keep watch, getting close enough without being seen will be almost impossible."

"What if we *want* them to see us? Or at least a couple of us?" Erno asked after a long pause.

"Why would we want that?" Liun scoffed, but Noah was intrigued.

"For a diversion while everyone else circles their camp."

"That won't work," Parel said.

"Why not?" Erno asked. "It worked on us. The barn burned down, and we didn't suspect any other trouble until it was too late."

Parel lifted both of his hands and touched his chest with his fingertips. "Look at us. They'll know we're Zakari."

Erno gestured toward Noah and Aterre. "Not if *they're* the diversion."

"No." Parel folded his arms over his tattooed chest and scowled.

Liun looked at Parel. "Why not? It's a good plan."

"What about it, Aterre? Noah?" Varelk asked. "Are you willing?"

Noah opened his mouth but stopped when Parel cut him off.

"Father. No. We can't trust them."

Varelk looked at his son. "Yes, we can. They aren't like the men of Bothar, and I don't believe for a moment that they're part of the abduction."

"You want to place our hope on the shoulders of two men we just met yesterday?" Parel's voice rose, and he stopped himself with obvious effort before continuing in a quieter tone, "Is that really a risk you want to take with your grandson's life?"

"I don't want to do any of this, but I believe the Creator sent them to us at the right time so that we can rescue all our children." Varelk spread his arms, palms open. "Do you have a better plan?"

Parel stared off into the treetops for a long moment before relenting. "No."

Varelk motioned to Aterre. "You don't have to do this."

Aterre nodded at Noah. "Yes, we do. We said that we'd do anything to help, so tell us what to do."

"Erno, what's your plan?" Varelk asked.

The tall man cleared his throat. "Noah and Aterre will act like travelers from the north who are heading to Bothar and need directions. So they will need to approach the campsite from the road. I think Aterre should do most of the talking since he sounds different than the rest of us."

"Forgive me for interrupting," Noah said. "But won't it seem odd if we see the children tied up and don't say anything about them?"

"Not necessarily," Varelk said. "If our suspicions are correct, they were kidnapped to be sacrificed in Bothar. Since you two will pretend to be heading there, you can ask if that's why they have them."

"Right," Erno said. "While the two of you distract the men, we'll spread out around the campsite, still hiding in the trees. Parel and Liun, you'll move behind the kidnappers, so that Aterre can see your sign when we're in position."

"What's the sign?" Parel asked.

"We'll each carry torches, but keep them dim and shielded. For the signal, get them blazing." Erno turned back to Aterre. "That's when you and Noah will position yourselves between the kidnappers and the children. Then the rest of us will show our torches. In fact, we should all light two of them. Since we'll be spread out, it'll look like there are at least 16 people surrounding the camp."

"And then what?" Liun said.

"Then Parel will call to them from the woods and tell them they're surrounded. If they walk away from the children without harming them, we'll let them go. And just to let them know that we're serious," — he lifted his bow — "I'll fire a warning shot into the ground near their feet."

Parel jerked his head toward Aterre and Noah. "And if they betray us, fire an arrow into them."

Frustrated by Parel's lack of trust, Noah sighed.

Erno put his arm in front of Parel as if to stop him from attacking Noah on the spot. "If everything goes according to plan, we can rescue our little ones without a fight."

"And if it doesn't?" Parel asked.

"Then we improvise." Erno motioned to Aterre. "You may have to put those skills you were teaching Noah to good use."

Aterre nodded. "If it comes to that."

"Let's pray that it doesn't," Varelk said. "In fact, if no one has anything else to add, we should pray and then move quickly."

The Zakari men lowered themselves to the ground in the same awkward pose as the previous evening. Noah and Aterre knelt, but this time neither copied the Zakari. Varelk offered a brief, but deeply heartfelt prayer, pleading for the safety of the children, protection for Noah and Aterre, and for a peaceful resolution. Following the customary silence at the close of the prayer, the men stood.

Torches were prepared and distributed. Varelk approached Noah and Aterre. "Please be careful. May the Most High be with you."

Parel placed a hand on Noah's shoulder. "I hope I'm wrong about you. And if I am, you'll have my respect and sincere apologies."

"Thank you," Noah said.

An agonized scream rang out in the distance and Parel stiffened. "That was Elam. We have to go now!"

Aterre and Noah hastened back to the trail and headed for the kidnapper's campsite. The stars sparkled in the early evening sky, and a crescent moon hung overhead. A light wind wafted through the night, evaporating the beads of sweat on Noah's face. On both sides of the path, insects chirped and buzzed, all but drowning out the sounds of their feet hitting ground and the pounding of Noah's heart. The peace surrounding them belied the gravity of their mission. *God, please guide our actions and protect those children.*

"Nervous?" Aterre asked.

"Of course. I've never been involved in something so dangerous. You?"

Aterre shrugged. "Definitely. But you can't show it or they may get suspicious. Just keep praying and follow my lead."

Moments later, they turned off the trail and trekked up a slight climb through the small patch of woods leading to the fire. For the first time, they clearly saw the situation. A moderately sized tent stood on the far side of a small bonfire. Three men sat on the ground around the blaze, while a fourth man stood nearby and jabbed a rod into the embers. The children were tied together to the left of the tent. They huddled closer together than their bonds required. With bowed heads, either in utter fear or defeat, a few sobs broke free. Elam rocked back and forth with his bound hands pressed against his upper left arm.

Aterre stopped behind a large tree several cubits before the clearing. "Are we sticking with the plan?"

"Yeah. It looks just how Parel described."

"Okay. Then act natural. If possible, don't let the children get a good look at you. They may give us away." Aterre smiled. "Loosen up. Don't be afraid to step on a twig or two. We aren't trying to surprise them."

Noah took a deep breath and slowly let it out. "Let's go."

Aterre led as they stepped out into the open. They continued forward until one of the men spotted them. "Evening peace, men," Aterre said.

The man stood and stepped around the fire. "Who are you?" His voice was gruff and threatening. While not a large man, his tenor indicated no lack of confidence. His dark, scruffy beard hid his mouth.

"My name is Aterre, and this is my friend, Noah." He turned his right foot outward and folded his hands together against his stomach in a peculiar manner that Noah had not seen before. Aterre's left hand enclosed two fingers of his right hand while his thumb stretched upward.

The man's face and stance relaxed as he copied the unique position. "And what's your business here, Aterre?"

Noah tried to make sense of his friend's action. *Is this some kind of secret Sepha greeting?* Although he desperately wanted to make sure the huddled Zakari were all right, he forced himself to keep his eyes on the man.

"No business, sir. We're on our way to Bothar for the first time and saw your fire. We decided to see if you might be headed that way too."

"Indeed, we are."

Aterre relaxed his stance, let his hands drop to his sides, and turned to Noah. He spoke loud enough to be heard by all the men. "I told you we were on the right path."

The kidnapper who had been poking something into the fire suddenly joined them. He was about a span taller and at least that much broader at the shoulders than the first man. Even with just the light from the fire, there was an unexplainable air of ruthlessness about him that made Noah want to protect the children even more. "You say you're making your first trip to Bothar?"

"Yes sir," Aterre said. "Is it much farther?"

"About two more days traveling by foot," Ruthless said. "Aterre, I've never heard that name before, and your speech is strange. Where are you from?"

Aterre motioned toward the fire. "May we join you for a bit and warm ourselves?"

"Have a seat," Scruffy Beard said.

Noah and Aterre found spots on the ground across from the four men.

"I'm from the land of Havilah, far away to the south." Aterre laughed. "And from my perspective, it's everyone around here who talks a little funny."

Ruthless relaxed only slightly and motioned toward Noah. "And what about your friend? Does he speak?"

"When necessary." Noah elbowed Aterre and attempted to keep his voice from shaking. "Now this one — he'll strike up a conversation with anyone."

Still seated, the man farthest to the left set a dish on the ground, and his soup sloshed over its brim. "You must be traveling to Bothar for the big Sepha festival. How long have you been part of the brotherhood?"

"I joined years ago in Havilah, and when I heard about Bothar and the festival, I knew I'd have to visit someday." Aterre tipped his head in the direction of the children. "Is that why you have them?"

Smiling, Ruthless pointed to his captives. "Them? Yeah, they're perfect for the sacrifice." At his words, a chill slithered its way down Noah's back.

Elam still rocked back and forth. A red and white burn covered the boy's upper arm. Noah's gaze drifted to the fire and he spotted the metal instrument used to destroy flesh. A large wooden handle encased the top, while glowing red hot at the bottom end of the rod was a tree-shaped piece of metal. *Was Elam just marked for sacrifice?* Noah swallowed his revulsion. He had to focus, had to be on the lookout for Parel's sign.

"So will all of them be sacrificed? Are there any more?" Aterre asked. The calm in his voice unnerved Noah.

"We have to mark the rest first, and then I guess it depends on the other group that traveled south, and how many. . . ." Ruthless's eyes drifted upward as he seemed to search for a word. A sinister smile spread on his face. "How many *recruits* they found."

"Did you buy these ones?" Aterre asked.

"Nah," Soup Spiller said. "We raided a little village last night." He playfully pushed the silent man next to him. "Sterk used to live there, so they were easy pickings."

Noah's eyes darted toward the surly fourth, then he looked away, afraid the man would read his emotions in his gaze. *How could he betray his own people, some of whom are probably his close relations?* A glimmer of light flickered in the woods behind the abductors. *Finally.*

Sterk jolted upright and pointed past Noah. "Do you see that?"

Noah knew what to expect, but jerked his head back to play the part.

"Over there!" Soup Spiller pointed to his right.

Aterre jumped to his feet. "And back there!"

"Don't move! You're surrounded!" Parel's voice carried throughout the campsite.

Ruthless picked up a knife and turned in the direction of Parel. "What do you want?"

"We want our children back. Now put the knife down."

"Over my dead body," the large captor yelled back.

Parel's laugh chilled Noah. "We can arrange that."

An arrow zipped past Noah and landed just short of Scruffy Beard.

"That's your only warning," Parel said. "I promise, the next one won't miss."

Aterre stood and put his arms up. "Wait! We aren't with them." He backed toward the children. "We're just passing through."

Noah slowly edged toward the young captives as well.

"Halt! All of you get on the ground!"

The abductors exchanged glances and slowly bent down. Ruthless mumbled something under his breath, but Noah could not make it out.

"On the ground!"

The kidnappers finally knelt.

"Now I want the man closest to the children to untie them."

Because Parel had singled Noah out, he stood and pointed at himself. "Me?"

"Yes, do it now."

Noah hurried over to the children, who stared wide-eyed at him. Tears streaked down Elam's face. Noah held a finger to his lips, urging the children to remain silent. "Your fathers are here. Run to that torch over there." Noah pointed in the direction of the road. He untied the two girls first, and then Erno's son. As he began to work on the knot that bound Elam, one of the kidnappers spat and growled.

"That one's already been marked. He has to die!" The man stood faster than Noah thought possible and bolted toward him in a rage.

Aterre sprang into action, but could not reach Noah in time. Bracing himself for the onslaught, Noah knew he only needed to buy enough time for Aterre to get there to assist him. Ruthless never slowed, lunging at Noah with a knife. Noah sidestepped to dodge the attack, but the blade caught his garment, cutting a long gash in the cloth. As the knife caught on the fabric, the man lost his grip on it. The force of the snag slowed him and yanked Noah into his aggressor, sending them both tumbling.

Noah scrambled to his knees, spotted the knife, and dove for it. The large man pounced on him just as Noah reached for the handle. Unable to grasp the weapon, Noah pushed it out of reach and rolled under the man's weight. Before Noah could react any further, a powerful fist landed a blow to his cheek. Noah blinked as a starburst flashed across his vision, but a sudden surge of energy coursed through his body. He planted one foot into the man's stomach, grabbed his shoulders, and then flipped him back over his head. Ruthless hit the ground with a thud.

Noah cringed in pain as Aterre leapt on the man and held his dagger-tooth knife to his throat. "Move and you die."

Clambering to his feet, Noah spotted movement out of the corner of his eye from the direction of the fire.

Scruffy Beard screamed and dropped to the ground several paces in front of Noah, an arrow sticking out of his leg. The other two men remained by the fire.

"Get the boy," Aterre said, still holding their assailant at bay.

Noah scrambled over to Elam and finished untying him, being careful to avoid his wounded arm. He helped the lad to his feet and pointed him toward the road. Then, picking up some of the rough rope, he moved back toward Aterre. They quickly bound the pinned man's hands and feet.

With arrow nocked and pointed toward the men at the fire, Erno stepped into the clearing. "If any of you makes a move, you'll go down like your friend."

Scruffy Beard still writhed on the ground. Blood gushed from his thigh as he grimaced in pain. Liun ran to the injured man and bound his hands while he screamed and cursed. Four more Zakari men emerged from the woods, drew their weapons, and circled the two men near the fire.

"I have all the children." Noah recognized the voice from the woods as belonging to Varelk.

Parel soon joined them. He marched straight to the two men at the fire and pointed to the one on the right. "Tie him up." He took a long look at Sterk. "How could you do this to your family? You'd sacrifice your own nephew for Sepha?"

Sterk's eyes filled with rage. "You're a fool, Parel! You have no idea what we're capable of." He spat in Parel's face.

Parel wiped away the spittle with the back of his hand. Then he raised his blade and thrust it toward Sterk, stopping the point just short of the man's chest. "You won't be capable of anything if we kill you."

"You don't have the guts." Hatred filled Sterk's words. "I don't know what my sister ever saw in you."

Parel's eyes glistened in the firelight. Without taking his stern gaze off Sterk, he simply said, "Bind him."

"Now what do you want to do with them?" Erno asked.

"I think we should treat them as they treated our children," Parel said.

Liun's jaw dropped. With eyebrows raised, he leaned forward and said, "You want to kill them?"

Parel shook his head and pulled the rod out of the fire. Holding it up, he looked closely at the glowing design on the end. "I think we should mark them."

"No!" Terror edged Sterk's voice. "You can't!"

Parel gave a knowing smile. "And why can't we?"

Sterk snarled and looked away.

"We could never go home," Soup Spiller said. "We'd be marked for sacrifice."

"Exactly." Parel pointed to two Zakari and then motioned to Sterk. "Gag him and hold him fast."

Liun drew Parel aside, his eyes questioning. "Are you sure?"

Noah wanted to object, but he saw the logic in Parel's decision. Freed kidnappers would return to Bothar and gather reinforcements to launch another attack. The Zakari were not a violent people, so executing the abductors was not an option, nor would it do to tie them up indefinitely so that they starved.

Oddly, Parel glanced at Noah before he replied. "It's the only way."

Sterk struggled to free himself, but the guards and ropes held him fast. Noah looked away, but he couldn't avoid the sounds. Sterk's whimpering, the sizzle of skin. The screams.

"Now you can never go back to Bothar or to Sepha," Parel said. "As much as I hate what you've become. . . ." He paused as if having second thoughts. "As much as I hate this life you now stand for, if you choose differently, for my wife's sake, I'd open my door to you — even though you mutilated my son."

Erno extracted the arrow from the wounded man's leg and treated it with some sort of powder he took from a pouch on his belt. Parel and the other Zakari quickly gagged and branded the remaining kidnappers, and this time Noah watched. Not the branding, but the Zakari, who winced and turned away each time, showing they did not relish their task. Then Parel ordered that the kidnappers be tied together.

He stood before the seared and seething men, holding up Ruthless's knife. "I'll leave this at the edge of the clearing. Once you figure out how to maneuver over there, you can cut yourselves free." Parel turned to leave, but stopped and looked straight at Sterk. "Know this. If you ever seek to hurt my family or community again, I will kill you."

CHAPTER 13

Varelk embraced Elam, but when Parel and the other men made it to the road, the boy ran to his father. Parel knelt down and squeezed his son like he would never let go. As Noah watched the reunions, his weariness faded into pure joy. Liun openly wept as he picked up his daughter and kissed her repeatedly. Holding a torch in one hand, Noah nudged Aterre with his other arm. "Makes it all seem worth it, doesn't it?"

"Absolutely." Aterre started when he looked at Noah. "Your face looks pretty sore."

Remembering the blow, Noah touched his cheekbone and winced. "I guess it does hurt. I was so focused on everything in the moment that I hadn't really noticed."

"Now you're just trying to act tough." Aterre pushed him and laughed. "You did great back there."

"You were pretty convincing yourself. You almost had me believing you were one of them. I half expected Parel to shoot us." Noah tilted his cheek toward his friend. "How bad is it?"

Aterre took a closer look in the flickering light from the torch. "Well, be prepared for girls to scream when they look at you."

Noah held his chin high, chest puffed out. "As if that's even possible."

"I'm kidding. They'll be too busy running away." Aterre smirked. "Seriously though, it'll be black and blue in the morning, but you'll be alright." He started to leave, but his attention locked onto the front of Noah's garment. "Might need to take a look at that though."

Noah's gaze followed Aterre's. A blooming line of blood marred his robe, tracing a long tear in the fabric. He lifted the cloth away from his chest to find the source. "I guess he must've cut me after all. It doesn't look very deep." Pouring some water over the gash, he flinched before tearing a piece of fabric from the end of his wrap and pressing it against the wound. "That's better."

"Noah, use a little bit of this on your wound. It will help stop the bleeding and keep it from festering." Erno handed him the pouch from his belt.

Noah withdrew a pinch of the powder and rubbed it into the cut, biting his lip at the sting. "Is that enough?"

"Should be. Check it in the morning when we have enough light."

"I will."

Parel walked Elam over to Noah and Aterre and then bowed before them. "I owe both of you an apology." He glanced down at Elam, placing a hand on the boy's head, and tears filled his eyes. "You saved my son's life. I'll never be able to repay you." He embraced Noah. "I'm sorry I misjudged you."

Noah flushed with satisfaction. He let the words sink in, warming his soul. At once, his father's voice rang in his head: *All we have comes from the Creator, Noah. Never forget that.* Feeling humbled, Noah mirrored Parel's bow. "I'm happy the children are safe and that the Creator gave us success."

Parel then embraced Aterre and apologized.

Noah bent down and looked into Elam's eyes. "How are you feeling?"

"My arm hurts, but I'm happy you came." He threw his good arm around Noah's neck. "Thank you, Noah."

"You're most welcome, Elam." Noah chuckled.

"I hate to cut this short," Varelk said, "but we'd better get far away from here tonight. I don't think those men will find the knife in the dark, so they probably won't be free until morning. But to be on the safe side, let's put some distance between us."

"Do you think they'll come after us, Grandfather?" Elam asked.

Varelk shook his head. "I doubt it. There are only four of them, and one won't be walking well for a while. But you never know what people might do when they're angry, so I don't want to take any chances. Parel, lead the way home."

Energized by their success, the Zakari walked as the darkness of night deepened into its stillest time. Noah estimated the deepest dark had long passed when they stopped at the small clearing they had used as a resting place earlier. With the exception of Elam, the other children had fallen asleep in their fathers' arms sometime during the long hike.

"Let's set up camp here," Varelk said. "Some of us can go no farther without sleep."

"We need two people to take the first watch," Liun said.

Noah's legs and face were sore, but his mind still raced. "I'd be happy to."

"And I'll join you," Parel said.

Varelk clapped his hands. "Good. It's settled. Let's get some rest. Elam, you can sleep next to me."

"I want to stay with my father and Noah."

"I'll bring him back here when he falls asleep." Parel put an arm around his son, and they led Noah a short distance down the trail they had just walked. Parel sat on a log and pulled Elam close beside. He patted a spot, inviting Noah to sit next to him.

Noah stared up at the litany of stars shining through the sparse canopy above, though the swelling around his left eye and his tiredness blurred the lights to some extent. He stretched and yawned before taking the seat. Feeling part of his skin catch oddly, Noah looked down and saw congealed blood on his midsection. Carefully he pulled the torn cloth from the laceration.

Elam yawned and snuggled into his father's side.

"Are you well? That's a bit of a gash you have there."

Noah suppressed a smile at Parel's concern for his well-being. "I didn't even notice it until after the rescue." He gingerly prodded the wound, feeling the blood stick ever so slightly to his two fingertips.

Parel shook his head. "Good thing it wasn't worse." He bent his head to look Noah in the eye. "And what about your face? Looks like he got you pretty good."

"Yeah, that was a strong man. I hope I never see him again."

"Same here." Parel sighed. "I hope never to see any of them again. Although I half wish Sterk would feel remorse and come home."

Surprised, Noah's jaw dropped a little and he winced. "What happened? Why did he leave Zakar?"

"I'm not really sure. He's my wife's older brother. My father-in-law used to travel a lot when Sterk was young, and he occasionally took his son along. I guess Sterk was seduced by what he saw of the world. Their father has never forgiven himself." Parel looked down and shook his head. "I've never seen such hatred in a man before. The way Sterk and those men acted tonight — they were more like beasts than men."

"I thought the same thing." Noah shuddered. "I'd like to think he can change."

"So do I." Parel rubbed his eyes.

Elam shifted to get comfortable and leaned against Noah.

Parel grinned. "I think he trusts you. And now, so does his father. It means a lot."

Noah returned the smile and draped a loose part of his robe over the boy.

After a long silence, Parel asked, "Do you agree with my decision to mark them?"

Noah nodded. "It's harsh, but given the circumstances, I can't think of a better solution. I'm glad you didn't execute them, even though they planned to sacrifice your son. But I'm also glad you didn't just set them free to strengthen their numbers and seek revenge against your people. You showed great wisdom in your judgment. Do you think they might still try to do something?"

Parel shrugged. "I wouldn't be surprised. We'll have to post a guard every night, especially if two strangers show up as a diversion." Parel chuckled softly so as not to wake the boy, and winked.

"You definitely can't trust people like that." Noah grinned but quickly turned serious. "What about his arm? If Sepha followers ever see that mark. . . ."

Parel shook his head. "I'm not sure. We can cover it for now. But I'll consult the elders. I don't want to do it, but . . ." He lowered his voice. "We may have to burn another design to mask that cursed one."

Noah cringed and glanced at the child resting comfortably against him. "Poor little boy."

"Listen, Noah, I'm truly sorry for misjudging you. You risked your life to help strangers, and you and Aterre gave me my son back. If you ever need anything, anything at all, please let me know."

Noah nodded. "There's one thing you could do."

"Name it."

"Could you give us directions to Iri Geshem from Zakar?"

Parel smiled. "I can certainly do that. There's a trail from the village that goes directly east to the Hiddekel, just over half a day's journey. On the third day of every week there's a boat that heads downriver. You could sail the rest of the way and be there in two weeks."

Noah yawned again but this time abandoned the stretch. "Two weeks? That's great. I thought we'd be walking for at least a whole moon."

"You're welcome to stay with my people until the boat leaves. We'd throw a great celebration to honor you and Aterre."

"I'll check with Aterre, but I'm sure we'd be happy to stay a few more days, especially knowing there will be good food. Plus, we could help rebuild the barn."

Casting a sly smile at Noah, Parel nodded. "Yes, my father always taught us to leave a place in better condition than when we found it. When you first visited, we had a barn, so we should probably have one when you leave."

CHAPTER 14

Taht nickered and shook her neck as Noah stroked her mane. With a slight catch in his throat, he turned and faced the dozens of Zakari who had formed a semi-circle to say their farewells. The cool morning air gave him a quick shiver.

Five activity-filled days had flown by. Extravagant in their joy, the Zakari had thrown a huge celebration on the night of the rescuers' triumphant return. In the following days, Noah and Aterre helped the villagers rebuild much of their barn — only the roof needed to be finished.

Mehul stepped forward, touched his forehead, and bowed slightly. "We're sad to see you leave so soon. You're always welcome here."

Varelk pulled Noah into a strong embrace. "May the Creator bless your journey." He had only just let go when Elam ran forward and wrapped his skinny arms around Noah's waist. "I'll miss you." The thick dressing around his upper arm hid the gruesome wound that looked nothing like the original mark. At his son's insistence, Parel had made the heart-wrenching decision to obscure the vile symbol by burning a large circle the size of a fist over it. Chewing bark from a wispy tree helped Elam cope with the pain.

Noah bent low. Carefully avoiding the bandaged area, he squeezed the boy who had followed him around for much of the last week. "I'll miss you too. You've got a lot of inner strength. Use it to serve the Most High."

Aterre mussed Elam's hair in farewell.

Pulling out a coiled object, Parel placed it in Noah's hand. "To show our gratitude."

Noah saw the distinct spheres of piks and pikkas laced on a cord and twisted into a loop. He shook his head and extended his palm. "No, this isn't necessary."

Parel held his arms out. "It's a gift for you and Aterre from all of us." Parel looked at his son, who now clung to Aterre. "It's the least we could do."

While his heart was ready to get back to the adventure that awaited them, Noah was sad to leave the Zakari, who had become like family in the short time they'd been together. He said nothing more, only embraced Parel again and held up a hand to the gathered villagers before turning away.

Their farewells said, Noah and Aterre set out at a brisk pace. The road to the tiny river town was far better maintained than the one that had brought them into Zakar. Wide enough for two pack animals pulling a wagon, the road accommodated the Zakari's supply runs to Novanam, which, according to Parel, consisted of nothing more than a few dwellings on the Hiddekel.

Noah secured the gift into one of their bags in the cart before rejoining Aterre next to Taht. He patted the animal's neck. "Just a short walk and then you get to ride on a boat again."

"I'm sure she'll love that," Aterre said.

Noah chuckled. "It took me a whole day to get my — what was the term Deks used? Sea legs? Maybe she'll get hers on this trip."

As he shifted his focus to the journey ahead, energy rushed through Noah's body, and he whistled a playful tune that matched the bounce in his steps. He felt ready to take on the world.

Throughout the early hours, scores of colorful birds and small reptiles made appearances along the way. But as the morning's coolness dissipated, a thick humidity blanketed the trail, bringing with it swarms of pesky insects to vex Noah's head and neck. By the time the sun had reached its zenith, his springy stride had flattened into a trudge. Noah found his mind wandering to home, thinking longingly of the cool breezes that played through the malid orchard, keeping heat and bugs alike at bay.

He perked up briefly when, at one point, a massive furry creature that was nearly twice Noah's height loped across the trail. Watching it walk on its hind legs and the knuckles of his front limbs, he almost laughed in spite of his discomfort. Taht stopped and tensed up, but the brown and white creature paid them no heed. It lumbered into the forest, snapping branches and twigs in its wake.

The excitement of the odd sighting faded quickly. Wiping his forehead clear of sweat with one hand and swatting another pest away with the other, Noah winced as the wound on his chest throbbed. He drew aside part of his garment to inspect it. The salve from the Zakari seemed to have sped the healing, but it didn't end the occasional ache or the persistent itch every time something rubbed across it. Focused on the injury, Noah stepped in a small rut and his ankle twisted, sending a sharp pain up his leg. "Ouch!"

"You alright?" Aterre asked.

Noah limped the next few steps as the soreness subsided a little. "I'll be fine." Truth be told, gone was the happy-go-lucky attitude of the morning. Instead, irritation mounted as discomfort and annoyance crowded his senses with relentless pursuit. He swatted at another insect. "Get off me!"

Aterre chuckled. "Settle down."

"These bugs are so annoying." Noah shook his head and wiped both arms in succession.

"Just ignore them."

"That's easier said than done. They aren't going after you." Noah tapped the side of the cart. "Let me ride for a while."

Aterre looked up from where he sat squeezed among their belongings. "We just switched spots a little while ago."

"My foot hurts."

"And you don't think my feet hurt? We've been on the go for weeks."

Noah scowled at him. "But I've been walking while you keep riding."

Aterre laughed. "What's gotten into you? I've walked just as much."

"You wish." Noah drew his garment back to reveal his wound. "I'm the one that risked my life to save those children."

"What's your problem?" Aterre pierced Noah with a gaze and jumped out onto the trail with his fists clenched. "I was right there, fighting with you."

Noah crossed his arms. "You mostly just let that mouth of yours run." Noah knew he wasn't making sense, but that just fueled his anger, his need to win.

"That's ridiculous. But if you need it, take the back of the cart." Aterre pointed and emphasized his words to leave no doubt that he thought Noah was being childish.

Noah tugged on Taht's lead rope. No way was he going to look weak. "Forget it. I'm good. Let's just get to Novanam so we don't miss the boat to Iri Geshem."

Time seemed to drag on Noah's thoughts, which eventually drifted back to his family. Loneliness filled him. What he would give to see them again. Like a cool breeze brushing against his skin, his father's final charge nudged at his mind, dampening the heat of his ire. *Don't forget your promise to follow the Creator.*

He looked back at Aterre, who walked in silence behind the cart. Noah shook his head. *My actions aren't honoring the Most High.*

Noah stopped the cart. "Aterre."

His friend ignored him and kept walking.

Noah put his hand on Aterre's shoulder. "I'm sorry about that back there. I don't know what came over me."

"And what? I'm just supposed to forget about the things you said?"

"I don't expect you to forget them, but I do ask that you forgive me."

Aterre stared at the ground for a few moments. "I guess I do owe your family one. Don't worry about it." Aterre smirked. "You're just lucky I didn't beat you up."

Noah shook his head but smiled. "I appreciate that."

CHAPTER 15

Iri Gesham — Noah's 40th year

I've never seen anything like it." Noah stood on his toes at the bow of the boat and leaned as far out as he could over the water. Reflected early-afternoon sunlight danced across the rippling surface that stretched to the horizon. Squinting, he looked past the water directly beneath him, beyond the riverside buildings of Iri Geshem on either side of the Hiddekel, and into the glistening expanse of sea before them. "It's spectacular."

Aterre put an arm around Noah's shoulder. "I knew you'd like it. Here we are at last."

After their adventure with the Zakari, the past two weeks on the Hiddekel had been tame to the point of boredom. Now, as they finally reached their destination, Noah yearned to get off the boat.

He pulled his gaze away from the Great Sea and focused on the ivory-colored buildings immediately ahead to their right. Numerous one-story structures lined the river. "Are those made out of stone?" he asked Farna, the vessel's captain.

"No, they're mud-brick," he said as he joined them at the bow. "They usually have wooden frames with the bricks placed around them."

"Look how many there are. This is so much bigger than Iri Sana."

Ahead, a dock built parallel to the river stretched along the shore. Farna's men slowly guided the boat alongside the wharf, while their captain tossed the mooring to a man on the shore, who quickly secured the line to one of the several tall posts jutting out from the water and evenly dividing the dock. A handful of men joined Farna's crew in unloading the ship.

Noah strode to Taht and stroked her mane, feeling her muscles slightly relax at his reassuring touch. "You made it, girl." He double-checked the cart to be sure their belongings were fastened inside and then hitched it to her.

"Noah, Aterre." Farna waved them over to him. He was a firm and demanding man when needed, yet fair and approachable. Noah admired the way he carried himself, and how he earned the respect of those around him.

Slowly and steadily, Noah guided Taht across the ship's deck.

Farna reached into a pouch and handed each man three copper pikkas. "You've earned some of your payment back through all of your help."

Noah smiled. "Thank you, sir. We appreciate all that you've taught us."

"You and Aterre are always welcome on my boat. Just don't bring that animal with you again." Farna chuckled.

Noah snorted. "I wouldn't dream of it." He pointed to the lane that led away from the dock and divided two rows of houses. "So we take this road until Sarie's Bakery and then turn left, and that'll take us all the way to Ara's shipyard?"

Farna nodded. "It will. Really, as long as you head to the coast, you'll find Ara. Since he's the one who builds all the boats, you can't miss it."

"Peace to you," Aterre said.

"I hope to see you at Ara's sometime," Noah said.

"Until next time then." Farna raised a hand, his attention already on the unloading process going on near the stern.

Noah carefully led Taht onto the dock and had to restrain her as she tried to hurry to the shore. "Easy. We'll be there soon enough." As soon as they stepped onto dry ground, she stamped her feet several times before snorting and shaking her head. She was finally at ease.

With all their belongings in tow, Noah and Aterre strode into town. Passersby greeted them with a nod or a smile. A group of young children played in the space between two of the buildings. An older woman stood on the roof of a one-story home, hanging clothes on a line tied to posts. A stone staircase ascended the side of the house.

"Farna wasn't kidding about this place," Aterre said. "They really are friendly. Not at all like Birtzun."

"I love it already. Look at all this." Noah gestured to one side and then the other. "At all this life."

Aterre shrugged. "I would've been happy to stay at the farm."

A stunning young woman, perhaps a bit older than they were, turned the corner. She smiled at them before ducking into a nearby house.

Aterre grinned at Noah. "On second thought, I could get used to this place."

Noah rolled his eyes and shook his head. As he tried to think of a clever response, the unmistakable scent of fresh-baked bread floated into his nostrils. He breathed it in deeply. "That must be the bakery." Ahead and to their left stood a two-story building. Faint smoke floated away from a nearby rooftop. A wooden sign over the door announced that it was indeed Sarie's Bakery.

They turned left before the shop, and from the top of the hill spied Ara's shipyard. At the end of the road, up against the shore of the inlet, the wooden frame of a boat rose a little higher than the mud-brick building not too far from it.

Noah tugged Taht's lead as he quickened his own pace. "Come on."

Aterre matched his stride. "Have you thought about what you're going to say?"

"To Ara?" Noah shrugged. "I haven't rehearsed anything. I figured it'd be better to just be natural."

"That's probably best." Aterre pushed him playfully. "Don't mess it up."

The closer they came to the shipyard, the larger the dwellings were, at least on the right side of the road. Spaced far apart, the two-story homes stood in yards adorned with a variety of trees and bushes. The district to the left was filled with small older homes; some wood and others mud-brick.

After crossing a wide dirt road, they stood at the gated entrance to the shipyard. Working on the boat frame, three men set a beam into place and fastened it with hammers and pegs, while another man cut a log with a saw. A hint of the sweet scent of sawdust amid the salty aroma from the water beyond, amplified Noah's senses. He took a deep breath and looked uncertainly at Aterre. "Time to find out if the journey was worth it."

"And if it doesn't work out," Aterre said, "remember, we helped save some lives."

"And had some adventures."

Once inside the gate, Aterre shut it behind them and Noah secured Taht's rein to a post near the building. "Think the wagon will be safe here?"

Aterre shrugged. "Farna said we shouldn't have to worry about thieves. The people still follow the Creator here."

Noah ascended the two small stone steps and stood before the front door. He knocked and waited.

"Can I help you?"

Turning in the direction of the gruff voice, Noah saw one of the men who had just been swinging a hammer striding toward them. He appeared to be in his third century, and black curls peeked out from under a snug covering on his head. Dark eyes complemented his sun-browned complexion, and his muscular build would probably intimidate most people.

"Yes, sir." Noah stepped down to the ground. "We're looking for Ara. Have we reached the correct place?"

The man's broad smile belied his husky voice. "Indeed you have." He stopped before them and bowed slightly. "I'm Ara. And you are?"

Noah gestured to his friend. "This is Aterre, and I'm Noah. We've come all the way from Iri Sana to meet you."

Ara bit his lip and furrowed his brow. "Iri Sana? That's beyond the rapids, right?"

Noah nodded. "Yes, sir."

He laughed. "Please, call me Ara. You say you came all this way to meet me? Do you seek to buy a boat?"

"Not exactly." Noah untied the band from his upper arm and handed it to Ara. "My grandfather is your cousin Methuselah."

Ara's eyes lit with recognition. He stepped past Noah and opened the door. "Please, come inside." He nodded toward Taht and the cart. "Your things will be safe there."

Noah and Aterre followed Ara into the building. Wooden furniture and shelves filled with trinkets, instruments, and tools nearly obscured the walls. A breeze carried the scents of the yard in through the small window in the front, which also afforded Noah a view of the back end of their wagon.

Ara moved behind a counter and withdrew a tall stool. "Here." He handed it to Aterre and then retrieved one for Noah before sitting down. He looked across the counter at them. "So you're Methuselah's grandson? How is my cousin? I haven't seen him in about half a century. He visited here not long after his father, my Uncle Enoch —" He looked away and tapped his front teeth with his fingernail a few times. "After his disappearance."

Noah could see the man was uncomfortable talking about what happened to Enoch, so he determined not to mention it. "My grandfather's doing well. He has 12 children and lives about a day's journey from us. My father, Lamech, is his third-born son."

"Well, I'm glad to hear that." Ara sat up straight and examined the armband as he slowly twirled it in his hand. "So how can I help you?"

Noah glanced back once more at their cart and swallowed the lump in his throat. "My father raised me to be a farmer, and even though I didn't mind it, the only work I truly enjoyed was found in my woodshop. I love building things, but there weren't any carpenters in our area that needed an apprentice. So my grandfather recommended that I travel here to work for you." Noah pointed to the band. "He sent that along as his pledge to you that he believes I can do the job."

Ara set the armband down and held Noah's gaze. "You wish to be my apprentice?"

"It would be an honor, sir."

Someone passed in front of the window, and Ara looked toward the door. "Excuse me for a moment." He bent down and pulled out a tightly wound scroll with a string tied around it. He walked around the counter, and as he crossed the room, the door opened.

Noah turned to see who had entered, but Ara's frame blocked his view.

"Hey, Emz." Ara handed the scroll to the person. "Please take this to Zain before heading home today."

"Of course, Baba."

At the sound of a female's voice, Noah craned his neck to see this "Emz." As she hugged Ara, her hands, forearms, and dark ponytail came into view, but nothing more.

He let go of her. "I'll see you tonight."

"Sounds good." The door opened again. "I love you, Baba."

"Love you too, Emz." As the door shut behind him, Ara returned to his place behind the counter. "That's my daughter, Emzara." He playfully hit himself on the forehead. "I'm sorry. I should've introduced her. That's alright. I think there will be time for that. Do you have plans for evenfeast tonight?"

"No, sir." Aterre said.

Noah shook his head.

"Great. I'd like you both to join us for the meal. We'll eat shortly before sundown." Ara pointed to his left. "Just follow this main road along the shore until it turns right to go up the hill and back into town. Instead of going up the hill, stay straight on a wide path that leads right to my house. Oh, and if you don't have a place to stay, you're more than welcome to stay with me."

"That's very kind of you. We'd be happy to join you," Noah said.

"Yes, thank you."

"Did you just get into town?" Ara asked.

"We did. We rode on two of your boats," Noah said. "Farna said many nice things about you."

"Farna?" Ara leaned back and put his hands behind his head. "He's quite the character. I trust the boat was nice and sturdy."

"It was," Noah said.

"Farna. We go way back." He chuckled and then stood up. "Noah, about that apprenticeship. I trust my cousin when he says you are qualified, but I already have an apprentice."

Noah's heart sank, and he struggled to hide his disappointment.

"But let me see what I can work out." Ara pointed toward the ship under construction. "We have enough men working on this project already, but if another order comes in soon, I could definitely use your help."

Noah nodded slowly. "I understand. I guess I should pray that you get another order soon."

Ara's gravelly laugh lightened Noah's mood a bit. "I need to get back to work. You should go explore Iri Geshem a little. I think you'll like it here."

"Thank you, sir," Aterre said. "I'm sorry to keep you from your work, but can I ask you one quick question?"

"By all means."

"Do you know any farmers looking for help?"

Ara pursed his lips and his gaze drifted upward. After a few moments, he said, "As a matter of fact, I think I do. Follow me."

They walked outside and Ara pointed back in the direction of the Hiddekel. "There are plenty of farms on the other side of the river. Go to the end of this road, and you'll find a man who'll ferry you across for a copper pik. Ask him for directions to Cada's farm. Cada is a good friend of mine, so tell him I sent you. I'm sure he'll find some work for you."

Aterre bowed. "Thank you."

Noah bowed slightly as well. "I look forward to seeing you tonight."

"Likewise," Ara said. "Give greetings to Cada for me too."

Aterre nodded. "We will."

Noah reached for Taht's tether.

"You can leave everything here if you'd like," Ara said. "We'll keep an eye on it. Besides, I'm not sure if the ferryman would be willing to take your animal."

"I hadn't thought of that. Thanks again." Noah scratched Taht's neck while Ara returned to the boat frame. "We'll be back in a little while, girl." He reached under one of the packs, withdrew the monetary gift from the Zakari, and tied the bag of piks and pikkas inside his robe.

"You ready then?" Aterre asked.

"I suppose. Hopefully, one of us will get to do what we love."

CHAPTER 16

Emzara fingered the cloth carefully, enjoying the feel of the soft folds as they rippled through her hands. She pondered the possibilities of what to embroider along the trim. *Unless* — her eyes sparked with a new idea. *No one says I have to follow the edge. I have this whole cloth as my canvas. What if* — A knock sounded below, breaking through her planning.

Setting the fabric on the low table in her room before rising from the floor where she had been sitting, she pushed past the heavy curtains blocking the doorway and pattered down the wooden steps to the main entrance below.

"Greetings, Bakur. What brings you here from the shop?"

"Good. You're home." Bakur was just as stoic while speaking as he had been while she welcomed him. "Your father sends word: Plan on guests for evenfeast."

"Oh wonderful! Who will it be?"

Bakur blinked. "Two relatives. From upriver."

"Hmm, upriver. I wonder how far, perhaps a long ways. Will they be staying longer with us?"

Bakur nodded.

"Then I'll get their rooms ready while Adira and Nmir prepare the meal. Thank you."

He raised his hand in farewell before traveling on the pathway back through the rows of trees that would usher him onto the road to the shipyard.

"Adira! Nmir!" She called the two servants — though perhaps *servant* was the wrong word. Nmir, her mother's old nurse and hers, had been part of the family for so long she practically was family. And Adira, well she was Emzara's closest friend.

The two women appeared in the doorway to the kitchen, Adira young and pretty; Nmir old and wrinkled. Vigor pulsed through Emzara at the challenge and excitement of not knowing if they'd finish before Father came home with the houseguests. "We've got company coming tonight."

* * * * *

Early in the evening, Emzara surveyed herself in the polished copper disk that hung in her room, large enough to reflect not only her face, but most of her torso as well. She checked to make sure none of her frenzied tasks from that afternoon would be evident in her appearance. She twisted and pushed one loose chunky curl back into its rightful place in the tiered bun she usually wore. Satisfied with the results, she replaced her coarse outer work garment with a finer threaded fabric, folding the pleats carefully before rolling down the top edge so that it was tightly situated just under her arms. Gathering what was left of the long cloth, she placed it over one shoulder and allowed it to flow down her back.

Adding two bangles to the four already adorning her wrist, she adjusted them and then held out her arm, pleased at the effect. She glanced critically at her reflection one last time, trying to still the nervous fluttering in her midsection.

You're a fraud. Her inner voice accused her. *You're play-acting hostess. They'll see it in the food or in a detail you've overlooked. There will be an awkward pause in the conversation and you won't get it flowing again, and it'll be your fault.* Her fingers trembled as she twined delicate earrings around her ears.

Without warning, Emzara's mind skipped back to a memory of childhood. Her father had come from the shipyard to find her in tears.

"What's wrong, Emz?" Concern showed in his face as he bent over her.

"Does Nmir love me, Baba?" Emzara barely choked the words out between her sobs.

"Why, of course she does." He picked her up and just held her close. "Tell me what happened."

Calmed in her father's embrace, Emzara said, "I was making a house out of the table. I had used some cloths for walls and I invited her to play with me. And she told me that it would be better for me to learn how to keep a real house than to waste my time on silliness. Then she took down the cloths, folded them, and put them away." She looked up at her father, watching him, waiting for him to make things in her world good again.

"My dear, Nmir is a woman who loves very few people, but those whom she loves, she loves with a very big heart. You're one of those special people."

"But my playhouse! She ruined it. How does that make me special?"

"She would prepare you for life, my love. She would see you grow to be a strong and capable young woman." He brushed a lock of hair from her face. "I understand why you hurt. But some people don't show how much they love a person by tenderness. Nmir is one of those people. You can see her love for you in how she takes care of you and teaches you. Look in her eyes. Trust me, you'll see love there when you least expect it."

She took a deep breath to focus her thoughts, and relaxed her brow. *Nmir has trained me well and loves me; I can do this.* She straightened her shoulders and marched downstairs. *Why so nervous? These guests are probably making one last pilgrimage to see family before they die. They probably won't even be able to see the food, much less taste it.* She skipped down the remaining steps and headed into the kitchen.

"Alright, Nmir, what's left to be done?"

"You just leave it to me. We don't need more bodies in here anyways."

"We have ample space. Tell me what I can do."

"It's almost done." Nmir turned, her exasperation palpable, but when she saw Emzara, her expression softened. Only briefly — the next moment she had moved away to check the contents of the oven — but Emzara thought again of her father's words, and her confidence rose.

"Good, I'm just in time to help then," Emzara said. "Let me lift the heavy things and you can take a break."

"Are you calling me old?"

Emzara grinned before taking the earthenware platter that the trusty housemaid held out to her.

Nmir was just as much a habit of the home as Emzara and her father were. She had been the nursemaid for Emzara's mother and had traveled with her when she married Ara and moved to Iri Geshem. Nmir had loved her first charge, and when Emzara entered the world shortly before her mother exited, Nmir extended her affections to her mistress's baby as well.

"Hold on. I'll take that." Adira relieved Emzara of the platter, interrupting her thoughts.

"How are things on your end of the preparation?"

"Just fine. After helping Nmir, I tidied some areas, made the cushions fluffier, things of that sort. But if you're going to do so much of the cleaning, why do you pay me to hang around?" Adira set the tray on the table.

"Ha. As if I could get along without you." Emzara followed her back into the kitchen. "You're the one who keeps me sane. Now that I spend half my time at the shipyard, someone has to be here for Nmir to boss around." She bent down and kissed the old woman.

"Humph." Nmir shook her head.

"So tell me, do you know anything about these visitors? Any handsome young men in the bunch?"

"I doubt it. Just a couple of relatives from upriver. Father must know them. I'm not sure how long they're staying."

"Bakur didn't chat about all the details?" Adira asked in mock surprise.

Emzara laughed. "Not so much."

"Well, you have to tell me everything. That's part of my contract as your friend."

"Oh, I will. You'll hear every detail about their aches and pains and how hard their journey was. You'll get all the stories. If I have to listen to them, so do you."

"Deal. I. . . ."

"Emzara." Ara's voice came from the front of the house. "Come and meet our guests."

"Here we go."

"Well you look lovely and you'll do fine," Adira said. "Whether they're 50 or 500, they'll be enthralled."

"Stop." Emzara made a face and pushed her grinning friend away. Turning to the doorway, she smoothed her clothing and went to join her father.

"Noah, Aterre, I'd like you to meet my daughter, Emzara."

Emzara stopped when she saw the men, and she fought to hide her surprise. A slight smile crept across her lips. *This just got a lot more interesting. Adira's going to like this.*

She stepped forward, extending her neck to touch cheeks with each man in the customary greeting among family. "It's nice to meet you both."

The taller man, Noah, smiled and glanced at her father before his deep brown eyes focused on her. "It's a pleasure to meet you too."

A confusing whirl of thoughts swept over Emzara, and she barely had the presence of mind to look away. "Um. . . . Please come to the table. You're both welcome in our home." Emzara glimpsed Noah once more as she spun around before leading them past the entryway to the well-lit banqueting room beyond. *Don't trip, Em.* She focused on her steps and took a deep breath. *What am I supposed to say next?* With a graceful gesture, she indicated the cushions around the table. "Please make yourselves comfortable." She leaned to kiss her father and then stepped into the kitchen.

"They're here. Let's get the warm dishes out." She leaned over a large clay container, which warmed over a firepot, and sampled the contents. She added several pinches of spice and stirred.

"So what were they like?" Adira asked.

Emzara shrugged. "Can you take the beverages out?" When her friend left with the tray of drinks, Emzara chuckled to herself, anticipating Adira's reaction.

Nmir, having already gone out with the bread, re-entered the kitchen and let out a low whistle. "Just a couple relatives from upriver, hmm? More like two handsome young men."

"Hmm?" Emzara focused on her preparations, feigning disinterest. "What did you say?"

The older woman put her hands on her hips. "I know you heard me. I said they were two handsome men from upriver."

Emzara faced her and raised her eyebrows. "Oh, I guess I didn't notice."

Nmir stared at her until Emzara could no longer suppress a laugh. "Well, I. . . ."

Adira burst through the door and rushed to Emzara's side. "Why didn't you warn me they were good looking?"

Emzara raised her palms in mock innocence. "What? And ruin the surprise?"

Nmir reached for the soup. Keeping her voice down, she nudged Emzara and flashed Adira a rare smile. "Looks like one for each of you girls."

Adira giggled. "I like the sound of that." She took Emzara's hand. "Let me guess. You like the taller one."

Emzara rolled her eyes and shook her head, but a flush crept up her neck. "How could I? I don't even know him." Though she downplayed the moment, Emzara found herself hurrying to see the men again. Using a thick cloth to place two dishes on woven-grass serving plates, Emzara finished gathering the last items and followed Nmir to the table.

"Ah, there she is." Ara gestured for his daughter to sit.

As Ara stood to pray, Emzara pushed aside thoughts about the food, the presentation, and performing her role. *Help me, Most High.*

When the prayer ended, she opened her eyes and found Noah looking at her. She blinked and he glanced away. Taking a deep breath, she passed each dish first to their guests and then to her father as the men continued their previous conversation.

"That was one of the most awe-inspiring moments of my life, being so close to a dagger-tooth," Noah said.

Ara leaned back. "I've never seen one of those beasts myself, but I've heard some of the boatmen talk about them."

"Look at this, sir." Aterre's impressive upper arm muscles became more defined as he set a knife made from what looked like a giant tooth on the table.

Ara's eyes grew wide. "You should thank the Creator that this was all you came away with in that encounter."

"We definitely did and do." Noah said. "I think that's the first time I've been truly scared."

Adira entered the room carrying a pitcher to refill their drinks. She bent low and filled the guests' cups first.

Ara looked at Emzara. "They'll be staying with us until they can find a place of their own. Aterre will be working on Cada's farm."

"For Cada?" She looked at Aterre. "That's wonderful. He'll probably send you home with fresh food every day."

Filling Emzara's cup, Adira said in a voice meant for her ears only, "It's time for me to go home. Tell me everything."

Emzara nodded and had to suppress a smile when Adira winked.

"Noah came all the way from beyond the rapids to work for me," her father said. "Apparently, he's pretty good at construction."

"Oh." She smiled at Noah, but her smile quickly faded, and she furrowed her brow. "Do we have a spot for him at the yard?"

"Not at the moment, but we might tomorrow. A potential customer stopped in today. I have to go into town to meet with him tomorrow morning. If he gives us his business, we'd have a few more ships to build, and we'd certainly need him then. Just in case, can you show Noah around in the morning? Introduce him to the men and give him a feel for the place?"

Emzara nodded.

Noah wiped his mouth with the small cloth set beside his plate. "I'm looking forward to the tour."

"My daughter is quite the wonder. I couldn't do without her. She was the only one that kept me going when her mother died. She's always helped our housemaid, and in the last few years, she's helped me with the administrative duties at work." Ara leaned back. "Emzara will be able to answer just about any question you have — maybe even better than I could."

"I believe it. This meal is a wonder." Aterre indicated his nearly empty plate.

Emzara bowed her head in acknowledgement of the compliment.

"Yeah," Noah agreed. "You don't know what I've had to suffer these last few weeks trying to work down whatever Aterre's scrounged up for us whenever it was his turn to cook. This is truly a treat."

"Sure, I wasn't the one who decided to try that new vegetable from that marketplace," Aterre said. "We boiled it overnight, but it never changed consistency."

"Guess I should've found out a little more about it." Noah laughed easily at his own expense, and Emzara found herself thinking it was a pleasant sound.

"Well, we're glad to welcome you. Emz has made up a room for each of you, and I'd be honored if you both considered this your home until you get your bearings and settle in."

"Thank you," Aterre said.

"If you would like to follow my father to the comfort of our sitting room, I'll fetch the leaf-brew."

Noah raised a brow. "What's leaf brew?"

"You haven't had leaf brew?" Ara asked as he rose from the table. "Then you're in for a treat. Thank you, Emz. Boys, let's continue our conversation out here."

As Emzara cleared the table, she heard Noah ask her father about his opinions on animals like the dagger tooth being given such frightening teeth if they were created to be vegetarian. She moved into the kitchen and grabbed the kettle from above the fire. Intrigued by the topic, she tried to eavesdrop as she poured the scalding hot water through the silver sieve attached to the kettle's mouth but couldn't make out her father's response.

She set the four drinks on a tray, stepped into the sitting room, and served the small rounded bowls, filled with a translucent, honey-colored liquid.

The men each took a sip of the steaming contents. Noah looked up. "This is delicious."

"Agreed." Aterre took a second sip. "What do you make it with?"

Emzara sat beside her father. "Well, I grow certain plants in the garden and dry their leaves. For others, Adira and I go outside of the city to the forest and gather. I blend them to get different flavors."

"Have you ever made a drink with roasted beans?" Noah set his empty cup aside.

"No."

"Well, it's a good thing we still have a bunch left in our cart. I'll make some for you."

"Beans? To drink?" Emzara looked at him and wondered if he was serious or if he was teasing her.

"Hey, at least beans are edible. Who eats leaves?" He cracked a small smile.

Emzara raised an eyebrow. "Doesn't everyone? How else does one make a salad?" As his smile faded, she wondered if she had said too much.

"She has a point, Noah." Ara laughed loudly and hugged her.

"Emzara, you should ask Noah what we planted in one of his father's fields last year for the family to eat." Aterre chuckled, clearly enjoying the opportunity to embarrass Noah a little.

Gaining confidence through the fact that Noah seemed to enjoy the light-hearted barbs, Emzara pressed on. "What was it, Noah?"

"We planted several crops. How am I supposed to know which one he's talking about?"

Aterre crossed his arms. "You know."

Emzara set her drink down and grinned. "Yeah, you know."

Noah shot a look at Aterre before sighing and sagging his shoulders in mock humiliation. He smiled at her, "Well, you see, uh, um . . . it was orb plants."

She gave him a knowing smile. "And what are orb plants?"

His face reddened before he said, "Essentially round bundles of leaves that we eat."

Emzara laughed along with everyone else.

As the evening waned, Ara got up slowly. "Boys, Emzara and I have rooms upstairs. Your two rooms are off this hallway over here." He looked at his daughter. "Emz, please take care of these bowls since Nmir went home. I'll help them unload their cart. Then we can all get some rest."

CHAPTER 17

Slowly the wick of the oil lamp caught fire and brightened the dim interior of the kitchen. Noah had extra energy this morning as he anticipated how his mission might go over. He looked around in wonder, surprised by the spaciousness. *Mother wouldn't know what to do with herself in here. This might take me longer than I thought.* Finding the oven wood pile in a dedicated bin to the left of the large clay oven, he snatched a couple of the smaller pieces and poked them into the still-glowing embers at the base of the yawning opening. Over that he littered several woodchips, which he found in a small crock. Bit by bit the embers sparked, and little flames appeared, before the fire awoke to full force — just as gradually and groggily as a person might.

Attempting to get all the necessary things in order before the others came down, Noah crushed a handful of Nuca's beans in a mortar and dumped the grounds into a fine cloth. He pulled the corners of the fabric together, tied them off, and set the pouch into an empty kettle. He found a pot positioned above the flame and, after filling it with water, replaced it so the contents could heat to a boil. Then he located four drinking vessels and placed them on the table.

With nothing left to do but wait, Noah leaned against a counter. *Creator, thank You for a safe and successful journey and please grant me guidance through the day.* Noah wondered if the other thing on his mind would be worthy to bring before the Most High. Before he could ponder that, he noticed the water was ready and poured it over the sack of beans waiting in the kettle. When he was satisfied that the contents had successfully diffused, Noah pulled the kettle from the heat and removed the spent grounds. He was searching for a place to dump them when Emzara entered the kitchen. He stilled. The room, which had been spacious only moments ago, seemed to shrink. He simply blinked at her, and felt his body temperature rise. Her wondrously large eyes looked at him in mild surprise.

"Oh, you're up early."

"Yes. Old habits die hard. We were always up early on the farm." *She's lovely in the morning, too.* Noah held up the cloth, the bottom firmly rounded from the contours of its contents. "Plus, I have this."

"Smells amazing." Emzara leaned closer and breathed in slowly before exhaling.

Noah concentrated on not dropping the bag and resisted the urge to lower his head so he could again inhale the spicy-sweet blend of her scent that had mystified and delighted him yesterday when she greeted him at the door.

"Wait until you taste it."

"This is the bean brew you talked about last night?" Emzara twisted a small curl on the side of her temple.

"It is, and I'll pour some for you soon."

"Well, you've certainly done a good job of making yourself at home. Although, we might not want to tell Nmir that there was a man in her kitchen." Emzara's eyes twinkled in fun. "She won't know whether to scold first or to rush and make sure all is still in order. Then again, that might be kind of entertaining to watch." She looked up at Noah and smiled.

"Nmir?"

"Oh, that's right. You probably saw very little of her last night since she went home to her own little place right up the road. Her official position is cook, but she's so much more than that. She fusses on the outside, but on the inside she's as soft as can be."

"If she helped with last night's meal, then she's an excellent cook."

"That she is. By the way, thank you for getting the fire going." While Emzara continued talking, she gathered the needed items for preparing firstfeast, and Noah admired the graceful, yet confident way she moved.

He drained the brew into the cups and then stirred some honey into her drink. "I'm almost done with this. Is there anything I can do to help you?"

"Well, the warmed oats are not quite ready to go on the table — they have to boil for a bit. Just to warn you, we usually eat a light first-feast around here, so there's not much else that needs to be done. I guess you can help by putting the dishes on the table." She glanced up at him as she spoke. "They're tucked away in this cabinet over here." Reaching above her head, she grabbed four shallow bowls and handed them over her head to Noah.

He took the dishes, and with hands still aloft, tried to step past her toward the dining area. Instead of reaching open space, he found Emzara had moved in the same direction. They bumped into each other. Trying to save the dishes and his balance, his arms lowered around her waist, hands still clasping the bowls.

Emzara dropped her gaze, and Noah detected a deepening in color at the edges of her cheeks.

"Whew, that was close." He smiled shyly as he eased away from her, trying his best to save the situation. "I'm glad these didn't break. Nmir won't have a reason to yell at me yet."

"Yeah, you're safe still." She smoothed her hands down her garment and then tucked an invisible piece of hair behind her ear.

"I'll get these on the table, and then you can try your drink." Noah made sure to give her plenty of room before hastening into the feasting room with the bowls. Upon returning to the kitchen, he handed Emzara a low rounded cup. "Try it. Tell me what you think." He watched closely while she took a sip.

"It's strong. I can see why you drink it in the morning." She took another sip. "I like it."

"I put a little honey in yours to sweeten it. I drink mine without, but my mother won't touch it unless there's something to reduce the bitterness."

"So yours is plain?" Emzara pointed at the cup near him.

"Yes."

"May I try it?"

"Of course." Noah offered his cup to her, glad she wanted to see how strong he preferred it.

"Whew." She shook her head and smiled. "That's something else. It might take a while to get used to." She handed the brew back to him. "Thank you."

Noah took the cup and deftly turned it so that he would drink from the same spot her lips had touched.

* * * * *

"Bakur, this is Noah." Emzara waved at a man who looked to be a few centuries old.

The scrawny, bare-chested man nodded but continued to push a hand plane in unbroken rhythm over a long, thin piece of wood Noah guessed would become part of the ship's hull.

"He'll be staying with us for a while." Emzara looked up at Noah. "How are we related again?"

"Your father is my grandfather's cousin."

Another man walked around the bow of the boat. Broad-shouldered, with a chiseled upper body and an unreadable expression, the man stepped toward Noah. "So, Noah, you're staying with Emzara?"

"I'm staying in Ara's home, yes." Noah shrugged. "For now at least."

"I'm Pennik. Ara's apprentice." He put a hand on Noah's shoulder and squeezed harder than necessary. "Welcome."

So this is Ara's apprentice. Noah ignored the man's attempt to intimidate him, if that's what it was. "Glad to be here."

Pennik looked past Noah and smiled broadly. "Morning peace, Emzara. You look beautiful, as always."

Bakur cleared his throat, and Emzara glanced at Noah with a sheepish smile. "Thank you, Pennik. Morning peace to you."

Suddenly Noah found himself irritated by Pennik. He moved toward Bakur. "Can you explain what you're working on here?"

"Strip of the hull." He gestured at the skeleton boat above him. "Today we start enclosing the frame. You here to give us a hand?"

"I'd love to." Noah clenched and released his fist as if by doing so, he could get to work faster.

"You can't have him." Emzara laughed. "He's here for a tour of the yard. I still have to introduce him to Fen and Tssed."

"Whatever you say, Boss." Bakur winked at Emzara and leaned toward Noah. "Make sure you stay on her good side."

Oh, I'd like nothing better. The surprising thought came out of nowhere, and Noah turned away to hide his sudden confusion. "Uh, thanks for the advice, Bakur. Nice meeting you. As soon as the boss gives the word" — Noah tipped his head at Emzara and she gave an approving nod — "I'll be ready to assist you."

Emzara set off again, looking over her shoulder at him as she picked up her pace. "Most of the construction goes on outside. We'd like to build shelters at some point, but for now, we have just two buildings. The smaller one is where Baba holds his meetings. I think you were in there yesterday. And this is the main building." She pointed to the modest-sized, two-story building made with the same mud brick as most other buildings in the city. "This is where I keep the ledgers on the days I'm here. Most of the tools and expensive supplies are kept in here."

"You aren't concerned about thieves?"

"Not in Iri Geshem. I've never heard of anything being stolen here."

She ducked into the doorway and Noah stayed close behind, looking around at the interior. On his left, broken only by a window, rows of various tools hung neatly on the wall. Some Noah recognized and he flushed with pleasure at the thought of working with them again. On the opposite side of the room stood various crates he assumed held the supplies. The morning's coolness still filled the air in this place.

"What's that?" Noah asked upon seeing a round wooden lid-like object in the corner.

"Oh, Fen made it. Kind of crazy, but it's an indoor well. Not only is it easier to get water during the day, but the men keep their midmeals here to keep them cooler." She picked up the lid, and Noah saw a small shelf jutting out not too far from the opening.

"And up those steps?"

"That's where I work. There's really nothing up there but a table and my accounts."

Curious to learn all he could about this young woman who had suddenly captured his thoughts, Noah asked, "Can I see?"

"Of course." Despite her shrug, she looked somewhat pleased and led him up the stairs. "Here it is. See? Nothing much."

As Noah's head cleared the threshold of the upper room floor, he saw tidily arranged and stacked pieces of wood, no more than a finger thick and all roughly the same size. "So tell me what I'm seeing."

She went over to one of the piles and lightly rested her hand on the edge. "These are made from the leftover pieces of wood. I keep records on them about our customers, the details of their order, and when we promised to deliver. I also keep track of all the supplies that come through and where we get them from. We cut down most of our wood. Baba owns a forest on the other side of the river. But we're also able to get other types of lumber from all over as traders come in with their wares."

"This looks like a strange customer. Did you draw this too?" Noah picked up one of the wood tablets and held it up for her to see.

"Oh, that. Yes, well," Emzara extended her arm to grab it from him, and for the second time, he saw the color in her face deepen. *This could be fun.* He held it out of her reach.

"I don't think I've seen someone with that long of a neck. Plus, that's a lot of hair coming out of his ears. And what are these horns in the center of his head?" Peering closer at the drawing allowed her the opportunity to snatch it out of his hands.

"This is a keluk." She looked at him with what seemed to be a hint of a challenge.

"I know what a keluk is. Those pesky animals kept getting into our malid orchard."

"You've seen them before?"

"Many times."

"Then I envy you. I wish I could see one. They don't live around here, but I've seen them on objects that some traders have brought and heard merchants talk about them. They're my favorites."

He nodded toward the portrait. "It's pretty accurate for never having seen one."

"I like drawing animals." She paused. "And anything else, really."

"Well, if that one is any indication, you're pretty good at it." Noah said.

"Thank you."

"So that's what you do when you're working then, huh?"

She feigned offense. "Yes, that's why Baba hired me, so I could spend all day drawing."

Noah smirked.

"I drew this during some free time." She hesitated as if not sure what to say next. "Well, should we go down and finish the tour?"

"Lead the way."

Emzara headed downstairs. "Do you have any questions about anything so far?"

"Seems straightforward enough. Why did you start working here?"

"I wanted to spend more time with my father." She paused and leaned her attractive figure against the frame of the open door. Tilting back her head, she closed her eyes briefly, welcoming the warming rays of the sun. Unable to look away, Noah couldn't decide what he liked better, the effect of her long lashes resting down or the playfulness in her eyes when they were open wide.

"As you know, my mother died right after I was born. Even though I was under Nmir's care, I spent much of my childhood here. I loved spending time with Baba and watching the bustling activities. I wanted to be near him, so I strived to be as helpful as possible. The energy here is invigorating: the hard work, the deadlines, the focus, and the people that come through. I love it all. The other men treat me like I'm one of their own daughters." She made a face. "Well, except for Pennik."

"They don't. . . ." His words stuck and he cleared his throat. Brushing at a speck in his eye, Noah suddenly felt out of sorts. "They don't mind taking orders from someone so young?"

"I don't really have any authority, but they treat me as if I do. I just do what I can to keep things on track." She crossed her arms. "Besides, I'm not that young. I'm 34, which can't be much younger than you."

"I turned 40 earlier this year. That was the day my father told me about this place. I'd been longing for some time to become a carpenter's apprentice, but it seemed like I was destined to work on the farm for my whole life. Then my father surprised me by telling me about a relative of ours who builds the boats that run the river." He ran his finger along one of the tools on the wall, trying desperately to keep from staring at her. "Did your father train you to do your job or did you figure it out along the way?"

"As I got older, Baba started teaching me little things about the business, and then a few years ago I started this system of keeping records. I split my time between working here and managing our home with the help of Nmir and Adira. It keeps me busy but I like what I do."

Noah joined her as she pushed away from the doorpost. "Speaking of what I do, I should probably turn you loose so I can get started on my duties." She walked toward the open shipyard and threw a grin back his way. "If you're able to get work here, do you think you'll catch on, or will Baba have to find someone else?"

He hurried to move alongside her. "Oh, I catch on pretty quickly. You won't get rid of me so easily."

"I guess we may find out soon enough."

With palms sweating and heart racing, he tried to respond, but something held his tongue. *What's wrong with me? I've never felt like this.* He stole a couple of glances at Emzara as they walked and it hit him. He was smitten. *So this is what it feels like.*

CHAPTER 18

"Hand me that piece of rope in the corner." Noah grunted as he used one arm to hold onto the roof's beam and dropped his free hand into the ceiling space of his and Aterre's future abode.

Aterre retrieved the requested item. "Here."

"Got it." Noah pulled himself up and double-checked the positions of the two beams that met at the apex of the roof to his left. "Does this look straight from down there?"

"Yeah, it's good."

"Okay." Noah carefully lashed the timbers together around a crossbar at the peak. Finding its way through the trees, a light breeze brought a welcomed coolness to an otherwise warm evening. The rhythmic lapping of waves on the shore joined with the irregular squawks of sea birds soaring over the large bay, creating a melody all its own. "Now I need the hammer." While he waited, Noah dug two pegs out of the pouch slung at his side and was ready when Aterre handed the tool up. *Bam, bam, BAM.* The sound echoed through the milknut trees. With the next peg in place, he squeezed the handle tight and drove the hammer violently against its mark. No longer focused on the peg, all he sensed was the impact each strike created.

"I said it's good!"

After three more blows, Noah lowered his throbbing arm. He grumbled as he tossed the mallet aside. Using the newly stabilized timber, he swung over the side and dropped to the floor.

Aterre gave him a clay drinking vessel filled with water and stared at him.

Sitting with his back against the mud brick wall, Noah savored the cool surface against his warm flesh. He took a long drink and then closed his eyes while massaging his tight neck muscles with his free hand.

"What's going on?"

"I'm so frustrated."

"With the building?"

"No, this is fine. But it's been two whole moons since we came here and I've got nothing to show for it. If only that order at the shipyard had gone through." Noah set the vessel down, and water sloshed over the edge.

"At least you still have a job and Ara allowed us to build a home here."

Noah scanned the small room, about 12 cubits square, just large enough for a kitchen and dining area and a place to sleep. Two more rooms would soon be built beyond the opposite wall. "Yeah, but I'm stuck farming again. I'm just not cut out for it."

Aterre slumped down beside him.

Noah wiped his forehead with the back of his arm. "It's great for you. You love what you're doing. But I was so close to fulfilling a lifelong dream, only to find it's still out of reach."

"But you only met Zara two whole moons ago." Aterre chuckled.

Noah glowered. "What are you talking about?"

"You're talking about your dream, so I figured this was about her."

"My dream of being a carpenter. Besides, what's the use of talking about her?" Noah let his head bump against the wall and blew out a breath. "I'm pretty sure she's interested in Pennik."

"I don't think you have to worry about him. But enough about that since you clearly weren't thinking about her." Aterre's sarcasm could not be missed. "I was wondering though. . . ." Aterre paused, becoming serious. "You told your father before we left home that you believed the Creator was guiding you down this path. Do you still believe that?"

Surprised, Noah sat up straight. Aterre had not discussed the Creator in weeks. "Of course I do. Why else would I have come all this way? Why would I stay?"

"If you truly believe that, why do you complain?"

"Because, I —" Noah cut short his instinctive reaction to defend himself as he realized the inconsistency between his actions and beliefs. He shook his head slowly. "You're right. Sometimes I wish He'd just tell me what I'm supposed to do."

Aterre nodded.

"But you're right. Just because this is taking longer than I expected, it doesn't mean God has changed the plan. I'll be a carpenter someday."

Aterre snorted. "I didn't say all that."

"No, but you said enough." Noah stood and dusted off the back of his garment before helping Aterre to his feet. "And I really needed to hear it. I'll try to remember it the next time I get angry about all this."

"You mean tomorrow morning."

One edge of Noah's mouth curled up. "Give it a couple of days at least. What about you? Have your thoughts about the Most High changed since the last time we talked about Him?"

Aterre pressed his lips together and shrugged. "Somewhat."

"Meaning?"

"I told you before that I wasn't sure if He existed, although I was open to the idea. But now, I'm pretty sure He does."

"Well, that's good. What changed your mind?"

"I'm not sure if I can pinpoint one specific thing. I know one of the reasons is your family — even after what I did, they took me in and loved me. And I saw the same thing with the Zakari and again here with the way Ara accepted us. If this is how people who serve the Creator act, then I figure there must be something to their beliefs, and to the Creator Himself." Aterre tilted his head back, apparently thinking about what to say next. "After our journey, the world makes more sense when I think of it being made by an all-powerful God. I hadn't really bothered to consider how everything came about, so I never took time to think much about the world around us. With all the amazing creatures and plants we saw, it just makes sense that God made everything. But . . ." Aterre paused and shook his head. "Never mind."

"But what?" Noah held up a palm.

Aterre's face turned sullen and he stared at the stone floor. "My family. I don't understand why the Creator would allow them to be killed or taken. I guess it'd be easy to trust Him when everything is going great, but when you've seen the evil things I've seen. . . ." He swallowed. "It's just hard."

Noah folded his arms. "I can see why that might make it harder to believe. But I don't agree that the evil in the world should be blamed on the Creator. My father said that the world was perfect until the Great Deceiver showed up."

"That's just it." Aterre leaned his shoulder against the wall. "Why would the Creator make anything bad in the first place?"

Perplexed, Noah shook his head. "I'm not sure. What if the Deceiver was originally good, like the rest of creation, and then chose to rebel, like Greatfather Adam did?"

"Hmm, if that's true," Aterre said as if speaking to himself, "then everything the Creator made would have been good originally, even people and the serpent. And the horrible things in this world could be traced back to their rebellious choices, right?"

"That's what my father taught me."

Aterre opened his mouth, but stopped before speaking. Instead, he bent down and picked up a long beam. "Let's finish a few more tonight. I'd like to move in while I'm still in my first century."

Noah wanted to continue the discussion, but he knew Aterre liked to think things through at his own pace. Resolving to broach the topic in the near future, Noah jumped up, seized one of the recently placed rafters, and pulled himself above it. "Let's do it." After steadying himself on the roof, he reached down to take the next piece from Aterre. "So why'd you say that about Pennik?"

Aterre chuckled. "I knew you'd bring things back around to Zara."

Noah settled the wood in place. "I didn't say anything about her."

"Then why'd you ask about Pennik?"

Noah shrugged. "I was just curious what you meant."

"Because you wanted to talk about Zara again."

"Is there something else you'd like to discuss?"

Aterre handed him some rope. "Not really. I'd just like to finish our home."

Noah bent low and tied the wood to the crossbeam and to a peg built into the outer wall. Standing and stretching his back, he spotted Ara walking toward them. "Evening peace."

"Evening peace, Noah." He pointed toward the door. "Is Aterre in there?"

Aterre stepped outside and greeted Ara with a nod. "I'm here. Noah's making me do all the heavy lifting."

Noah rolled his eyes. He sat on the edge of the roof, allowing his legs to dangle, and then dropped to the ground. "How are things at the shipyard?"

Ara inspected the roof, running his finger along the ends of the timbers. "They've been better."

"Is something wrong?" Noah asked.

Ara shrugged. "I guess that depends on you."

"I don't understand."

Ara looked at the roof again. "My cousin was right. You do fine work. And that's good, because, as of today, I'm in need of an apprentice."

Noah wondered if his imagination was playing tricks on him. He shot a look at Aterre. "What about Pennik?"

"That's why it was a rough day. He quit on me without any warning."

"Did he say why?"

Ara's mouth quirked in a smile, and he looked Noah in the eye. "No, but I think I can guess the reason."

"So Pennik's gone?" Noah asked, trying to hold his excitement in.

Ara nodded. "So if you're still interested in being —"

"Yes!" Noah's response came out louder than he planned. "Sorry — yes, I'd love to work for you."

"Good," Ara said. "And I appreciate the enthusiasm."

Aterre laughed. "You *sure* you don't want to continue farming at Cada's with me?"

Noah slapped Aterre's back hard enough to make him "oof," and grinned. "Not a chance."

Ara peeked inside the unfinished house, peered closely at the joints between doorposts and lintel, then turned back to the young men. "Why don't you two get cleaned up and join us for evenfeast? Whatever Nmir's making, it smells wonderful. We can discuss the terms of your apprenticeship after the meal."

CHAPTER 19

"There and back." Aterre pointed to a small ship anchored in the bay several hundred cubits down the coast.

"Do you need a head start?" Noah asked, knowing full well Aterre was faster than he was.

Aterre laughed. "Just say when."

Noah bent his knees and dipped beneath the water to acclimate himself to its coolness. He emerged from the sea and pushed his hair back. Licking the saltiness from his lips, he took a deep breath. "Ready? On three. One."

Noah plunged forward and glided under the water for a long stretch. Breaking the surface, he kicked hard and quickly settled into a steady pace. *One, two, three. Breathe. One, two, three. Breathe.* Every so often, he pulled extra hard on a stroke to lift his head up and check his trajectory. Knowing the lead from his early start would not last, he focused on keeping a rhythm.

As he reached the boat and turned for the home stretch, he spotted Aterre from the corner of his eye. Determined to hang on to his body-length lead, Noah felt a surge of energy and increased his tempo. He came up for a breath and sensed Aterre straight across from him. Kicking furiously and drawing every ounce of strength from his arms, Noah strove to keep up. But it was no use. Aterre grabbed the lead, and Noah's strength flagged.

Struggling to settle back into an easy rhythm, Noah rolled onto his back and tried to catch his breath as slow and deliberate strokes carried him back to the starting point. A splash from Aterre let him know he had made it, and he allowed his legs to sink until his feet hit the bottom.

Breathing hard, Aterre said, "I'm still faster."

"Not by much. I'm gaining on you."

"Only because you had a head start and I wasn't trying very hard." Aterre grinned.

Noah stepped closer. "Well, if you're so fast, then why can't you dodge this?" He lunged forward and locked his arm around Aterre's waist. Planting his feet, Noah lifted his friend above the water and then slammed him under it.

When Aterre pushed to break free, Noah released him and quickly stood again, wary of retaliation. When none came, he wiped his eyes and raised his arms in triumph.

Noah spun at the sound of familiar laughter from the shore, where Emzara and Adira sat giggling. He kept one arm raised in a greeting to them, but Aterre slammed into him and drove him under. The surprise attack caused him to swallow a bit of seawater, so as he staggered to his feet, Noah coughed and gasped for air.

"Now we're even," Aterre said.

"Yes, we are. Truce?"

Aterre nodded and then flashed a sly grin. "For now."

Noah waved at Emzara, but she and Adira were talking to each other. He looked back at Aterre. "She must be here to watch the sunset."

"So when are you going tell her how you feel about her?"

"I don't know." Noah crossed his arms, pleased that their intense race had caused his muscles to look larger and more defined, at least temporarily. "It's tricky since I work for her father. What if she doesn't like me that way? Could I still work for him? And even if I could, how awkward would it be?" Noah looked back at her and sighed. "I'd love to be the one she watched sunsets with."

Aterre laughed. "You're so blind. Why do you think Pennik disliked you so much? Everyone else can see that she's interested. She flirts with you all the time."

"And what if you're wrong?"

"Well, there's only one way to find out. Ask her." Aterre started for the shore. "Come on."

"Wait, you mean right now?"

Aterre looked back and shook his head. "Coward."

Trudging through the water toward the beach, their speed increased as the water shallowed. Noah checked to make sure his garment was tied tightly about his waist. The girls stood and sauntered toward them as the men reached their robes on the shore. Picking up his outer wrap, Noah quickly dressed himself.

"Evening peace," Adira said.

Noah smiled at her and then at Emzara. "Evening peace. How long have you been here?"

Emzara grinned. "Long enough to know who the faster swimmer is."

"And that would be me." Aterre used both hands to point at himself. "Were you two here to watch the sunset or to see him lose?" Aterre gestured to Noah with a nod of his head.

Emzara pursed her lips and held up a bundle of squared black objects, each about a span in length. "Actually, we went to town to pick up some new drawing sticks for my artwork and then decided to enjoy a walk on the shore."

"Yeah, it's the first time that we've had a chance to — ever since you moved here," Adira said. "But since you moved into your own place last week, we finish our chores earlier. Plus, the days are getting longer."

"Do you like your new home?" Emzara asked.

Noah brushed some sand off his robe. "It's coming together." In just three whole moons, they had constructed their small home, but there was still much to be done. "But I confess I miss the meals."

"That's not all you miss." Aterre's words were almost mumbled, and Noah hoped they weren't clear enough for Emzara to hear. Aterre looked at him and the left side of his mouth curled up.

Oh no. Please don't.

Aterre's grin spread across his face. "Zara, you know, Noah was just telling me that he wishes you'd watch the sunsets with him instead."

Fear gripped Noah, and he barely withstood the urge to pummel Aterre, who now beamed with his arms crossed. Sheepishly, Noah looked away as Adira laughed. He struggled to find the right words to extricate himself, but he only said, "I didn't say that."

"So," Adira said, "you're saying you don't want Zara to watch them with you?"

Noah felt his face warm even more. He couldn't deny it without lying, and if he answered truthfully, she would certainly know his feelings. He was stuck. His gaze dropped to the ground, and then he spotted his way out. Aterre had not finished wrapping his robe and part of it lay on the ground near his feet. Noah stepped on the end of the cloth and shoved him. When his robe caught, Aterre lost his balance and tumbled backward into the shallow water, landing on his backside with a splash.

Adira squealed in delight and then laughed along with Emzara. Satisfied that the last question was abandoned for now, Noah walked to Aterre and held out a hand to help him up.

"I deserved that." Aterre smiled and took Noah's hand. "Nicely done."

Noah nodded. "You know?" He spoke loud enough for the girls to hear. "This reminds me of how we met."

"You met in the water?" Adira asked.

Noah wanted to embarrass Aterre some more, but he remembered his promise that he wouldn't tell others about Aterre's past, particularly his shady activities while on the run. "Something like that. It's a long story for another time."

Emzara pointed to Aterre as he rewrapped his garment, though he stopped when he realized that much of it was wet. "What's that mark on your back?"

Aterre sighed. "Another long story for another time."

"Sounds like you have a lot of stories," Adira said.

"Too many, but they're in the past." Aterre walked toward the trail that led to their house. "Looks like I need another robe."

Seizing the opportunity to avoid the potentially awkward questioning again, Noah hurried behind Aterre. He looked back briefly at Emzara. "I'll see you tomorrow."

"If you're lucky," she said.

Noah bit his lip to stop a smile from escaping. "Evening peace."

The trail wound through a patch of milknut trees and led all the way to Ara's house, but they turned off the path to go to their new home, just a few hundred cubits from the beach.

Noah followed Aterre through the door and closed it hard. He hurried to his room as Aterre strode to his. Noah changed out of his wet undergarment. With a clean and dry robe on, he rejoined Aterre, who had already changed clothes, in the tiny dining area that had yet to be furnished. Noah walked to the wall and slumped to the floor. He buried his head in his hands. "I can't believe you did that."

Aterre laughed. "Did what? Tried to help you out?"

"Help me out?" Noah held his hands out and glared at him. "You made me look like a fool in front of her."

"Calm down. You should thank me."

"Thank you?" Noah raised his voice. "If you ruined my opportunity with Emzara, I'll —"

"I didn't ruin anything. Stop overreacting." Aterre sat next to him and spoke softly. "Didn't you see her reaction?"

Noah shook his head. "I was too afraid to look."

"You really love her, don't you?"

Rolling his eyes, Noah asked, "Whatever gave you that idea?"

"Um, maybe it's the fact that when she's around you suddenly freeze up, stutter, and act like a little boy."

"It's that bad?"

"Worse than Jerah with Pivi." Aterre chuckled. "No, not that bad, but you do change. You just need to be yourself around her."

"I try, but can't help it. She makes me so nervous."

"That's because you're trying too hard, but you don't need to. She already likes you."

Noah ran his fingers through his hair. "Why do you keep saying that? And since when are you an expert on women?"

"I didn't know there was such a thing." Aterre stood and gazed out the window. "When you were too scared to look at her, she was smiling wider than I'd ever seen before. And that's saying a lot, because she always smiles when you're around."

"Probably because she thinks I'm a fool."

Aterre shrugged. "Could be, but I doubt it." He lowered his voice. "Speaking of Zara."

"What about her?"

Aterre put his finger to his lips and shushed him. Then he gestured to the front of the house.

After a long pause, three soft knocks patted the door. "Noah?"

"Just a moment." Noah jumped up.

Aterre grabbed his arm and stopped him. "Take a deep breath. Act natural."

He closed his eyes and inhaled slowly and let it out. *Don't make a fool of yourself, Noah.* Taking another deep breath, he opened the door. Emzara stood with her arms in front of her carrying a small covered basket. Her outfit perfectly complemented her lithe figure. The bottom of her robe ended just above her ankles, which were wound about by the leather straps of her sandals. Her hair, no longer pulled back and tied behind her head as it had been at the beach, draped over her shoulders. A stray lock hung down the left side of her face. Standing in the doorway in the fading daylight, she had never looked so breathtaking. "Emzara. I didn't expect to see you again tonight."

Holding up the basket, she smiled and her eyes sparkled. "You said you missed our cooking, so I brought you some leftovers from tonight."

"I'll take that." Aterre stepped between them and grabbed the basket. "Thanks, Zara."

"You're welcome. Just be sure to share it with Noah."

"I won't," Aterre said over his shoulder.

"He probably won't." Noah wracked his brain for something worthwhile to say during the long pause that followed. Emzara looked expectantly at him, adding to his mounting frustration. *Just say something. Tell her she looks nice.* "You —"

"Adira already left for home. Did you want to watch the sunset with me? There's still time."

Noah fought to control his excitement; he did not want to overreact. "Sure, I'd be happy to." His heart racing, he stepped outside and closed the door.

Emzara led him up a small hill between the shipyard and the beach. "It looks better up here," she said. "The edge of the harbor doesn't block the view."

"Is this where you'd normally watch it?"

"Most of the time. Although, I think it'd be better on Superglider Cliff." She pointed to the edge of the coastline. "That's what we call it."

"Have you seen a superglider up close?"

"Not yet, but I'd love to. I want to draw one for my collection."

"You're a very talented artist. Other than technical drawings, I can't draw anything. But the Creator gave me the ability to make things out of wood."

"That's what my father says." Emzara pushed aside a low branch and allowed him to pass by. "He said that you do a great job. Do you like working for him?"

"I do. It's hard work, but when you love what you're doing, it's not really toilsome."

"That's what I think about art. I love watching the animals and drawing them. It takes time, but it's so rewarding." She pointed to the grassy outcrop ahead. "That's it."

After allowing her to pick out her spot, Noah sat about a cubit away. He stretched his legs in front of him and leaned back on his hands, approximating her pose. The bay extended to the south, opening into the Great Sea. To the southwest, the sun hung just above the horizon, and immediately to its left, Superglider Cliff climbed above the edge of the water. The boat that he and Aterre had raced to lay in the water ahead of them.

"It's perfect." Noah said.

A slight breeze blew her hair across her face. She closed her eyes and breathed in. "It sure is."

Noah watched her. It seemed impossible, yet she grew more beautiful each time he saw her.

With her eyes still closed, she asked, "So did you say that earlier?"

"Say what?" Noah asked, hoping she was not referring to Aterre's embarrassing revelation.

She turned, fixed her gaze on him, and her lips curved slightly. "That you wished I would watch the sunset with you instead."

Her dark eyes drew him in and he couldn't pull away. Not that he wanted to. A spark of courage flashed inside of him. *Maybe Aterre's right. Maybe she really is interested in me.* "Those weren't my exact words." The spark grew into a flame that filled his body, and in his mind, he crossed the point of no return. He would never get a better chance. He held her gaze. "I think I said that I'd love to be the one you watched sunsets with."

Her lips spread into a wide smile and her eyes danced. "I was hoping you'd say that." She moved her left hand and placed it on top of his.

Every fiber of his being sprang to life, and his whole body tingled at her touch. He turned his hand over and allowed her fingers to cross between his. Feeling as though he would burst from emotion if he continued looking at her, he turned his attention to the setting sun along with the bands of orange and pink that stretched across the southwestern sky.

Moments later, Emzara scooted closer and leaned her head against his shoulder.

For a while, neither of them spoke. Words were not needed for the moment.

When the sun was almost gone, Emzara tilted her head up at him. "You're right. It is perfect here."

Noah glanced down and their eyes met briefly. "It is now."

"Sadly, I need to get home before it gets too dark or my father will be upset."

"I understand." He stood and helped Emzara to her feet.

Hand in hand, they walked down the hill and too soon they were back at the trail between Ara's house and the beach. Noah walked her most of the way back to her home.

"Would you like to do this again tomorrow night?" he asked.

"Definitely." Nodding, she pulled away slowly. "I'll see you at work in the morning."

"I can't wait."

She smiled and then turned, humming a tune as she went to the front door.

Noah walked back to his home with a lively bounce to his step. He forced himself to stop smiling and then went inside. He spotted Aterre at the counter scraping the last bit of salad out of Emzara's bowl.

He held up the empty dish. "I'm really sorry. I ate everything. It was too good."

Feigning anger, Noah crossed the floor and stood before Aterre, glaring at him. When he could no longer suppress his joy, he reached out and hugged Aterre tight. "Thank you!"

Aterre laughed and pushed himself free. "I guess that stupid grin on your face means I was right."

"For the first time, I'm glad you were right and I was wrong." Noah turned and put his hands on his head. "This is the best night ever."

Chapter 20

"A whole day together." Emzara shifted her hand within Noah's warm grasp and leaned slightly against him, enjoying the feel of his strong presence. "I'm so excited."

Noah regarded her and a thrill coursed through him. He squeezed her fingers gently. "I've been looking forward to spending this much time with you."

She grinned. "Me too." She hung on to those words, making both of them a few syllables long. "So what's the adventure for today?" She pointed at the full satchel that hung from Noah's shoulder.

"Well —" Noah paused.

"Tell me." Her eyes begged him as she rocked on her toes.

"I thought that since we have the time we should finally check out Superglider Cliff instead of just talking about it." He held up the leather bag. "This is in case we get hungry."

"Oh, how fun! We've never crossed the river for an outing before. Do you know the way?"

"Aterre's been there before. He said it's not far from Cada's farm. I think we can find it. We have to go through your father's land, and then past all the fruit trees."

Emzara swung their joined hands and skipped a little in her excitement.

"Did you hear what happened to Fen at work two days ago?" Noah asked as they left the grassy knolls beyond the river and entered a lush tropical forest.

"No. Tell me."

"After midmeal, Bakur sneaked away and retied Fen's nuzzler in a hidden spot. And since Fen lives far away from the shipyard he certainly didn't want to walk home."

"Yeah. What happened?" Her eyes sparkled in merriment at the joke.

"After work, of course he couldn't find her. He went to the market-place, thinking his wife had taken the animal to load up supplies, but he came back just before dark, concerned that neither his wife nor the nuzzler were at the market."

"Just before dark? What were you still doing at the shipyard?"

"Bakur and I were finishing up the stern."

"You're really getting the hang of things, aren't you?" she asked.

"I love it. Time seems to whisk by whenever I'm working." He looked at her as he had so often, and Emzara instinctively knew he was telling her she was beautiful. "And whenever I'm with you."

A warm feeling spread over her and she spoke softly. "These moments go by too fast, but when I'm with you, there's no other place I'd rather be."

They were silent for a while, connecting with each other in spirit. As they picked their way through the uneven terrain, sounds of exotic birds and occasional flashes of brightly colored feathers added to their enjoyment. Soon the ground veered upward as they approached the rear of the cliffs.

"Ready for a bit of a climb?" Noah asked.

"Absolutely. Mind telling me the rest of what happened to Fen?" Following his lead, she started up the steep incline of the hillside.

"Oh, so he traveled all the way home, ready to give his wife a piece of his mind, only to discover that she didn't have the nuzzler either. When he arrived at the shipyard yesterday, his animal was right where he usually ties her."

Emzara laughed in delight.

"Fen eventually saw the humor in it, and Bakur was thrilled — for him, anyway. He even cracked a smile. However, I know that Fen is planning a way to pay him back. Bakur's going to have to watch out."

She laughed again, picturing the exchange between the two men that were like family to her. "Good thing they never did something like that to Pennik. He had an even longer travel each day than Fen does. And not nearly as good a sense of humor."

Noah tilted his head and gave her a questioning look. "Whatever happened to him? Don't get me wrong, I'm glad he's gone."

She sighed. "He always assumed that I was interested in him. And I guess I was a little at first, but it didn't take long to see that he thought too highly of himself. Once you came along, I think he felt threatened."

"By me?" Noah smirked. "He could have crushed me."

"I'm not so sure about that." Emzara squeezed his upper arm. "He could tell that I was interested in someone else. In fact, I think everyone knew, except for you."

Noah kissed her hand. "Well, I know now. So what happened with Pennik?"

"He heard me talking to Baba about you one morning, so he came to my office around midmeal. He told me flat out that I needed to stop talking about you because I was supposed to be with him."

"I'm glad you didn't agree."

Emzara threw her hair back. "Me too. I told him that I wouldn't marry him, and he stormed away. That was the last time I saw him."

Noah paused before speaking. "So I should thank you for my apprenticeship then?"

"I can't really take credit. I was annoyed with Pennik at the time, but it wasn't my intention to hurt him. And I didn't expect him to quit."

Noah smiled to himself. His frustrating start in Iri Geshem had been well worth the trouble. "Be careful of that step there." Noah pointed to a rocky area. She gathered up the hem of her dress and readjusted it, giving her knees freedom to make the climb up the hill. Noah reached his arm out to help her navigate and she grabbed it with her free hand, letting him pull her up. He pulled her close, steadying her, and she fell easily into his embrace. "Maybe we don't need to go any farther." His words were only partly in jest.

"No way. I'm enjoying this adventure. No complaints from me." After a pause she softened her tone, "Although, I'm quite fond of being in your arms right here."

He tightened his hold before letting go. "I think I can force myself to release you just long enough to make it to the top."

She smiled, marveling that someone could come to mean so much to her in so short a time. Every time she saw him, her heart danced in pure joy, and she imagined that her existence before his arrival was simply that.

Existence. With Noah near, she felt more alive than ever before, and did not want to know life without him again.

She had been nervous to invite him to watch the sunset with her for the first time, hoping that Aterre was not playing a cruel joke. But on the whole walk home from the beach that evening, she'd contemplated all the little moments between them, replaying each to get a better understanding of what they meant. What did it mean when he rapped a pattern on the doorway every time he had to pass by the building she worked in? Was that his way of flirting with her, or was he simply saying hello? And what about the time he offered to help her pull a splinter from her small hand and held it in his? Or the time when his foot tapped against hers and he didn't move it away during the rest of midmeal? Was he even aware that that had happened?

After thinking things through, she decided that maybe they added up to more than just random occurrences. Asking him to watch a sunset wouldn't be too much — if he said no, or if things didn't go well, it wouldn't make life around him awkward for too long. She could shrug it off and walk away as if she was used to randomly inviting people to watch sunsets with her. Emzara smiled to herself in the afternoon sunlight, glad she had taken that small, uncertain step.

Since then, seldom did a day go by where they did not have some time together, even if it was only a quick conversation at the shipyard. The more they talked, the more she pieced together an understanding of him. And the more this happened, the more she valued him. Notwithstanding his dark, handsome features, or his strong physique, she found herself also attracted to his way of thinking, to his sureness in decisions, and to the pride he always took in his work. She liked the strength he displayed while building, but more importantly the strength of his faith in the Creator. With him around, she felt both at peace as well as strangely astir. Somehow, in his presence as she was today, she just felt complete.

"Here we are." Noah shouldered the satchel before helping her up the last step.

She looked at the expanse of grassy plain, broken only by a smattering of large rocks here and there. To their left in the distance, one of the cliffs jutted high overhead, and from it gushed a sparkling waterfall that crashed into a large pool. Another cascade fell to the sea from the opposite side of the pond. "It's breathtaking up here."

151

"Yes, you are." The edge of Noah's lips twitched upward.

Her cheeks warmed, and she pulled his hand toward her lips and kissed it. "I said this place is breathtaking."

"I wasn't disagreeing with you."

"Come on, let's get a closer look." She tugged at his hand, and together they ran to the pool. "Look, a rainbow!"

Noah gave her a knowing smile. "We've seen several of them together, haven't we?"

Emzara leaned her head on his shoulder and nodded, her cheek rubbing against the gathered fabric of his garment. "I like watching sunsets with you on clear days." She wrapped her arm around him. "And on the days when it's cloudy or rainy. Although I questioned your sanity a little bit the first time you invited me to see the sunset when it was pouring."

Noah laughed. "But we got both a sunset and a rainbow at the same time."

She remembered how pleasant the surprise was to them both when the dismal clouds suddenly burst apart to reveal a crimson sun along with the most brilliantly colored arc tracing its way across the sky. "Best ever. Although this is already a close second and we just got here." She settled on one of the large, smooth boulders that created the edge of the natural pool and reached up to Noah. "I'd like to draw this while we wait to see the supergliders. May I have the scroll I gave you and a drawing stick?"

Noah fumbled around the sack for a bit before handing her the two objects. He sat down next to her and inched a little closer, then scooted back, only to readjust and settle to where his knee was just a hair's distance from hers. He sighed a little. "So I had a good talk with your father last night after we closed up shop."

"Is that why he was so late to evenfeast?" She looked at him, but his gaze was on the water. He drummed his left hand fingers on the rocky surface. "What did you two discuss?"

"He told me that he's been very pleased with my work, and also my, uh, well, he said he's happy with my integrity too."

"He's told me how much he values you."

"I'm glad. I really enjoy the work. And your father is a great teacher."

"He says you're quick to pick things up and already work like you've been there for years."

"With all I've learned, sometimes it feels like I have been. But we didn't focus on my past last night; we talked about my future." Noah paused. "He told me that if I'm interested, within a few years he'd begin turning some of the management of the business over to me. But before that time, he'd continue to mentor and groom me."

Emzara laid down her artwork to clasp her hands together in excitement. She leaned toward him earnestly. "What did you say?"

"I told him that there's no place I'd rather be, but that I had one condition."

Suddenly feeling nervous, she glanced away. "So you might leave?"

"Well, we worked it out that I'll continue as his apprentice until he makes me his right hand man, and possibly someday, the future owner." Noah suddenly turned his gaze to her and she caught the faint hint of a smile on his lips. "But I have to work for more than five years before we can really talk more about any of that."

"Why five years? That's longer than the normal time for an apprenticeship."

"That's true, but it's the right amount of time for something else."

"What do you mean?" She shook her head, "I don't understand."

Abruptly, Noah shifted the conversation. "I have something for you here." He searched through the satchel, taking care that she couldn't see inside. "I made this." He held out a delicately carved figure of a keluk.

"My favorite." She accepted it eagerly and turned the animal over, fingering the expertly whittled ridges, when suddenly she became aware of a leather strap looped around the animal.

"What's this?" She glanced up at Noah.

"Look at it."

Slowly she unwound it from the carving and saw a little wooden disc attached in the center of the length of leather. She turned the front of the circle to face her and held it in her palm. A delicate outline of a rainbow rested on a small line of land. She blinked, not fully comprehending, when Noah gently took her hand in his and pointed to the token.

"I carved it. The land on the bottom here is from my father's symbol. But instead of having a stalk of grain coming out from it, I thought it might be nice if we had a rainbow." He clasped both of her hands in his. "Zara, you're my one condition. And you're the reason for the five years." His chest heaved and he spoke rapidly. "I care for you so much

153

that I want you by me always. A thousand years if the Creator gives us that long." His hands trembled in hers. "I know you're not of age yet and won't be for another five years. But when that time comes — I talked to your father, but Em, I need to know if —" For the first time he paused the rush of his words and beheld her eyes. "If you want to be my wife."

"Noah," her eyes filled with tears. "I can't think of anything I'd rather be."

"So that's a yes?"

Emzara looked at him, emotions inside her swelling and feeling as if they would pound forth, just like the waterfall that surged into the pool beyond them. Angling in toward him, she rested her hand on his chest and tilted her head. "Yes."

He wrapped an arm around her and pulled her in closer. As he slowly leaned in, her heart pounded as both delight and contentment overwhelmed her.

"ARRWAK!"

The sudden piercing cry startled her, causing her to pull her lips away from his. They both jumped to their feet and looked around. Emzara's hand flew to her chest.

Noah laughed. "We have company."

Soaring above them, two supergliders nipped and squawked at each other. She had seen them flying over the bay several times, but they never ventured too close to the city. Now, up close, she staggered at the magnitude of these creatures. Whisper-thin leathery wings spread out at least five cubits to either side of their slender yet powerful bodies. The pointy beaks in front and long crests protruding from the back of their heads made them somewhat comical in appearance, but with their fierce temperaments, no one would dare tell them they looked funny.

As the pounding of her heart subsided, the humor in the moment made Emzara laugh. She watched as the two animals tumbled in the air. "Guess we did come to see them up close." She grinned and twined her fingers with his as she leaned into his body. "Think we'll ever squawk at each other like that?"

"With your spunk and my self-assurance?" He winked at her. "Perhaps."

"Noah, I —" Suddenly her heart was too full to give way to the words she wanted most to express.

"I know. Me too," he finished softly.

Chapter 21

Land of Havilah — Noah's 45th year

Naamah tucked her veil a little more over her face before leaving the relative safety of the tree trunk. The night was full of shadows and stars. Crossing the few paces between the edge of the forest and the clearing where the little house stood, she wished for just a few more clouds to aid in her concealment. She darted to the door and rapped lightly on the wood, huddling up against the cool mud exterior as if she might somehow be swallowed into the wall itself.

The door opened and an aged man stooped his head under the top of the frame and looked about. "Good sir. Could you help me?" Her voice was soft and held just as much of a plea as did her eyes.

"Come in. Tell me what you need," he said in slow, measured tones.

"I need your help."

"So you said." He held out a hand, pointing at the small fireplace across the single, cozily lit room. "Sit. Be warmed and at peace. And tell me what you seek."

She sat on the low, hard stool by the fire, twisting her hands in her lap before speaking, trying to figure out where to begin. "I need answers. I need to know what to do."

"Sounds like you have a story to tell. I'm here to listen. Tell me your troubles, child." His caring voice soothed her nerves and did more to comfort her than the friendly flames.

"My father is someone who's very important to the city I come from. His —"

"I know who you are, Princess of Havil, and I know who your father is." He settled into a high-backed wooden chair, its gnarled posts looking almost as if they had grown in their current position. Behind him, a glimmering figure caught her eye. A carving of the familiar Sepha tree rested on a shelf, but there was more. A golden serpent wrapped around the trunk and became entwined in some of the branches. "Don't worry, daughter of Lamech, your words will not leave this place."

How could he know me? I'm so far from home. Maybe he really can access the Creator's knowledge. Naamah loosened her covering and lowered it behind her head. "No need for pretenses then. I have your word? Our meeting is secret?"

He raised his hands and pressed them together beneath his chin and nodded. "Always."

She rubbed her arms to warm them. "Well, as I was about to say, my father's power grows each year. And each year, I'm wounded by it. I'm his only daughter and will be of age when I turn 35 next year, and yet I'm just a means to an end. In his eyes, my existence only matters because of what power he might gain through me." Her words tumbled out now as if compelled by the fears that had gripped her for so long.

"There have been about half a dozen suitors—warriors and important men—who have come, seeking his permission to take me as their wife. In most of them, I see only a hunger of temporary desire. In one of them, there lurked something monstrously sinister. Yet there was another." At the memory of him, her voice softened.

"He actually saw me for who I was and not just how I could advance his station in life. He spent just as much time with me as he did trying to win my father's favor. And yet, he, like the others was rejected. My father called me to him and said with contempt that one such as he wasn't worthy of my beauty. But I could see the greed. I could see that my father hoped for one still greater to align with.

"I'm frightened. I don't want to be mercilessly handed over to someone who cares only for himself. And yet, I long to be married. To have someone good. Someone I can love and adore. Someone I can give myself to and not fear. And that's why I've come. I've heard you can see what's ahead. Please tell me. If I go back to my father's house, what will become of me?"

The man leaned closer and looked at her, yet Naamah sensed that he was not so much seeing her, as seeing past her. He blinked rapidly, almost as if that action would bring his being back to the body that loomed before her. "Child, there's mystery surrounding you. And greatness. But I lack clarity. To learn what may be, I need some of your blood. Once blood and ground meet, only then will the voice of He who formed the ground truly cry out."

Naamah bit her lip. She had not expected this. She pulled away.

"Relax, it'll just be a tiny cut on your finger. You'll barely feel it."

She looked at her hand. *The minor pain will be nothing compared to the pain of not knowing.* She weighed her options carefully then timidly extended her hand. The seer gently held her finger steady and with his other hand, removed a small sharp blade from atop the mantle. She watched in mingled horror and fascination as he sliced a small groove in her tallest finger and then squeezed several large drops of blood, which landed decisively on the hard-packed dirt floor.

He breathed deeply, his eyelids slowly sinking. The silence seemed endless until his eyes rolled back, leaving only narrow slits of white.

"A storm brews in the north with thick, dark clouds, vexing your father. But a ray of sunshine pierces through it, lighting up your face." As he spoke, his voice rang out in confident tones. His eyes popped open — clear and intently focused.

A tingle traveled down Naamah's spine. *What did he mean? Does the storm represent a person? An army? Or simply a storm? Did any of it have to do with getting a good husband? Hmm . . . the sea lies to the north, so there isn't anyone in that direction, is there?* She stood and gathered her things, placing a strand of piks on the mantle as she did so. Puzzled as she was by his words, for the first time in a long time, she breathed freely. Absently wrapping her finger with a bandage the seer handed to her, she pondered this new feeling and realized what it was. Hope.

CHAPTER 22

Iri Geshem — Noah's 45th year

Noah held his drink up toward Aterre, who lounged across from him in Ara's sitting room after evenfeast. "To your first harvest of Nuca's beans."

"Drink up." Aterre beckoned to them as if he were the master of a feast, joining Noah in being overdramatic.

Breathing in the aroma of the brew, Noah took a sip. The expected bitterness was largely absent, and in its place, a smooth and mellow taste enveloped his palate. He took another sip and it achieved the same result. "Outstanding."

"It's better than Nuca's." Emzara's face lit up. "It's not so strong."

Ara leaned back. "You're to be commended, Aterre. This is very good."

"How did you make it taste so different?" Noah asked.

Aterre shrugged. "I'm not sure. Maybe it's the soil here, or maybe I didn't roast them long enough. I was afraid to burn them so I didn't follow the directions perfectly."

"Well, whatever you did, this is delicious," Noah said.

Aterre set his cup down on the small table next to his chair. "Cada said that once we sell enough to cover his initial investment, he's going to split the profits with me evenly."

"Sounds like he made you a pretty good deal," Ara said before turning to face Noah. "Guess that's a good reminder to me that with patience, getting a better product is possible."

"I've been fiddling with it," Noah said. "I think I've narrowed down the problem, but I'm not any closer to a solution."

Emzara sighed. "If you two are going to talk shop, you might as well clue Aterre and me in."

"We're trying to figure out how to make bigger boats." Ara said. "We've been making the same two models for nearly 20 years, but sooner or later, someone's going to make something larger, and when they do, we'll be out of business."

"I know some of the riverboat owners would like to be able to transport more goods, but if you make them too big, will they be able to maneuver much?" Aterre asked.

"They might get stuck in the shallows," Ara said. "But we're not really talking about boats for the river."

"For the sea?" Aterre raised an eyebrow.

Emzara scooted up against Noah. "Why would you want something to cross the sea?"

Ara held up a hand. "Merchants and explorers want ships that can carry enough supplies and are strong enough to survive on the open sea. There are several cities along the coast that they could trade with. But our current boats can't handle the waves during a storm. That's why they hug the shoreline all the way, but doing so can add weeks to the trip, depending on how far one is going. So it's really not worth it."

"Is it even possible?" Aterre asked.

"Well, I'd like to find out," Ara said.

After grabbing a blanket from the open seat to her right, Emzara pulled her feet up on her chair and covered up. "What prevents you from doing it now, Baba?"

"Good question." Ara cracked his knuckles. "Do you remember when you were a little girl and one of my ships sank?"

Emzara shook her head.

"An adventurer bought a boat from me and planned on sailing all the way around the land to map it out. I warned him about taking it out in the big waves, but he didn't listen. A few weeks later, he returned to town and tried to ruin my business by telling everyone that my boats can't be trusted."

"What happened?" Aterre asked.

"He went east, trying to navigate all the way to the land of Nod, but he got too far from the shore. A storm came along and ripped the ship apart."

"He's lucky he didn't drown," Aterre rubbed his brow and blew out a breath.

"No question about that. He said he hung onto one of the boards throughout the night and swam to shore in the morning. He came back here determined to blame me for his stubbornness."

"Is he still around?" Emzara asked.

"No, he eventually left town." Ara smirked. "I think he decided to explore on land."

Aterre laughed. "Maybe he should've done that in the first place."

As Noah rubbed the back of her neck, Emzara asked her father, "You said the boat sank in the storm, but were you able to ascertain what went wrong?"

Ara shrugged. "Maybe. I tried to talk it through with the man, but he wasn't interested in working things out. Still, he said something that's stayed with me. He mentioned that the joints gave way first. Noah's agreed to help me figure out how to get past the added strain to the joints."

"What about using some sort of metal?" Emzara asked.

"I've thought of that." Ara scratched his head. "Copper isn't strong enough. It would bend too easily. Silver is too expensive and isn't strong enough either."

Aterre jolted upright. "I have an idea."

Holding up his cup, Noah said, "No, we aren't going to use your crop to make them."

"Ooh, there's a thought." Aterre smiled. "But in all seriousness, I think Emzara's right. Metal might be the answer."

"It hasn't been so far," Ara said.

"Maybe." Aterre pointed in the direction of town. "We may not have anything here that's strong enough, but in Havilah, where I grew up, they had figured out how to get another metal from rocks in the ground. They called it iron, and it's much stronger than copper."

"How much stronger?" Ara asked.

"I don't know for sure, but they make weapons out of it." Aterre looked away. "I can tell you this much, it doesn't bend like copper. It's very sturdy."

Ara stroked his beard with his thumb and index finger. "Hmm. That would require a trip to Havil, which poses a couple of problems."

"Like the time it takes to get there?" Aterre asked.

"That's one of them. We'll see at least two whole moons before completing the trip." Ara downed the last of his drink. "Although if the boats could survive the open sea, it'd be a lot faster."

"I'll go," Noah said.

Emzara squeezed his arm. "No. You can't leave for that long. We're getting married in less than a year."

Noah kissed the top of her head. "And that's why I must go. To secure the business for the future, so that I can provide for us and someday, our family."

Quiet and motionless, Emzara stared at her feet. Noah knew he would hate the separation as well, but at the same time, the thought of an adventure in Havil made his skin tingle.

"We're ahead of schedule right now, so I think I could spare you for that amount of time." Ara nodded toward Emzara, "That is, if my daughter will allow it."

"I understand it." She sighed and looked up. "But I don't have to like it."

"That's one of the problems," Noah said, eager to conquer any obstacle. "What's the other one?"

"This is a matter that needs to be brought to the town council," Ara said.

"Why?" Aterre asked.

"Because we don't have any official trade agreement with the land of Havilah, right Baba?"

"And I'm not sure our council will want to start one," Ara said.

Noah furrowed his brow. "Really?"

"There are rumors that the major city, Havil, has grown quite wicked. The elders don't want any of that influence here."

Emzara sat up and smiled. "Well, I guess you aren't going anywhere then."

Ara held up his palm. "Hold on. Noah and I will go to the next council meeting." He glanced up and used his fingers to count days. "I believe it'll be in eight days." He pointed to Noah. "If they're open to the idea, then you can go. They'd probably want to send a representative with you. And you'd need someone to help with the boat." He turned and looked at Aterre.

Aterre nodded. "I'd do it, but I'll have to check with Cada. The harvest is almost over, so he may let me once that is finished, as long as I'm back before the planting season."

"It's settled then. If the council approves, you two will leave for Havil to see if we can procure some iron."

Emzara grabbed Noah's hand with both of hers. "And what if I could persuade Noah not to go?" The tone of her voice made it clear she was only partly serious.

Ara laughed. "Then I could just order him to go. I am his boss, after all."

"You don't play fair." Emzara folded her arms across her chest, but the tiniest smile escaped her lips.

Noah's feelings were mixed too. Leaving Emzara for so long seemed unbearable, especially after they had seen each other nearly every day for the past five years. He placed a hand on her shoulder. "Before we make any decisions, we need to ask the Creator for clear directions in these matters." He looked over at Ara. "If the Most High wants me to go, then there's no use fighting it." He turned back to Emzara. "But if He wants me to stay, then I'll certainly not object."

Emzara kissed his hand that she still held tightly. "That is a plan I can't argue with."

Ara stood and held out his arms. "Then let us pray."

CHAPTER 23

Their long morning shadows kept stride ahead of them as Noah and Ara strolled through Iri Geshem's downtown. Two-story shops — many with residences on the top floor — lined the outside of the rectangular district. In the center of town, a small fountain featured a stone sculpture of a sea creature with a hole on the top of its head, which perpetually sprayed water a few cubits in all directions. Powered by an underground spring, the fountain produced the pleasant ambience of a light rainfall. The sunlight passing through the mist created a small color band. On the far end of the street, the recently completed three-story administrative building rose above the rest. Five stone steps led up to a large entryway highlighted by two wooden pillars stretching from the floor to the overhanging flat roof.

"Is this what Iri Sana looks like?" Ara asked.

Noah chuckled. "Not unless it's had some major renovations in the past five years. There's only a main street with about 20 small homes and shops. It looks much older than Iri Geshem."

"How far out of town is your family farm?"

"It's south, right on the Hiddekel, not too far."

"I see." Ara gestured to the large council building looming in front of them. "Zain told me the council was quite appreciative of your assistance with carving the pillars. They look very nice."

"Let's hope they'll remember that as they consider our request this morning." Noah draped the excess of his formal robe over his left arm.

They climbed the steps, and Ara stopped to examine Noah's handiwork on the wooden pillar to their left. Chiseled filigree designs wrapped around the town's name on the massive pole. "Emz described this to me, but it's better than I imagined. You definitely have a gift."

"She helped me figure out the design. She's quite an artist."

Ara nodded, still admiring the woodwork. "She's an exceptional young woman and deserves an equally amazing man." His eyes measured Noah, and then he shrugged and smiled. "But I guess you'll do."

Noah laughed then became serious. "I may not be her equal, but I love your daughter more than life itself."

"I know. So do I." Ara placed a hand on Noah's shoulder before stepping toward the entrance. "Come on, let's find out what the council thinks of our proposal."

Inside the new town hall, stairways along the left and right walls of the foyer wound to the second and third floors. The small, polished white and gray stones which comprised the flooring recreated the designs in the pillars. Ahead, a wide double-door led to the main hall. Ara opened it and allowed Noah to proceed into the back of the main room.

Four long benches lined either side of the space, and only one of them was occupied. An elderly man sat in the second row. *It's nice to live in a town blessed by the Creator where troubles are so rare.*

In the front, on a raised platform, five men sat behind a long curved desk. Noah recognized them all, but had only met three of the men, including Zain, who sat to the right of the center position. Zain had visited Ara's house and shipyard several times, and Noah appreciated his straightforward manner.

An old woman stood near a podium on the left, listening. Ara stopped short of the first row of benches and Noah stood behind him.

"Yes, you and your husband will still be able to access the well near the tanner's place when the improvements are made." Akel, the chairperson, who sat in the middle, held out an arm toward the woman. "In fact, it'll be even easier for you to get there. Did you have any other matters to raise today?"

"No. That's all. Thank you." The woman slowly turned, and using a walking stick, made her way back to her husband. She tapped his leg with her cane. "Let's go home, dear."

He stirred and then struggled to his feet. "What did they say about the well?"

Noah turned his attention to the matter at hand as Ara walked up to the podium and gripped the edges of its flat top. "Morning peace, honored councilmembers." Noah stepped to his side.

Akel smiled. "Welcome, Ara. It's good to see you."

"Likewise. I believe you know my apprentice, Noah."

"Indeed, he did great work on this building." Akel grunted as he shifted his seven-hundred-year-old body in his seat. He had been on the council for over two hundred years and, according to Ara, he had gladly stepped aside for the required amount of time every decade. His wisdom helped guide Iri Geshem in peace and prosperity. Most importantly, his insistence on following the Creator's ways had made the city safe, and every citizen was encouraged to worship the Most High. "And if I'm not mistaken, he's not far from becoming your son-in-law."

Noah couldn't hold back a smile at the thought of Emzara being his bride.

"That's true," Ara said.

"Well, what business do you have with us today?" Akel asked.

Ara paused and looked at each member. "We seek your permission to travel to the land of Havilah following the harvest."

Akel drew back and furrowed his brow. "Why would you need the council's approval to travel to Havilah? You're free to come and go as you please. Although, I didn't expect that you would want to travel so far."

"It's true, I don't intend to go. But my apprentice has offered to lead the trip."

"I see." Akel extended his arm with his palm up. "And that brings us back to my question. Why do you feel the need to ask for permission?"

Ara stood up straight. "We've recently learned that the people there have a technique to work with a metal much stronger than copper."

Akel raised his eyebrows. "Surely, that could be of great benefit to us in many ways. But what interest do you have in such an innovation?"

"I'd like to try building a larger ship. One that carries more cargo up and down the river, and if it works, one that could maybe even survive the open sea."

"You're aware of our desire not to open up trade with Havil?" the man on the far left asked. Having met him only once, Noah could not recall his name, but he was the only one on the council who lacked facial hair. "They do not honor the Creator."

"Yes. Hence my reason for coming today. I seek the council's wisdom on this matter." Ara pursed his lips. "Would it be a violation of the council's desire if we acquire this knowledge from these people?"

Several moments passed as the councilmembers spoke quietly, yet animatedly, amongst themselves. Akel listened. Zain pointed to himself and spoke more than the rest. Ashur, the youngest member, sat on the end next to Zain and said very little. Akel held out his palms when he talked and the others sat silently.

"Thank you for your patience with us," Akel finally said. "You've raised an interesting question. While we still don't desire an official alliance with Havil, your proposed endeavor doesn't violate our policy. Therefore, we'll not forbid your apprentice from making the trip. We do have one request we'd like you to observe, however."

"Of course," Ara said. "Name it."

Akel gestured to Zain, who cleared his throat. "I offer my assistance on this venture as a representative of Iri Geshem."

"I'm sure we'd be happy to oblige." Ara turned to Noah. "Isn't that right?"

"You'd be most welcome." Noah bit his lower lip and looked at the ceiling. Something was amiss, but he couldn't put his finger on it.

"You have some reservations?" Akel asked.

Noah hesitated briefly and the issue became clear. "Just one, sir. I have no problem with Zain coming with us. I'd enjoy his company. But if he joins us as an official representative of the city, would that not give the Havilites the impression that we seek to establish official ties with them?"

Akel lifted his head in understanding. "Ara, your apprentice has some wisdom beyond his years. Indeed, it could be seen that way."

"Then it's not worth the risk," the beardless man said.

"There's an easy solution." Akel looked at Zain. "You're a merchant, so you can go in that capacity. You'll be our eyes and ears, but the people of Havil don't need to know that you're an official representative of our city."

"If it pleases the council." Ashur glanced at the other men before he focused on Noah. "And if you'd permit it, I'd also like to make this journey." He pointed to himself. "I'm curious to know how inns and dining halls operate in other places to see if I can gain any insights about my own business. While I do have a private interest here, I may be able to acquire knowledge that can benefit our city. Of course, I'd also go as my own agent instead of an official representative."

Akel scratched the side of his head, where his thinning white hair was thickest. "And you'd submit to Zain's leadership?"

"Certainly."

"Do you have any qualms about this arrangement, Noah?" Akel asked.

After meeting Ashur a few times, Noah found him to be affable enough. "As long as these men are willing to help with the various tasks on the boat, then I welcome their company."

Akel fixed his gaze on Ara. "Are these arrangements acceptable to you?"

Ara studied Noah for a moment. "Yes sir. Your conditions are acceptable."

"Good, it's decided," Akel said. "After the harvest, Zain and Ashur will travel with Noah's crew to the land of Havilah to find out how they make stronger metals. Did you have any other business with the council this morning?"

"Actually, I have one more question about the previous matter." Ara spoke up. "If the people of the land require some form of payment in exchange for the knowledge we seek, would it be a violation of policy for Noah to offer fair compensation for their services?"

Akel glanced at his colleagues, but no one spoke and a few shook their heads. "As long as he uses your resources and makes it clear that he is acting on your behalf instead of the city's, then there will be no infringement."

Ara nodded. "That's all. Thank you for your time and guidance."

"Thank you, sirs," Noah said. "I'd ask that Zain and Ashur would visit the shipyard sometime soon so that we can finalize plans and prepare for the voyage."

"We'll certainly do that," Zain said.

"This concludes our matter today," Akel said. "May the Creator guide your path, Noah. Thank you for seeking our counsel on these matters, Ara."

Ara and Noah bowed slightly to the council, left the hall, and walked through the foyer before either of them spoke. Once outside, Noah said, "That went better than I anticipated."

"It did. Yet two things concern me."

"Two things?"

"Yes." Ara spoke softly. "Something about Ashur's request troubled me. I don't know what it is, but please keep a close eye on him. I don't wish to speak ill or imply something unbecoming of one of our town's leaders, but be on your guard."

"I will," Noah said. "What's the second one?"

Ara grinned. "I wonder if I'll still have an apprentice after you tell my daughter that you're really leaving for so long."

Noah smiled again at the thought of Emzara and chuckled. "Guess there's only one way to find out."

CHAPTER 24

The gentle, steady rocking of the boat nearly lulled Noah to sleep as he leaned against the side of the cabin. The sail just behind and above his head stretched tight in the strong, warm breeze. To his left, the coast lay in the distance beneath the late afternoon sun. To ensure their safety if a storm rose up, they remained within eyesight of the shoreline, yet not close enough to risk running aground.

Stretching far beyond his sight in the direction of Iri Geshem, the undulating water sparkled, but the scenery had long since lost its appeal in the tedium of the voyage.

Noah yearned to see Emzara again, to talk to her and hear her laugh, and to feel the warmth of her embrace. *Creator, please comfort Em during this time and keep her from harm. I give You praise for the safe travel afforded us so far and ask that You'd continue to watch over us and show us favor.*

Raucous laughter shook Noah from his contemplation. He turned to see the others laughing at Zain, who playfully tossed his game pieces into the middle of the group. Zain pointed at Aterre. "You got lucky this time."

Aterre smirked. "I think four games in a row is skill, not luck."

"I'll beat you one of these times, but not now." Zain shook his head. "That's enough for me."

"You're quitting?" Ashur asked.

"I don't need any more humiliation today."

Ashur held up both palms. "Come on. Just one more round."

Farna reached for the pieces to set up the next game and glanced at Ashur. "You just don't want us to gang up on you next."

Thankful for Ara's direction in hiring Farna to captain the voyage, Noah looked around at his crewmates. Farna's men were handling his usual river run in his absence, and Noah had come to appreciate the depth of the man's expertise in every aspect of sailing. Before setting out, Noah had been confident that he could captain the voyage himself, but after less than a day on board, he had discovered just how far in over his head he would have been. Humbled, he had set out to learn everything he could about sailing in open water, and Farna had readily accepted his role as teacher, even showing Noah how to use the stars to navigate.

With five people on board, the small ship felt nearly full, although they still had plenty of room below deck. Originally designed for a three-man crew and cargo, this particular model had undergone renovations before the voyage. Noah had expanded the small cabin to accommodate another double bunk, which had cut down on deck space, but simultaneously created more storage space above the sleeping quarters.

Zain joined Noah near the mast. "Still missing her?"

Noah nodded. "Sorry if I'm not much fun to be around."

"You're doing fine. I remember my first few solo trips after being married." He crossed his arms and leaned against the mast, a nostalgic smile creasing his face. "I was a wreck. I couldn't concentrate on my work because I missed Kmani so much. It got better as the decades passed. Now, although I love her more than ever and I still miss her, being away isn't as difficult as it used to be."

"I'm glad to hear it gets better." Noah sighed and stretched his arms above his head. Anxious to change the subject he asked, "Have you always lived in Iri Geshem?"

"We both grew up in a small town east of the city — about a four-day journey. After we married, I wanted to find a more strategic place for my little textile business. At the time, Iri Geshem was barely bigger than my hometown, but I knew it could become so much more. It's in a perfect location, right on the sea and at the mouth of a major river. So we packed up and moved there." He shrugged. "It was difficult for a while. I spent much of the daytime farming and made clothes at night, with Kmani's help, of course."

"Your business does very well now," Noah said.

"The Creator's been good to us." Zain rubbed his eyes. "Everything changed when Ara moved to town. Back then, his property was just a small farm. I still remember when I first heard about this newcomer building a boat by the sea. I wanted to meet him to see if he was crazy or if he could really do it. I knew if the rumors were true, we could buy and sell goods from all over the place. And there he was, this young man all by himself, building a craft about half this size."

Noah stomped his foot on the ship's deck. "Obviously, he wasn't crazy."

"No, he knew what he was doing. Emzara's mother, Biremza, invited me to stay for evenfeast, which I happily accepted." Zain pursed his lips and looked away. "You would've liked her. Emzara reminds me of her so much. She loved the Creator and was such a sweet woman. She became my wife's best friend and we spent a lot of time with them. It was such a tragedy to lose her."

"I wish I could have met her." Noah paused as the painful memory spread across Zain's face. Although he enjoyed hearing about Emzara's mother, he could see how difficult it was for Zain. "So did that first boat float?"

Zain raised his eyebrows. "It did. It tilted a little, but he compensated by putting more weight on the other side." He chuckled. "It wasn't much more than a rowboat, and it wasn't long before it started springing leaks. But he learned from his mistakes and soon drew up plans for a larger one that would actually carry cargo. By then, I believed in him, so I helped finance the business. Best investment I ever made."

"So that second model worked?"

"It floated perfectly, but it didn't have any means of propulsion. And it was too big to row, so it just sat on the shore for about a year." Zain tapped the bottom of the sail. "That's when he added a sail for propulsion and a rudder for steering. Before long he was making boats to run the river or the coast. Of course, they were still small and couldn't carry much."

Noah gestured to the deck under their feet. "When did he start making them this size?"

"If I remember correctly, it was shortly before Emzara was born." Zain pointed to the three men playing their game. "Farna was actually the first person to buy one."

"Really? No wonder Ara told me they go way back."

"Whoa!" Ashur suddenly jumped to his feet and pointed past the front of the boat. "Look at that."

The other men stood and Noah and Zain quickly joined them. Noah could not believe his eyes. Several hundred cubits ahead, an enormous splash of water shot high into the air, the only remaining visible marker of the thing that caused it.

"What was that?" Zain asked.

"A sea monster jumped out of the water." Ashur's eyes remained wide open. "Did anyone else see it?"

Noah shook his head "Just the splash."

Farna flashed a mischievous grin. "You boys better find something to hang on to right now."

No sooner had Noah grabbed the mast than the first wave slammed into the boat, causing boards to creak while the ship lurched sideways. Water sprayed over the port side, dousing him and the others. He tightened his grip and steadied himself for another surging blast. His short-lived wait ended as a second and then third wave crashed against the hull.

While Noah held on for dear life, Farna taunted the sea, laughing uproariously between shouts of, "Is that all you've got?" and "Send another one!"

As the surf returned to normal, Noah loosened his grip and looked at each of his shipmates, who all stared at Farna.

"You're crazy," Ashur said.

"You didn't think that was fun?" Farna asked.

Ashur shook his head side to side and then shrugged. "Well, maybe a little."

Noah quickly surveyed the rest of the ship. The top two crates above their sleeping quarters had shaken loose. After rapidly ascending the ladder on the right side of the cabin, Noah grabbed the nearest loose box at his head level and strained to slide it into position.

"Thanks, Noah," Farna said. "Be sure to tie them down tight. Aterre, lower the sail so that we don't drive right into that beast."

"Got it," Aterre said.

"There's another one!" Zain pointed ahead and to their left.

Noah traced the trajectory of Zain's finger. His eyes grew wide while his jaw dropped. A creature twice the length of their boat launched most of its massive body out of the water, then twisted in the air and crashed back into the surf. As it slammed into the sea, a gigantic spray shot up, followed by the thunderous sound of the splash. Noah looked around to brace himself before the first wave hit, but nothing on top of the cabin offered any promise of safety.

Gripping the tie-down rope, he looked at the approaching swell. *I think I can reach the mast.* Just then the boat pitched forward and Noah staggered, his grip on the rope the only anchor keeping him from falling to the deck. The hull creaked and the whole ship reeled sideways. Everything seemed to slow as Noah spotted the source of the upheaval from the corner of his eye. His heart leapt into his throat when he realized one of the sea monsters was under the boat. He turned to renew his grip when another jolt shot the heavy box toward him. All of the air in his lungs instantly discharged as the crate hurtled into his chest, and he flew backward through the air. He tried desperately to reach for anything to stop his impending appointment with the deep, but his arms disobeyed his thoughts. Before hitting the water, intense pain from the crushing blow to his ribcage finally registered. He opened his mouth to yell, but no sound escaped.

Terror seized Noah as he plunged into the water. His arms still failed to respond, and the pain in his chest nearly caused him to pass out. Emzara's face raced through his mind, but imagination was instantly replaced by the reality of a long, scaly tail sweeping past him. Noah's kicks were too weak to propel him upward, and the fear of drowning or becoming a small meal for the sea monster gripped him. His mind flashed back to Emzara and then his family. *Creator, please —*

As his consciousness began to fade, he felt himself being yanked upward by a powerful arm wrapped across his chest. Light filtered through his eyelids as his head breached the surface. He begged for air, but his breaths were limited to short gasps.

"I got you, Noah. Stay with me."

Still fighting to inhale, Noah rolled his head back on the water and saw Zain's face next to his. The pain in his chest radiated through his body.

A nearby splash caught his attention, but his tension eased at the sight of Aterre's head and shoulders emerging from the sea. While Zain shifted to one side, Aterre grabbed Noah's other shoulder, and together the friends raised Noah's torso. Already the buoyancy kept him better afloat in his new position, "Just breathe, Noah. We've got you."

As they moved him toward the boat, Noah's gasps brought in a little more air. With the side of the hull looming overhead, Aterre and Zain lifted his arms up to where Farna and Ashur could grab them and lift him aboard. They pulled him onto the deck and he rolled to his stomach, coughing and pleading for his lungs to fill.

Several moments passed before he inhaled anywhere close to normal. Coughing yet again, Noah felt like he had swallowed the contents of the entire sea. Each breath came with a price as the agony emanating from his ribs nearly caused him to wretch. Slowly, he rolled to his back and all four of his friends stared down at him.

"Are you okay?" Zain asked.

Noah nodded weakly.

Ashur looked concerned. "Zain got to you just in time."

"Now you've got a story to tell the grandkids someday." Farna mussed Noah's hair and winked. "Welcome aboard. I think I'll give you the rest of the day off."

Noah thought about giving a short laugh, but his ribs reminded him it would be a bad idea. Tears filled his eyes. Not knowing if his voice would work again, Noah glanced at each of them and mouthed, "Thank you."

"Ashur, get that sail up," Farna said. "Let's get out of here as soon as we can. Zain, give me a hand with those boxes."

Aterre put his hand on Noah's arm. "I thought we'd lost you. Emzara would've killed me if I came back without you."

Hearing her name brought a smile to his face and he closed his eyes. *Thank You, Creator.* After several more breaths, Noah struggled to a sitting position with Aterre's help.

"Whenever you're ready, I'll help you to your bunk."

CHAPTER 25

Havil — Noah's 45th year

So big." Noah put his hand on his head, wincing ever so slightly as the bruising in his chest from a week earlier reminded him to move slowly.

"The city or that building?" Aterre asked.

"Both. I've never seen anything like it."

Farna whistled. "It's grander than I imagined, and I've heard all kinds of stories."

The city of Havil spread before them as the boat sped toward the shore. Still at least a thousand cubits away, the enormity of the place dominated the view. Buildings stretched far down both sides of the coast, but all were dwarfed by a massive stone edifice resting on a hill behind the city.

"What is that place?" Noah asked.

Zain shook his head. "I'd guess it's some sort of administrative building, but it's at least five times the size of our new hall. What else could it be?"

Ashur squeezed his hands together. "Looks like we came to the right place to learn some business tips."

"Just remember, we are not officially representing Iri Geshem," Zain said. "In fact, do your best to avoid mentioning where we're from."

"Understood," Ashur said.

"I think we're going to create a scene." Farna swept his arm in front of him. "There aren't any larger boats out here at all. Just a few solo rigs."

"You would think a city of this size would have some," Zain said. "Maybe Ara is the only one who knows how to make boats like this."

Farna nodded. "We'll need to be extra careful. I'll stay with the ship while you all head into town. Aterre, grab one of the poles and make sure we aren't going to run aground too soon. Ashur, get ready to lower the sail at my word."

Zain picked up his bag and slung it over his shoulder. "Noah and I will seek out a metalworker. Ashur, you and Aterre check out some inns. Learn what you can, and we'll meet back at the boat before sundown."

"Got it," Ashur said.

Farna raised his arm and then swung it down sharply. "Now."

Ashur dropped the sail, and the boat coasted easily toward the shore. A small group of people gathered on a dock, pointing and staring in their direction. Tied to the side of the dock, a narrow vessel bobbed. The waves grew larger as they reached the shallows, and Noah heard them breaking and slapping against the hull.

Farna, manning the rudder, steered them closer to the pier. "Aterre, slow us down. Zain, ask them for permission to dock. If they let us, then you can get off there, and I'll take the boat out and anchor in deeper water for the day."

Aterre jabbed his pole into the water and strained to stop the craft. He pulled it out and thrust it back into the sea, holding them steady and turning them perpendicular to the dock roughly ten cubits away.

Zain stepped up to the bow and cleared his throat. "Peace to you. We are merchants and have come from far away. Is this the city of Havil?"

A young man in a green-hemmed robe stepped forward. "It is. Where are you from?"

"Far to the north," Zain said. "May four of us unload here?"

Confused, the man looked at his fellows and then shrugged. "What's your business here?"

"As I mentioned, we are merchants. We are interested in seeing what your city has to offer." Zain gestured to Noah. "He and I are interested in metalworking while these other two men would like to visit your eateries and an inn. May we dock?"

"I suppose. We don't have any laws against visitors — we've just never had them come from the sea before."

"Thank you, sir."

Aterre and Farna brought the boat up softly against the pier. Noah looped a rope around a post at the end of the dock, and then walked across the deck and gingerly picked up his pack. "Time for another adventure."

Aterre set his pole on the deck and grabbed his own bag. "You feeling well enough for this?"

"I think so. I'll just need to take it slowly."

Farna slapped Aterre on the back. "You boys be careful. I'll see you back here tonight."

Noah nodded. "We'll return by sunset."

Noah followed Aterre as he stepped down onto the dock. Zain and Ashur stood near the men of Havil, conversing in a friendly manner. Noah turned around and looked up at Farna. "Are you ready?"

"I'm always ready." He untied a rope on the mast.

As Farna hoisted the sail, Noah slipped the loop from the post and tossed it on the ship's deck. "See you later." Noah shifted his attention to the men on the wooden dock.

"Thank you for your help," Zain said to those gathered about him.

"You're welcome," one of the men said. "Enjoy our city."

"I'm sure we will," Ashur said.

Noah stepped past the group and joined Aterre. Havil, the greatest city of the south, lay before them. Two small boats, if it was fair to call them that, rested in the water beside them. "Where do we even start?"

Aterre shrugged. "Your guess is as good as mine."

Loud footsteps and creaky wood alerted Noah to Zain's and Ashur's approach. "Did you find out where we need to go?"

"They were most helpful." Zain pointed ahead and to their right. "Noah, you and I will find our metalworkers on the western side of town. And Aterre, you and Ashur will find eateries and inns all around town, especially in the market district just ahead. Learn what you can and meet back here. Be sure to get some provisions for our return trip." Zain took a step and then stopped and turned back. "Oh, and be careful. We don't know who we can trust around here."

They stepped off the dock onto a sandy beach littered with tiny broken seashells. An older couple strolled hand-in-hand and barefooted along the waterline, while a large group of boys chased each other around farther up the shore. Several young people played in the water while a handful of adults watched. Happy to be on dry ground once again, Noah inhaled deeply, but the stitch in his ribs cut it short.

As they crested the beach, Havil's enormity and busyness grew more evident. A wide street ran straight ahead into the city, fringed by an assortment of shops and vendors on either side. A smaller road ran to their left and right, but it was no less busy. People swarmed everywhere and paid little to no attention to the newcomers.

The familiar scent of roasted nuts captured Noah's attention. "Should we eat before splitting up?"

Ashur shook his head. "I'd rather wait until we visit one of the larger establishments, but you two can go ahead."

"Fair enough." Noah motioned toward the vendor selling the fragrant nuts. "Zain?"

"Sure, I could go for some. We'll see you tonight?"

Aterre stopped and gripped Noah's forearm. "Stay safe."

"And you do the same, my friend." He glanced at Ashur, who stood several paces away, and leaned close to Aterre's ear. "Ara wanted me to keep a close eye on him. Watch him and tell me if he does anything unbecoming a city official."

Aterre furrowed his brow. "Ara must have his reasons. I'll be on the lookout. I also plan to ask about a possible slave trade around here. Who knows? Maybe I'll get word about my family." He released Noah's arm. "Farewell."

"I pray your search will be successful."

Noah and Zain purchased some of the sweet-smelling food and enjoyed it as they moved through the town. Along the way, Noah spotted fruits and vegetables he had never seen before. The marketplace eventually gave way to a string of homes larger than Ara's sizeable estate. The doors of the residences boasted ornate designs fashioned out of an unfamiliar yellowish metal. Beyond the final home, rows of young skarep trees in full bloom lined both sides of the street leading to a massive stone wall rising more than 15 cubits high. Spreading far to their left and right, it seemed designed to protect whatever lay behind it, but the expansive opening before them gave the impression that protection was unnecessary.

"This must be what the men at the dock mentioned," Zain said. "We need to go right once we pass through the entrance."

Wide-eyed, Noah stared at his unique surroundings. "I've never seen anything like this."

"Nor have I." Zain looked at the stones high above their heads as they passed through the gap into a sprawling courtyard. "It's certainly impressive."

"That's an understatement. The metalwork on those homes and the stonework of this wall. . . ." Noah shook his head. "Simply incredible."

Zain smiled. "Yeah, but can they match your skill with wood?"

"Based on what I've seen here, I'm sure they can."

"Looks like they hold public gatherings here." Zain pointed to his left. "My guess is that the leaders sit up there."

A massive stone edifice rose to the height of the wall and leveled off at the top, creating a large platform highlighted by a pyramidal structure that rose even higher. Three wide, intricately carved stairways, one on each side and one in the middle, scaled the structure's façade.

"This place is unbelievable." Noah scanned the rest of the square. Opposite their position stood another, taller wall with a large double door placed at its base. Two men stood at attention, one on each side of the opening. "That must be the building we saw from the boat. I wonder how they —" Noah's words stuck in his throat as he spotted a large ska-rep tree in the middle of the expanse, with another guard stationed next to it. He nodded in the tree's direction. "Does that look familiar to you?"

Zain shook his head. "No, but it sure looks strange all by itself. You've seen it?"

Noah scrunched his forehead while staring at the lone tree. "I'm not sure. It seems so familiar, but obviously I've never been here before."

"Come on. Let's find ourselves a metalworker." Zain put an arm on Noah's shoulder and guided him to the right as he continued staring. "It's just a tree, Noah."

Noah broke off his gaze and looked ahead. "I know. I'm not sure why it grabbed my attention like that."

The courtyard stretched for hundreds of cubits in front of them, but was fairly nondescript other than the colossal walls on either side. Noah glanced back at the tree and another image instantly popped into his mind. *Aterre!* He bit his lip and breathed deeply as a wave of realization swept over him — *the Sepha mark on Aterre*. Was it merely a strange coincidence or did Sepha hold sway over the city of Havil too? Noah looked at the large ceremonial platform again and a chill shook him as he thought about the activities that might be held there.

"The metal shops are supposed to be just beyond this wall," Zain said.

"I'm glad we're almost there."

They walked through an opening on the western side of the square that matched the one they had entered moments ago. And just like the other entrance, this one featured skarep trees along the road. Noah's stomach tightened as he considered the evil these might symbolize. Still, he had not seen any hard evidence of Sepha's presence, so he forced himself to focus on the task at hand.

The street descended into a small marketplace, far different than the one near the beach. Instead of vendors peddling all sorts of food, the buildings featured a variety of silver, yellow, and black metals fastened to their wooden sides. Dark smoke billowed from the roofs of the shops, filling the air with an acrid odor.

"I think we've found it," Zain said.

Noah nodded. "Well, this is why we came all this way. I hope they can help us."

Zain gestured to the first building on the left, which was considerably larger than the rest. "Why don't we start with this one?"

Noah stepped forward and opened the door for Zain and then followed him into the shop. The pungent smell from outside intensified, as did the temperature. A high-pitched clanging echoed from the back of the shop at regular intervals.

"What can I help you with?"

As his eyes adjusted to the darkened room, Noah discerned the figure of a man several cubits away. He seemed to be nearly a span shorter than Noah but very strong.

"We're interested in talking to someone about a metal called iron," Zain said.

"Let me check if the boss has time." The muscular man turned and took a few steps. "Hey, Boss, there are a couple of men who want to talk to you."

"I'll be right there," said a man working next to a hot furnace. He struck a metal rod with a thick hammer a couple of times, turned the rod, and repeated the process before setting the mallet down. Next, he plunged the metal into some water, and as the water briefly sizzled, steam rose in the air. As the man strode toward them, he grabbed a cloth from a shelf and wiped the sweat from his face and brawny shoulders. He smiled broadly as he sized Noah and Zain up. "What can I do for you?"

Zain bowed slightly. "My name is Zain, and this is my friend Noah."

"I'm Tubal-Cain. It's good to meet you."

"It's good to meet you as well," Zain said. "I'll get right to the point. We've heard that the people of Havil have learned how to work with a metal called iron, and that it is much stronger than copper. Based on what I see in here, I assume the rumors are true."

"Yes, it's much stronger than copper."

Noah pointed to the spot where Tubal-Cain had been working. "Is that iron you were working with?"

"It sure is." Tubal-Cain wiped his face again and set the cloth on a nearby workbench. He picked up a metallic bar that was about a cubit long, a handbreadth wide, and less than a finger tall. "Here, look at this."

Noah grabbed the metal and ran his fingers along its surface. "It is heavy. You said it's stronger than copper?"

Tubal-Cain grinned. "Try to bend it."

Gripping each end of the bar, Noah exerted downward pressure on the ends while trying to force the middle to bow upward. He increased his force until his ribs reminded him of his recent brush with death. The metal would not budge.

"Use your knee," the assistant said.

Noah glanced at Tubal-Cain who gave him a go-ahead nod. Noah put the middle of the bar above his knee and grunted as he strained to push both sides down. The bar held fast. He gave up and nodded at Zain. "Much stronger."

Noah set the bar on the counter next to a small, shiny figurine. He touched the yellowish ornament. "May I ask what this is made from? I've never seen a metal that looks quite like this before today. It has an appealing quality to it."

"We call it gold. It's pretty common around here."

"Is it strong like iron?" Noah asked.

181

Tubal-Cain chuckled. "No, it's very soft. Sounds like you must not have it in your city. Speaking of that, where are you from?"

"We've traveled from the other side of the sea to find out more about iron," Zain said.

Tubal-Cain raised an eyebrow. "All that way for iron? What do you need it for? Weapons?"

Zain shook his head. "We've no need of weapons where we're from."

"Truly? I wish I could say the same about Havil — that's what a lot of our iron is for."

"Why?" Noah asked. "Do you have enemies?"

"No foreign enemies, but we arm our guards to keep the peace within the city. We've grown so quickly in the past decade that we've had to triple the number of troops." He shrugged and looked at his assistant. "Guess that's good job security for us."

The other metalworker nodded. "Indeed."

Noah stretched his fingers to relieve the minor cramping in his forearms. "So where do you find —" The door behind him swung open. Noah turned to see four armed guards file into the shop. Instinctively, he backed up and stood next to Tubal-Cain.

The guards wore the same uniform he had seen on the two standing by the massive door in the courtyard. Long light brown leather tunics with strategically placed pieces of shiny armor attached to them covered the troops from their thighs to their shoulders. One man stepped forward and removed his helmet. He stood tall and dropped his gaze. "Sorry for the intrusion, Master Tubal."

"No need to apologize, Kenter. What do you need?"

The man's eyes drifted from Noah to Zain before settling back on Tubal-Cain. "Four men arrived in our city asking where they could find the ironworkers."

"Have they done anything wrong?" Tubal-Cain asked.

The soldier shook his head. "No sir. The king would like to speak to them and welcome them to Havil."

Tubal-Cain crossed his arms. "And why would the king trouble himself with four men inquiring about metal?"

The man furrowed his brow. "Metal? No, it's not that. It's how they entered the city. The men came from the sea. "

"How is that possible?"

"They arrived on a large boat. The king is curious about their vessel and wants to invite them for evenfeast."

Tubal-Cain turned to Zain. "Did you come on a large boat?"

Zain nodded, and Noah easily read the disquiet in his face. "Yes, sir."

"And the other two men?" Kenter asked.

"They are merchants," Zain said. "They stayed in the marketplace to visit some of your inns and to purchase supplies for our return trip."

The soldier gestured for Noah and Zain to follow him. "We'll take them to the king."

Tubal-Cain held up a hand. "Hold on, Kenter. We were in the middle of a good discussion. I'll take them myself. You can look for the other men if you'd like."

"As you wish, Master Tubal." Kenter turned and led his men out the door.

Curious, Noah gave the blacksmith an inquisitive look. "If you don't mind me asking, why do the king's guards take orders from you?"

Tubal-Cain smiled. "Oh, didn't I tell you? I'm the king's son."

CHAPTER 26

I'm heading out for the day," Tubal-Cain said to his assistant. "Why don't you finish what you're working on and take the rest of the day off too?"

The burly man's face lit up. "Really? Thanks, Boss. I'll see you tomorrow."

Tubal-Cain nodded. "Greet your family for me." He opened the back door of the shop and gestured for Zain and Noah to move past him.

Noah shaded his eyes as he stepped into the sunlight. "Thank you for showing us the rest of your forge and for explaining where to look for iron and how to separate it from the rocks."

The king's son moved alongside them and guided them to a trail that led straight to the giant stone wall. "I'm glad I could help. It would be a shame for you to travel so far and not find answers." He stopped and looked up, rubbing his bare chin with his thumb. "You know, if my father would allow it, I would be willing to accompany you back to your city and train some people to work with iron."

Stunned by his offer, Noah noticed that Zain appeared to be equally surprised.

"Do you really mean that?" Zain asked.

"Of course. I've never been very far from here before. Just to a few small nearby towns and the mines."

Zain held up both palms. "And how much would it cost us?"

Tubal-Cain motioned to the enormous edifice rising before them. "Cost?" He chuckled. "My family owns all of this. I think I could manage to cover my own expenses. Well, I may need you to prepare some of my meals. I'm not much of a cook."

"Thank you for your very generous offer. We'll definitely consider it." Zain glanced at Noah, who nodded slowly.

"Fair enough." Tubal-Cain moved quickly toward the wall. "I'll take you to my chamber. You'll need to get cleaned up before meeting my father."

Noah and Zain followed him as he led them alongside the wall for about two hundred cubits. The wall doubled in height before they arrived at a small door. Tubal-Cain pulled a thin metal object from a pocket on the front of his robe, inserted it into a slot in the door, and turned it. He withdrew the object and opened the door.

Noah pointed to the item as Tubal-Cain slipped it back into his pocket. "What is that?"

"Oh, it's a key. Something we invented around here several years ago to lock and unlock doors."

Noah peeked inside the door. "I suppose I'll see plenty of new things this day."

Tubal-Cain grinned. "You probably will. Let's go inside and find out."

Zain and Noah entered the doorway, and Tubal-Cain stepped in behind them. He closed the door and turned a small knob above the handle. "Now it's locked again. Follow me."

He led them through a short hall and then up three flights of stone stairs. The stairway ended at a wide hallway. Tapestries and paintings lined the walls. Sunlight spilled in through openings on the roof and oil lamps burned to light otherwise dark areas.

"We just finished building this whole complex earlier this year. I requested that my room be built near Blacksmith Row. I'm the overseer for all the metalsmiths in town." He gave a goofy smile. "Now I can truly oversee them." He stopped and opened a door on the left. "Welcome to my room."

Noah stepped inside and his mouth fell open as he scanned the spacious room. A large bed rested against the middle of the far wall. Metal weapons hung from the walls along with paintings and technical drawings. In the middle of the stone floor lay a massive furry rug from an unfamiliar creature. "Incredible."

"You like it?" Tubal-Cain asked.

"It's very nice. Just a little bigger than mine." Noah laughed. "Actually, it's larger than my house." Noah studied one of the hanging weapons. "This is extraordinary work. Did you make this?"

Tubal-Cain nodded and reached into a large cabinet set against the near wall. He pulled out two luxurious robes and set them on the bed. "You may wear these tonight. I need to go find out when my father would like to meet with you." He pointed to a door past his bed. "There's a wash closet in there. Go ahead and get cleaned up, and I'll be back soon."

Zain and Noah looked at each other but neither moved.

"It's fine," Tubal-Cain said. "Make yourselves at home. I'll be right back." He closed the door behind him as he left.

"So." Zain kept his voice low. "What did you think about his offer to return with us?"

"I was just going to ask you that. I think he seems very genuine."

"I do too."

Noah glanced at the door. "How would the council react if they knew the king's son returned with us?"

"I'm not sure. I haven't really seen much to be concerned about yet. Our meeting with the king should be quite informative." Zain rubbed his eyes. "If our blacksmith is as honest as he seems, he may be willing to view this trip as if he is simply providing a service for us rather than establishing diplomatic ties. In that case, I would give you permission to accept his offer on behalf of Ara, as long as you understand this is not an official offer from Iri Geshem."

Noah nodded. "I'll think about it." Noah looked at his well-worn wrap. "We should probably wash up if we're to meet a king."

Zain tilted his head toward the washroom. "You go ahead."

"Can you believe this place?"

Shaking his head, Zain said, "I've never even imagined something like this. And our host is so friendly. I wonder if his father is the same."

"I do too." Noah grabbed one of the robes from the bed and strolled into the wash closet, which he soon found out was incorrectly named. The closet was larger than Noah's bedroom. A considerable basin full of water rested on a stand in one corner near the stool. *I've never seen one of those indoors before.* Along the far wall lay a lavish tub. An array of towels hung from a nearby rod. Noah dipped one of the smaller towels in the basin and wrung it out. He quickly undressed and cleaned himself thoroughly. When he finished, he put on a clean undergarment from his pack and placed his wrap in the bag before spreading the towel over the rim of the tub. He held up the ornate robe and examined it before putting it on. A shiny metal sheet on the wall reflected his image. He turned to the side and admired how the outfit appeared on him, although the robe had no belt, so he had to hold it to keep the front closed.

Knowing they may not have much time, Noah opened the door and moved back into the bedroom. "Your turn." He smiled. "Don't get lost in there."

When Zain closed the wash closet door, Noah moved toward the robe cabinet to find a belt. As he reached the animal rug, the door to the hallway opened and he froze.

"Tu, help me out." A young woman stepped into the room and stopped when she spotted Noah. Something about her reminded him of Emzara, and it wasn't just the fact that they were both beautiful. Her light green gown appeared to have been made from the same fine material he now wore. Hanging from the edge of her shoulders down to her ankles, it perfectly accentuated her attractive figure. She scanned from his head to his feet and smirked. "What are you doing here?" The words were more of a demand than a question.

Noah quickly closed his robe and tried not to blush at the awkwardness of the moment. "I'm sorry. I was looking for a belt."

"Where's Tubal-Cain?"

"He said he had to find out when the king wanted to meet with us and then he would be right back. And we're here because he said that we needed to get cleaned up before we could see his father."

"Wait." She pointed at him. "Are you one of the men from the boat that everyone is talking about?"

Noah nodded. "I see news travels fast around here."

"All day everyone has been buzzing about the sea people. That's what they're calling you." She crossed her arms and leaned against the wall. "Where are you from?"

"We're from a small town on the north side of the sea."

"You said 'we.' Is someone else here too?"

Noah gestured to the wash closet. "My friend Zain is getting ready."

She furrowed her brow and looked down as she pushed a lock of hair behind her ear. "Did you say you were from the north?"

Noah nodded. "Yeah, we left a few weeks ago and just arrived today."

She shook her head as if clearing her thoughts. "I'm sorry. I never introduced myself. My name is Naamah." She walked toward him.

"It's very nice to meet you, Naamah." He gave her an easygoing smile. "I'm Noah."

"Noah?" She pushed her lips to one side and gave a puzzled look. The young woman was playful like Emzara too. A tinge of green matching her dress gleamed from large, otherwise brown eyes, and her smooth brown skin dimpled in the middle of her cheek. "I don't ever remember hearing that name before. What does it mean? Wait, let me guess." She twisted a strand of hair around her finger. "Storm?"

Noah chuckled. "No, actually it's quite the opposite, although storm would be more intimidating. My name means rest."

She bit her lip, almost as if she were disappointed. Then she brightened and laughed. "I wasn't even close. Well, Noah, how about I help you find a belt, since my brother didn't leave one for you?"

"Thank you." Noah started for the robe cabinet again and then stopped suddenly. "Tubal-Cain is your brother? Then that would make you the king's daughter."

Naamah gave him a half-smile and nodded slowly.

"Forgive me. Is there a title I should use to address you?"

She snorted lightly and shook her head as she walked to the wardrobe. "How about Naamah?"

Noah breathed a sigh of relief. "That sounds good to me, Naamah."

She reached into the large cabinet and pulled out four stylish belts. She held them up in front of Noah to see which one would match his outfit. She handed him the last one she checked. "This one."

Noah quickly wrapped it around his waist and tightened it. "Thank you."

"Of course."

"What are these robes made out of?"

She raised an eyebrow. "They're silk. You don't have silk where you are from?"

"Not that I can recall."

She placed the other belts back in the wardrobe and then turned to face him. "I wonder if you would be so kind as to help me."

"Sure. What do you need?"

"I was going to ask my brother, but obviously he's not here. I'm trying to get ready for tonight too, but my necklace has a knot in it. Would you see if you can untangle it for me?" She turned her back to him and pulled her hair up, revealing that the neckline in the back of her gown plunged beneath her shoulder blades.

Noah took a step closer and caught a whiff of her appealing fragrance. Her raised arms were well-toned and the skin of her neck and upper back was perfectly smooth. Noah spotted the knot in the necklace and tried desperately to focus on it. Wishing he hadn't agreed to help her, he reached for the knot and carefully avoided touching her. He pulled it back slightly to give himself some slack. With his heart racing, Noah untangled the knot, and while holding a loose end in each hand, he quickly put his left hand over her shoulder and grabbed the end of the necklace with his right and pulled away.

She let her hair down and turned around. "Thanks."

Noah did a double take upon seeing the pendant in his open palm. The image of Aterre's mark flashed through his mind, followed by the memory of the tree in the courtyard. *Sepha!* Noah thrust his hand toward her but avoided making eye contact. "Here you go."

Naamah ran her fingernails across his palm as she snatched the necklace. "Now I can finish getting ready. You really helped me, and I'm glad you're here."

He nodded. "Thanks. It's been quite a trip."

"Well, I hope we can make it even better." She grinned and then turned away. "I'll see you tonight."

As Naamah headed for the door, Noah glanced once and caught her striking figure before averting his eyes. He had already seen more than he should have. He walked over to the bed and sat down on the softest surface he could remember. Noah closed his eyes and Naamah's smile popped into his thoughts. He opened his eyes and stared at the rug. Struggling to block the images of Naamah from his mind, he forced his thoughts back to Iri Geshem and Emzara. He finally relaxed when he could focus on her. *Em, how I wish you were here now.*

Zain opened the wash closet door at the same time as Tubal-Cain entered from the hall. "Is there a belt for this thing?" Zain asked.

Noah laughed to himself as Tubal-Cain hurried to his wardrobe and found the appropriate strap. He retrieved an outfit for himself as well.

"Looks like you both are ready." He walked to Zain and handed him the belt. "I'll wash up, and then we'll go see my father."

CHAPTER 27

The closed golden doors before him stood at least twice his height and were equally broad. Noah marveled at the fine detail displayed in the animals and people engraved on panels. He snorted when he saw his reflection distorted by one of the figures. Just then, the door to his right opened slightly and Tubal-Cain slipped through and closed it behind him.

"How can you even move these things?" Noah asked. "They must weigh as much as an earth shaker."

"They're not quite as bad as they look," Tubal-Cain said. "They are made of wood and overlaid with gold. That's one of the great things about this metal — it can be beaten so thin."

"Fascinating."

Tubal-Cain adjusted his robe. "Okay, they are ready for you. Just a couple of things to remember. First, don't speak unless my father asks you to. He's in a good mood today and eager to see you, so he'll probably be a bit relaxed in this regard. And second, a slight bow is considered a sign of respect here. You ready?"

Noah nodded and then followed his new friend through one of the massive doors. He quickly glanced around the room. Elaborate tapestries and gleaming weapons decorated the room's side walls. White stone pillars with oil lamps attached to their sides lined their walkway toward a small set of black stairs that climbed to the platform against the back wall. On the stage sat the king on a golden high-backed throne. He wore an exquisite robe bedecked with precious stones, and a golden crown speckled with jewels rested on his curly brown hair. Noah guessed the man was probably about his father's age. One woman with long black hair sat on a similar, but smaller chair to his left while another woman with shorter brown hair sat in an identical chair to his right. Both wore daintier versions of the king's crown. Two guards stood at attention on either side of the second step.

Tubal-Cain led them to within a few cubits of the first stair and stopped. "Greetings, Father." He looked to his left. "And Mother." Then he nodded to the other woman.

The king leaned forward. The soft light of the lamps revealed a scar running from close to his nose all the way back to his right ear. "Greetings, Son, how are the metalworkers today?"

"Busy as always, Father, but they are keeping up with demands. In fact, they are ahead of schedule."

"That's good to hear. But I didn't really invite you and your guests here to discuss smithery. Let me meet our guests."

Tubal-Cain stepped to the side. "Please, introduce yourselves."

Zain and Noah bowed slightly as Tubal-Cain had suggested. "Greetings, sir. Thank you for meeting with us. My name is Zain. I'm a merchant, and this is my friend, Noah."

"Zain and Noah, allow me to welcome you to the great city of Havil, the jewel of the sea. I am King Lamech."

Noah raised an eyebrow when the king mentioned his name. He realized that he should avoid drawing attention to himself so he tried to put on a straight face, but he was not fast enough.

"Did I say something you didn't like?" the king asked.

Noah felt all the eyes in the room turn on him. He shook his head. "No sir." His voice came out weakly, so he cleared his throat. "It's just that I had not heard your name until now, so I was surprised to learn that you have such a fine name — the same as my father's."

A small grin crept across the king's face. "Well, then I must agree. Your father has an excellent name." He nodded to the woman on his right. "This is my wife, Zillah." He gestured to the other woman. "This is my other wife, Adah."

Noah wanted to react but remained expressionless. He was a guest here and did not believe it was his place to tell the king that the Creator had established marriage at the beginning as a union between a man and a woman. If the king flagrantly violated such a basic part of God's created order, what else might he be willing to do?

He pulled himself forward and sat up straight. "Are you a merchant as well?"

"No sir, but I do work with them regularly. I am a shipbuilder."

"Are you?" The king raised his head and smiled. "Then I have found my man. Did you build the boat that you came in on?"

Noah nodded. "I was part of the crew that did."

The king pointed up and to his left. "I have only seen it from the roof. It's too far away to for me to really know much about it, but I've heard reports. Is it true that you crossed the sea in the ship with five people?"

"We didn't really cross the sea." Noah drew a semi-circle in the air with his finger. "We had to stay pretty close to the shore."

"Why? If it floats, which it clearly does, why can't you go straight across?"

Noah nodded. "We could've done that if the water remained calm the whole time. But the joints aren't strong enough to survive in stormy seas. The boats are really made for running the river. That's the reason we made the trip to your city."

The king tilted his head slightly to the side. "What do you mean? Havil only has a few tiny boats. How can we help?"

"We heard that you had figured out how to use a metal much stronger than copper, and that it might be useful for making stronger joints. We decided to find out if the rumors were true." Noah glanced at Tubal-Cain. "That's how we met your son."

The king stroked his chin slowly as he eyed Noah and then Zain. "Son, you have spent time with these men. What is your impression of them?"

"I haven't known them for long, but I believe they are honest."

"Indeed." The king pointed at Noah. "How can I purchase a boat like the one you brought here?"

"Well, you could order one and we would build it in our shipyard. Or —" Noah looked at Zain who nodded in return. "You could send an ironworker with us to teach us how to use iron."

"A boat in exchange for a blacksmith?" The king pursed his lips and seemed to consider the offer.

Tubal-Cain glanced at Noah and his eyes brightened. "Father." He stepped forward. "I'd like to volunteer to travel with these men and teach them."

The king raised an eyebrow. "Who would supervise the smiths here?"

Tubal-Cain stood tall, exuding confidence. "Demek could do it. He's ready."

"And why would you want to go?"

"As you know, Father, I've never really traveled anywhere before, except for the mines and the nearby towns. I would like to see some more of this world." Tubal-Cain scratched the sizable muscle on his upper right arm. "Perhaps I could find other metals while there."

"Perhaps." The king turned to Noah. "How long would it take you to build me a ship like the one you have?"

Noah looked up as he counted on his fingers. "It takes about five whole moons to build the boat, plus up to one whole moon of travel each way."

"Seven total?"

"Eight, sir. There is another I must add to the total. I am getting married soon after we return."

The king grinned. "Congratulations, young Noah."

"Thank you, sir."

He extended an arm toward each wife and let out a short laugh. "As you can see, I like marriage. So in exchange for my son's services, you would deliver a boat like yours to these shores in eight whole moons?"

Noah glanced at each of the man's wives; neither seemed to find his joke funny. "Yes."

The king leaned back and looked at Tubal-Cain's mother. "Zillah, how many whole moons until the festival?"

The woman hesitated before speaking, apparently searching for the answer. "Just shy of eight."

The king pointed at Noah. "If you can guarantee delivery of my own ship like yours before the festival, then my son can go with you."

Tubal-Cain clasped his hands together. "Thank you, Father." He looked at Noah. "Will you have room for me and all my gear?"

"How much do you have?" Noah asked.

"Well, besides some personal items, I'll need to bring a load of iron pellets and a full complement of tools."

Noah shrugged. "We should have enough space."

"Great," Lamech said. "Return in time for the festival, and you will be our honored guests."

"That sounds like quite an honor, sir," Zain said. "Thank you."

"You're welcome." The king stood abruptly, allowing his decorative robe to fall onto his throne. He motioned toward a large open door on the side of the room opposite of where they entered. "Instead of spending all evening in here, I'd like for you to join us for evenfeast." The two guards and Lamech's wives followed the king down the stairs. He approached Noah and warmly clapped him on the shoulder. "Come."

Noah walked with the king. The man was a little shorter, but his broad shoulders, barrel chest, and thick arms made him quite intimidating.

"You never said where you were from," Lamech said.

Noah grinned. "That's because the king never asked. We are from a small city on the other side of the sea."

"I gathered as much. What's the name of your city? I wonder if I've been there."

"You've been on the other side of the sea?" Noah asked.

"Of course. I was born in the city of Enoch."

They walked into another spacious room. A long dining table stretched across the middle of the floor. Ten chairs lined each side, although only about half of the places were set with silver dishes and golden drinking vessels. Ornamental oil lamps hung above the table. A large purple curtain draped from the ceiling to the floor above a low platform in the middle of the far wall. As Noah marveled at the richness of the room, Lamech continued.

"My father was heir to the throne of the Nodite Empire, but his younger brother wanted the throne, so he framed my father for murder." The king stifled a cough. "We were exiled and decided to move far away from Nod. Sadly, my father became very sick and died along the way."

"I'm sorry," Noah said.

Lamech held up a hand as if to tell him it was in the past. "I moved to Havil and soon became involved with the town council. The city grew rapidly so we had to keep building. The council must have seen something in me. About five years ago, they decided to make me the sole ruler. It's hard to believe how much Havil has changed since we arrived. It's now the greatest city of the South."

"From what I've seen, it's a magnificent city."

The king gave him a sly smile. "Just wait until you see what else we have to offer."

A guard ushered Noah to a chair on the near side of the table. "Remain standing until the king is seated."

Noah watched as the king stood behind his chair on the far left until his wives reached their respective spots on either side of him. Lamech motioned for the women to sit, and then he followed suit. Noah sat to Tubal-Cain's right, and an empty spot remained to Tubal-Cain's left, between him and his mother, Zillah. A guard directed Zain to a chair across from Noah, with two open spaces between him and the king's other wife.

Lamech cleared his throat. "Noah and Zain, we would like to thank you for joining us for evenfeast. But before the meal is served, we have prepared a little entertainment."

A guard entered the room behind Noah. He hurried to the king's side and whispered something.

Lamech nodded. "Bring him in."

A second guard led Ashur into the room and directed him to sit near Zain.

Ashur, wearing a new outfit, bowed to the king before taking his seat. "Thank you for allowing me to join you for evenfeast, sir."

"We want to thank you for visiting our city. It's the least we can do as your hosts. I understand that you are a merchant as well."

"Yes, sir. I run an eatery and inn back home."

"And what did you think of Havil?"

"Marvelous. Spectacular." Ashur shook his head. "I don't know if I can find the right words."

Lamech chuckled. "I'm glad you enjoyed it. I understand your companion was not with you when my guards located you."

"Yes, that's right." Ashur gave him a half smile. "He left to take a load of supplies back to our boat. His loss. I'm sure he would've loved to be here."

"Well, maybe next time. Now for some entertainment." As the wife to his left turned around in her chair, the king turned and gave two loud claps.

Young twin boys dressed in elegant gold-trimmed robes stepped out from behind the curtain. The first carried a thin wooden rod, and strapped to the front of the other boy was a wide wooden tube with some sort of animal skin stretched across its top. They took their places along the wall on the edge of the platform.

Tubal-Cain leaned close to Noah. "My little brothers."

With his hands, the second boy beat rhythmically on his instrument. After a few moments of steady pounding, the other lad put one end of the wooden rod in his mouth and covered some of the holes in the top of the instrument with his fingers. As he blew into the rod's end, a high-pitched but soothing sound echoed through the room. The twins continued to play in perfect harmony. Noah had never heard such pleasant music, and it was even more impressive to hear it from children who could not have been more than six years old. Eventually, their tune ended and everyone at the table clapped.

The king extended an arm toward the boys. "My sons. Outstanding as always."

The boys nodded in acknowledgment and then started into a new and much faster song. The curtains parted slightly and four women moved through the opening, their dancing seamlessly synchronized with the music. Wearing different colored veils and dressed in fine matching silk gowns that revealed more than Noah believed to be appropriate, the women moved in ways that exuded sensuality. From left to right, they donned red, yellow, blue, and purple, respectively.

Not wanting to appear rude, Noah tried to make it seem as if he were paying attention. He looked past the women at nothing in particular.

Just then the music became softer, and a powerful and captivating voice rang out from behind the curtains, which slowly parted farther as the singer came forward. She moved effortlessly to the center of the platform, almost as if she were walking on air. Her soft brown skin complemented her light green silken gown and veil, which, like the outfits of the dancers, revealed too much of her flawless figure. Everything about this young woman seemed perfect. Incredibly, the loveliness of her voice surpassed her arresting beauty.

Temporarily lost in the enchantment of the moment, Noah became conscious of the fact that he had seen her outfit before. *Naamah.* He blinked when he realized he was gaping at her. Closing his mouth, Noah looked away and quickly checked to see if anyone else had seen his reaction, but they were entranced too. He chanced another glimpse at

Naamah, and her eyes met his. With considerable effort, he broke contact and willed himself to focus on the twin musicians instead. He smiled as he watched the young maestros, wondering how the boys could be so skilled at their age.

The song eventually came to an end, and Noah joined in the applause. The twins set their instruments down and sat between their mother and Zain. Two of the dancers moved around the table and sat to Noah's right, while the other two sat next to Ashur, who enthusiastically greeted them. Naamah strutted behind her father and sat between her mother and Tubal-Cain.

Servers quickly moved in and placed a variety of food in front of each person. Lamech's large plate included an array of fruits, and two fish. Noah shifted his eyes to his own plate, trying to hide his confusion and disgust at the meat before the king. *Eating animals? Does he follow any of the Creator's ways?* Relief swept over him as he realized the plate set before him contained only an assortment of spiced grains and colorful fruits and vegetables, some of which he recognized only from the marketplace that afternoon.

Lamech introduced the twins, Jubal and Jabal, to their guests. "And this beautiful young woman is my daughter, Naamah."

Naamah smiled congenially at Zain and Ashur as they acknowledged her. She turned to Noah, and her eyes glistened as she flashed a smile. "It's wonderful to see you again, Noah."

"Likewise," Noah said. "You're a fantastic singer."

"You've already met?" the king asked.

Naamah bit her lower lip and nodded rapidly. "Yes, Father. I went to Tu's room earlier, but I found Noah there instead. He told me that they came from across the sea."

"We've already heard much about it," Zillah said.

Tubal-Cain placed his hand on Naamah's shoulder. "Amah, you'll never guess what lies in my future."

She coughed. Noah thought he saw her shoot a glance at her father before focusing again on Tubal-Cain. "Hmm?"

"I'm going back with them to teach them how to use iron."

Her eyes shot wide open. "What?" She leaned forward and looked past him at Noah. "Then you're taking me too."

Tubal-Cain laughed. "Why would you want to go?"

"Because I've never traveled anywhere before."

"But I need you here," Lamech said. Noah turned away as the king shoved rectangular flakes of fish into his mouth. *It looks like woodchips.*

"For what, Father?"

"To plan the annual festival."

Naamah held her palms up. "But that's not for another seven whole moons. How long is he going to be gone?"

"They agreed to bring me a boat like theirs before the festival," Lamech said.

"It's not fair." Naamah crossed her arms and pouted.

Noah quietly let out a sigh of relief, then he wondered at himself and frowned. Naamah had done nothing to deserve his disapproval. *Maybe it's the Sepha pendant.* He looked across the table to see Ashur enjoying a lively discussion with the dancers.

"Can't someone else do the planning this year?" Naamah asked.

"You'll be 35 years old," the king said. "It'll be your first one as an adult, and you'll have so much to do. The whole city will be watching for you."

An adult at 35? Noah rubbed his forehead. *So many differences here.*

She leaned toward her father. "What if I came back early?"

"How would you do that?" Lamech asked.

"You could send a couple of guards with me, and we could walk or ride back."

Tubal-Cain snorted. "Do you know how far it is?"

She scowled at him. "I don't care. I want to go."

"I don't want to speak for their city," Tubal-Cain said, tapping a finger against his lips. "I don't know if it's possible, but maybe they can send her back on another ship and return with more of my supplies. I don't know how long it might take to locate some iron there, so I'd like to have as much as possible."

Lamech took a sip of his drink. "What do you think, Zillah?"

The woman studied her daughter. "I've learned by now that if she wants something bad enough, then it's best to stay out of her way. Tubal-Cain can look out for her until it's time for her to come home."

The king leaned back in his chair and shook his head. "Fine. You can go too, but I'm sending two of my best guards with you."

Naamah squealed in delight. "Yes. Thank you, Da."

Lamech smiled at his daughter and then shifted his gaze to Zain, but pointed at Ashur. "What's his name?"

Zain elbowed Ashur to draw his attention away from the dancers. "It's Ashur, sir."

Ashur spun quickly in his chair and faced the king. "Sir?"

"You said that you own an inn?" Lamech asked.

Ashur nodded. "I do."

"Is it a nice place?"

Ashur gestured to the spacious room. "It's not like this, but it's one of the finest places in the city. I'd be happy to host your son, daughter, and guards while they are in town, if that's what you were going to ask."

"That's precisely what I had in mind."

Noah searched for a way to prevent this plan from becoming final. "Sir, may I point out a difficulty with this idea?"

Naamah fixed her gaze on Noah as concern spread across her face.

"By all means," Lamech said.

Noah scratched the side of his head. "I don't mean to cause offense, but I don't think we have enough room on the ship to accommodate your daughter and two guards."

"I think we can make room for them," Zain said. "As long as Tubal-Cain's supplies don't fill up the entire cargo hold, we can set up some sleeping quarters below deck."

Noah furrowed his brow but conceded defeat. "I'm not sure, but we can try to rearrange things tomorrow to see if there will be room."

"That sounds fair to me," Lamech said. "Now let's eat."

CHAPTER 28

Naamah stepped around her brother's many crates full of tools and iron pellets, and left the small curtained-off area in the hull. Although she was not accustomed to such tight sleeping quarters, she was thankful for the privacy. Tiptoeing as quietly as possible to avoid waking her guards, she slipped up the steps to the main deck. She arched her neck, glad to be able to fully stand, and looked around. The deep hued sky, strewn with a myriad of stars, beckoned to her like an old friend while the moon hung low and large as if it longed to be near. Having dropped to the mild temperature she liked best, the evening air filled her lungs, and she succumbed to the dangerous invitation the wind gave as it softly whispered through her hair and the light folds of her dress. She smiled, knowing that the elements were on her side and would accentuate her beauty tonight. Looking over her left shoulder, she saw her brother and the farmer along with two others from Iri Geshem; all were engrossed in a game of sorts. She scoffed at the raucous noises they were making near the stern and headed toward the front of the ship.

Her foot caught on something and she stumbled forward, barely staying on her feet. "Oops." She put a hand up to her mouth. "I didn't see you there."

Noah, lying flat against the deck, lifted his head slightly off his arms. "Oh. Evening peace, Naamah. I meant no harm."

"Please, don't get up." She waved him back to his more comfortable position, her many bangles starting a cheerful chorus. "It was my fault. Mind if I sit?"

Noah shrugged before resting his head back against his crossed arms. "Not at all."

Naamah settled close to him, where she was sure to been seen and hardest to ignore. She laid a hand gracefully on her knee and dipped her shoulder ever so slightly toward him. "What are you doing here?"

"Watching the stars. This is the perfect evening for it."

"Mmm, I completely agree. It's absolutely enchanting out here." She gave him her most engaging smile.

"Indeed. But I'm also using them to track our movements. Right now, we're heading east."

"How can you tell?"

Noah pointed to his left just above the horizon. "See that bright star over there?"

"Yes."

"That one always leads north, so since it's to our left, then we're pointed east." Noah returned his hand behind his head.

His muscles bulged and shifted as he moved. *The physique of a warrior.* Not for the first time since meeting him, she recalled the words of the seer: *"A storm brews in the north, with thick, dark clouds, vexing your father. But a ray of sunshine pierces through it, lighting up your face."* The words had become like a litany, running through her mind again and again, shaping her thoughts and even her dreams. Now the question that had plagued her for weeks returned: *Could Noah be the storm as well as the sunshine? Maybe he doesn't have cause to harm my father yet, but I could give him plenty of reasons.*

Since their voyage began, she had searched for insights about him, but he seemed to go out of his way to avoid her. She was surprised he had not fled to the safety of the other men's company in the stern. Perhaps he was finally abandoning his reticence. Excitement rippled through her. The more she gleaned of his character, the more she was drawn to him, and not just as a means to further her ends.

Eager to extend this unexpected chance to be near him, she leaned in, letting her eyes widen in what she'd long ago realized was her most irresistible look. "What else do you learn from the stars?"

Noah quickly looked at the entirety of her and paused as he swallowed.

She hid a smile. *So he likes what he sees.* By shifting her long frame occasionally, she forced his eyes to keep peeking at her. He discussed names and how travelers used the stars' locations to keep their bearing. Stifling a yawn, Naamah blinked and tried to look interested. Suddenly, the ship hit a small swell, and she used the unexpected motion to her advantage. Feigning a loss of balance, she hitched forward and placed her hand firmly on Noah's chest as if to regain her equilibrium.

"Thank you." Allowing her thumb to lightly stroke him in the same spot, she let the curtain of her hair brush against his torso and peered at him through her lashes. "I'm glad you were there. I'm still learning how to steady myself on one of these."

Noah shifted away and sat upright. "You get used to it. The pitching and rocking become barely noticeable after a while."

Concealing her displeasure, she smiled demurely. "It's been several weeks and yet I'm still clumsy, while you manage so well."

"You don't seem clumsy to me."

She blinked slowly and tilted her head. "It's easy to feel at ease around you. Are you always this nice?"

"Ha. You should ask Aterre; he'd tell you the truth."

"Well you've been nothing but kind to me this whole time. I'm so glad I've come. I'm thrilled to see new places." Her fingers extended to their full length, as if they too could not contain their excitement. She almost brushed against Noah's hand with hers and he looked at the near contact before turning his attention back to her face.

"I know what you mean," he said. "I couldn't wait to see more of the world than the tiny corner where I grew up."

"And now, here you are."

"Yeah. I would've never thought I'd get to come this far in so short a time."

"You're a driven man, full of greatness. Noah, I —" She paused and looked down as if suddenly shy.

"What is it?"

She traced the edge of her garment and let the silence do its work. "Tell me."

She smiled inwardly. "You and I are cut from the same cloth." Holding up her hem to make her point also revealed the skin just past her knee. She released slowly, letting the fabric flutter back — not quite into place. "We both long to know what's out there and to make something of ourselves. And" — she dropped her voice to a whisper, forcing him to lean closer to hear — "I confess, I also want to know you in a deeper way. I can see that you're not entirely indifferent to me."

"Naamah, I should —"

She softly put her finger on his lips. "Let me finish, please. Maybe it's out of place for so young a girl to speak this way, but I think we'd be good together as" — she gave him an alluring glance — "as husband and wife."

He gently placed her hand away from him. "I'm getting married once we return to Iri Geshem. I thought you knew."

She drew in a sharp breath. "No, I didn't." Silence took over once more as she pushed emotion aside and rapidly tried to find where her advantage lay. She chose to play the innocent victim. "You've been so attentive, I thought — I guess I thought you felt the same as I do. I thought you found me beautiful." She bent toward him. "Don't you think I'm beautiful?"

"Naam — uh, you certainly are. That's not it. It's just that —"

"You're promised to some girl," she interrupted. "I get that. But it's such a shame. You're ambitious and focused, and with your passion and my position, don't you see how far we could go? I have the money to finance your dreams. You'd have your ships and we'd sail the world, always searching for the next adventure. And we'd have each other; we'd have it all."

"Naamah, please listen. I did promise myself to Emzara, but it's not something I dread. I love her and long for her. I never meant for you to think that you and I had a future together." Noah stood, smoothed his wrap so it hung back down to his knees, and then offered to help her up. She could read concern in his eyes. "I don't know if you've thought much about him before, but Aterre is available."

Pretending not to see his hand, she stood and stepped back. Though her heart seethed with anger and hurt, she forced a little low laugh. "It's hard to notice the moon when it's always next to the sun. But thank you. I wish you — and her — all the best. Please, let's speak no more of my silly nonsense. Shall we see what the others are up to?"

Noah nodded, and she allowed him to pass by her before following him to the rear of the ship. The noisy game had ended, and only two figures remained, each using a large barrel as a makeshift stool. The illumination of a nearby oil lamp revealed the features of her brother. Quickly she hopped up next to him, leaning her head on his shoulder so he could not see her face.

"Amah. I thought you were asleep already."

Forcing her tone to be light, but still hiding her countenance, she spoke softly. "No. It was so beautiful out here, I just had to soak it in."

"Aterre." Tubal-Cain turned to the other man. "Let's catch these two up before you finish your story."

He paused and she sensed his hesitation. "I can leave if I'm not wanted here."

"She's fine."

Noah's words warmed her as he sat next to his friend.

"Your brother asked about my background. I told him I grew up very peaceably with my family in the western part of Havilah, and I was just to the part where all that changed."

For the second time that night, Naamah found her mind wandering. As bits and pieces of Aterre's story floated in and out of her conscious thought, she revisited the words of the oracle. *What good are they now?* Battling the emotions and willing the tears back, she bit her lip and forced herself to pay attention to the farmer's words.

"I thought I was done for. After a desperate attempt for freedom, I slashed into the darkness and felt his blood drip down my arm and heard my attacker yell. He released me to move his hands to where my blade had met his face." Aterre's shoulders shuddered as if the memory haunted him often.

Silence and uneasiness shrouded the group, but Aterre eventually filled in the blanks with quiet, but intensely spoken words. "My dreams often bring back that night and torment me with their vividness. I don't know what I'd do if I really saw him again."

"Have you come close to finding him?" Tubal-Cain asked.

"No. That was seven years ago, and I'm not even searching for him. I'd still like to know what happened to my family, though." He shot a glance at Noah and Noah gave a tiny shake of his head as some meaning passed between them.

Oblivious to the exchange, Tubal-Cain furrowed his brow. "But after everything that villain did to you?"

"I know." Aterre shrugged. "But, because of those events, I fled and ran straight into Noah and his family."

"Literally." The two men shared a small chuckle.

"And it's through them that I've come to have a greater understanding of the Creator." Aterre's voice cracked.

"It's been a long time in coming, I can tell you that." Noah shouldered his friend playfully. "This one is almost as hardheaded as I am. But after ever so many questions, he's pledged to learn and follow the ways of the Creator."

"Good has come out of my tragedy."

Naamah stared at him. How could he talk so? His mother and sisters dead or enslaved, and he sits here rambling about trusting God? Did their lives mean nothing to him? She jumped down from the barrel and moved to stand by the railing, looking out over the black and silver expanse of sea.

The men sat in silence for a long moment before Tubal-Cain cleared his throat. "That's quite a life you've lived already. I'm honored you'd share some of your pain with my little sister and me."

Naamah sneered at the water, then pasted on a smile and turned, brushing her hair out of her eyes. "Yes, thank you for including me, but it's time I headed downstairs. Evening peace to you three."

Later, while she lay in bed, her tears finally made their little paths down her cheeks and opened the door to the inner torrent. Aware of the tightness of the quarters and the thinness of her curtain wall, she sobbed into her pillow, her shoulders silently heaving. The pain of rejection gripped her chest, familiar and fresh all at once. The old scar, the one that appeared the day her father came back with a new wife, throbbed in dull counterpoint to the new wound. *I expect it of him, but not you, Noah.* She balled up her fists. *And how can you so easily dismiss me to the farmer? He's no better than my father. He found a new family too.*

She would never consider Aterre as a potential mate. Though she could never pinpoint why, he had repulsed her from their first meeting. And now — what she'd heard tonight only deepened her revulsion.

Something poked at the recesses of her memory, something about his story. Swallowing her tears, she replayed Aterre's words, but the connection eluded her. *Think.* She stared at the boards of the deck, which comprised her ceiling. *Noah probably worked on those. No, don't go there. Focus on Aterre's story. Why does it bother you?*

She sat straight up and clutched at the thin sheet covering her. *Her father's scar! Could it be?* Wildly, she pondered the ramifications. Seven years ago a new wife was not the only thing her father brought home. *The wound on his face.* And seven years ago, Aterre lost his mother and gave a scar to a raiding man. *Could Father be that man? Impossible. The timing is the same, but Father claimed his was a defensive wound. Of course, he would say that to keep the respect of the people.*

Just when she had convinced herself that these were crazy thoughts, born of her intense emotions from Noah's refusal, she straightened her shoulders and her eyes shot open. *His accent! Aterre's accent is the same as Adah's. My disgust of him is connected to her.*

Pondering the usefulness of this information, she lay back down, her mind spinning.

CHAPTER 29

Iri Geshem — Noah's 46th year

Sweat dripped from his cheek as Noah strained to bend a strip of wood for the hull of Lamech's ship. Just nine days remained before the wedding, and the week-long preparation rituals would soon commence. Looking forward to his two weeks away from work, Noah poured himself into his labors, trying to finish as much as possible before his departure. He held the wooden strip in place as Bakur lashed it to the stern with a temporary leather strap. Eager to use the iron binders, Noah remembered Tubal-Cain's admonition that they would need to be greased to prevent rusting. A hint of doubt touched his mind, but he pushed it away. No matter how much maintenance the new ships required, it would be worth it if they could sail the open sea.

The days had blurred together since their return from Havil, with Lamech's commission keeping everyone busy. Ara added another employee, allowing them to prepare the wood and completely frame the vessel in only two whole moons.

In addition to overseeing that project, Noah helped Tubal-Cain set up his forge — next to the shipyard, at Ara's request. After they constructed the new building, Tubal-Cain spent much of his time venturing to outlying regions around town, searching for a source of iron ore. He also showed Noah how to convert certain lumber to charcoal that would burn hot enough for ironworking. Before long, the blacksmith's shop opened for business.

During this construction, the long workdays left little time to spend with his beloved or their friends and guests from Havil. Thankfully, Naamah had put the awkward moment on the boat behind her, and she got along with the others well, even spending considerable time with Emzara and Adira. Earlier that day, they had all traipsed down to the shore to see her off as she departed for home with her guards on another Farna-led voyage.

"Steady. That should hold for now," Bakur said, bringing Noah's attention back.

"I'll get the next strip." Noah strode over to the stockpile and on the way picked up the container of water and drank deeply. The waves lapped the shore behind him, and a slight breeze carried only minor relief from the day's heat.

"Hey!"

Noah recognized Tubal-Cain's voice and spun to see the blacksmith jogging toward him with a larger than customary grin on his face. "Good news?"

Tubal-Cain closed the gap between them and stopped a few cubits away. "Great news, actually. We found deposits not far from Superglider Cliff. The hills there are full of iron ore."

"That is great news." Noah handed the water to his friend. "What's the next step?"

"It'll take a lot of work to mine and extract the ore, but I'm sure I can find a couple of apprentices that'll help."

"When I have the time, I'd love to learn how to do it," Noah said.

Tubal-Cain crossed his arms. "I'm sure you'd make a great blacksmith, but your woodworking ability is unmatched."

"Thanks." Noah stretched his arms out and yawned. "Maybe after this ship is delivered to your father."

Tubal-Cain shook his head. "I was hoping you'd do that. I don't anticipate moving back there anytime soon."

Noah drew back. "You aren't going back?"

He shrugged. "Maybe someday. I am the king's oldest son after all. But for now, I'd rather live here. I love the smaller town feel, and the people are honest and much kinder."

"That's good news. We'd love to keep you around." Noah grinned and then added. "I guess it doesn't hurt that Adira's here too."

Tubal-Cain snorted but cast Noah a sheepish glance. "She might've factored into my decision, although she doesn't know that yet."

"I'm sure we can figure out a way to let her in on it. That seems to be Aterre's specialty, actually." Noah chuckled and then looked to the side and lowered his voice. "What'll your father say?"

"Well, that'll be the tough part. But if Demek's doing a good job back home, then I'm sure my father will let me stay here for a while, especially if he thinks it'll help his chances at opening up trade opportunities with Iri Geshem."

Noah raised an eyebrow. "Not likely. No offense, but I know the council here doesn't wish to establish —" He stopped as he noticed Tubal-Cain staring at the water behind Noah instead of listening. "What is it?" Noah turned around.

"A boat."

"Usually they unload at the docks on the river." Trying to get a good look at the craft being pushed into the shallows by crewmen on either side using pushpoles, Noah squinted against the light continually reflecting from the water. "There are quite a few people on there."

"Who are they?"

Noah opened his mouth to speak, but stopped when he caught his first clear view of the ship's occupants. His heart leapt and he shot an excited glance at Tubal-Cain. "It's my family! Come on." Sprinting across the beach, he spotted his sister waving her arms frantically as the boat softly ran aground. "Misha!"

"Noah!" Misha jumped up and down.

His parents beamed next to her as they watched Noah dash into the shallow water. His mother held the hand of a very young girl, and to her side stood Jerah and an attractive young woman.

As Noah reached them, Misha leapt off the deck into his arms. He squeezed her tightly, trying to make up for six years' worth of hugs. "I missed you so much." He kissed her cheek.

"I missed you too."

Noah set her down gently in the ankle-deep water. No longer the small girl he remembered, she was now a beautiful young woman. "Where did my little sister go?"

"All grown up." She hugged him around the waist. "Well, almost. Where's Aterre?"

"He's working on a farm right now. He'll be back tonight."

His father climbed out of the boat and turned to face him.

After gripping Lamech's forearm, Noah grabbed his father in a tight embrace, with Misha still latched onto his waist. When they separated, the two men reached up to help Nina out of the boat. "It's been so long. What're you doing here?"

Jerah bounded over the edge of the hull and splashed into the water. He helped the young woman disembark.

Noah raised an eyebrow at the size of Jerah's arms as he lowered the woman to the shore. Before he could comment, though, he recognized her. "Pivi?"

Jerah blushed. "Although you already know her, I'd like to introduce you to my wife."

Noah reached forward and embraced Jerah. "Congratulations, little brother, or not-so-little brother. Looks like all that constant flirting eventually paid off." He stepped back and smiled at Pivi. "And my condolences to you."

Jerah shook his head and laughed. "Same old Noah."

Noah shrugged and winked at Pivi. "When was the wedding?"

She blushed. "About six whole moons ago."

"I'm sorry I missed it. Congratulations to both of you."

"Mother, I need help." The little girl that had been holding his mother's hand stood above them, peering at the water with a determined frown creasing her forehead.

Noah stared at the youngster and then back to his parents. "Another sister?"

His father nodded. "Meet your newest sister, Elina."

"Elina." Noah reached his hands up to her. "Can I help you down?"

Her huge brown eyes locked in on his, but she stood fast.

"It's okay, baby," Nina said. "He's your oldest brother, Noah."

"Noah?" She carefully extended a hand toward him and leaned forward.

Noah swept her up in a joyous embrace and spun around. "A baby sister." Still holding her, he looked at his father. "I can't believe you're all here."

"You think Mother was going to miss your wedding?" Jerah said.

"My wedding?" Noah scrunched his brow. "How could you know?"

"We received a message many weeks ago," Nina said, smiling and taking little Elina from his arms. "We wanted to surprise you."

"Well, it worked." Noah hugged his mother. "I missed you."

She kissed his cheek and squeezed him tight. "It's so good to see you, Son."

Suddenly remembering his friend, Noah glanced up and saw Tubal-Cain standing on the shore watching. He released his mother. "Oh, I'd like you all to meet my good friend, Tubal-Cain. He's the best metalworker around."

As they greeted Tubal-Cain, Noah asked, "So who sent the message to you?"

"Your future father-in-law," Lamech said. "The letter mentioned that he wanted it to be a surprise."

"It sure is. The best surprise ever." He glanced toward the shipyard's taller building. "I'll be right back. Don't go anywhere." Noah sprinted toward Emzara's office. "Em!" Opening the door, he hurried into the darkened lower floor. Momentarily unable to see, he stopped a few steps into the space. "Em!"

"What's wrong?" Emzara padded down the stairs from her office.

"Nothing." He blinked hard and she came into focus. "Come here."

"What's all the yelling about?"

He blinked back tears of joy and grabbed both her hands as she joined him. "You have to come with me right now." He pulled her along as he ran outside. King Lamech's half-built boat stood between them and his family.

"What's the big rush?"

"You'll see in a moment."

"This had better be good. I was right in the middle of something important."

"Stop. Close your eyes. It's better than good." Noah readjusted his grip on her hand and walked backward in order to lead her carefully. "Your eyes closed?"

She bit her bottom lip and nodded.

Noah led her around the ship and toward his family who busied themselves unloading their belongings and chatting with Tubal-Cain. Jerah stood on the deck of the boat and passed a crate to Tubal-Cain on the shore.

"Keep them closed." He gently placed his left hand over her eyes. "We're almost there."

Misha ran toward them. "Noah."

"Who's that?" Emzara asked cocking her head.

Noah stood in front of her to block her view. "Open your eyes." He grinned and stepped aside. "I'd like you to meet my family."

Misha sprinted right into Emzara and wrapped her arms around her. Startled, Emzara held her and giggled.

"This is my sister, Misha. I think she likes you already." Noah put his hand on Misha's shoulder. "Meesh, this is Emzara."

She let go and rolled her eyes at Noah. "I figured that much. It's so great to meet you. Now I'll have two big sisters."

Emzara kissed her cheek. "And I'll finally have a little sister."

Noah pointed to his mother and Elina walking toward them. "Two little sisters."

"Two?"

Noah held his hands up and shrugged. "I was surprised too."

Misha grabbed Emzara's hand and pulled her. "Mother, this is Emzara."

Nina's smile grew even wider. She handed Elina to Misha and then stopped to look at Emzara. "I'm Noah's mother, Nina."

"It's wonderful to meet you, Nina."

Nina pulled her close and kissed her on the cheek. As she released Emzara, her eyes welled up and she looked at Noah. "Oh, Son, she's gorgeous." She grinned as she turned back to Emzara and spoke quietly to her.

Emzara's cheeks reddened but her smile broadened and she glanced at Noah.

Pivi joined the group, and as the women became better acquainted, Noah spotted Ara walking toward the ship. Noah hurried over and arrived in time to introduce him to his father and brother. "Father, I want you to meet my mentor. This is Ara."

Lamech gripped Ara's forearm. "It's great to meet you. Thank you for the invitation."

"I was hoping it'd reach you in time, and that you'd be able to come. You and your family are most welcome here. How is your father, my cousin?"

"Very well." Lamech hitched his thumb toward Noah. "I trust my son has been helpful."

A wry grin crossed Ara's lips. "He's not so bad."

Noah chuckled. "Well, your daughter's opinion is the one that counts." He turned around. "I'll help Jerah unload."

As he stepped back into the shallow water past Tubal-Cain, he overheard Ara. "He does great work. He's very talented and hard-working."

"This is the last one," Jerah said as he lifted a chest and handed it to Noah. "I was wondering if you were going to do some work here."

Noah grunted as he lowered the crate to his waist. "Who do you think built that boat you're standing on?"

"You made this?"

"Not by myself, but I did a lot of it."

"Impressive." Jerah jumped down into the water. "It's really great to see you again."

"Likewise." Noah carried the box to the shore and set it next to the others. "Where are we taking these?"

"My house, but just leave them there. I'll get a cart." Ara walked away toward his office.

Emzara, walking arm-in-arm with Misha, arrived at the pile of luggage with the other women.

Lamech stepped toward Emzara. "You must be my future daughter-in-law."

"And you must be Noah's father." Emzara hugged him. "It's a pleasure to meet you."

"And you as well," Lamech said. "I'm glad we could make the journey for your upcoming covenant."

"How were your travels? And with Elina, too?" Noah asked.

"Quite an adventure. And we met some friends of yours along the way."

"The Zakari?"

Lamech nodded. "We stayed with them for two nights. Great people. They spoke very highly of you and Aterre. They said you were heroes."

"Heroes?" Tubal-Cain cocked an eyebrow. "This sounds like a story I haven't heard."

Lamech explained. "When the boys passed through the remote village of the Zakari on their journey here, the place was attacked in the

214

night and four children were kidnapped. Noah and Aterre helped the Zakari men track down the assailants and rescue the children."

Feeling Emzara's arms wrap around his waist and squeeze him tight, Noah lowered his head, embarrassed. "You'd have done the same thing, Father."

"Perhaps. But young Elam said you risked your life to save him from some crazy man with a knife. He wondered if your cut healed up properly."

Emzara pulled away and looked into Noah's face. "You never mentioned that part."

Noah pulled his wrap up slightly and gestured to the horizontal scar above his stomach. "It's fine."

Lamech put his hand on Noah's shoulder. "I'm proud of you, Son."

Noah held his father's gaze. "Thank you."

"Oh." Lamech reached into a pocket in his wrap and pulled out a small cloth with Noah's name stitched into it. "Elam made this for you. Apparently, he's quite the seamster."

After examining the cloth, he smiled as he thought about his young friend. "How was his arm?"

"It's scarred," Lamech said. "But they said it looked so much better than before."

"That's good to hear."

"They also said our return trip will probably go much faster. The people of Novanam and one of the neighboring towns upriver were nearly finished clearing boulders out of the river and installing a system that will allow boats to sail that stretch."

"That's right," Nina said joining them and standing close to her husband. "Now it won't take as much time for you to come and visit."

"Wonderful. I'd love to show Em where I'm from."

"And then you can make good on your promise to show me a keluk," Emzara whispered.

Noah nodded, staring into her eyes and thinking of how much he enjoyed life with this woman by his side.

"Taht?" Jerah asked as Ara led an animal pulling a wagon up to the pile of luggage.

Noah nodded just as the creature raised her head in recognition of her name.

"You still have this old beast?" Jerah scratched Taht's neck. "It's good to see you again, girl."

As they loaded their belongings, Noah watched as Nina lifted Emzara's hand. "So, newest daughter, I want you to know that I'm here to be of any assistance I can."

Emzara nodded and brushed the corner of her eye. "That'd be wonderful. I'd love to have your help. Thank you." She hugged Nina tightly before both turned to help with the remaining few items.

The cart loaded, Noah came near to his wife-to-be and tried to put his arm around her, but Misha jumped between them and wrapped an arm around each of their waists. He shared a smile with Emzara over the young woman's head, and the three of them walked linked together toward Ara's house, the rest of the crowd following along behind them.

CHAPTER 30

"I finally get to see you. Seems there's hardly been a chance all week." Emzara reached a hand up to Noah's face.

He rested his cheek against her palm. "There's been so much to do and so many people to see."

"You won't believe all the food that we've prepared. And to have your mother here, organizing it all — I can't express how much that's meant to me — how much she's meant to me. I wish they didn't have to leave so soon after the wedding."

"I do too. You know, my mother's quite taken with you."

"Having her around has been so good." Emzara blinked faster. "I —" She cleared her throat and tried again. "I didn't know all that I missed, but this week's given me a glimpse of what having a mother would've been like."

Noah kissed her hand. "You have all the qualities to be a great mother. And after tomorrow. . . ."

She blushed, but then looked back up at him.

Holding her tightly against his chest, he didn't speak for several moments as he took in the softness and eagerness of her gaze. Even the pounding of the waterfall in the background could not rival the intensity of his heartbeat. "Tomorrow."

"Yes."

Forcing himself to pull away from her, Noah gently touched the leather band on her upper arm and then gestured to the landscape around them, softly illuminated by the retreating sunlight. "Five years ago, at this spot, you agreed to be my wife."

A breeze from the cliff's edge danced around them and ruffled through the loose curls framing Emzara's face. "It's remained almost the same."

He scanned his surroundings, taking in not so much the details, but remembering that day, which somehow seemed ages in their past and yet, also felt strangely like only moments ago. He had been so nervous before kissing her for the first time.

"Although tonight, I don't see any pesky supergliders to bother us." Her eyes held the familiar spark of fun and invitation before closing as she pressed her lips to his.

Leaning back, she looked up at him. "No supergliders and now these stones that you've assembled. I can't believe you went to all that work this week."

"I know it's different, but I thought it'd be fitting."

"I love that you seek the Creator's favor for our marriage." She joined her hand to his.

Noah kissed her fingers. "You're one of a kind. Not many girls would want to spend the last night before their marriage sacrificing an animal. And that's just another reason that I love you and can't wait to marry you."

"Tomorrow is simply a day. What's more important than the ceremony is how we'll spend the rest of our lives living before the Most High."

Noah squeezed her palm. "You ready?"

"Yes."

They walked to the altar. Noah's arms still ached from lugging those stones out of the pool, and placing them just right. But the time spent with his father, Jerah, Aterre, Ara, and even Tubal-Cain had been worth it.

Kneeling, he caught the woolly bleater he had tied to a stake a few hours earlier. He quickly flipped it on its back and bound its four legs together before loosening the lead rope. Hating what came next, he paused and looked at Emzara, who shuddered and held her arms tightly around herself before nodding. His first sacrifice came to mind. Though thankful that the motions came easier, it still saddened Noah to watch the animal bleed out and to feel it go limp.

Walking over to the shallows where the water did not churn as much, he bent and washed the blood from his arms. Returning, he lit the high stack of branches and then stepped back to Emzara, receiving the dry cloth she held out to him. Rubbing himself dry, he dropped the cloth and spoke the words that came to him. "Creator of the heavens and earth, we thank You — for the life and mercy that You bestow. We are Yours. Guide us and lead us in Your ways as we walk in them together."

* * * * *

Noah stood alone in the center of a large circle created by the several concentric rings of standing guests, and waited nervously for the formal procedures to commence, officially uniting him with Emzara. The gray mid-morning fog, which gave a soft appearance to their surroundings, exposed at least four rows of people, with close friends and family in the central rings. Standing atop a large, low-lying grassy knoll just outside of town, he slowly turned, taking in the faces of those he loved. Aterre beamed proudly at his friend, and Noah gave him a nod. *I owe you.* Tubal-Cain stood to his left along with Zain and his wife, Kmani. Next Noah looked at his sister, Misha, and the lump in his throat grew. It had been so good to be around her this week and see the young woman she had become. Next to her, Jerah and Pivi smiled with the delighted, knowing expressions that usually accompanied those who recently experienced this ceremony for themselves.

He vaguely noted Nmir, Farna, Fen, and Bakur before he caught the look of approval from his father. Lamech stood alongside Ara on a small, slightly raised platform in the place of honor. Tradition dictated that Lamech initiate the ceremony, and Noah wished it would happen soon. He tried to look past the sea of faces to catch a glimpse of Emzara, but the fog made it impossible. Turning back to face his father, Noah saw him give a slight nod to someone beyond him before stooping at his feet and picking up a large clay jar. *Here we go.*

Solemnly, Lamech brought the vessel toward Noah and held it under his nose. Noah closed his eyes and breathed in the heavy scent of the incense.

Lamech spoke the customary words. "The Creator fashioned our Greatfather Adam out of the dust of the ground and breathed into his nostrils the breath of life. It's by that breath, each of us is alive and gathered today to celebrate this sacred rite."

Noah had heard this retelling of the first man every time the village had gathered to commemorate the union of a new husband and wife, but it suddenly hit Noah that these words were being spoken for him. He turned his attention back to his father's voice.

"Just as the Most High placed Adam in a deep sleep, so we symbolize that today." His father held up a thick cloth and placed it over his eyes.

As Lamech tightened it around his head, a knot grew in Noah's stomach and his knees trembled slightly. He opened his eyes but could only see a small slit of light, not even large enough to discern shapes or colors.

"The Most High said that it was not good for man to be alone. Noah, my son, it is not intended for you that you should be alone." His father placed a hand on his shoulder. "You need a helper." Lamech withdrew his hand and his words grew fainter, and Noah knew his father had returned to his place. His pulse quickened in anticipation, and again he tried in vain to peer beyond the cover. He sensed someone standing nearby and felt small hands working to unwind the cloth at his temples. A hint of Emzara's familiar spicy-sweet perfume reached his nostrils. He smiled and breathed it in deeply.

In soft, clear tones, Emzara said, "I can be a helper fit for you."

As the last strip fell from his face to the ground, Noah blinked and beheld the form of his beloved. His breath caught and he stood in stunned silence. Pulled back behind her head and held in place with two wooden pins he had given her the night before, Emzara's hair fanned out before dropping beneath her shoulders. The colorful wrap Kmani fashioned for her glistened as the scant sunlight reflected off the shimmering beads along the upper hem. Noah's eyes welled up as he regarded true beauty. Slowly, his mind prodded him to respond. Custom offered this opportunity for the man to accept or reject the woman standing before him. He always scoffed at the pause some men had taken, thinking that it would seem long indeed for the woman awaiting the response. Now, standing here, he finally understood the reason for the delay.

He licked his lips. "Here, at last, bone of my bones, and flesh of my flesh." The words leaped from deep inside of him. "You are truly the helper created for me. You are mine and I am yours."

At this juncture, Ara stepped forward with a sealed scroll in his hand. With tears in his eyes, he gave it to Emzara. "I've been saving this for your wedding day. Your mother would be so proud." He looked aside and swallowed. After a couple of deep breaths, he faced the guests. "As the father of this lovely woman, I get to pronounce my own blessing on the couple and initiate their vows."

Ara turned again and placed one hand on Noah's shoulder and the other on Emzara's. "Emz, before you were born, your mother and I prayed that one day you'd unite with someone who loved and served the Creator and loved you more than life itself." He deftly wiped away a tear. "You're everything we hoped you'd become and so much more. I love you more than my words could ever express."

Emzara sniffed. "I love you too, Baba."

Ara squeezed Noah's shoulder. "Noah, I've witnessed your devotion to the Most High, and I know you love my daughter. Will you vow before those assembled today to ever serve the Creator and to remain steadfast in your love for Emzara? And if the Creator blesses you with children, will you raise them to follow His ways?"

Holding Ara's gaze, Noah nodded slowly. "I promise each of those things before you and all those gathered here." He looked down into Emzara's eyes, their faces less than a handbreadth apart.

Ara stood next to his daughter and raised his hands high, "You are all witnesses to the forming of a new couple."

To complete the ceremony, Noah slowly unwound the length of leather cord around his waist and cinched it between himself and Emzara at rib level. He wrapped it around them, causing her to stand closer. As he pulled the cord, the space between them quickly disappeared. Her eyes shone brightly and she blushed. He never wanted to let her go.

She raised her mouth close to his ear. "Most couples wrap it pretty loose."

He winked. "Well, I guess we aren't most couples."

CHAPTER 31

Havil — Noah's 46th year

Naamah glanced in the reflecting plate hanging on the wall near her bed. She grabbed a small pot, and in confident strokes applied the dark contents to the contours of her eyes. Peering closer, she wished the metal disk showed more details. *Does my unhappiness really show as Mam intimated yesterday?* Unable to tell, she brushed on more of the dark liquid, hoping to hide whatever she failed to see. Just then, a knock sounded at her door.

"You may enter." She set down the items and turned to face the newcomers.

Two guards bowed and then stepped aside as one announced, "Your father, the king, wishes to speak with you."

Lamech entered and stood looking around as the guards backed out and shut the door.

You may be in control everywhere else in Havil, but this is my room. She donned a smile. "Da, this is unexpected. What brings you here?"

He remained silent as he continued to look about.

What? Just tell me what you don't like and get out. "Won't you please join me?" She walked over to the window and sat on the end of a long cushion that spanned the width of the opening. Her father followed her, and she was pleased when he sat on the other end.

"Naamah, I'm here to discuss the upcoming ceremony and your role in it."

"Yes, the dancers, I —"

"Where are you with those preparations?"

"There will be 13 of us total and —"

"You know this is a very big part of the celebration."

Frustrated at being cut off, Naamah clenched her teeth and let out a breath. "Yes, I —"

"I'm not sure that you do. This will be unlike any other festivity we've ever hosted at Havil. This will be the one that all future celebrations will hope to live up to. I have grand plans for it."

Realizing that her father just wanted to hear himself speak, she folded her hands in her lap and tried to look interested as he talked of his accomplishments. He droned on of how he not only made himself great, but also made the city of Havil rise to prominence.

"People look to us to lead the way, and that's what this ceremony will do. Up until now, Sepha's been an option for the masses, a way of living their life if they so choose." He pounded his fist on the wooden window ledge. "But these people are weak. They have no passion. They just go through the motions of life and if Sepha happens to fit in, then they shrug and allow its presence. But all that must change."

Naamah wondered why he focused on Sepha now since he rarely mentioned it. Sure, many of their guards had been through Sepha training to fight, and the famous tree stood in the square, but to him, it was nothing more than a means to an end. *Just like me.*

"The people have a strong leader." As he spoke, he stroked the front of his impeccable garb, which sported large feathers and gold bangles sewn in tight rows. Lamech smiled as if pleased, "Yes, a very strong leader, but they need a strong belief. And with that, they'll learn strong devotion." He turned his focus away from the city street below and looked at her. "I have something for you, my daughter. This will be part of that new beginning." He placed a necklace in her hand.

Her curiosity building, she looked down. Multiple strands of gold and silver beads the size of her smallest fingernail formed a large teardrop, which featured a large gold medallion at the point. Even though the pendant almost took up the whole of her palm, she imagined how nicely it would look, draped around her neck. The familiar crooked tree of Sepha was beautifully carved on it, but she noticed something else entwined up the trunk and into the branches.

"A serpent, Father?" *Like the seer's.*

"Yes. The ancients tell stories of long ago, when a serpent named Nachash, the wisest and most beautiful of all creatures, offered the knowledge of the gods to men."

"Yes, but —"

"And with Nachash added to the tree of Sepha, we'll have a new, improved religion to offer the people. They can have a better life and as we grow in knowledge, we will grow in power. The two elements are now fused."

Naamah snorted. "You really believe all that stuff about Nachash?"

Lamech arched an eyebrow. "It doesn't matter if I believe it. What matters is that the people believe it. That's why this ceremony is of such importance. We will enlighten the people and open their eyes to the way life could be." He pointed at her. "And you, my daughter, with your dancers, will lead the procession. It's a great honor I'm giving you. Make sure that you live up to it."

Feeling the familiar pressure rise to her throat, she got up and moved toward the small table beside her bed. Thankful to gain some distance from her father, she set the necklace on the low-lying carved wooden square. The ornate designs made her again think of Noah, and her failure to win him. *Don't think about him.*

As if reading her thoughts, her father continued. "Now, tell me about your time in Iri Geshem."

With her back toward him, Naamah rolled her eyes. Knowing that ignoring him was not an option, she slowly returned to her spot, sank back onto the cushion, and exhaled. "It's small compared to here."

"Good, good, I thought so."

"The people were welcoming. Tu really liked —"

"As they should have been to the offspring of a great man. But about the city itself. Was it as grand as Havil? Did it have large gates and walls?"

Naamah looked at him quizzically. "No. No gates or walls."

"And the city leader?"

"I don't know."

"Did he have a place like ours?"

Feeling neglected, as usual, Naamah glared at a spot on the floor and clenched a fist. "I don't know."

"Did you not see him? What of their feasts and marketplaces and weapons?"

She worked to control her response, "I spent most of my time with Tu. And he spent most of his time creating a forge. There wasn't much for me to do."

He looked pleased. "Ah, yes, for all your desire to explore, you realized that I've brought the best part of the world right here at your door."

This place will never be the best as long as you're around. If only Noah had chosen me instead of Emzara. She realized her arms were crossed tightly in front of her and loosened them. *Stop thinking about him.*

"Well then tell me about that young man, Noah. You must have at least seen him. How far along is he with my boat?"

That's right. He's coming back here. Naamah heard her father's voice, but her thoughts remained on Noah. *I don't ever want to see him again if I can't have him. No! I will have him. But how?*

The king placed a heavy hand on her shoulder. "Naamah? Is Noah going to deliver my ship on time?"

"I don't know and I don't care!" She swatted his hand away. "I don't want to talk about the ship or the people or anything else about Iri Geshem. Especially not Noah." She leapt to her feet and paced across the room. "Surely the guards you sent with me have given you all the information you wanted. Now leave me alone. I need to work on the songs I'm singing for the ceremony." Angry, she added as much bitterness to her voice as possible. "So they can be *perfect* for you."

Lamech stood. "Actually, I gave the singing for the ceremony to Navea."

"What?" Naamah stopped and put her hands on her hips. "How could you?"

"She's a lovely girl with a lovely voice."

"I know that. But just because she was one of my dancers when No—" She stopped before completing his name. Her temperature rose as she tightened her fists. "Ahh!"

Lamech cocked his head and watched her closely until she calmed. "This is my decision and it's been made. She will sing."

"But I wanted to."

He scratched his brow. "Yes, but you still get to dance."

"Before I left, I was going to do both. I'm a much better singer than she is."

"That was before. She came here while you were gone, I assume to spend time with you. And I realized that with you being away for so long, she'd have more time to practice. She's been up here several times to perform for guests, and I must say, she's perfect."

Hurt, Naamah backed away. *I need it to be me.* "She's perfect? Or her voice is?"

"What?"

"You just gave her the part because of her looks."

Lamech folded his arms and gave her an incredulous look. "That's ridiculous."

"Oh really?" Her voice grew louder. "Then why ask her to come here so often? Was it really to practice or did she 'earn' the part some other way?"

Lamech's hand flew quickly and struck her face.

Stumbling, she caught herself on the bedpost. She raised her hand to her cheek and glared at him.

"No one speaks to me in that manner. Ever! I'm the king and whether you like it or not, you're my daughter, and you will do what I say." He glanced toward the door.

That hit a nerve. Was there some truth to it? She recklessly proceeded. "What are your plans for her? Make her your third wife?"

"Of course I'm not —"

She was on dangerous ground, yet his anger fueled her boldness. She pushed harder, using what little leverage she had. "What are you going to do with Navea's family? Are you going to raid her house too?"

"What?"

"Murder her parents and siblings just so you can take her?"

"What are you talking about?"

"Watch out. She has a brother."

"Naamah, what on earth is wrong with you?"

"When you go to kidnap her, watch out for her brother. He might just jump out of the shadows and slash you to add a matching scar to your face."

His eyes grew wide and he raised his hand toward her again. "Stop!"

She flinched and ducked. *I've finally gotten to him.*

"What's all this about?" He lowered his arm without striking.

She danced away from him and, drunk on her success, continued. "Oh, let's just say that I met the man who gave you that scar."

He shifted his weight to his rear foot. "I was attacked."

"That's not what he says." She practically sang the words in glee. "You went into their house at night and attacked them. You killed his

226

family, at least that's what he thinks. But I know that you spared his mother since you wanted her for your own. You would've killed him if he didn't get away. He tried to defend them." She pointed to his face and slowed her words to emphasize each one. "And that's how you got that scar. And that's how you got Adah." She folded her arms and smiled smugly. "And that's what I learned on my trip to Iri Geshem."

"Who told you all this?" His voice was cold. "What's his name?"

"I'm not telling. But now you know that I know the truth."

Stepping forward, he came a mere handbreadth away and glared at her. The muscles in his cheeks tightened as his jaw clenched.

A tingle traveled down her back as she caught the fury in his eyes. *I went too far. What price am I going to pay?*

Suddenly, his countenance changed. Lamech stepped back and broke out in laughter.

Confused, she stared. "What's so funny?" Her frustration grew as his amusement continued.

Slowing his laughter, he pointed directly at her face. "You are."

"What did I say?"

He shook his head. "Ah, my little tempest, you're just like me."

Shocked, Naamah drew back. "I'm nothing like you."

"I never realized it before. But like me, you crave power, and you'll do anything to get it. You manipulate people to get what you want." Lamech grinned. "Tell me I'm wrong."

Naamah opened her mouth, but nothing came out when she realized he was right.

Stunned by the revelation that she acted so much like the man she had grown to despise. Naamah sat on the edge of her bed, pouting, and crossed her arms tightly against her body.

"The reason you get so angry with me is because you're just like me."

She shook her head and looked up at him with pleading eyes. *It can't be.*

His smile flaunted his victory. "The difference is that I've mastered it, and you have so much to learn."

Naamah pulled her legs up and hugged her knees, absently tucking the end of her long garment under her feet. Blinking back tears, she tried to focus on the floor.

"You think that I took Adah as a second wife because I desired her, but you're wrong."

She furrowed her brow and sniffed. She had not cried since that night on the boat after Noah rejected her.

"I did it to demonstrate to the world that I'm above the old ways. The ancients claim that the so-called Creator established marriage to be for one man and one woman. Well, I make my own rules. I'm the lord of this land, and *no one* tells me what to do. No man, no woman, and no god sets my agenda."

Lost in her thoughts, she barely heard his boasts. *And Noah's married by now.* Several tears dripped from her cheeks, and she watched them land on the lap of her blue silken gown.

Slowly, he stepped to her bed and sat beside her. "Naamah, I have big plans for you. If you're willing to learn from me." He leaned in front of her to catch her gaze. "If you're willing to learn from and obey me, you'll have more power than you've ever imagined. And you can use it to get whatever you want."

His words echoed in her head. Her eyes flashed and she raised her head. "Whatever I want?"

He put his hand on her shoulder again.

Instinctively, she started to pull away, but then stopped. Perhaps this man she had scorned for so long actually held the solution. She looked at his hand and then raised her gaze to his face, a question in her eyes.

"*Whatever* you want."

Reading the implication in his gaze, she allowed one side of her mouth to curl up.

He squeezed her shoulder. "And that starts with leading the dancing *and* the singing at the ceremony." He rose and moved toward the door.

The conversation was over. Though he was the one walking out, she felt dismissed, and for a moment the old hurt reared. But instead of crumbling, Naamah wiped her eyes and drew herself taller. "What about Navea?"

Pausing, the king looked back, a small, knowing smile on his lips. An ugly smile. "You decide where she fits best." He turned again toward the door. "I need someone I can trust to lead our new religion. Prove your loyalty to me, and I'll make you the first high priestess of Nachash."

Chapter 32

Havil — Noah's 46th year

"Those were amazing." Emzara brushed her fingertips together to remove the salty remains of roasted nuts. "I wish we had them back home."

"I do too." Taking Emzara's hand, Noah pointed with his free hand across Havil's busy marketplace. "Let's check out that one."

"A metal shop? Very well, but then I get to pick the next one."

"We've already been to three that you wanted." Noah pinched her side, then wrapped his arm around her waist and slowed to allow a group of young people to pass before them. "I should get to pick at least one place while we're here." He pulled back so he could glare at her with the full force of his mock indignation. "*And* don't forget, yesterday I took you to that farm with all the unique animals."

Unrepentant, Emzara slipped her arm around his waist and nestled her head against his shoulder. "And I loved every minute of it. I still can't get over that bird that copied all the noises it heard, even speech." She squeezed him tight. "Thank you for taking me on the trip this time."

Noah kissed the top of her head. "I don't ever want to be apart again."

As they approached the shop, he looked back toward the sea and spotted the two boats they arrived in tied to the dock. Unlike the first time around, Noah had enjoyed every minute of the voyage to Havil with his new bride. Once they landed, they had been met by a delegation from

Lamech, who welcomed the group and escorted them to two comfortable guesthouses. Everyone found something to do. Farna agreed to train a few of the king's select men in how to handle their new ship and immediately set about fulfilling that commitment. Zain spent time gathering details about the city's construction. Ashur and the other crew members frequented multiple establishments and markets, while Noah and Emzara simply took in the city together. Tonight, Noah, Emzara, Zain, and Farna would be guests of honor at Havil's annual festival.

Opening the door to the smith's market and then following Emzara inside, Noah expected an acrid odor to assault his nostrils but instead encountered a pleasant berry scent. As his eyes quickly adjusted to the well-lit interior, he scanned the room, surprised to see shelves laden with trinkets with no forge in sight.

"Welcome to the Gallery of Gifts and Gold." Standing next to a counter, the middle-aged woman wore a dark blue wrap, and her black hair draped evenly around her head, except where it was cut in a straight line just above her brows. Her eyes shifted from Noah to Emzara. "How may I help you?"

Emzara shrugged and hitched a thumb at Noah.

"Greetings. I'm looking for items made by Merka the goldsmith."

"Oh, nothing but the finest for your woman, right?"

Noah glanced at Emzara. "Well, she certainly deserves the best."

"Right this way, please." The woman stepped past the counter and moved to the wall along the left side of the store.

As they followed her down the aisle, Emzara glanced at the price of a pikka-sized golden pendant on a shelf. Her hand flew to her chest and she quietly gasped. She looked at Noah and shook her head.

The clerk stopped at the door along the back wall. "We keep Merka's items in a separate space for our wealthier customers." She barred the door with her arm. "Before allowing you into the showroom, I need you to prove you can afford one of the items inside."

Emzara leaned in close to her husband. "If they're more than that pendant, then there's no way we —"

Noah held up a finger, winking at her. He pulled out a tiny scroll from his pouch and handed it to the woman. "Here."

"What's this?" The clerk examined the scroll.

"You recognize the seal?" Noah asked.

The woman nodded. "I do."

"Go ahead and open it." Noah said. "I believe it's addressed to you."

The clerk looked askance at him and then broke the seal. She unraveled the tiny document and quickly read it. "And what's your name?"

"I'm Noah, and this is my wife, Emzara."

The woman smiled at Emzara and opened the door. "You're a lucky woman. The king's son says you may pick any item you wish."

Emzara's eyes grew wide. "Tubal-Cain did this?"

Noah kissed her forehead. "It's his wedding gift to us. He said you'd find the middle shelf particularly interesting." He nodded toward the opening. "Shall we?"

Holding an oil lamp, the clerk led them into the showroom. She reached up and lit a circular metal tray nearly one cubit in diameter. The flame spread around the ring, and the room filled with light.

Emzara's jaw dropped.

Three shelves lined the left, back, and right walls of the space. Resting on the top shelf, massive, intricately designed gold and silver plates, statuettes, and daggers sparkled in the firelight.

"Look at these!" Emzara pulled Noah to the left and pointed to the middle shelf. "Tubal-Cain was right."

Noah watched Emzara gaze in wonder at the wares before her. The amazement spreading across her face could never be matched by works of metal, no matter how spectacular. Finally, his curiosity got the best of him and he turned his attention to the shelf. Dozens of exquisitely crafted golden animals stood before him. Most were recognizable, but there were a few mysterious creatures he could not identify. He shook his head in astonishment at the quality of the work. "Fantastic."

Emzara squealed. "That one!"

Noah smiled when he spotted the item she pointed to. A golden keluk nearly a span in height stood behind several other flawless sculptures. "That's the one you want?"

She grabbed his arm with both hands and nodded. "Absolutely."

Noah turned to the clerk. "I believe she's made up her mind."

The clerk carefully removed the item from the shelf and handed it to Emzara. "Let me get a box to protect it."

As the woman searched for the proper container, Emzara asked, "How much does one of these cost?"

"It's best if you don't know." She held out a simple wooden box lined with soft scraps of cloth, carefully took the statue from Emzara, and gently placed it in the case. "It's also best if you don't let anyone around here see it. Keep it safe." When the figure had been secured, she motioned them toward the door.

Stepping back into the main area of the shop, Emzara grasped Noah's hand. "I don't need to see any other stores." She raised the box before him. "This has been more than enough. Let's just head back to our guest house."

CHAPTER 33

O nly a short walk from the city square, the guesthouse he now shared with Emzara and Zain had been familiar — he recognized the gold-trimmed doors from his previous trip. Noah smiled as he lounged on a cushion in the meeting room of the large guest house. This was a far cry from the cramped quarters on ship.

Emzara slept against his chest. Absently massaging her head, Noah studied the wooden craftsmanship on the trim near the ceiling and the massive railing lining the staircase leading up to their room.

Zain returned from the kitchen with a drink in his hand. He lowered himself into a spot across the low table from Noah. "Looks like the shopping trip wore her out."

Noah yawned. "Me too. We thought it'd be good to get some rest before the ceremony."

"That's not a bad idea." Zain adjusted his wrap as he got comfortable against a cushion. "Noah," he said after a pause. "Do you have any concerns about this evening? I don't get the impression that this celebration will elevate the Creator."

A small knot in Noah's gut twitched and grew tighter. "I was thinking the same thing." Even though he was sure they were alone, he looked around before continuing. "I haven't heard them talk about it, but we know Sepha has influence around here. I told you before about their symbol on Naamah's necklace, and then there's that Sepha tree in the square."

"I thought about skipping the event," Zain admitted, "but I don't want to upset our host. The king's been very gracious, but, between the two of us —" He broke off, his gaze slipping out of focus as if his thoughts had taken him elsewhere. After a moment he gave a single emphatic nod. "We will go and observe. We'll need to be careful. Thankfully, we're leaving in a couple of days, and I can't think of any reason to come back here anytime soon."

Noah opened his mouth to speak, but a knock on the door interrupted his thoughts.

Zain stood quickly. "I'll get it." He strode to the front door and opened it. "Hello."

"Are you the special guests from Iri Geshem?" The man's firm and familiar voice carried through the expansive room.

"Yes, how can I help you?"

"We're looking for the shipbuilder — the man named Noah."

Noah perked up at the mention of his name, causing Emzara to stir.

"Is something wrong?" Zain asked.

"Is he here?"

Noah carefully wriggled away, unsuccessful in his attempt to not wake her. Sleep still clinging to her eyes, Emzara mumbled, "Where are you going?"

"Someone's at the door. I'll be right back."

Zain turned toward him. "Noah, these guards want to speak with you."

As Noah stood he saw Zain back away from the door. "Hey, be careful."

Four guards hastily entered the room and turned their attention to Noah. The leader stepped forward and pulled off his helmet, and Noah recognized him as Nivlac, one of the guards who had accompanied Naamah on her round trip to Iri Geshem. He pointed to Noah and turned to his fellows. "Seize him."

As the three soldiers advanced, Noah backed up but quickly ran out of space. "Nivlac, what's this all about?"

"Did you think you'd get away with it?" Nivlac asked.

"Noah, what's going on?" Emzara asked.

Noah glanced at his wife. "I don't know. There must be some mistake." He ran a hand over his head. "Get away with what?"

Nivlac remained silent until his men cornered Noah. The guard in the center drew his weapon and pointed it at Noah's chest, while the other two each grabbed one of his arms.

Emzara screamed. "What's happening?"

"Why are you doing this?" Noah asked.

Zain stepped in front of Nivlac. "I demand to know what this is all about."

Trying to free himself, Noah twisted and bucked, but the large men held him fast. "What have I done?"

As the guards pulled him toward the door, Nivlac looked straight at Emzara and raised his voice. "Noah, shipbuilder from Iri Geshem, you are guilty of assaulting our princess, Naamah."

"Naamah? Assault? What are you talking about?"

"There is but one punishment for attempting to lie with the princess."

"I never —" A guard struck Noah in the side of the head, causing him to stagger.

"No!" Emzara screamed. "Nivlac, you can't do this. It's not true!"

"Oh, but it is true, Emzara. I saw it with my own eyes on our voyage to your puny city."

"You lie." Enraged, Noah dove toward him but the guards restrained him just before he reached Nivlac. "Ask Naamah. She'll tell you the truth."

Nivlac jerked his head and one of the soldiers landed another blow to Noah's ear. "Don't worry, Emzara. He won't suffer — the execution will be swift. Get him out of here."

"No!" Emzara rushed Noah's assailant and jumped on his back, trying desperately to pull him away from her husband. The man grabbed her arm, bent forward, and flipped her over his head onto the hard floor. She landed flat on her back with a groan.

Zain shoved Nivlac to the side and then slammed into the man who had thrown Emzara, driving him against the door frame. Suddenly freed from one of his captors, Noah whirled in front of the soldier who held him, clutching the man's arm and pulling back with all his might. The force of his spin threw his adversary against Nivlac, and both men tumbled to the floor next to the stairs. Noah dodged a thrust from the guard who had drawn his weapon and now stood between Noah and his wife.

Emzara staggered to her knees. "Noah, run!"

With his back to the door, Noah spun and bolted outside. Sprinting toward the gate, he glanced over his shoulder and saw three men exit the house. His mind raced. *Not the city square — too many guards. Where can I go?* He hurried across the road and ducked between two skarep trees, pausing to draw a few deep breaths before turning right and dashing away from the center of town.

Behind him, shouts rang out, the guards calling out his movements as they gave chase. Noah only half listened, his mind flipping from one plan to another like a fish on dry land. After discarding half a dozen ideas, he decided to hide at the edge of town until nightfall and swim to the boat under cover of darkness. To that end, he turned away from the water and the luxurious homes bordering it, and soon found himself darting between smaller buildings and dodging trees. Before long he encountered a road teeming with crowds moving in both directions. Noah turned onto it and tried to lose the men trailing him among the masses of people.

His heart pounding and lungs burning, Noah glanced back to see two of his pursuers step into the road and turn in his direction. Rapidly surveying his options, Noah cut in front of an animal pulling a tall cart and walked ahead of it until an opportunity to sneak away presented itself. He did not need to wait long. From the opposite direction, a large beast reminiscent of Meru lugged a bulky wagon with several passengers aboard. Noah waited for it to pass and then immediately snuck behind it and bounded down a narrow alley between two buildings.

Rancid air filled his nostrils and he soon realized its source. Garbage and rotting food filled the huge containers lining the alley. Pulling his wrap across his face to block some of the odor, Noah squeezed between two of the receptacles and pressed himself tight against the wall. Struggling to catch his breath, he tried to figure out why Nivlac had falsely accused him. What could he possibly gain from such a lie?

Unable to settle on any explanation, his mind drifted back to Emzara and the soldier who had hurt her. Suddenly a horrifying thought struck him. *Emzara.* She'd attacked the guard. Could they arrest her for that? What if they tried to use her to get to him? Anger welled within him. *Creator, please protect her.*

"Mister, what are you doing?"

Noah searched for the source of the voice. Glancing up, he saw a young boy standing on a balcony above him on the other side of the alley. Noah raised his finger to his lips.

Confusion spread on the lad's face as he looked back and forth between Noah and the busy street. Then his expression changed and his eyes grew wide. Pointing at Noah, he turned to the street. "He's here! Right here!"

Noah shook his head rapidly and then peeked around the edge of the container. Two guards cautiously moved toward him. He took a deep breath and darted out of hiding, the soldiers yelling behind him as they followed. The alley quickly came to a dead end, and the walls around him were too high to climb. He spun to face his foes.

They drew their short swords and stepped a few cubits apart from each other, cutting off Noah's only hope of escape. "There's no way out," the soldier to his right said.

For one fleeting moment, Noah rashly thought to give his life trying to exact revenge. He studied their faces, hoping, but neither was the man who had thrown Emzara. He deflated. The guard was right. There was no escape.

"Put your hands above your head."

Noah slowly raised his hands and put them on his head as one guard placed the tip of his weapon under Noah's chin and the other circled behind him. Out of the corner of his eye, he spotted the man raising his arm. Suddenly, a sharp pain struck the back of his head and Noah fell forward before all went black.

* * * * *

Groggily, Noah opened his eyes. His head throbbed and he felt himself being dragged along by his arms, which were tied together at the wrists. Blinking hard, he scanned his surroundings and recognized the city square, but it was surprisingly empty, given the huge ceremony scheduled for that night. *Am I being taken to the palace?* Noah briefly closed his eyes in an attempt to focus and block out the pain. *At least I'd have a chance to explain myself and Naamah could set the record straight.*

Nivlac stepped into view. "Ah, you're awake. Good." His gaze flicked to someone beyond Noah's head. "Put him down right there."

"Where's Emzara?"

237

His captors pulled him a few cubits farther and then dumped him on the ground.

Nivlac grinned. "You should be worried about yourself. Not your pretty little wife. She'll be taken care of."

Noah's gut clenched. "Why are you doing this to us? You know I'm innocent of the charges."

"I know what I saw." Nivlac crossed his arms and nodded to one of his men. "Put him in position."

One of the men flipped Noah around and pulled him to his knees. "Stay right there."

From his new position, Noah could see the large ceremonial platform, where several dancers practiced a routine. As his eyes darted to his right, he jolted when he realized exactly where he was. The lone skarep tree, the symbol of Sepha, stood just a few cubits away. His gaze traced the trunk upward and then caught on something amiss among the branches. Coiled around one of the lower limbs, an unmistakable sculpture of a serpent wound its way from the branch around the back of the trunk, ending with its hideous face looking directly at him.

Noah shuddered as he realized the true root of Sepha's evil. It was the same source that tempted Greatmother Eve at the beginning of the rebellion.

Moving between Noah and the tree, Nivlac pulled out a large blade. "Hold him fast." He turned his body and gestured to the serpent. "How does it feel, knowing you'll be the first human sacrificed to the Great Serpent in Havil?"

Fear's tendrils started to worm their way into Noah's mind, but quickly dissipated as a peace came over him. Noah held Nivlac's gaze. "You worship the Great Deceiver. I serve the one true God, the Creator of heaven and earth."

Nivlac burst out in laughter. "You believe in ancient stories created by men of the past to control others through fear. But don't worry, you won't even feel this." Nivlac nodded and one of his men slid a box under Noah's upper chest while another looped a rope around his neck and pulled him forward across the crate.

Creator, I'm Yours. Please protect Emzara. Images of his wedding day flashed through Noah's mind. Seeing Emzara with his family behind her brought a smile to his face.

"O Great Serpent," Nivlac said. "We offer this man's blood to you as we seek your favor. May all of your enemies share his fate."

"Stop!" A woman's voice pierced the air. "Don't move!" The familiar voice came from the direction of the ceremonial platform and echoed off the cavernous walls of the square.

Noah twisted his head to see Nivlac standing near him with his blade held aloft, poised to strike. His heart rate skipped forward as the certainty of death came into question once more.

"Stop!"

Beyond his would-be executioner, a woman hurried toward them. *Could it be?*

Nivlac turned and instantly knelt. "Princess?"

Naamah.

The princess stormed forward and stopped just before the kneeling soldier. "What are you doing, Nivlac?"

"This man needs to be executed for a capital offense."

"And what has he done?" She looked past Nivlac and her eyes grew wide. "Noah?"

"Naamah." Noah's voice cracked. *Thank You, Creator.*

"Release him." She folded her arms as Nivlac slowly climbed to his feet. "Now!"

"Yes, Princess." With a gesture, Nivlac ordered his men to comply.

"And just what crime was he charged with?" Naamah asked.

Nivlac looked toward the ground and spoke softly. "For assaulting you, of course."

She drew back in surprise, and Noah's hope flared into confidence. "Assaulting me? Where did you hear such nonsense?"

"On the voyage to Iri Geshem." Nivlac glanced at Noah. "I saw the two of you alone on the ship one night, and then I heard you crying afterward. Anyone who hurts my king's daughter like that deserves to die."

Naamah put a hand under Noah's elbow and helped him stand. She touched the side of his face, her exquisite face twisting in sympathy as he winced. "Are you badly hurt?"

"Just bruised. Thank you for saving my life."

"I'm very sorry about this." She turned around, and her voice grew icy. "Nivlac, how dare you presume to execute someone without orders! You've disgraced yourself and our city. Go back to the palace and confine yourself to your quarters until I can speak to my father about what to do with you."

Nivlac hung his head. "I'm sorry, Princess. I was only concerned about your honor."

"Honor, maybe, but not truth." Naamah took a deep breath. "Did you do anything to his wife or companions?"

Nivlac shot a glance at Noah, who took a step forward, fists clenched. "What have you done with my wife?"

Ignoring Noah, Nivlac focused on the princess. "One of his friends got violent, so we have him locked up. I posted a guard outside their quarters to make sure the others didn't go anywhere until the ceremony. The woman is unharmed."

Noah closed his eyes and turned away. *Thank You, Creator.*

Behind him, he heard Naamah giving orders to one of the other guards. "Go immediately and release his wife and friends, including the one you incarcerated. Reassure them that Noah will be reunited with them soon and that this was all a terrible misunderstanding. They're free to go wherever they want in the city."

"Yes, Princess."

Noah collected himself in time to see the man turn and run toward the large opening to the north.

"And you." Naamah pointed to the remaining soldier. "Take Noah inside, get him cleaned up, and then let me know when he's ready for the ceremony. I have a wedding gift for him before he goes back."

The soldier nodded and offered Noah a small bow as he gestured for Noah to accompany him toward the large doors at the front of the palace.

Noah swallowed, relief warring with resentment in his heart. Focusing on the former, he looked at Naamah. "Thank you, Naamah. I owe you my life."

She winked at him. "Just remember that."

CHAPTER 34

B^{e} *calm.* Emzara repeated the words again and again, but still the waves of panic rose and threatened to strangle her. She placed a trembling hand over her heart. "Most High, I won't make it. Guide me as You once walked with my father's relative, Enoch. I can't —" Tears flooded her deep brown eyes and overflowed down her cheeks. "I can't make it on my own." Attempting to wipe away the droplets, she realized it was in vain and sank to the floor, sobbing.

Farna! Renewed hope rushed over her. *Yes, I must find him. He's been here before. Maybe he can help me find Noah.* She stood and gasped at the pain from landing on the floor during Noah's arrest. When the spasm passed, she slid on her shoes and rushed to the front door. Stopping short, she backed up and peered out of the window, scarcely daring to breathe lest she be heard through the opening. A guard stood out front. *Now what?*

Walking past the two opulently decorated front rooms, she hastily pressed on until she reached the hallway adjacent to the kitchen. Her feet clapped against the ornate stonework of the floor. She had marveled at the designs upon arrival, but Emzara now wished for dirt surface so she could move more quietly. A large window at the end of the hallway provided light and fresh air to the kitchen. The aperture stretched from just above Emzara's knees to nearly touch the ceiling. Privacy curtains made of layered lengths of a delicate cream fabric obscured all but faint lines of what lay outside while still allowing in light.

Pulling back one layer, she barely made out the forms of the tall shrubs that lined the garden walk behind the house. She shifted another layer and more details emerged. *There's no guard back here.* Removing the third and final layer, she timidly stepped onto the ledge, glancing both directions before jumping down to the lush grasses below.

The lodging Farna shared with the rest of his crew lay next door. Danger awaited in the open space between the two buildings should the guard out front chance to look behind him. Reaching the corner of the house, she dropped to her knees and peered around the edge. *All clear for now.* Lowering herself even farther into the grass that reached mid-calf, she crawled forward slowly on her belly until she reached the back wall of the neighboring house. Shielded again, Emzara stood and quickly brushed her sore and scratched forearms.

She hurried to a much smaller window than the one she just exited. She jumped and attempted to hoist herself over the chest-high sill, but slipped and fell back to the ground. Determined, Emzara kicked off her shoes and took a few steps back. This time, her momentum gave her the needed boost to hook her right elbow over the edge and grip it with her left hand. Grunting and kicking her feet, she slowly inched her upper body onto the sill. Emzara allowed her legs to dangle as she rested and glanced around the room. Several large pots sat in the far right corner. Immediately below where she clung, a shallow table housed several herbs growing in little containers. *It's the kitchen. And no one's here.*

After a deep breath, Emzara slung one foot up. She heard footsteps coming from within and froze.

Farna appeared in the doorway. "Emzara? What are you doing?"

"Farna, you don't know how glad I am to see you."

The man rushed to help her through the window. Back on her feet, she readjusted the top of her wrap and tightened the fold. Between Farna's concerned look and the relief of seeing him, she felt the tears spring up once more. *Be strong, for Noah's sake.*

"What's going on? Why in all the wide river didn't you use the door?"

Gathering her composure, she shook her head and tried to speak, but her sentences came out forced and fast. "Nivlac and some guards came. They tried to take Noah, but he ran, and I don't know if he got away."

"What?" Farna gripped her upper arms and stared into her face as if he could read the history of the last hour in her eyes. "I don't understand."

Her frustration mounted. "I think they're going to kill him. They took Zain too, because he tried to stop them. They have guards out front now, and I need your help."

He started and released her. Moving quickly, he led her to the front of the house and peered out the window without showing himself to anyone who might be outside. He must have seen the guard because, when he returned to her, his face was grim. "Slow down. Start at the beginning."

She forced herself to take a deep breath, then recounted the main points of everything that had happened.

"Did they say why?"

It was the question she hadn't wanted to consider. She swallowed. "Naamah. Nivlac accused Noah of trying to . . . I can't even say it." She sniffed, trying not to acknowledge the tinge of doubt that had crept into her mind. "Wait, you were there. Did Noah ever . . . act inappropriately with Naamah on the boat?"

"What? No, not that I ever saw. He didn't spend much time with her at all. I even thought at one point that he seemed to be avoiding her." Farna shook his head. "Why would Nivlac say that?"

Encouraged a little by his words, Emzara turned her frustration on herself for allowing a doubt about Noah to find its way into her thoughts.

Farna took her arm and gently led her back toward the kitchen. "Do you know where they're going to take him if they catch him?"

"No. It — it all happened so fast."

"My first guess would be the palace. But if he escaped, he'll probably try to work his way back to the boat." He grunted. "None of this makes any sense. We just need to —"

Loud knocks on the front door caused them both to freeze. "Hide in the sitting room." Farna whispered, nudging her to his right.

Emzara rushed behind a large grouping of indoor plants.

Farna returned to the front and opened the left side of the gold-leafed double doors only a hand's width. "What can I do for you, sir?" His gravelly voice came out completely composed.

"We're looking for Lady Noah. She's not in her estate."

More guards. What have I gotten Farna into? Emzara shrank back and sank to the ground, clasping her legs tightly.

"Why are you looking for her?"

"We have important news for her."

Emzara's stomach tightened into a knot during the speaker's pause, the wait for his next words nearly unbearable. *O Most High, please don't let him be dead.*

"And?" Farna spoke with authority, like a man who was used to having people follow his orders.

"There was a mix-up with her husband and a couple of our guards, but it's all been straightened out. I was sent to find her and report that Noah is well and will be escorted to your specially reserved seats at the ceremony."

Emzara almost knocked over one of the taller plants in her hurry to get to the door. "My husband is fine?"

"Lady Noah." The lead guard's face remained placid, unaffected by her sudden appearance. "Yes. And the palace offers its apologies for the misunderstanding."

"He's alive?" Emzara gripped Farna's forearm for support.

"Yes, and he's being well taken care of."

"And Zain?" Farna asked.

"Your friend has been released and will also be escorted to the ceremony. Speaking of which." He snapped his fingers and one of the three guards behind him rushed forward, holding folded garments. "Garments for your group to wear at the festival. Again, the palace offers its sincerest apologies. To see that no harm comes to you, we'll wait here and personally escort you when you're ready."

He's alive. He's alive. Emzara grabbed the colorful gown from the top and headed for the other guest home, trying to ignore the unsettling sense that she was still under guard in a foreign land. Home had never seemed so far away.

Chapter 35

Walking between two guards along the hallway on the top floor of the palace, Noah pointed ahead. "Is Tubal-Cain's bedroom down there?"

"You've been up here before?" Garun, the other guard who had accompanied Naamah to Iri Geshem, furrowed his brow.

"Just once. I guess I have a pretty good sense of direction."

"Indeed." Garun turned toward a large entryway set into the right wall. He stepped toward a massive wooden door decorated with elaborate metalwork. He rapped sharply three times and waited. When no response came, he cracked open the entrance and called into the room. "Princess?"

So this is Naamah's room. Creator, thank You for sending her at the right time today.

Garun pushed the door open wide. "Follow me."

Like in Tubal-Cain's quarters, a large window flooded the expansive bedroom with light, only Naamah's view faced north, allowing her to see the city below and the sea beyond. Long strips of colorful cloths stretched across the ceiling, creating an interesting starburst pattern emanating from the center of the room. Expensive gowns hung on the near wall next to two expertly painted landscapes, and beneath them stood a low desk with a couple of scrolls and several pieces of jewelry. Covered in cushions and exotic fabrics, Naamah's large four-poster bed sat against the far wall next to a short latticework partition separating the corner from the rest of the room.

"Wait right here," Garun said as they reached the middle of the space. He nodded to the other guard who turned and left the room.

Noah stared out the window at the crystalline waters of the Great Sea. Floating through the room, a light breeze pressed portions of his silk robe against his chest. Thankful for the long bath in the servants' quarters to wash away the grime and stench from his earlier flight, Noah closed his eyes and breathed deeply. Even though they had just arrived two days ago and were to be honored at the ceremony that evening, Noah could barely wait to leave Havil for good.

Remembering Naamah's intervention in the scene beneath the Sepha tree, Noah shuddered as the image of the serpent jumped into his mind. Equally beautiful and grotesque, but all evil, the presence of the Deceiver meant that Havil had grown far more vile than he had imagined. *O Most High, I pray that the people of this city would turn from their perverse religion and serve You alone.*

"Noah. You're looking better."

Noah opened his eyes and turned in Naamah's direction. She stepped out from behind the latticework and moved purposefully toward him. The hem of her long black gown hovered just above her feet as she walked.

"I feel better. I know I said it earlier, but it's worth repeating." Noah bowed slightly. "Thank you for saving my life."

"It's nice to have people indebted to me." She tipped her chin at an angle and softened her gaze upon him. In this light, the green tints in her eyes gleamed strongly. She flicked her wrist in Garun's direction. "Wait outside."

"Yes, Princess." Garun pivoted and marched out.

"I'm just glad I happened to be in the courtyard at the time. We were rehearsing when I saw you."

"Will you be part of the ceremony tonight?" Noah asked.

"Part of it?" A full smile spread across her face. "Father put me in charge. Ten thousand people will pack into that square down there, and I'll be leading the singing and dancing."

"I'm sure you'll do an amazing job." Noah rubbed his wrist, massaging the soreness caused by the rope bindings. "You have an extraordinary singing voice."

"Thank you. It's a very important night for our people." She stood tall, raised her chin, and pulled her long dark hair behind her shoulders. "And for me."

Glimmering on her chest, a golden pendant bore the familiar shape of the Sepha tree, but it was markedly larger than her previous necklace and, on this one, tiny reddish jewels formed the unmistakable shape of a serpent. Noah tried to hide his disgust. "I can see why. Sounds like a lot of responsibility."

"It is. I've never performed before such a large audience." Naamah walked to the window and looked down. "It's filling up. See?"

Noah joined her and scanned the sprawling courtyard below. Droves of people spilled into the expanse through the huge northern and western gates. Several guards stood around the Sepha tree in the center. At the edge of the yard to their right, three stairways led up to the expansive stage for the ceremony. The middle of the platform housed a massive object, perhaps 15 cubits tall, shrouded by a large white cover. *I wonder what —*

Naamah pointed toward the base of the massive edifice. "Down there, that row of seats on the dais between the center and left stairways is where your group will be sitting." Her eyes sparkled as she smiled at him, and she gently brushed his shoulder as she turned and moved away from the window. "We know how to treat our guests of honor."

Noah snorted while searching the crowd for Emzara. "Other than that near fatal misunderstanding with your guards, I'd say that your family has hosted us graciously on both our trips."

"Your people were kind to me. You know, I really enjoyed my stay in Iri Geshem." She paused, and when she spoke again, she sounded a little closer. "It wasn't everything I hoped it would be, but what is?"

Noah shrugged. *Marriage to Emzara.* Staring at the sea, he spotted the two vessels against the dock. "Hey, I can see your new ship from here."

"Noah, about that conversation we had on the boat. I —"

Noah shook his head. "No need to apologize again. It was a misunderstanding." He smiled to himself. "And although I was flattered that you were interested in me, I'm glad we were able to put it behind us." Noah stepped back from the window and turned. "You know, the view from up here is awe —" As soon as he saw her, Noah averted his gaze, and stared at the floor to his left.

Naamah had removed her gown and stood fewer than ten cubits away, wearing only her far-too-revealing undergarments and that profane necklace. "I haven't put it behind us, Noah."

He sensed her moving closer and willed his eyes shut.

"In fact, I'd like to offer you a second chance." She moved around to his right as she spoke. "You were going to say the view up here is awesome. Open your eyes and tell me about the view now."

Stunned by her brazen indecency, Noah stood speechless. He wanted to run, but remembered the guard at her door.

Circling behind him, she ran a fingernail along his bare upper back causing him to flinch and turn his head to the right. "What's wrong, Noah? I know you find me attractive." She traced above his ear while speaking in almost a whisper. "I'm right here. Yours for the taking."

Noah clenched his teeth and took a deep breath. Suddenly, an urge to open his eyes rose from deep inside the recesses of his mind. He shook his head. *No! Creator, give me the strength, please*. He trembled. "I'm already married."

She chuckled softly. "Yes, I know. Emzara is lovely, and we got along so well. That's why I'm willing to be your second wife." Naamah slid the back of her hand along his cheek and then down the side of his neck. "I'll admit, I'm envious that she found you first, but just think, Noah, you could be married to two beautiful women."

"Naamah, please."

She stopped directly in front of him and forcefully pulled his chin to face her, yet he kept his eyes shut. "My father has two wives. Why shouldn't my husband?" She paused. "Look at me!"

Noah shook his head.

She put her finger on his lips and then ran it down his neck to his chest. Grabbing the back of his neck with her other hand, she pulled his head down.

Feeling warm breath on his face, he cracked open one eye ever so slightly and yanked his head back an instant before her kiss could land. "No."

Naamah laughed. "You're proving to be quite the challenge, Noah. That will only make our union that much sweeter."

"I will never be unfaithful to Emzara." Noah stood tall and exhaled. "And I will not sin against the Creator in this way."

A sharp pain struck his cheek, and he realized she had slapped him. "The Creator? You believe those ancient myths? Don't you know who you're talking to?"

Noah cocked his head.

"That's right. I am the high priestess of Nachash. Join me, Noah, and he will guide us into true wisdom and show us real power."

Pity joined Noah's range of emotions. *How can Naamah believe these things?* "I follow the Creator's ways, and I will not turn from them. And if you were truly wise, you'd do the same, instead of following the Great Deceiver."

Naamah's laughter told him she had moved farther away. "Yes, your quaint little village follows the Creator, and what's that done for you? Look at this great city, Noah. Why do you suppose we're so much greater than any other in the world? Because our god is the true source of wisdom. And tonight, the high priestess of Nachash will be revealed."

She stepped close to him and grabbed his hand, pulling it up to her cheek. "Do not deny me. Open your eyes."

Noah steeled himself during a long, awkward silence.

"I'm sorry for hitting you." Her words came out softly. "Seeing you again, here in my room — Noah, I need you."

Keeping his head up, Noah shook it slightly.

Naamah sighed. "Why do you have to be so stubborn? Just imagine all that we can be together. And it can start right now." She shifted her hold on his hand and pulled it toward her body.

Noah yanked his arm back. "Stop."

Her voice turned sullen. "After all I did for you today, this is the thanks I get? You owe me. You said it yourself. If it weren't for me, you'd be dead by now."

"And for that I am thankful, but —"

"Don't you realize I could order Nivlac to finish the job?"

This time the coldness in her tone made Noah shudder. He nodded. "I'd rather die than violate my vow to Emzara and my Creator."

"Aaah!" She slapped him again, her long fingernails scratching the left side of his face.

"Garun, get in here."

Immediately, the guard entered the room. "Yes, Princess?"

"Get him out of my sight and out of the palace."

A strong hand gripped Noah's arm. "Let's go."

* * * * *

Naamah stood still. Her chest rose and fell with her rhythmic, labored breathing. Closing behind Noah, the ornate door represented so much more than its ordinary function. Its bulk seemed insurmountable as it stood in the way of all her hopes for the future. Freely allowing Noah passage back to his life, it kept her trapped.

"Aaaah!" Her yell echoed through her chamber. She ran to the door and pounded it with the bottom of her fists, giving full vent to her anger, welcoming the throbbing pain from her blows. If only it could replace the pain in her heart. Finally tiring, she crumpled to the floor and leaned her back against the door. *How dare he refuse me!* She stared aimlessly at the rug. *He won't get away so easily. I can just have him brought to me after the ceremony.*

Fixing her attention on the black gown that lay crinkled in a small pile in the middle of the room, deep emotions welled within her. Hot tears emerged and descended her dark cheeks. *You're better than this. Don't cry over him.* She wiped back the moisture with her palms, then paused and stared at the site where the seer had pricked her hand. *I haven't lost only him. The oracle deceived me, gave me false hope. Now what? There's no storm from the north to destroy my father. It's all a lie.*

Large sobs racked her body, and she mourned the loss of everything that she had clung to. She gave way to the torrent of tears. Finally worn out, Naamah sat with her head bowed against her knees. Slowly opening her eyes and drying her face, she gazed at the pendant from her father. *Whatever I want? You couldn't even give me Noah. Why should I serve you?* Suddenly angry, she grabbed the chain, ripped it from her neck with a jerk, and hurled it across the room. *I hope you break.*

The adornment struck the narrow section of wall between the window and her bed. It ricocheted off the mud-brick and landed on the low table below. Naamah closed her eyes and leaned her head back, allowing it to hit the door with a soft thud. *How am I supposed to lead the ceremony like this?*

A bright light suddenly assailed her eyelids, causing her to squint hard. Shielding her eyes with a hand, she peeked out to see the brightness originating from the pendant.

Placing her palms on the floor, Naamah winced. "Ow." Gingerly, she got up and walked over to investigate. A small ray of early evening sunlight shone through her window and reflected off the medallion. She picked it up and inspected it. "Hmm, not a scratch."

Shaking her head, Naamah let the jewelry slip from her hand and fall back to the table. The piece landed on the sheet of parchment she had placed there after returning from the seer's house.

A ray of sunlight pierces through it, lighting up your face. The words of the oracle jumped out at her.

She glanced out her window just as the sun disappeared behind a cloud low on the horizon. "Ray of sunlight, hmm." Scrunching her eyebrows, she pondered the familiar words again. "A storm." She picked up the document and held it in both hands. *My little tempest.* Her father's voice echoed in her head. *Why would he call me that? A tempest is. . . .* Her pulse raced as she turned her back to the window. She imagined her father's room on the opposite end of the palace's top floor. *He's on the south side, which would make my room* — She spun and looked out of the opening toward the sea. "The north!"

Holding the page aloft, she softly read aloud. "A storm brews in the north, with thick, dark clouds, vexing your father. But a ray of sunshine pierces through it, lighting up your face." She clasped her hands around the parchment. "It's me. I'm the storm. I'm the one who'll vex my father."

She gazed at her discarded gown and then back at the spot Noah had recently vacated. She snorted in derision. "All this time I thought you were the answer. I don't need you, N—" His name stuck in her throat. With a huff, she grabbed the necklace, retied it, and slipped it over her neck.

She clutched the pendant tightly in her hand and glanced back at the page. *I am the storm in the north.* Slowly she opened her palm and traced her finger along the jeweled serpent. A grin crept across her face. "And you are my light, Nachash." *Allowing her gaze to drift past the adornment, Naamah spotted the throngs of people below assembling for the ceremony.*

"All-wise Nachash, I will follow you. I will perform my best this evening. And I'll be yours." She closed her long lashes and tilted her head toward the ceiling. "Make me great — even more powerful than my father, and I'll devote my energy to you and show the people how to follow you." Opening her eyes, she scowled at the reserved seating near the base of the stage. "And about the one who rejected me . . ." Naamah smiled.

Turning back, she removed the jade dress for the ceremony from the hook where it hung in readiness. As she dressed, she smiled and shook her head at the symbolism. In one evening, her very being had been transformed as starkly as the change from her discarded black gown to the outfit she now donned. Her shattered soul now reshaped itself into her new purpose and new self. She stared at her reflection in the shiny silver plate on the wall. *Even though I might look the same, I hardly recognize myself.* She laughed. "How fitting that this night of all nights, I have truly come of age."

As she finished wrapping the fresh outfit around her torso, someone knocked on the door. Straightening the silk folds, she gathered herself. "What is it?"

The door cracked open slightly. "You have a visitor, Princess."

"If it's Noah, I don't want to see him."

"No, it isn't Noah. He says he's an old friend."

An old friend? "Bring him in."

The guard allowed a tall older man dressed in a dark robe to step past him. The man's right hand held a gnarled wooden staff topped by a golden serpent. "You sent for me, Princess of Havil?"

Having only seen the man in his darkened house, she failed to recognize him until he spoke. *The seer.* She nodded. "Your timing couldn't be more perfect."

CHAPTER 36

In spite of the unsettling afternoon, Emzara smiled as she neared the large north gate. The sun hung low in the sky, casting long shadows to her left. The balmy summer air warmed her skin, but not nearly as much as the news of Noah's safety warmed her soul. The burgeoning crowd scurried out of the way of the two guards escorting her and Farna.

Straight ahead, the lone tree in the courtyard stood defended by the king's protectors. Beyond that, the palace rose high into the air. She studied the giant façade. *I wonder if Noah is in there or already in his seat.*

"This way, please." The guard guided them to the left.

Emzara marveled at the dimensions of everything from the towering walls to the massive platform ahead and sprawling yard around her. An air of enticing mystery and celebration pervaded the atmosphere. As they passed groups of people, she noticed jewelry-clad women who had donned so many trinkets that their bare arms were almost covered in glittering objects. Feeling insignificant, she turned her attention to their guide. "How many people are you expecting tonight?"

The guard shrugged. "It'll be packed."

She raised her eyebrows and gestured to the entirety of the square. "This whole place will be full?"

"It should be. I suspect it won't be large enough to let everyone in."

Emzara looked around again, stunned at the thought of so many people in one place.

Several moments passed before they reached the reserved seating area. To her left, a grand stone staircase climbed up to the top of the massive stage above her. An equally impressive staircase to her right ran from the ground to the center of the stage.

"Right up here." The guard pointed and stood aside to let her pass.

Five short wooden steps led to a decorated platform which held about 20 seats, most already filled. As she reached the top, she quickly scanned the chairs for the familiar form of her husband. "Noah's not here."

"I'm sure he will be soon," the guard said. "In the meantime, I suggest you and your friend take your seats and enjoy the festivities. Help yourself to any of the food or beverages on the table."

Raising her eyebrows, she looked back at Farna. At his reassuring nod, she proceeded to a chair near the waist-high railing. The view from this angle was spectacular. Once she was comfortable, she shifted to observe the people below. "Now that I know he'll be here any moment, I might actually enjoy this." She grinned at Farna.

"Too much fuss for my taste."

As Emzara poured herself some water from the pitcher on the table, the scent of roasted nuts reached her nostrils. She quickly found the delicious items and grabbed a handful as she waited.

The crowd continued to swell. People began to pull out their own food items, and as they partook, laughter and conversation echoed. As time passed, she noticed several hand-sized jars being passed from group to group. Wisps of thin smoke curled up from the center of each. Every time a person accepted the jar, they inhaled deeply before handing it off. Curious, Emzara continued to watch as a rotund man maintained possession of one of the jars and continued to contentedly breathe its contents.

People to the far left began shifting quickly and Emzara peered in their direction to try to understand what was causing such excitement. A muscled man led a beautifully clothed girl to the outskirts of the crowd where a cluster of men stood against the wall. The men yelled to the strong man, and a few tried to touch the woman while she averted her face. Emzara turned away, sickened. *Those men are offering to buy the girl!*

She focused again on the portly man but saw that he no longer had one of the jars. He merely stared in front of him at his outstretched hand and made no comments when a few around him looked as if they were initiating conversation. *How strange. I wonder why he's acting that way?*

A few feet away from him two people cavorted and at one point almost tripped over the man; still he didn't budge. After the pair recovered their balance, their interactions became clear, and Emzara turned her head swiftly, feeling her cheeks warm. She focused on her lap for several moments and determined to restrict her people-watching to the more sedate people seated around her. Zain soon joined them, expression tight, but as the evening sky grew darker, there was still no sign of Noah. Twisting in her seat, Emzara looked every direction for him, doing her best not to recognize anything but the form of the man she knew so well.

A woman in front of her with long black hair turned and asked, "Are you alright, dear? You seem a bit restless."

Emzara knew the woman must have been quite important. In addition to sitting in the reserved seats, she wore an expensive-looking gown and a thin gold tiara rested on her head. "I'm sorry. I'm just waiting for my husband. I thought he'd be here by now."

"Oh, I see." She twisted and patted Emzara's knee. "I'm sure he'll be along soon. He wouldn't want to miss the ceremony."

A loud clang of metal reverberated through the yard. Emzara turned as two large doors at the base of the palace opened, allowing a number of dancing girls to sashay their way toward the center of the square. The leader wore a beautiful jade-colored gown, while the performers trailing her were bedecked in white. Dozens of servants walked beside them, bearing torches to illuminate the scene. Emzara had grown accustomed to the noise of the crowd by now, but suddenly the melodic tones of a musical instrument captivated her. Drums joined, and their sound swelled, drawing everyone's attention to the scantily clad figures weaving their way gracefully in and out of intricate formation.

"You know, I think I've changed my mind," Farna said. "I'm starting to like this place."

"Farna." Emzara playfully hit him on the shoulder.

"I wonder if one of them would want to travel with me." He pointed his large index finger toward the dancers.

Rolling her eyes, Emzara shook her head and struggled to hide her smile. As the dancers reached the tree, they whirled around it, bending low, before righting their torsos, arms outstretched to the heavens. Then suddenly everything paused in dramatic silence. Before long, the drums slowly picked up the pace and volume, causing Emzara's chest to pound with the beat. The dancers leapt into action and wove toward the focal point of the ceremony atop the main platform, each girl following the one directly before her. They slithered first to the right and then left while proceeding to the base of the stone stairs.

"They almost look like a serpent moving on the ground," Farna said.

"Yeah." Emzara watched the procession snake toward the front, and for the first time, she gained a clear view of the woman in the unique gown. *Naamah?* She glanced at Zain and pointed. "It's Naamah."

The serpentine formation climbed the central staircase to the top of the stage. Uncomfortable because of the way their movements accentuated their barely covered bodies, Emzara looked away.

Noah should be here soon. What's taking him so long? Her eyes searched the terrace when suddenly the drums stopped and clear strains of the most beautiful voice filled the air. All the dancers were gone, save one. Although she cared little for Naamah's dancing and attire, the princess's powerful voice captured Emzara's attention. A young boy drew close and accompanied her on an instrument Emzara had never seen before. *This part is beautiful. If only Noah were here to share it with. Most High, bring him soon.*

* * * * *

"I'm very impressed," Garun said. The middle-aged man hurried as he led Noah down the stairs that led to the side door not far from Tubal-Cain's forge.

Still deeply disturbed by Naamah's actions, Noah kept silent.

"We could hear almost everything. I can't imagine how hard it must've been to refuse her — again." He blew out a short whistle. "I admire your convictions."

"Thanks, Garun."

"Thank you for honoring the Creator. I prayed you would remain faithful."

They turned to head down the last flight of steps and one of the knots in Noah's gut loosened. "You follow the Creator?"

"Keep your voice down." Garun reached the landing and unlocked the door. "I'm one of the few around here who still do. But it's becoming more dangerous for us. I fear that things will only get worse after tonight."

"If Naamah's going to lead the people to worship the serpent —"

Garun held up a hand. "That's part of her plan, but I'm afraid she may have more in store for you." He looked around before speaking. "I don't know what more she and Nivlac have plotted, but your arrest this afternoon and the mock execution were just part of a scheme to drive you away from your wife and right to Naamah's waiting arms."

Noah frowned. "Is Emzara in danger?"

"She's safe, for now." He faced Noah squarely. "But you and your people should leave immediately. I wouldn't be surprised if she tries something directly after the ceremony."

"You mean we should walk out during the event?" Noah flexed his fingers to loosen his hands up. "Won't that draw too much attention? We'll be in the front."

Garun nodded. "Try to pick the right moment, though it would be better to create a scene than let the princess detain you again."

Noah grabbed Garun's shoulder. "You should come back to Iri Geshem with us."

"I've thought about it, but I believe my place is here for now." He held Noah's gaze. "If that changes, I know where to find you."

"I'll pray for your safety then."

"Thank you." He pushed the door open. "Let's go. Stay close to me." Grabbing Noah's arm with one hand, Garun drew his sword and held it aloft with the other. "Make way for the king's guard!"

The people near them stopped surging forward and created slight gaps. Garun repeated this multiple times, loud enough to alert those nearby, but not so loud as to create a scene. It took some time, but they finally reached the gate. Behind them tinges of orange streaked the lowest part of the horizon as the sun hid itself for the night. The swarm of people stretched farther back than Tubal-Cain's forge. *I don't think they'll all fit in here.*

Garun continued pulling Noah through the crowd as the last vestiges of sunset faded. Along with thousands of stars, the whole moon lit up the crystal clear sky and bathed the city in its cool glow. On the opposite end of the courtyard, the massive stage rose above the crowds. The swarm of humanity remained quiet, captivated by the song echoing through the expanse. One glance at the woman in green on the distant platform sent chills down Noah's spine. Naamah's magnificent voice, which once

257

enthralled him, now only grated in his ears as thoughts of her brought disgust.

They picked their way through the sea of people toward the north wall, where the crowd thinned slightly. Naamah's song ended with a flurry of drumbeats accompanied by fire and smoke effects. Applause exploded from every direction.

Naamah held out both arms and waited for silence. "People of Havil, thank you for coming to the most important ceremony we've ever held. I am Naamah, Princess of Havil." Her strong voice reverberated against the walls surrounding the throng. "And as you'll learn soon enough, I've recently been given another title, but I'll allow my father to tell you about that."

"Did she get married?" a man next to Noah asked the woman at his side.

"I don't think so," the woman said.

Naamah turned slightly and gestured with both arms to her father on an elevated throne behind her. "I have the honor of introducing you to the most powerful man in the world. People of Havil, this is the reason you came here tonight — to hear from your ruler. Here he is, my father, King Lamech."

The massive assembly roared their approval, forcing Noah and Garun to stop momentarily. People soon chanted the king's name in unison until he stood and motioned for them to be silent.

Lamech stretched his arms out wide. "My people." His voice boomed across the space. "Welcome to our annual Sepha celebration. Tonight is a very special evening for many reasons." With his luxurious robe wrapped loosely around him, Lamech paced as he spoke. "You know that Sepha has been tremendous for our people. Under my rule, and through the disciplines taught by Sepha, we've achieved much in the past few years. Just look at this place." He swept an arm toward the palace to his left.

Cheering resumed along with chants of "Lamech" interspersed with shouts of "Sepha!"

"But I believe we can do more. We must do more." He stopped pacing. "Under my reign, Havil has quickly become the most powerful city on this side of the sea, but we have much to do if we're going to surpass the city of Enoch in the Nodite Empire."

Noah and Garun finally reached the north gate and pushed through the influx of people forcing their way into the congested square. Once they passed the cross traffic, they moved a little easier toward the reserved seating.

"To surpass Enoch, we need to learn all we can about this world. We must commit ourselves to seeking knowledge, wherever it can be found. To assist us in this endeavor, I'm implementing three important changes. First, tomorrow we begin construction on the House of Knowledge on the other side of this wall." Lamech directed an arm to the space behind him. "Our goal is to store all of the world's knowledge in this consecrated place and make it available to you, the citizens of Havil."

Applause broke out again as Noah finally reached the base of the stairway that led up to his spot.

"Thank you for the escort, Garun, and for everything else."

The guard nodded. "Be careful."

Noah gripped his new friend's forearm. "You as well. I hope to see you again." He glanced around. "Just not in this place."

Garun let a half grin form on his lips. "Farewell."

Noah turned and bounded up the wooden stairs. A sheer curtain fluttered in the light breeze, obscuring the guests from the view of those behind them. Noah stepped around the drape and located Farna a few seats away from the edge. Zain took up the chair next to him, and then following an open seat, Emzara. Slipping behind his friends, Noah slid into the empty spot and gently put his hand on her shoulder. "Em."

Emzara spun. "Noah." She threw her arms around him.

Wrapping her in a tight embrace, he closed his eyes and silently thanked the Creator for giving him the strength to resist Naamah. After kissing Emzara's forehead, he whispered in her ear. "We have to leave right now."

She drew back, looked in his eyes, and nodded.

Noah looked around, noting that one of the king's wives sat directly in front of Emzara. He then surveyed the stage.

The king now stood about four steps down the center staircase. "And our quest for knowledge will be greatly enhanced due to our honored guests from Iri Geshem." He pointed toward Noah. "Thanks to the ship they've made for us, we'll be able to travel farther and faster than before." He pressed his palms together and pointed them in Noah's direction with a slight nod. "Thank you."

After a brief ovation, the king continued. "The second change I am making has to do with my daughter, the lovely Naamah." He returned to the top of the platform, where she joined him.

Noah grabbed Emzara's hand and kept his voice down. "We have to go. It's not safe for us here and we have much to discuss. Come on."

"What's going on?" Zain asked.

"I'll tell you on the way. We need to leave the city. Tell Farna."

As Zain spoke quietly to Farna, Noah glanced back to the stage.

Lamech stood in front of the towering covered object. "In addition to being your princess, Naamah will also serve as the high priestess of our enhanced faith." He raised her arm as the citizenry shouted their praise and approval.

Noah looked past the father-daughter duo to the covered object that took up much of the stage. A shiver slinked down his back when he discerned the shape under the cloth. He cupped Zain's shoulder. "Right now."

Noah led his group off the platform and headed for the north gate, while keeping his ears tuned to the king's voice for any warning that their absence had been detected.

"The third change follows naturally from the second," Lamech said. "Sepha taught us great discipline. We learned how to fight and control our feelings. But if we're to achieve a deep understanding of this world, we need call upon the source of that knowledge."

Noah's stomach turned. The Great Deceiver was about to strike again.

"Many of us grew up with the story about the first man and woman being deceived by a serpent. Our ancestors used this story to create rules to control us — to keep us from doing what we wanted and to take away our freedoms. But our ancestors lied to us."

A nervous energy flowed through the crowd. Some of the onlookers they passed seemed confused, while others hung on every word in an attitude of eager anticipation.

"The Serpent wanted to help the first people acquire the knowledge of the gods. He told the truth, but the so-called Creator punished them for their desire to learn. As the years have passed, the one they call the Creator has become weaker and weaker, while the Serpent has grown in power and in knowledge. If we're going to become the greatest people in the world, then we need to serve the god who can lead us to those heights."

Noah turned and tapped Farna's shoulder when they reached the exit. "Head straight to the ship and get it ready to leave. We'll gather the belongings and the others and meet you there."

Farna nodded.

"People of Havil." Lamech's voice resounded more powerfully than before. "You have the distinct honor of being the first people to serve the giver of true knowledge. It is a great pleasure to introduce you to our new god, the Great Serpent."

Wild cheering erupted from all directions.

Noah, Emzara, and Zain stopped at the exit and turned back for a final look.

Naamah's dancers twirled around the cloaked object, while she and Lamech each picked up a rope connected to the covering.

Lamech held his arms upward. "People of Havil, feast your eyes on your god. I give you, Nachash!"

Lamech and Naamah pulled their ropes, and the huge cloth fell from the image. Coated in glimmering gold from its coiled base to its terrifying face, poised as if ready to strike, the towering statue of the Great Deceiver dominated the massive stage.

Naamah faced the multitude. "Bow down in reverence." She turned and fell on her knees before the image. Waves of people in the crowd followed her example.

Tears dripped from Emzara's eyes as she looked at Noah.

"I know." Noah grabbed her hand and pulled her through the open gate. "Come on. We must get onboard as soon as possible. We'll need the Creator's wisdom to stand against this abomination."

Enjoy a glimpse of Book 2 in the compelling Remnant Trilogy

Chapter 1

Naamah twirled, her bare feet tracing the same intricate steps to the dance that she performed earlier in the evening. Tap, tap, tap-tap-tap. In the final steps of the choreography, her toe gracefully patted against the sandstone flooring that lined the gardens on top of the palace. She dipped her left shoulder and glanced over it to where the seer lagged slightly behind, his lanky frame dark against the backlighting of the torches. Laughing, she ran back toward him and swirled around several potted kalum trees, enjoying the spicy aroma their flowers gave off.

"How did I do tonight?" she asked, looking up at him and hoping he approved.

"Very well, my child." The old man lightly patted her cheeks, as a father who was proud of his child would do.

"Did I?"

"Yes, your singing mesmerized the people. Hearing your talent in person was greater than I imagined."

"I'm so glad." Unable to keep still, she spun as they walked toward the waist-high parapet marking the edge of the expansive rooftop garden.

"You're a natural leader, and tonight you received some of the recognition you deserve."

Naamah glowed under his high praise and leaned against the low stone wall. "There were so many people. Look at all the lights below, even this late at night."

They both peered out at the city, which still bustled. Pockets of people moved about the streets below, laughing with their companions and calling out good-naturedly to other groups that passed by. The sheer number of lit windows indicated that the celebratory atmosphere moved beyond the streets. Music and drumbeats sounded out from a variety of places.

She flung her hands wide. "Isn't the city magnificent?"

"It's quite a sight. And you are its only princess."

"Yes, I am. Everyone got to watch me."

"And as priestess." He stroked the serpent image atop his staff. "Introducing them to Nachash was your greatest achievement tonight. Against the backdrop of your talents, the people saw the beauty in following him."

Naamah pressed her hands together and trembled with excitement. "I can't wait for next year's celebration. I'll dazzle them even more."

The seer gave a patient chuckle. "I have no doubts, but listen to me." He grabbed her hands. "Tonight was only a first step for you. With my guidance, you can achieve power you've never dreamed of. The success you now feel — and deserve — is only a glimpse of what is to come."

"More?"

He swept his arm out. "All that you see here — the might of your father's soldiers and the skill of your craftsmen." He shook his head slowly. "It's nothing compared to the power available through Nachash."

Intrigued, Naamah looked up and rubbed her chin, pondering the implications.

"The first time we met I saw greatness and giftedness in you. And power — that few can possess and even fewer will be able to resist."

Naamah leaned in closer. "Show me. Teach me everything."

A crooked smile spread across his lips. "Patience. It takes time. I'll guide you in the ways of Nachash, and as you learn, your power and wisdom will grow."

Hearing the rustle of leaves, Naamah stepped back as she glanced around. "Who's there? Speak."

Nivlac stepped forward from the foliage into the well-lit patio area, accompanied by Tsek, a mountain of a man. Nivlac bowed. "Princess, the king's captain has a message for you." Nivlac retreated to his post a short distance away.

Tsek bowed. "Evening peace, Princess. I'm here on behalf of the king. He wishes to inform you that he's pleased with your part in the festivities. Because of your efforts, the people learned how great of a leader they have. Now they have a god worthy of the leader who has done much to build this city into what it is. And you, Naamah, played a part in that."

Naamah stiffened as Tsek droned on. *It's just like Father to take what should've been a simple compliment and make it all about himself.* Discouraged, she looked up at Tsek's strong jaw line as she waited for him to finish. *Power? Can I really be as powerful as the seer promised? Could I turn Tsek's loyalty to me instead of my father? Imagine that. His own captain following me.* She grinned.

"I'm glad that you're pleased with your father's report of the evening's successes."

Pulled suddenly from her reverie, Naamah blinked quickly, attempting to speed up her brain's responses. "Of course. I'm happy as long as my father is happy."

Tsek bobbed his head. "Do you have anything you want me to take to the king in reply?"

She looked at the seer, who had taken a seat a short distance away, while she searched for the right phrase. Stepping close to Tsek, she brushed an imaginary speck from his broad, tanned shoulder, being sure to let her hand linger longer than necessary. She cast him an alluring look as she backed away. "Tell the king that my victory rests in his vast accomplishments."

Tsek searched her face before replying. "I shall relay that. And may I say that, personally, I thought you were the highlight of the evening."

She flashed him a broad smile. "You are most kind, Tsek. Thank you for bringing words from my father." She dismissed him with a small wave of her hand.

He bowed and looked back at her twice as he walked through the garden.

The seer rejoined Naamah, wearing a slight frown. "That was not the type of power I was alluding to."

With a flip of her head, she tossed her hair over her shoulder. "Oh, I care nothing for him, but it wouldn't hurt to have his complete loyalty." She turned around to look at the city again. "There is, however, someone that I'd like to bring to his knees before me. Do you think you could help with that?"

"Perhaps. Tell me what's on your mind."

"A man slighted me twice. He dismissed me once a while ago and again just today." She let tears gather at the corner of her eyes, playing the role skillfully and without hesitation.

"Would this be the man your guard mentioned this evening? Noah? The shipbuilder?"

She bit her lip and nodded.

"And just what do you want to do?" He gently touched her shoulder.

She wanted vengeance. *But how?* "I, I . . . never mind."

"Capture this man's wife so that he has to beg you for her life."

Once hidden in the recesses of her mind, her darkest thoughts became clear. And yet, the seer spoke them calmly and with even tones, as if he were simply discussing what would be served for the next meal.

Naamah's eyes widened. "How — how did you know?"

The seer looked steadily at her. "I've been trying to tell you that the power I can teach you is beyond anything you've imagined."

Still awed by his ability, she stared into the wrinkled face before her.

"If you're bent on making this man pay, then call your guards to go get his wife. But I must say, you're setting your ambition too low."

She shook her head, brushing off his disapproval. "Maybe I am. But if I put this behind me, then I can focus more fully on what you have to teach me." She raised her voice so that the sentry stationed on the terrace might hear her. "Nivlac!"

Her most dependable guard hurried across the roof and stood before her. "Yes, Princess."

"I have an urgent mission for you."

BEHIND THE FICTION

The first part of this non-fiction section, "Answering Questions Raised by the Novel," is designed to address certain questions that readers may think of during the story. Many of these issues will be apologetic in nature. That is, in this portion of the book, we will respond to numerous challenges raised by skeptics and critics. The goal is that these novels will also help you defend the truth of Scripture.

You may have noticed as you read the novel that several things didn't line up with what you may have expected. This was done on purpose to help break certain stereotypes about Noah and the pre-Flood world that many Christians assume are from the Bible, but aren't actually found there. We want you to see clearly what comes directly from the Bible and what comes from traditions people have developed over the years.

The second feature in this non-fiction portion is what we call "Borrowed from the Bible." Since the Bible only includes scant details about Noah's life and times, we must use artistic license to flesh out his story. We certainly do not wish to be seen as adding to Scripture and understand that these are works of fiction, with the exception of the few details that come straight from the Bible. Some places, we curbed the amount of artistic license taken by drawing from other biblical accounts instead. In "Borrowed from the Bible," we highlight certain events and customs in our story that will be somewhat familiar to those who know their Bibles.

The third special feature is entirely unique to this series. We had the incredible opportunity to work behind the scenes at the Ark Encounter for the past few years. Tim was involved in the planning of nearly every exhibit and was responsible for writing or overseeing all of the content while K. Marie took part in designing various aspects of several spaces on the Ark. We wanted to use our experience to bring this series to life in a creative manner. As such, many of the objects and animals described in the book are on display in the Ark Encounter, so visitors to the theme park can see part of what Noah witnesses in our story. The "Encounter This" section lets the reader know what these items are and where they can be found.

We hope you've enjoyed reading about what may have been, while learning to better discern between fact and fiction.

ANSWERING QUESTIONS RAISED BY THE NOVEL

Did the people before the Flood really live over 900 years?

The Bible tells us that Noah lived to be 950 years, and all of his male ancestors, with the exception of Enoch (365 years) and Noah's father, Lamech (777 years), lived over 900 years. Lifespans of this length are difficult for us to fathom, because people in our day do not exceed 120 years. But how is it possible for people to live so long?

Before listing the various theories to explain such longevity, the reader should be aware that the Bible is not the only ancient text that assigns great ages to the earliest people. The Sumerian King List, from one of the earliest post-Flood civilizations, describes a series of rulers before the global Flood who lived and reigned for many thousands of years. While this fictional list includes people living over 20,000 years and is not inspired by God like Genesis is, such an early document shows that people who lived soon after the Flood believed their pre-Flood predecessors lived extraordinarily long lifespans.

Various theories have been proposed to account for such long lifespans. Perhaps the most popular idea among Christians who accept the ages as accurate is that the pre-Flood world had some sort of vapor or water canopy around it that filtered out harmful radiation and allowed people to live for 900 years. There are numerous scientific problems with the canopy model, and it is not explicitly taught in the Bible but was just one possible interpretation of a passage. As a result, many creationists who once held it have now abandoned it.

Another proposal is that something happened genetically to reduce man's lifespan. In studying the Genesis genealogies, we see two drastic drops in lifespans. At the time of the Flood, life expectancy dropped from roughly 900 down to about 400, based on the small sampling of people mentioned. Then after three generations, the life expectancy dropped to around 200 years. This decrease is often associated with the rebellion at Babel. Then the lifespans slowly dropped over the next dozen or so generations to what we experience today. In support of the genetic argument, one can point to Lamech, Noah's father, who died five years prior to the Flood at the age of 777. Is this a hint that there was some genetic factor in Noah's line that would lead to reduced lifespans? Also, at the time of the Flood, humanity's genetic diversity was reduced to the information carried by eight people. This "population bottleneck" was somewhat repeated at Babel, as a large population was suddenly split into about 70 small groups that went their separate ways. Perhaps these two "bottleneck" events enabled a problem within Lamech's genes to become pronounced throughout all humanity. Of course, Noah still lived 950 years, so this may not be the best solution either.

The answer to why man does not live nearly a millennium anymore may be found right in the Bible's Flood account. Genesis 6:3 states, "And the LORD said, 'My Spirit shall not strive with man forever, for he is indeed flesh; yet his days shall be one hundred and twenty years'" (NKJV). While many Christians believe that the "one hundred and twenty years" refers to a countdown to the Flood, the text does not necessarily make that point, as the Flood is not mentioned for another 14 verses.

A cursory reading has given many people the impression that the "one hundred and twenty years" refers to a new limit on man's lifespan. But how could this be since Noah lived 950 years and his son, Shem, lived 600 years? Before dismissing the lifespan view based on this argument we should consider what the Bible reveals about lifespans from the time the announcement was made until the time it was written down by Moses. The following chart shows the lifespans of the people from Noah to Moses.

Name	Lifespan	Name	Lifespan
Noah	950	Terah	205
Shem	600	Abraham	175
Arphaxad	438	Isaac	180
Salah	433	Jacob	147
Eber	464	Levi	137
Peleg	239	Kohath	133
Reu	239	Amram	137
Serug	230	Moses	120
Nahor	148		

Man's life expectancy from that point in history steadily dropped from over 900 years to 120 years in the 16 generations from Noah to Moses. Lifespans continued to decrease after Moses. Joshua lived 110 years, and before long, it seems that few lived beyond 80 years.

It is quite interesting that the Bible records the ages of the people in the genealogy from Adam down to Moses. As soon as the lifespans decreased to 120 years, the Bible stopped recording how old a person was when they died. It is as if Moses showed the fulfillment of Genesis 6:3 by listing all the ages, but as soon as this passage was fulfilled, there was no longer a need to record the ages. Yes, Joshua lived to 110, but the ages of his immediate ancestors are not given, and there may be another reason why his age was specifically given. The Egyptians of that time believed the ideal age for a person was 110 years. As such, it is rather ironic when Jacob tells Pharaoh that his 130 years had been few compared to his ancestors. Moses outlived this "ideal age" and Joshua reached it.

Also, notice that in modern times we see a handful of people live beyond 110 years, but they do not reach 120. Much more could be said about this issue. Interested readers can learn more from my article, "Did Noah Spend 120 Years Building the Ark?" It is available at http://midwestapologetics.org/blog/?p=1445.

Does this mean that they matured at a slower rate?

When a person lived over 900 years, what would their maturation rate have been like? Certainly a 100-year-old person at that time did not look like a modern centenarian. Noah had children and built an Ark while in his 500s. Another potential clue related to the maturation rate can be found in Genesis: the youngest recorded age of a pre-Flood person having children is 65 (Mahalalel in Genesis 5:15 and Enoch in Genesis 5:21). Of course, they may have had other children prior to the sons mentioned in the Bible, but since Scripture is silent here, we have the opportunity to incorporate some artistic license on this point in the story.

Our novel depicts a person's development into adulthood as taking about twice as long as in our day. The early part of the story revolves around Noah's 40th birthday — when he would be considered a man and have the opportunity to set out on his own. From that point on, a person would age considerably slower, and once they reached about 250 years of age, you could divide their age by 10 to picture how they might look compared to people today. In other words, a 400-year-old man would look about the same age as a 40-year-old man today.

How many siblings did Noah have?

Our story begins with Noah having a brother, Jerah, and a sister, Misha, but these will not be his only siblings in the story. Genesis 5:30 states that after Noah was born his father Lamech lived another 595 years and had sons and daughters — at the very least, Noah had four siblings. The Bible does not specify how many brothers and sisters he had, and it does not name any of them.

We portray Noah as the oldest of Lamech's children, but the Bible is silent on this point as well. Some interpreters have assumed that each of the men listed in the lineage from Seth to Noah were the firstborn sons, but this is highly unlikely. We know Seth was not Adam's oldest child, so there is no reason to assume all the other men listed were the oldest either. Also, Genesis frequently focuses on someone other than the oldest son (e.g., Isaac rather than Ishmael, Jacob instead of Esau, and Joseph rather than Reuben). Noah may have had older siblings, but the Bible says nothing about them.

What does the Bible really teach about Enoch?

In the novel, Noah's great grandfather, Enoch, is a bit of a mysterious figure, and his sudden disappearance gave rise to multiple legends. The Bible sheds just a little light on him. Genesis 5:21–23 tells us that Enoch lived 65 years before his son, Methuselah, was born, and he had other sons and daughters over the next three hundred years. Then verse 24 states, "Enoch walked with God; and he was not, for God took him."

Scripture does not say much else about him, but Hebrews 11:5 clarifies what Genesis 5:24 means. "By faith Enoch was taken away so that he did not see death, 'and was not found, because God had taken him'; for before he was taken he had this testimony, that he pleased God." Enoch was a faithful man who walked with God. This does not mean that he took strolls with his Creator, but that he faithfully followed the Lord.

The final point that we learn about Enoch from the Bible is that he prophesied judgment against ungodly individuals. Jude 14–15 states, "Now Enoch, the seventh from Adam, prophesied about these men also, saying, 'Behold, the Lord comes with ten thousands of His saints, to execute judgment on all, to convict all who are ungodly among them of all their ungodly deeds which they have committed in an ungodly way, and of all the harsh things which ungodly sinners have spoken against Him.'" This is a quote from Enoch 1:9. The Book of Enoch was a popular writing in the first century A.D., but the fact that Jude quotes from it does not mean it should be included in Scripture. It simply means that Jude, whose writing was inspired by God, believed this particular verse was a genuine prophecy.

Much more could be said on this issue, but the important point for our purposes is that Enoch prophesied against wicked people. Approximately 70 years passed from the time God took Enoch until Noah's birth. Our story opens with many people still following the Creator, at least in the region in which Noah lived, but there are reports that certain places have become quite wicked. One of these places is the land of Nod and its primary city, Enoch, named after a different Enoch — Cain's son (Genesis 4:17). We envisioned this city as one of the places that Noah's great grandfather would have prophesied judgment upon the wicked.

What is the difference between land of Eden and Garden of Eden?

Genesis 2:8 states that "God planted a garden toward the east, in Eden" (NASB). The garden is where He put the first man, Adam, and where the Lord made Eve from Adam's rib. It was in this garden that God made two special trees: the tree of life and the tree of the knowledge of good and evil. And it was in this garden that Adam and Eve rebelled against God when they ate the forbidden fruit.

But the garden was just a part of the land of Eden. We do not know how large either one was. And we also do not know where they were located, only that the land was apparently in the east, although some Bible translations have the garden in the eastern part of the land. Many people have assumed that the Garden of Eden must have been in the Middle East, near the Tigris and Euphrates Rivers because these rivers are mentioned in Genesis 2:14 in connection with the garden. However, the description given in Genesis does not match the Middle East since it describes one river flowing out of Eden that divided into four rivers: the Pishon, the Gihon, the Hidekkel (Tigris), and the Euphrates. The modern Tigris and Euphrates Rivers are two separate rivers that come together before emptying into the Persian Gulf. We need to keep in mind that the global Flood described in Genesis destroyed Noah's world and completely reshaped earth's geography. And it would make sense for Noah's family to rename some of the places in the new world after the places they knew from before the Flood.

Was Noah the one to bring rest as Lamech thought?

Upon Noah's birth, his father Lamech uttered the following words: "And he called his name Noah, saying, 'This one will comfort us concerning our work and the toil of our hands, because of the ground which the LORD has cursed'" (Genesis 5:29). Lamech's longing for an end to the Curse on the ground formed the basis of our decision to have Noah grow up on a farm. This verse seems to indicate that Lamech had grown weary of working the ground. And since Noah would one day be required to provide for thousands of animals, it seemed natural to have him learn to grow crops and care for certain creatures at a young age.

Lamech apparently suspected or hoped Noah would be used by the Lord in a very special way, but was his utterance a prophecy, a blessing, or simply an ancient convention appearing frequently in Genesis?

Some commentators (Skinner, von Rad, Westermann, et al.) have suggested that this statement found fulfillment in Noah's discovery or advancement of viticulture (growing of grapes, particularly for wine). It is argued that Lamech's generation did not see an end to the Curse, but they were wiped out by the Flood. So the comfort from the Curse came through wine derived from the grapes. It's difficult to believe that Lamech's words would be fulfilled in such a seemingly trivial manner. Of course, these scholars do not truly view Lamech's words as being prophetic, and generally see them being attributed to Lamech after the fact.

Henry Morris viewed Lamech's words as a prophecy, although there are significant problems for this view. First, the text does not indicate that his words were prophetic, nor is Lamech ever cited as a prophet. Second, if it was a prophecy, how was it fulfilled? How did Noah provide comfort (or rest) from the work and toil of people's hands? All the remaining people in Noah's and Lamech's generations died in the Flood, except for those on the Ark. Obviously, the Curse was not lifted.

Two plausible fulfillments could be considered, but they do not seem to match the text. First, a massive amount of wickedness was washed away from the earth during Noah's lifetime, but so were all of Lamech's family members except for Noah and seven others. So how was the Flood a comfort to "us" from Lamech's point of view? Perhaps he was speaking of his family in general — Noah would bring relief/comfort/rest from the vast wickedness on the earth. With the restart after the Flood, certain effects of the Curse were lessened, yet the Curse on the ground remained, as did death and man's wickedness.

The other view is that Lamech's words pointed forward to the Messiah, Noah's distant descendant. Certainly, Jesus is the One who will do away with the Curse and bring comfort, but Lamech's words seem to imply something that would happen in Noah's lifetime — that Noah would bring about this comfort.

A third view is that Lamech just followed a typical naming convention seen frequently in Genesis and occasionally in other books of Scripture. These could have been prophetic in nature, although they are not necessarily so. For example, in Genesis 3:20, we see that "Adam called his wife's name Eve, because she was the mother of all living." Adam's naming of Eve did not require any special knowledge of the future from God, so it was not truly prophetic in that sense. He simply needed to know that they were the only two people on earth and that they were to populate the planet.

A child would often be named based on their appearance or actions at birth. For example, when Rebekah gave birth to Jacob and Esau, we read the following:

> So when her days were fulfilled for her to give birth, indeed there were twins in her womb. And the first came out red. He was like a hairy garment all over; so they called his name Esau. Afterward his brother came out, and his hand took hold of Esau's heel; so his name was called Jacob (Genesis 25:24–26).

Wordplays are involved in the naming of the boys. The word *Jacob* is related to the "heel," and *Esau* uses some of the same sounds for "hairy" (*se'ar*), and note that Esau's descendants would live at Mt. Seir.

At other times, children were named based on the emotions of one or both of the parents. With the birth of Isaac, whose name means "laughter," both parents had laughed upon hearing the announcement (Abraham in Genesis 17:17 and Sarah in Genesis 18:12). The naming of Jacob's sons provides a dozen examples of this (Genesis 29:31–30:24, 35:18).

Of course, God is fully capable of speaking the future through the lips of the godly and ungodly. So there are no theological problems with Lamech uttering a prophecy at Noah's birth, but the text does not specify that his words were meant to be a prophecy. Also, applying his words to the Flood would seem to stretch their meaning, perhaps further than can be allowed. Lamech and his immediate family (save Noah and his family) were not comforted from the ground God had cursed. The ground was (and is) still cursed following the Flood, so just how were his words fulfilled in Noah's life?

If Lamech's words must be understood as a prophecy, then it would seem that the words of each of the other parents in Genesis who used this naming convention should be understood as prophecy. However, if that is the case, then it seems that numerous false prophecies were uttered. The best solution seems to be viewing Lamech's words as a statement of what he hoped would take place rather than as an actual prophecy. Seeing Lamech's words as a typical naming convention would be in line with the practice that appears throughout Genesis in which parents often expressed what they hoped would occur as a result of the child's birth. In the text, there is an indication in his words that life was difficult and he sought relief from his toil. There is a bit of irony in his statement. The land would receive a reprieve from the violence of man for a time; however, the ground itself was destroyed with the Flood, and the Curse remained upon it.

When did carnivores become carnivorous and scavengers become scavengers? Also, how did attack/defense structures come about?

Genesis 1:29–30 explains that human beings were given green herbs for food. The same is true with "every beast of the earth," "every bird of the air," and "everything that creeps on the earth in which there is life." It is not until after the Flood that God gives man permission to eat meat (Genesis 9:3). But what about the animals? Did they begin to eat meat after the Flood or were they permitted to do so long before God destroyed the world?

The Bible is silent about when certain animals turned to carnivory or became scavengers. In rock layers deposited during the Flood, we occasionally find fossils with bite marks, and some fossils have been discovered with the remains of another animal in its belly region. So carnivory and scavenging seems to have occurred prior to the Flood, but when did it start?

One possible answer is that these activities began soon after Adam and Eve sinned. When He cursed the serpent, the Lord said, "Because you have done this, you are cursed more than all cattle, and more than every beast of the field; on your belly you shall go" (Genesis 3:14). The serpent may have undergone certain changes at this point, which may hint at other animals changing at this time as well. Adam's sin wrecked this world, so it makes sense that the animals were corrupted at this time too.

Another possibility is that the animals gradually became predators over the centuries from creation to the Flood. Just as mankind's wickedness seemed to gradually increase until it reached a climax at the time of the Flood, certain animals may have gradually started to eat meat and scavenge. This is how we portray them in our story because we thought it would be another way for Noah to vividly see the wickedness of sin. If he had grown up with carnivorous animals, then he may have thought of it as normal, but this activity is an intrusion in God's creation. Witnessing animals killing and eating other animals, and then seeing people eat animals shows Noah that the world is broken due to sin.

This raises a related issue. If these animals were initially designed to eat plants, then when and how did they acquire their various attack and defense structures? The Bible does not directly address this question, but at least three plausible answers have been proposed. First, since the serpent seems to have been altered in some way at the time of the Curse, it is possible that other animals were changed at that time. Second, the animals may have been created with these structures but originally used them for different purposes. Third, God may have created these animals with the genetic information for the attack and defense structures, but these were not displayed immediately, remaining latent until sometime after Adam's sin.

When did people start to eat meat?

As mentioned in the previous answer, man was originally instructed to eat vegetation (Genesis 1:29), and it was not until after the Flood that God gave mankind permission to eat animals (Genesis 9:3). However, the people before the Flood had grown exceedingly wicked. Consider the following verses to see how the Bible describes the people of that time:

> . . . the wickedness of man was great in the earth (Genesis 6:5)

> . . . every intent of the thoughts of his heart was only evil continually (Genesis 6:5)

> The earth also was corrupt before God, and the earth was filled with violence (Genesis 6:11)

> . . . it was corrupt; for all flesh had corrupted their way on the earth (Genesis 6:12)

> . . . the earth is filled with violence (Genesis 6:13)

It is not hard to imagine that many of these wicked people would have violated God's dietary instruction and were killing animals for food. In the story, we made sure that the righteous people, like Noah and some of his family members, did not eat meat. This detail also explains why Noah is disgusted by the fish served to the king. Up until this point in our story, he had not witnessed anyone violating this instruction.

Was Enosh's generation godly?

Genesis 4:26 states that when Seth's son Enosh was born, "men began to call on the name of the LORD." This verse seems rather straightforward in teaching that mankind began worshiping God around the time of the birth of Adam's grandson, Enosh. Based on Genesis 5:3–6, we learn that Enosh was born 235 years after Adam was created.

In our novel, we portrayed Enosh's generation as one that was largely faithful to the Lord. Given their 900-year lifespans, these people would have been the elders in many places in Noah's early years. This is most clearly seen in the city of Iri Geshem where a 700-year-old man named Akel leads the town council. Certain places lacking this godly influence became more evil as younger generations held sway.

Some Christians have claimed that Genesis 4:26 should be understood in the opposite way. That is, at the time of Enosh's birth, men began to turn away from the Lord. This is based largely on an ancient

Jewish work known as the Genesis Rabbah, which instead of having the verb "call on" uses the verb "pollute." So these people believe this verse teaches that men began to pollute the worship of the true God, probably through the worship of idols. In the Genesis Rabba, the "generation of Enosh" is a wicked one. However, the Hebrew text is accurately translated in all major English versions: the people of Enosh's generation began to call on the name of the Lord.

Was there one continent before the Flood?

Many creationists believe that earth initially had one large supercontinent. This conclusion is the result of an inference made from Genesis 1:9, in which God states, "Let the waters under the heavens be gathered together into one place, and let the dry land appear." If all the water was gathered into one place, then it seems as if the land would have been gathered in one place as well.

At the Creation Museum and Ark Encounter, this massive C-shaped continent is named Rodinia. Modern continents are made up of pieces of the original earth. These pieces, called cratons, can be put together like a jigsaw puzzle to give us a clue as to what the world may have looked like before the Flood. For more details about the original continent and how it was transformed into the seven continents we have on earth today, please see "Noah's Lost World" by Dr. Andrew Snelling, available at https://answersingenesis.org/geology/plate-tectonics/noahs-lost-world/.

Why are the animals described in the novel different than what we observe today?

You may have noticed that we avoided using modern names for the creatures and plants Noah encounters in our story. Let's look at the animals as examples to see our rationale behind this decision. First, and perhaps the most obvious reason, is that Noah would have certainly called them something different than what we do today. Even after accounting for language differences, people in different cultures often call animals by names that do not necessarily mean the same in another culture. For example, one people group may name an animal after the way it looks; another may name the same animal after the sound it makes, a third culture may name it after its behavior, and a fourth group may call it by its scientific classification.

Second, the animals would not have looked the same as they do today. The creatures Noah knew were the ancestors of our modern animals before those original kinds developed into the various species we recognize. For example, we are familiar with wolves, coyotes, jackals, dingoes, and regular dogs, but these varieties of the dog kind probably did not exist in Noah's day since they are descendants of the two dogs God sent to board the Ark.

The third reason we avoided using modern names for animals is that we wanted the pre-Flood world to have an otherworldly feel to it. Many of the animals were named based on appearance or their behavior. So the bounder on Noah's farm is part of the rabbit kind, and the supergliders spotted by Noah and Emzara are a type of pterodactyl, as shown on the cover.

How could Tubal-Cain and his siblings be about the same age as Noah if they were in the eighth generation and Noah in the tenth?

Three of the major characters in our story are members of Cain's line mentioned in Genesis 4. Lamech is in the seventh generation (Adam, Cain, Enoch, Irad, Mehujael, Methushael, Lamech), and his children, Tubal-Cain and Naamah, are in the eighth generation. Yet Noah is in the tenth generation through Adam's son Seth, and we portray Noah as being roughly the same age as Tubal-Cain and Naamah. How can this be if they are two generations apart?

The answer is really quite straightforward, but since we have had people ask about this, it is worth addressing here. The simple answer is that the men in Tubal-Cain's lineage were older on average when each one had his son of record. Let's explore that just a little bit.

We know the age of each patriarch from Adam to Noah when his son of record was born (an average of 117 years), but Genesis 4 does not include the ages of Cain, Enoch, Irad, et al., when their son of record was born. Assuming Cain was born one year after Adam and Eve were created (have you ever considered that Cain may have been just one year younger than his parents?), then the average age upon having their son of record of the men from Cain's son, Enoch, to his descendant, Lamech, would need to be around 175 years. Since Methuselah, Lamech, and Noah were all older than 175 when each had their son of record, this average age is well within biblical precedent. In fact, if one man in Cain's line was approximately 500 years old (like Noah was) when his recorded son was born, then the rest of the men could have averaged about the same age at the birth of their son as the men in Seth's line.

Did Lamech lead a pre-Flood empire?

While studying Genesis for the Ark Encounter, an interesting thought occurred to me (Tim). At the end of Cain's line in chapter 4, we read about a man named Lamech. This man is the first polygamist mentioned in Scripture, and he also boasted about killing someone. Four of his children are named: Jabal, Jubal, Tubal-Cain, and Naamah. The three male children are all cited as being leaders in particular industries: livestock, musical instruments, and metalworking. In the back-of-the-book section of the second book in this series (*Noah: Man of Resolve*), we will explain why we made Naamah a gifted singer.

Why would one family feature leaders in at least three industries? Perhaps they were exceptionally smart and creative. However, many people prior to the Flood were surely very intelligent. Perhaps the reason is that Lamech ruled over a particular area, and he placed his children in charge of these trades.

In our story, we made Lamech a ruler in the land of Havilah. He is an ambitious man who manipulates people to do his bidding. When Noah first encounters him, Lamech is friendly to him because he sees an opportunity to improve his own situation through trade. We will see much more of Lamech and his family in the second book.

Why does Havil have so much gold?

In our story, the city of Havil features a large amount of gold. It can be seen in decorations on buildings, in the expensive gift gallery, and throughout the palace. The basis for this is found in Genesis 2:11–12. There we are told about the first river that flowed out of Eden. Named the Pishon, this river skirted the land of Havilah. The Bible states that there is gold in this land, and that the gold of this land is good.

Since Tubal-Cain was known as an instructor of metalworkers, we made Havilah's capital city, Havil, a place where all sorts of metals, including gold, were readily available.

In our novel, Noah marries the daughter of his grandfather's cousin (his first cousin once removed). In our day, this would be considered incest in many places, so why was it acceptable for so many biblical characters to marry close relations?

Skeptics have long attacked the biblical account of creation because we are told that God made Adam and Eve. Then Adam and Eve had Cain and Abel. After killing Abel, Cain moved away and had children of his own. So who was Cain's wife?

The most natural answer to this famous question is that Cain married his sister. Although it is possible that he married a niece, the objection remains because he married someone very closely related to him. And to make the objection even stronger, the skeptic reminds us that the Bible forbids marriage to a close relation in the book of Leviticus, so how can we claim that many of these people married their kin?

First, we need to understand that the law against close intermarriage in Leviticus 18 was not instituted until two-and-a-half millennia after God created the world. The main reason incest is outlawed in many places is because it can be harmful to the offspring of such a union. Since brother and sister share many of the same genetic mistakes passed down through their parents, these mistakes would be passed down and likely amplified in their children. But early on, marriage to close relations would not have caused these sorts of problems for the offspring because humanity did not have as many genetic problems. As the centuries passed, more and more mutations occurred in our genes, and this genetic load eventually reached the point where it became dangerous for the offspring of closely related parents. This is why the law against such relationships was necessary in Leviticus 18.

Second, the Bible tells us that Eve was to be the mother of all the living (Genesis 3:20), and it also states that after Seth was born, Adam and Eve had sons and daughters (Genesis 5:4). Originally, brother married sister. It sounds gross to us today, but there were no other options, and it would not have the same stigma attached to it as it does today.

Third, some Christians object to this answer because it seems like incest. Some have claimed that God created a different people group so that Adam's children had someone to marry. But such an act would mean that Eve was not the mother of all the living. Also, this objection ignores the fact that Abraham married his half-sister, Sarah. Their son, Isaac, married his first cousin, Rebekah. And their son, Jacob, married two of his cousins, Leah and Rachel. So there are plenty of examples in Genesis of close intermarriage.

Finally, before you get the idea that creationists have a big problem on our hands, you should consider the incest problem we would have if evolution were true. Not only would all of humanity have needed to come from a single pair, or a small community of early humans, but every single plant, animal, and microbe supposedly evolved from the first one-celled organism. Why do skeptics think it is a problem for all of humanity to arise from two people when they believe that all of humanity and every plant and animal came from a single organism?

If it never rained before the Flood why did the story include rain and rainbows?

In our story we mention several instances of rainfall in the pre-Flood world. You may wonder why this deserves mention in this section. Well, many Christians believe the Bible teaches that it never rained prior to the Flood. The primary argument comes from the second chapter of the Bible.

> This is the history of the heavens and the earth when they were created, in the day that the LORD God made the earth and the heavens, before any plant of the field was in the earth and before any herb of the field had grown. For the LORD *God had not caused it to rain* on the earth, and there was no man to till the ground; but a mist went up from the earth and watered the whole face of the ground (Genesis 2:4–6, emphasis added).

Yes, the text states that God had not caused it to rain on the ground. But what period of time are these verses describing? The answer is that these verses state that up until the sixth day of the creation week, God had not caused it to rain on the earth. Is it a safe assumption to extrapolate from this verse through the next 16-plus centuries and claim that it never rained until the Flood? Perhaps, but the text certainly does not demand such a view.

Another argument is based on Hebrews 11:7, which states that Noah built the Ark by faith after being warned by God of "things not yet seen."

Some supporters of the "no rain before the Flood" position claim that the "things not yet seen" refer to rain and other effects associated with storms. But Hebrews does not necessarily have ordinary rainfall in view. In all likelihood, the phrase in question refers to the Flood and its effects.

A third argument used by those who do not believe it rained prior to the Flood is based on the idea that the early earth had some sort of water canopy around it. This is based on a certain understanding of the events on the second day of creation when God separated the waters below the expanse (or firmament) from the waters above it (Genesis 1:6–7). This proposed canopy somehow created an ideal environment around the globe, blocking harmful rays and permitting longer, healthier lives. However, there are numerous scientific problems with the canopy theory, such as the fact that it would have created a massive greenhouse that would have destroyed life on earth. Even more important is that Genesis 1 also states that the sun, moon, and stars are in the expanse, so that would mean that "the waters above" should probably be understood as being beyond the stars instead of some sort of canopy around our planet.

The final argument given to support the "no rain" position has to do with the rainbow. Following the Flood, God made a covenant with Noah and all the inhabitants of the earth, human and animal, that He would never again destroy the earth with a Flood (Genesis 9:9–11). Regarding the sign of this covenant, the Lord stated, "I set My rainbow in the cloud, and it shall be for the sign of the covenant between Me and the earth" (Genesis 9:13). Supporters of the idea that it never rained before the Flood claim that this was the world's first rainbow, so it must not have rained before.

There are at least three big problems with this statement. First, we know it had rained for 40 days and 40 nights beginning at least a year before God announced this covenant. And it undoubtedly rained following those first 40 days, so if sunlight shone through at all during this time, then we should expect a rainbow to appear as well. Second, rain does not even need to fall for a rainbow to form. If waterfalls existed in the pre-Flood world, then a rainbow would appear in the mist that inevitably forms if sunlight reached the water droplets in the air. Third, and most importantly, the Bible does not claim that this was the first rainbow. God used the rainbow here as a sign of the covenant He made. Nothing in the text necessitates this as the world's first rainbow.

If rainbows had appeared before, then what we see here is an example of God attaching special meaning to them at this point. He did the same thing with the Passover lambs roughly a thousand years later. When the Lord told Moses and the Israelites to sacrifice lambs at Passover, He did not invent lambs at that point; He attached special significance to them at that point in history.

In our view, the arguments used for the "no rain" position are not compelling enough to adopt such a position, but at the same time we want to acknowledge the plausibility of such a view. However, since many creationists have heard and repeated these claims as found in the Bible, we wanted to take the opportunity to challenge these assumptions and encourage readers to look closely at the biblical text so that they could learn whether their beliefs are based on Scripture or tradition.

Why does Noah have anger and pride issues when the Bible describes him as a righteous man?

The Bible certainly tells us several times that Noah was a righteous man, but we have several reasons for giving him these character flaws. First, the Bible's description of Noah as being a righteous man had to do with his character at the time God called him to build the Ark. He may have sinned regularly in his first several centuries, and undoubtedly struggled with sin throughout his life.

Second, every story needs to see the protagonist change during the course of his journey. This is especially true in a coming-of-age tale like this one. Readers want to relate to a character, so they need to see a realistic person instead of an idealistic one. They need to see him struggle with difficult situations, make mistakes and learn from them, see the consequences of his decisions, and grow as a person as a result of his experiences.

Third, the fact that Noah needed God's grace (Genesis 6:8) reveals he was not perfect. While it would be nice to think of him as never struggling with any sin, we realize he was just as human as we are, and surely battled the desires of the flesh regularly. This made things tricky for us because the Bible only tells us about one mistake made by Noah, and that episode of drunkenness happened years after the Flood (Genesis 9:21). Many novels about Noah use this event in his life as justification for giving him a disposition toward drinking alcohol. While this may be reasonable, it is a bit overdone in these books, so we decided to give Noah a couple of other sinful issues to struggle with.

The two main areas where our Noah struggles are pride and anger. The pride issues are more subtle in the book, but they can be seen a few times as he admires his own appearance or focuses too much attention on himself. Pride also rears its ugly head in the way Noah is tempted by Naamah, although he does a great job in handling his most difficult encounter with her.

The anger issues are more noticeable. He allows his frustrations to boil over in chapters 14 and 18. But in each case, his temper subsides before too long. Why would we give him such a temper?

We decided to borrow characteristics from the Apostle Paul for aspects of Noah's personality. Like Paul, Noah was a preacher of righteousness (2 Peter 2:5), something we will see him become in the next two books. In the Bible, these men seemed to share a common boldness, willing to stand before anyone at any time and proclaim the truth, regardless of personal harm that may come to them. Paul endured flogging, imprisonment, and many other punishments because of his desire to spread the gospel (2 Corinthians 11:24–27). While the Bible doesn't give us any specific instances about Noah's boldness, there is little doubt he strongly contrasted with the rampant wickedness of his day.

People with this sort of boldness seem to share a righteous anger toward sin, which is a good thing, but there is a fine line that can quickly be crossed when that righteous anger is personalized and becomes a sinful temper. There are signs that Paul had a fierce temper. Prior to his conversion to Christianity, we read that Paul was "still breathing threats and murder" against Christ's disciples (Acts 9:1). Years after his conversion, the high priest ordered Paul to be struck. In the next verse, Paul immediately responds with a strong insult, saying, "God will strike you, you whitewashed wall!" (Acts 23:3). It is hard to overstate how offensive that remark would have been at the time. After being informed that this man was the high priest, Paul recognized his outburst was wrong (v. 5).

Like so many other sins, if not all of them, temper stems from human pride, and Paul was not immune to that. He had a major falling out with Barnabas because of John Mark, whom Paul refused to travel with, thanks to John Mark deserting them on a previous missionary journey (Acts 15:36–41). Paul highlights his prideful failings when he openly admits his daily struggle to do what is right and not do what is wrong (Romans 7:15–19).

If this godly man who wrote 13 books of the New Testament can struggle with pride and anger, then it is certainly believable that a fellow preacher of righteousness, Noah, could struggle with the same issues, particularly at a young age.

Why is the serpent god called Nachash?

By the end of the first book, readers learn about the false god Nachash (pronounced nah-KOSH). Bible readers may be familiar with some of the other pagan gods and goddesses mentioned in Scripture, such as Dagon (1 Samuel 5:7), Ashtoreth (1 Kings 11:5), or Molech (1 Kings 11:7), but Nachash is not mentioned — at least not in English Bibles.

Genesis 3 describes man's rebellion in the Garden of Eden, typically referred to as the Fall. The serpent deceived Eve, and she ate from the tree of the knowledge of good and evil — violating the one prohibition God had put in place. Then she gave some to Adam and he ate. Adam's sin brought sin, disease, suffering, and death into the world. God also cursed the serpent and the ground at this point.

So where does Nachash fit into all this? Nachash is a transliteration of the Hebrew word used for serpent in this passage. This explains why we chose to use a serpent idol to represent Nachash and have Noah refer to him as the Great Deceiver.

Christians generally recognize the serpent as Satan (Revelation 12:9), but Genesis does not make this identification for us, and somewhat surprisingly, neither does any other place in the Old Testament. So readers should not expect Noah or anyone else in the novels to refer to Nachash as the devil or Satan, which leads to the next question.

Why did Noah seem to have a fairly limited understanding of God and the things described in Genesis 1–5?

Early in our story, Noah and Aterre have a conversation about the Creator, and Noah doesn't seem to know how to properly address each of the issues. Some readers may wonder why we portrayed this faithful biblical hero in this way, but we have two major reasons for this decision.

First, at this point in our story, Noah is a young man who has not encountered beliefs contrary to those he was taught from his childhood.

He does not have years of experience to draw from in knowing how to respond to challenges to his beliefs. In our day, this situation would be like an average recent high school graduate being drawn into an important philosophical and theological discussion.

Second, modern readers often assume that biblical characters knew much more about God and His plans than what they may have. We tend to think that they should be aware of everything the Bible mentions about the people and times in which they lived. Some Christians assume that these characters even knew about teachings that would not be revealed until the New Testament.

The main problem with this latter idea is that the Bible describes a concept that has come to be called progressive revelation. Numerous verses could be cited to illustrate this, but the following passage explains it well.

> Now to Him who is able to establish you according to my gospel and the preaching of Jesus Christ, according to the revelation of the mystery kept secret since the world began but now made manifest, and by the prophetic Scriptures made known to all nations, according to the commandment of the everlasting God, for obedience to the faith (Romans 16:25–26).

As he frequently did, the Apostle Paul spoke of a "mystery" that had now been made manifest. When using this term, Paul refers to a concept that God had hidden from the generations before him but had been revealed in his day, such as God's plan to establish His church (Colossians 1:24–27), end times teaching (Romans 11:25; 1 Corinthians 15:51), and the content of the gospel (Ephesians 6:19).

As far as we know, there is an enormous amount of biblical information that Noah was not privy to. It is possible that God had revealed some information to him or others that is not recorded for us in Scripture, but even if this were the case, we cannot know the details of this revelation.

So if Noah was unaware of later revelation, would he have been familiar with all the things written in Genesis 1–5? Many creationists have adopted a view known as the tablet model, which states that the Book of Genesis was written by multiple people, including Adam, Noah, Shem, Abraham, et al., and then later compiled by Moses. Personally, I believe there are some strong arguments against such a view, but even if this model turns out to be correct, it would not guarantee that Noah, as a young man, would have been familiar with all the details at that time. After all, the earlier records may have been passed down to him hundreds of years later.

Another assumption made by many creationists is that Adam knew Methuselah and that Methuselah would have passed this information down to his grandson Noah. It is true that Adam lived 930 years, long enough to be alive during the first two centuries of Methuselah's long life. However, this fact does not guarantee that the two men would have known each other. Methuselah was the seventh generation after Adam. Given their very long lives, it is very possible that these people had dozens of children.

For the sake of argument, let's assume a minimum number of children for each of the men listed between Adam and Methuselah. The Bible names at least one son for each of these men and then states that after they had other "sons and daughters." So each of these men had at least five children — an extremely low number for people living over 900 years. If each generation had five children on average, and each of those children averaged five children, then by the time Methuselah was born, Adam would have had more than 78,000 descendants. But remember, that number is assuming a small number of children for people who may have been capable of producing offspring from at least age 65 (Genesis 5:15, 21) to over 500 (Genesis 5:32). If each family averaged a dozen children, which is probably still a low number in such a long lifespan, Adam would have had over 35 million descendants at the time Methuselah came along. Why should we assume that he happened to know one particular great, great, great, great, great grandson named Methuselah?

The truth is, we cannot know for certain how many people were on earth at that point, and we cannot know if Adam knew Methuselah. In fact, we cannot even be sure that Methuselah and Noah knew each other. In keeping with our goal of challenging stereotypes, we decided to minimize the amount of biblical information from Genesis 1–5 that Noah may have known, at least as a young man. In our story, he is aware of some of the key events in these chapters, such as creation and the Fall, but he does not know all of the details. If these events were not faithfully recorded or passed on to him at this point in his life, legends based on the events would surely develop, making it hard for him to know what really happened. For example, he knows of Enoch's disappearance, but he is not entirely sure what happened to him. Since the time of Babel, many cultures passed their histories to the next generation through storytelling and song. Perhaps some of the people living prior to the Flood did the same.

Traditions would be another way to hand down this information, but as is often the case, a tradition gets passed down while the meaning behind it becomes muddled or lost. An example of this is seen with the Zakari assuming a strange position while praying. This practice comes from a tradition handed down to them derived from a key event in Genesis, but they have lost the truth behind it. Readers will need to wait until the third book in the series to learn why they do this.

Finally, one tricky element in our story has to do with the way in which an individual related to God prior to the Flood. As Christians, living after Jesus Christ's death, burial, and Resurrection, and after the Holy Spirit came on the Day of Pentecost, we have the advantages of hindsight and having the Spirit dwell within us. We also have 66 books in the Bible to guide us as we seek to live in a way that pleases the Lord.

The people of Noah's day did not have these advantages, so how could they know what they should do to please the Lord? They would need to rely on the truth passed down to them, however much that may have been. Some people, like Cain (Genesis 4:6) and Enoch (Genesis 5:21–24; Jude 14–15), had the opportunity to hear directly from God, just as Noah would in the years leading up to the Flood. Perhaps other people had this privilege as well. Even if the people did not have access to these first two options, they still had a God-given conscience to help them discern between right and wrong.

We see examples in the early chapters of Genesis that people made sacrifices to the Lord. Abel offered the "firstborn of his flock" (Genesis 4:4), and after the Flood, Noah offered sacrifices from every clean animal and clean bird (Genesis 8:20). So these individuals must have had some comprehension of their sinfulness and that the cost of sin was death. This practice almost certainly came from the first sacrifice when God killed at least one animal to provide "tunics of skin" to clothe Adam and Eve (Genesis 3:21). These sacrifices may have become mere ritual for some people, but in the cases of Abel and Noah, we know they were righteous men (Matthew 23:35 and Genesis 7:1), so we have every reason to believe that the proper reasons for offering sacrifices were passed down to Noah. Our novel depicts Noah's recognition of the right reasons to offer sacrifices at his coming-of-age ceremony and just prior to his wedding.

ENCOUNTER THIS

Since we worked on the Ark Encounter project, we had the unique opportunity to include details in our story that can be seen in various exhibits. We were also able to influence the design of certain elements so that they connected with our story. If you visit the Ark Encounter in Williamstown, Kentucky, you will be able to see the following items that were included in the story.

Chapter 3: As Noah looks over the family farm, he recalls memories of daydreaming at the top of Sacrifice Hill as he watched boats travel the river. An illustration of young Noah watching a boat on the river while carving a small boat out of wood is shown in the *Who Was Noah?* exhibit on the second deck. This illustration also includes some earth shakers (sauropod dinosaurs) on the other side of the river. In Chapter 9, Noah told Aterre that he had occasionally seen earth shakers when he was younger.

Chapter 4: Meru, Lamech's pack animal, called a lunker in the story, is an extinct animal known as a macrauchenia. Two theosodons, a smaller variety of this kind of animal, can be found in an animal enclosure on the second deck.

Chapter 5: Noah's father, Lamech, and grandfather, Methuselah, appear early on in the story, and Lamech appears later as well. Portraits of these two men can be viewed in *Noah's Study* on the second deck.

Chapter 6: In our first scene from Naamah's point of view, we learn that her father, another man named Lamech, has married a second wife. In the *Pre-Flood World* exhibit on the second deck, there are six large panels depicting the world's descent into darkness. The second panel depicts a man with two wives and includes the Bible verse that mentions Lamech's polygamy. Later in the same exhibit, this king and his wives can be seen in a large diorama depicting a drunken feast.

Chapter 10: The knife Noah and Aterre fashioned from the large tooth can be seen hanging on a wall in the *Library* on the second deck of the Ark Encounter. Although Noah and Aterre never see the animal it came from, the description of the scene and the details provided by the Varelk make it obvious that the "dagger tooth" creature is a type of Tyrannosaur. Two juvenile tyrannosaurs are on display in an animal enclosure on the second deck.

Chapter 14: After Noah and Aterre leave Zakar, a large animal lumbers across the path in front of them on their way to the river. This awkward creature, unnamed in the story, is called an anisodon. This creature can be found in a large animal enclosure on the second deck.

Chapter 18: Noah travels to Iri Geshem to become an apprentice shipbuilder. After months of frustration, he finally gets his opportunity. The *Who Was Noah?* exhibit on the second deck includes an illustration of Noah learning the trade of shipbuilding from Ara. In *The Interview* film, Noah mentions learning the trade from Emzara's father.

Chapter 20: In the chapter where Noah proposes to Emzara, he hands her a carved animal called a keluk in our story. This carved animal can be found in the *Library* on the second deck of the Ark Encounter. A keluk is what we named the pre-Flood version of the giraffe, and we made it Emzara's favorite type of animal. This fact is mentioned by the animatronic Noah in *Noah's Study* on the second deck, and there is a picture of her guiding two of these animals into the Ark in the *Doors of Bible* exhibit (part of the *Why the Bible Is True* exhibit) on third deck.

Chapter 30: During her wedding, Emzara's father hands her a letter he had written when he offers his blessing on her and Noah. Emzara can be seen reading this letter in *Noah's Study* on the second deck. Three of the items used in the wedding ceremony can also be seen on a shelf in that exhibit: the blindfold around Noah's head at the start of the ceremony, the engagement armband Noah made for Emzara, and the cord used to wrap the couple at the end of the ceremony.

Chapter 36: In the final scene of the first book, the massive idol of the serpent is revealed in Havil. Each of the following exhibits include artwork showing a version of the serpent idol in pagan cities: *The Pre-Flood World* (second deck), *Who Was Noah?* (second deck), *and Flood Geology* (large mural on third deck).

These statements are accurate as of the opening of the Ark Encounter. Exhibits may be modified in the future, so certain details may change.

BORROWED FROM THE BIBLE

Since the Bible does not give us details about Noah's early years, we needed to use artistic license to tell the story. To keep the story more closely tied to the Bible, we decided to borrow and slightly adapt some of the concepts found in the novel from other portions of Scripture. The Question and Answer section explained that we borrowed aspects of the Apostle Paul's personality in our depiction of Noah's personality. Here are some other examples where we borrowed ideas from other portions of Scripture.

Chapter 12: When the Zakari develop a plan to rescue the children, Erno tells them to spread around the camp and pull out two torches to make the kidnappers think there are more people in the woods than there really were. This plan is loosely based on Gideon's strategy for defeating the Midianites found in Judges 7. With an army of only 300 men, Gideon's men spread out into three companies, surrounding the Midianite camp. Each man held a trumpet and a torch hidden inside a pitcher. When Gideon blew his trumpet, the 300 men blew their trumpets and smashed the pitchers. The cacophony confused and scared the Midianites and the Lord used Gideon to win an important battle.

Chapter 20: Noah agreed to work for Ara for more than five years, at which point he could marry Ara's daughter. While we set up Noah's working relationship with Ara as an apprenticeship, the concept was borrowed from Genesis 29. Here, we read the account of Jacob working seven years for Laban for the right to marry Laban's daughter, Rachel. Of course, Laban deceived Jacob by giving him Leah instead, so Jacob agreed to work another seven years for Rachel. Another similarity to this account is the fact that Jacob traveled far to stay with a relative. In our story, Noah travels a long distance to work with Ara.

Chapter 21: Naamah's visit to the seer is loosely borrowed from 1 Samuel 28 where King Saul consults a medium in order to find out from Samuel what his future will be. At this point in our story, Naamah knows some things about the true God, but she does not have a good understanding of His ways. She desperately hopes that the seer will tell her that she will not always be under her father's rule, which she has grown to despise. His words will play a huge role in her life as she seeks to find the one who will fulfill them. Saul's visit to the medium would end in tragedy as Samuel appeared and told him that he would die later that day. Readers will need to wait to see how this encounter turns out for Naamah. For a detailed explanation of this passage about Saul and the medium, please read my two-part article, "King Saul, a Witch, and an Elohim," at http://midwestapologetics.org/blog/?p=1273 and http://midwestapologetics.org/blog/?p=1382.

Chapter 30: Some of the wording and symbolism found in the marriage ceremony is taken right from the creation of Adam and Eve. As Noah's father explained, the cloth over Noah's face represented the deep sleep Adam was put into by God. Emzara repeats God's words about the woman being a helper for the man. The use of the cord to bind husband and wife together at the ribs is drawn from the fact that Eve was made from Adam's rib.

Dear Reader,

Thank you for choosing this book. We hope you've enjoyed the story so far and are looking forward to the next installment in the series. In the novel, Aterre had plenty of questions about God. While trying to make sense of our world, perhaps you've wondered about many of the things Aterre questioned. Noah did not have all of the answers for his friend, but he trusted in God and believed that answers could be discovered. And he was right. The answers are available if you are willing to search for them.

Today, we have access to details about God and His plan that were unavailable in Noah's time. We have the Bible, God's written Word that tells us all we need to know about God and His plan for our lives and this world. The Bible tells us that we have all sinned against God. In other words, we have rebelled against our Creator. The Bible says that the wages of sin is death. That is, what we have earned through our sin is God's judgment. We need His mercy and forgiveness.

If you really want to know what God is like, then look at Jesus Christ. The Bible explains that Jesus, God's Son, came to earth as a man and lived a perfect life. He died on the Cross and rose again to life to pay the penalty we owe for all our sins. In order to be right with the Most High, you need to acknowledge that you have failed to live up to God's expectations — you've sinned and stand in need of a Savior. Trust that Jesus' sacrificial death and Resurrection are enough to cover you, and ask God to forgive you of your sins.

In light of what God has done for you, commit yourself to living for Him. Read the Bible to learn more about our Creator and how to follow Him faithfully.

> Jesus said to her, "I am the resurrection and the life. He who believes in Me, though he may die, he shall live. And whoever lives and believes in Me shall never die. Do you believe this?" (John 11:25–26).

ABOUT THE AUTHORS

Tim Chaffey is the Content Manager for the Ark Encounter and Creation Museum. A former pastor and teacher, Tim is also a leukemia survivor and competes in half-marathons with his wife and son while his daughter cheers them on. He has earned advanced degrees specializing in apologetics, theology, and church history. Tim maintains a popular blog (www.midwestapologetics.org/blog), contributes regularly to *Answers* magazine and the Answers in Genesis website, and has authored over a dozen books, including *The Truth Chronicles* series and *In Defense of Easter: Answering Critical Challenges to the Resurrection of Jesus*.

K. Marie Adams has an obsession with words that once resulted in her being grounded for reading too much. Later, it served her well as she worked for many years at a bookstore and as a literature and grammar instructor. Now, as a graphic designer, her love of language goes by the fancy name of typography. K. Marie also volunteers for several ministries dedicated to rescuing young girls from modern-day slavery.

40 POWERFUL EXPLANATIONS
to prove the Bible is accurate and **without error!**

VOLUME 1

A powerful team of contributors lead a bold defense for the accuracy of Scripture, providing core biblical truths to help refute over 40 claims regarding the inaccuracy of God's Holy Word.

VOLUME 2

Biblical evidence disproves the toughest of critics and brings to light the indestructible power of God's Word. Contributors led by Answers in Genesis highlight the answers to these debates and more.

$12.99 • 978-0-89051-600-3

$12.99 • 978-0-89051-649-2